ORION'S BELT:
Birth of the Hunter

BOOK ONE IN A SERIES

John Peter Ferris

DEDICATION

This novel is a work of fiction loosely based on historic events and is dedicated to the fighting men and women of the United States. My inspiration includes the events of 9-11 and the global unrest we currently face. In troubled times we have always looked to our military for defense and strategy, and this is especially true at this point in our nation's history. It is our warriors in harm's way whom we herald as our heroes. Stay safe.

CONTENTS

ACKNOWLEDGMENTS

First of all in the inspiration of this book came about after my 34 years of construction work as a mason, carpenter, and other careers in the building industry. Because I became disabled by arthritis and an accidental injury, I decided it was time to try to accomplish my life's passion to write Science Fiction thrillers that are exciting enough for the Silver Screen. Helping me along with this project, I give a fond and great thank you to my for-matter, book cover illustrator, and website designer Holly Chervnsik. Also to one very patient and fantastic editor and project consultant, Melanie Saxton. Also to my business manager and loving daughter, Melissa Padro. But the one who gave me the greatest inspiration of them all, my dear & sweet kind mother Ellen Ferris, who without her, my daughter, and my two new friends, this would have not been possible.

PREFACE: THE FLIGHT OF ICARUS

Following are the last words of Daedalus, the alchemist and necromancer, as he speaks to his beloved son, Icarus:

"My son, the Gods have made me aware of all I have accomplished. They have warned us to beware of personal valor and accreditation, as thy creations may turn on thee."

His son Icarus rebukes and disclaims his father. "The Gods did not help thee as thou copied the creatures of the sky, but yet thou didst, and now thou hast conquered man's inability to achieve the heavens and fly. Where are the Gods now?" Icarus then dons the wings his father created.

Daedalus implores his son to wait because the test flight was but 100 feet above the ground. He pleads, "Son, we have only tested the boundaries at a safe distance and need more time."

Icarus bellows to his father, prideful, "Father, we will show the world what Zeus has bestowed on me. Absolute power, my father. This world is for the taking."

He spreads his mighty wings and shouts to the universe, "Dare defy us now and ye will be the masters of thine own fate." Icarus flaps his wings and flies towards the sun.

INTRODUCTION

Captain James Malloy (retired) heard that an old Navy surgeon with whom he served in Vietnam had a problem. To help solve that problem he called on an ex subordinate officer named Johnny Orion, a Lieutenant under him in S.E.A.L. Team 2. Orion had opened a private investigator's office, and Malloy explained that Dr. Jeffrey Pearson's daughter had taken off to the south Bronx and was hooked on heroin. An old girlfriend of hers had found this out through the grapevine. She also said that Pearson's daughter was being pimped off when she was drugged out.

The daughter's name was Kendra. Months before, she had a blowout with her father and ran away to New York City to start a new life. Seems it didn't work out that way.

Dr. Jeffrey Pearson was a Commander in the Navy during Vietnam. Captain Malloy had witnessed him saving several lives (including his own) and told Orion he felt compelled to help Pearson. But Orion couldn't do this gratis and needed funding — business was slow. "I'd do it for free if I could," Orion told Malloy. "We owe this man for what he's done."

"Money is no object," Malloy assured Orion. "Dr. Pearson is very wealthy." Indeed, his civilian practice coupled with his research and development laboratory had brought the doctor prominence and prosperity over the years.

Orion ticked off a list. "I need smoke and tear gas grenades, 45 caliber ammo and police scanners," he told Malloy. "It's Wednesday 1850 hours and contact me at 0615 hours on Friday for confirmation. Then expedite to the rendezvous point." The plan included time for recognizance before Orion infiltrated and achieved the mission.

"Do whatever it takes, and I don't need to know the particulars," instructed Malloy.

"Hey, you trained me, and I don't think you want to know," responded Orion. Just before leaving, he turned. "IF ANYTHING DOES GO WRONG, GET A HOLD OF TRUDY FOR ME, SKIPPER."

"Just do your job, shithead, it's just another evolution." With that, Malloy hung up his cell phone.

1900 hours: Mission begins.

Malloy directed Orion via text message to place and time for ammo, tear gas and smoke grenade pickup, along with police scanners and code frequencies.

1 THE RAZOR'S EDGE

Damn alarm clock going off again. Time to get up and hit the bricks. Orion was groggy. Can't wait till this Friday is over. The shit I had to go through to clear my mission yesterday . . .

Orion knew the mission was incomplete. He still had to transport two 19-year-old girls out East to the Hamptons. His old Commanding Officer from S.E.A.L. Team 2 had asked for help in initiating this adventure. The scenario: The Commanding Officer's rich doctor friend was in dire straits after falling out with his daughter Kendra. The girl complained that she didn't even exist in his life and that his work and research were more important to him than his love for her. Worse, ever since her mother died of breast cancer he completely shut himself off from the world.

Kendra knew some girl who was dating somebody in the Bronx. This girl told Kendra to come live with her and her boyfriend, and that her boyfriend would introduce her to "Joaquin." Problem: This was eight months ago and Joaquin was bad news.

The intel Orion got on these two assholes were they were pimps and heroin dealers. They lured young girls from prominent families and got them so hooked that they were out their minds. This was about all Orion had when he executed his infiltration scenario.

Now at 0500 hours, November 26, 2010, Orion got himself out of bed and headed towards a little kitchen area in his warehouse located in Garden City Park Long Island, New York. The coffee machine went off and he grabbed a plastic 7-11 coffee container purchased the night before during recon as he surveilled the drug dealer's tenement.

Orion poured himself a cup and heard in the front of the warehouse, "Let me out of here, you fuckin' scumbag." Picking up a balaclava hood and putting it on, he headed toward the noise. Both girls were restrained and blindfolded.

1

"Did you sleep well, your highness?"

Kendra screamed, "How could I? I'm handcuffed and blindfolded to this iron monstrosity you call a bed."

"I'd take off your restraints if I knew you'd behave. Look at your girlfriend; she seems to be in compliance."

Kendra screamed, "What a dick you are, I'm blindfolded, you stupid mother fucker."

Orion placed duct tape over her mouth, having fun in his own sick little way. Her friend's mouth was duct taped the night before.

Heading for his tactical locker in the warehouse basement, he took his cache bag with him. Orion removed the keys in his pocket and unlocked a giant padlock at the right side base of a giant bookcase. This particular book case had small roller bearings on the bottom, and he rolled it to the right to lock it into the hidden mortise on the other side.

There, a security keypad lay hidden in the entrance of his weapons & ordinance room. Orion entered his private code that only he and one other person knew. Failure to do so would set off an M-26 trip grenade right next to ten pounds of C4 explosive, which was enough to level anyone trying to get in. Inside a cache of weapons and ordinance awaited. On the wall hung one M.P.5, and next to it was an empty space. Orion reached into his tactical bag and retrieved the other M.P.5, putting it next to the other one. He looked over to an M-16 with 203 grenade launcher. Next to that perched an AK-47 and one M19 30-caliber machine gun. As he look at the back wall, a M-2 (Ma deuce) 50 caliber machine gun hung. Right next to that were his two babies— a McMillan 50 caliber sniper rifle and his favorite, the M107 Barrett assault and sniper rifle. Next to this powerful array of weaponry was small metal locker. Inside were battle tactical vests and one Biv-pack with comm. unit. Orion stole the damn thing before he got out of the Navy. He pulled a Mossberg shotgun off the wall and put it in his tactical bag. He also loaded his S-37 2000 combat knife under his coat. Better be safe then dead; the hell with sorry.

He exited the hidden room and rolled the bookcase back to the left, padlocking the 2-inch steel rod against the bookcase. On the outside behind a picture on the wall was an embedded key lock. Orion took off the picture and put in the key, reactivating the alarm.

Orion headed upstairs to get his two passengers ready for transport. At the front of the warehouse were his two vehicles, one a 12-passenger armored van. The other vehicle, a 1969 Plymouth black armored Roadrunner. When battle situations occur, or someone tries to steal it, a flood of purple L.E.D lights activate with a siren; After all, it had a 440 high performance engine. Special compartments were hidden throughout the vehicle.

Orion got his New York pistol permit when he got his Private

Investigator's license. He contemplated what went down last evening.
****

Time: 2130 hours, November 25, 2010.

Orion approached the back of the tenement, working his way toward Kendra Pearson. He dimmed his head lights and departed the van. The air was heavy and smelled like dogs in an alley. This made sense as two pit bulls jumped and growled like no tomorrow. Pulling out his Sig-Sauer 45 with silencer (known as a hushpuppy in the Team), he dropped both animals. Back tracking to his van, he opened the side sliding door and pulled out a truck battery. He put it on the stoop by the back door.

He then pulled out a curling iron, switched up with car battery clamps attached. Orion clipped the curling iron to the back door knob and clamped the battery. One more quick recon was needed before he executed breach and recovery. He checked the only small back window and saw the car clearly. At the side of the tenement he checked the side-bedroom window and saw it was all clear, but with a small TV blaring loud as hell. He then crept toward the front of the house to the other bedroom window.

The second bedroom was clear, as well. Orion went to his van and quickly retrieved a battery powered screw gun and small tripwire. He snuck up to the front door, taking out two Phillips' head screws and two washers.

As he wrapped one end of the trip wire around the screw, he secured it with the screw gun. The one end was 10 inches from the bottom of the door. The next screw and washer went only half way, and Orion pulled the trip wire over and wrapped it tight. Then he sent it all the way in. He reached into his coat pocket, withdrawing a battery-operated bullhorn siren with remote control. He placed it on the front stoop and stealthily made his way to the front window. Peering inside, Orion saw one man smoking crack from a glass pipe. The other male drug dealer was on the couch to the side of the room with two groggy-looking females on either side of him. Next to the couch was an AK-47 assault rifle. On the coffee table were a 9mm Glock, needles and spoons. The crack smoker relaxed in small recliner with a Mossberg shotgun at his side.

All of a sudden a toilet flushed and another male entered from the kitchen combination room on the left of the building.

Hmmmm….. Orion knew the guy wasn't there when he reconned the place last night. Oh well. No matter; I'll accommodate.

Out of the blue one of the female spoke. "Joaquin, you promised to get us some food. You promised, poppi."

"Shut the fuck up bitch, you've had too much dope, and you'll puke it all over my apartment, asshole," answered Joaquin. "Be more like your friend and go to sleep 'till I'm ready for you."

All three men burst out in laughter.

Orion decided it was time to expedite his plan. He glided to the side of the building toward the back bedroom with the blaring TV.

He checked the window, surprised it was open. Orion crawled through very quietly, noticing the putrid stench of unwashed sheets, sex and drugs. He opened his coat and located two tear-gas grenades and four smoke grenades. Removing the filthy sheet from the bed, he tied one end in a big knot. Then he carefully lifted the small TV in the air and placed the knot to the back. He sat the TV down on the rest of the sheet.

Orion pulled a spool of fishing line from his coat, tying the line to the other end of the sheet. Then he began releasing the spool while prowling down the hall to the front bedroom. When he arrived at to the other bedroom, he cut the line and prepared himself for the assault.

Orion pulled out one tear gas grenade and pulled the pin. At the same time, he hit the remote control for the bullhorn siren at the front door. Orion donned his gas mask as all hell started breaking loose.

He threw the other tear gas grenade to the rear of the building.

"IT'S THE PIGS, let's get out the back," he heard as they choked and panicked. Joaquin yelled to Carlos, "Check to see if we can go out the back." Carlos (the one previously in the bathroom) flew blindly past the bedroom that concealed Orion, who couldn't help but notice the lowlife's AK-47. Carlos dropped and began crawling just before reaching the back door.

As Carlos groped for the doorknob, he hadn't a clue that it was red hot. He grabbed hold and it practically stuck him to the door.

Orion pulled on the fishing line, causing the TV in the other room to crash to the floor.

"Julio!" yelled Joaquin, "Someone's coming into the back bedroom; go kill him!"

Julio came choking down the hall, barely able to see. He turned his shotgun into the bedroom and started firing. Orion, right behind him, put the tip of this combat knife at the base of Julio's neck, slamming it in right below the skull. Julio dropped silently, like a rag doll.

Through the commotion Carlos screamed in agony as he pulled hard to free himself from the red hot door handle. When he finally unfused his hand, he noticed the ripped flesh and looked up just as Orion was upon him. The pistol to his skull dropped Carlos to the floor like a ton of bricks.

Meanwhile, Joaquin, overwhelmed by the sounds and smell, took his chances and ran out the front door, leaving the two girls behind. He ran out shooting on fully automatic, then got hung up in the trip wire. He tumbled to the floor and managed to shoot himself in the stomach.

At that exact moment Orion felt the buzz from the police scanner. "Time to go," he announced, heading for Kendra. But as he entered the front room, the other girl made a break for the front door. Orion came up behind her and used a sleeper hold to knock her out. As he turned around, he beheld a helpless-looking female staring straight at him. He tossed the first girl onto the couch and grabbed Kendra, turning her over and handcuffing her. Hefting her onto his shoulder, he toted her out to the van. Then he returned for the second girl. Orion dropped all four smoke grenades as he drove off and removed his gas mask, not realizing that Kendra could see him. Four miles out he heard the other girl starting to moan. Pulling off to the side of the road, he got out and opened the side door. She was starting to wake up, so he turned her over and handcuffed her, too. He decided to duct tape her mouth and blindfold her. As he finished, he heard from the back of the van, "Won't do you no good. I know what your face looks like, mother fucker." He blindfolded and gagged Kendra, as well.

Time: 2235 hours.

****

Time: 2345 hours.

John Patrick Orion had just completed the first part of his mission and pulled into his warehouse in Garden City Park, Long Island, New York. As he exited his van, his two loyal and trained hybrid wolf and German Shepherd dogs came to greet him. "Good boys," he shouted to his dogs. "Come, I'll give you some water and dinner in just a minute."

Orion opened all the doors to the van. He wrestled each girl, one at a time, out of the vehicle and laid them on an iron bed with a half way decent mattress.

Then he headed toward a little cubicle in the warehouse and returned with a cot, on which he deposited the other girl. He draped her torso with an army blanket and did the same for Kendra on the bed.

Time: 0540 hours.

Orion stopped daydreaming about the night before and got to the business at hand. Captain James Malloy, the one who hired Orion for this job, gave him Sodium Pentethol for Kendra's transport so she would sleep through the journey. He administered the drug to both of them.

Little to anyone's knowledge, at the same time in New Jersey five men were on a mission: To meet and cast a terror plot.

Orion, oblivious as the rest of the world to this plot, attended to his guests. He finally got Kendra comfortable, turned on the TV and finished his coffee. The news reported the police investigation about a shootout in the Bronx. Two well-known drug dealers were killed and the assailant (or assailants) got away by covering their escape with military-type smoke grenades.

Orion laughed and joked out loud, "What do you expect? It's the Bronx." Time: 0550 hours.

Orion shut the front warehouse door and headed for the Long Island Expressway, finally reaching it at 0615 hours. His cell phone started playing

"Popeye the Sailor Man," and on the other end was Captain Malloy.

"Orion, do you have the package?"

Yes sir, actually two special packages wrapped with ribbons of love." Malloy barked loudly at Orion, "Ribbons? What the fuck have you done?" Orion interrupted, explaining, "Don't worry Jim. I've got all bases covered. I'll explain to you in a bit. Don't get all crazy, Skipper. I had no choice but to bring an extra gift to the party and will explain at Rendezvous Point A." Then he added, "Captain, you didn't pick me as team leader back then for nothing." Malloy replied, "Okay, Lieutenant, you're running the ball." With that he hung up.

Immediately another call came through with the ring tone "Sweet Emotion" by Aerosmith. That told him his girlfriend of eight months was trying to reach him.

"Hey Stud. Are you coming by for lunch today? Maybe I'll give you a little dessert, too."

Orion laughed and replied, "I bet you will, baby doll, but it will have to be dinner. I'm delivering construction equipment out east."

Lanny Beatrice Cromwell. He liked the sound of her name and the fact she was crazy about him.

"What time do you think you'll be here so I can prepare you something good?"

"About 1900 hours, baby doll."

"What the hell is 1900 hours?" she wanted to know, bewildered.

Orion laughed. "That's 7 o'clock, sweetheart."

Lanny, full of joy, replied, "Okay, Johnny, don't be late!"

"I'll be there baby, by hook or crook."

His delight in hearing from her also brought with it a sigh of despair. He didn't want her to know his past. He also knew he would never lie to her. Then he remembered Captain Malloy's words: "Never feel bad about any mission you go on. It's for the greater good that we stay clandestine."

It was just about 0630 hours and Orion was still on the Long Island Expressway, ETA 0830 hours.

2 JIHAD IN JERSEY

Inside an old, abandoned warehouse in Kearney, New Jersey a meeting was about to begin. In this meeting were five men — three Yemenis nationalists and two Iranian fundamentalists. The taller of the two Iranian men was Kassim.

He began with a question. "Have the New York newspapers announced when the Emir of Kuwait will make his speech at the United Nations?"

The eldest looking Yemenis man replied, "Our sources have only told us that it is confirmed for Wednesday."

The other Iranian man, whose name was Milan Safir, asked Kassim, "This man that Rajhid has told us about, can he be trusted?"

The obese Yeminis man next to the eldest said, "We were told by a very high and reliable source that this man, Fashir, is the most credible Jihadist of our country."

Milan Safir responded, "What is your name and how do we trust what comes from your interpretations?" He pointed to the eldest and pelted, "Abdullah, who is this fat piece of shit that seems to speak for you?"

Abdullah retorted, "How fuckin' dare you question anyone who comes with me to these meetings."

All of a sudden, the little fat chubby one pulled a dagger from his robe, firing it at Milan Safir. It whipped past his right ear and caused a little blood to trickle.

The rotund knife thrower said to Safir, "Please allow me to introduce myself. My name is Omar Khaldif." He continued, "I was once the bodyguard for the Mullohur in Afghanistan. Do you have a problem with this?"

As the ruckus escalated, Kassim, the taller of the Iranian men, reached for his HK-P30. Before he could completely get it out, the third Yemenis man had a Mossberg shotgun pointed at his head. He said to Kassim, "On top of that, I am Omar's brother, Mustafa."

7

With that, Milan Safir said, "All right, all right, and all right. I'm sorry ,Abdullah, but you can never be too careful."

Abdullah watched his two compatriots lower their weapons. "If I didn't need you real bad for this Jihad, I would have had your heads cut off right now." Kassim implored Abdullah, "Please, I beg your forgiveness, Excellency. We are noble to the cause." Kassim then bowed his head to him and said, "We are all Hezbollah, the Party of God." He then reiterated, "We do this for the glory of Islam. Allah Akhbar, God is great."

All five stood and screamed at the top of their lungs, "Allah Akhbar, God is great."

With that, Omar Khaldif said, "Let's get down to brass taxes, as the Americans say. Mustafa, will you show our plan to our Iranian brothers?" Mustafa Khaldif was an expert in computers and circuitry gadgets. He also had a master's degree in Robotics and studied at a French university in 1999. He later joined his brother in Afghanistan in 2000. After 911, they both fled to Yemen and joined al-Qaeda. It was now November 26, 2010.

The plan of the two brothers from Yemen had been approved by Osama Bin Laden, himself. As the clock struck 0910 hours, Mustafa pulled out three giant blueprints. The first print contained all bridges and tunnels in and out of New York City. The second print disclosed all railways and shipyards throughout the five Burroughs. The third print showed all power stations, financial and Theater Districts and roadways.

Omar Khaldif stepped up to the table and pointed to the blueprints. "We have studied all access into New York City and tried to configure the best possible target to our plan."

His brother Mustafa broke in. "We have picked the Holland tunnel because it connects with out of state shipping and travel. This is a checkpoint coming into the city, and they will stop and detail any truck or vehicle that gives out a radioactive signal."

With that Omar cut in. "At approximately 1715 hours on Tuesday, November 30, three trucks and one passenger car will be set to enter the city."

Just as Omar tried to speak again, Milan Safir interrupted. "That is the stupidest thing I have ever heard. That's the first place to get caught; you are making us the lambs being led to the slaughter."

All witnessed Abdullah's face turning scarlet red. He walked right up to Kassim and demanded, "Tell your moronic brother to shut up and listen. If he doesn't and interrupts us once more, I will cut out his tongue."

Everyone at the meeting knew that the mission was to sneak weapon-grade plutonium into the city without being detected. "I'm sorry, Your Excellency, it won't happen again. Milan, please let them speak. Osama would never approve of it if it wasn't plausible."

"Thank you," said Omar, and proceeded to give details. "You will have truck number 1 in the front. With the passenger vehicle, we will have women and children in this car. The third vehicle will be the one with plutonium. The truck will be allowed to pass along, but it will only move 35 feet at which time you will hit a cut-off toggle switch and make it stall. From there, you will hit a switch in your truck that will lower a platform located in the center of your truck. At the same time, the truck behind the car will lower the same type of platform. The only difference is that one of Mustafa's little robot contraptions will pass under the car and onto the first truck that has been let through."

Abdullah cut in, "Now remember, everyone must do this precisely as soon as the truck has been detected with radiation. When the package is loaded safely and quickly, the third truck will try to pass the second truck, creating a diversion. The driver of the third truck must yell out 'I'm in a hurry! I have to get my cargo into Manhattan on time.' This will create more confusion. Kassim, you will be in the first truck. The passenger vehicle will be filled with women and children we have already picked from mosque in Jersey. They will have no idea what is going on. Tomorrow they will be told they are going to a play in the Theater District. Now, with the confusion going on at the truck stop, the first truck will proceed to the rendezvous point in the Theater District. This will be a big boom for Broadway."

They all burst out laughing.

With a face that was evil incarnate, Abdullah said, "Make no mistake. We are the salvation of the people of Islam. We will do this during the rush hour on Tuesday evening. Omar, you will tell this man, Fashir, on Tuesday morning to meet you at 1615 hours. He will be driving the third truck. I do this to ensure that the plan goes off without a hitch. The less people know, the better to initiate the success of the operation. Omar, you will communicate with Fashir at 1655 hours, and if you don't know what that is, its 4:55 p.m. You will tell him we are moving computer units to a warehouse in Tribeca. That will be our front because we will also be carrying computer units in the last two trucks. This will be an explanation of the radioactive detection."

Mustafa explained that if they don't buy it, well, too late, because the plutonium was already on its way. "Mission accomplished," he added, leering at the others.

Abdullah added, "Make sure all vehicles are in perfect working order and gassed up completely."

Omar looked at the two Iranian brothers and scolded them. "Do not get arrested over the weekend with your drinking and whoring around. Be smart and go to the mosque and pray to Allah for help and wisdom in our finest hour." With that, Milan walked to Omar and told him, "Seems like me and my brother are doing all the dirty work while you sit on your ass."

Abdullah walked between the two and said, "Please. We are all sharing in the glory of this Jihad. Now Milan, you must not say what you are saying. You see, it was Omar and his brother Mustafa's plan. They have figured out every detail down to how many feet the first truck must be to the extraction of the plutonium with Mustafa's robot. These things are all calculated to the rush hour traffic, so they will try to hurry everybody through. I do not think men of great minds and importance should be comprised at any cost."

With that Kassim strode over to Abdullah. "As always, you are correct, Excellency. Our minds will be clear as our hearts."

Abdullah responded, "You and your brother go forth and prepare for our destiny. Yours and Milan's name will be spoken on every tongue throughout the Islamic world."

Satisfied, the two Iranian men headed out the back door of the warehouse, both yelling "ALLAH AKHBAR." The door closed behind them. Omar Khaldif looked at his leader, Abdullah Musheen, and snorted, "Go forth and prepare our destiny? Those two assholes couldn't prepare burgers at McDonalds. Those fuckin' idiots get caught and everything will blow up in our face."

Abdullah explained to Omar and Mustafa, "They will not get caught. I have already taken those precautions."

Mustafa commented, "Kassim is not that bad, but that sissy-dressing friend of his, Milan, is definitely a risk."

Abdullah answered Mustafa, "That Kassim is the biggest ass kisser I've ever seen. If I had to suddenly stop short, his head will be stuck in my ass."

All three broke out in hilarious laughter.

"Don't worry, Omar, I'm going to let them know that their part of the mission is over as soon as we safely have the package tucked away. They would never contradict my word. After all, they will never know where the first truck went. Now, when you get a hold of our friend Fashir Salaam on Tuesday, make sure you don't forget to tell him he must stay in the truck at all cost. Tell him he must pretend to not understand English too good. Even if the police have to drag him from the truck, it will give the diversion time to work. All right, any more questions?"

Abdullah looked at them both. They said nothing. "Good, then I'm going into Manhattan to get laid at the infidel's many cat houses."

They all rose, laughing, and left for the front door.

"Allah, where has Rahjid been?"

Abdullah answered, "He's back in Yemen. Friends of Fashir are setting up a Jihad for him in Israel."

Fashir Salaam, the person of whom the three Yeminis terrorists spoke, was really Benjamin Kraemer. He was part of Orion's unit for six years. After all the years of blowing up buildings, he had decided to leave the

Navy and go to Architectural School. He was always an expert at taking them down; now he was an expert at putting them up. He had friends in the Mossad in Israel.

Last year while visiting the Holy Land on vacation, Joshua Golon, a captain in the Israeli Defense Force, came to him for help on a problem with a couple of Hezbollah extremists. This was because Benny was fluent in Arabic and Farzi. He looked more Arabic than Jewish. Therefore, he was able to infiltrate into a faction of Hezbollah run by a terrorist named Rahjid Hussein. Within the last week, Benny had tricked and had him captured by the Mossad.

Benny found someone else in the Arab world with the same name. He gave this person $5,000.00 in US currency and sent him on a vacation to Yemen. Obviously, the former First Class Petty Officer in the Navy S.E.A.L.S still showed he had the thrill of the hunt in his blood. Benny was also a computer expert and cryptographer.

Back in New Jersey, he tried to break a code in the computer of Abdullah Musheen, but it wasn't easy going. Just when he had it almost figured out, he heard someone coming down the hall. Benny opened the window and got out in the nick of time. It was the cleaning lady. As she opened the door, he barely got away. The cleaning lady's name was Roberta. She's been employed at the mosque for the past eight months.

"Oh look at this, Mr. Musheen has left his computer on and his window open." She turned off the computer and closed the door, then proceeded to clean Abdullah's office. After 15 minutes she finished, locked the window and door and turned on the alarm.

She won't come back till Tuesday. I'll have to try again when the alarm is off. I won't risk the life of the poor woman who has no idea what's going on, Benny thought to himself.

Time: 1300 hours. Friday, November 26, 2010.

JOHN PETER FERRIS

3 DELIVERANCE

On the road, an exasperated Orion shouted in his armored van, "Jesus, Mary, and Joseph! I've been off the expressway for well over an hour now. Damn it, how much longer?"

He looked at his diver's watch to check the bezel mark, noting he didn't have the patience he once had when he was with the team. Well, according to Malloy, I've got ten minutes to arrival time. Why the fuck doesn't he just say where instead of this recon practice. All of a sudden, Orion's phone played "Popeye the Sailor Man."

On the other end was Malloy. "You're only four minutes away from extraction point."

"No, fucking way. According to your time setting on my watch, I've still got 5 minutes and counting."

Malloy, in a woman-like voice, teased, "Oh, please don't come like Superman, I want to enjoy it." Then in his normal tone he said, "I forgot, you have a real lead foot. Slow down, a friend is going to say hello."

Just as Malloy hung up, a helicopter appeared 500 yards ahead.

Ah shit, it's the Suffolk county cops, I'm fucked. Just then, a familiar voice came over the chopper's loudspeaker. "You know kidnapping is a crime in this here country, ya'll."

Orion opened his van and ran towards the chopper. The door opened as the blades started slowing down. He yelled, "The only crime here is that some fuckin' fool who didn't know how much of a scumbag pirate you are, let you become a cop."

They both hugged each other like there was no tomorrow.

"Bobby, how you been, brother?" Orion picked him up by his legs and asked, "Can you still H.A.L.O. jump, or did you lose your balls?"

The pilot replied, "Can you still get up, old timer?"

"Ask your old lady, she had no problem last night."

Robert Palladin the G.O.D of Orion's team, replied, "My old lady's dead, you mother fucker."

Orion immediately hung his head down and replied with sorrow, "Bobby, I didn't know."

"Well don't let it get to you . . . Ha! I got you again. My old ladies are all whores."

Orion whacked the back of Palladin's head. "You'll never fuckin' change, will ya?"

At that moment, Captain Malloy pulled up in another van that looked even more fortified than Orion's. "C'mon, Johnny be bad, we ain't got all day. Play fuck fuck with him some other time. Got to finish your mission, Orion."

Palladin looked at Orion. "He hasn't changed much, old prick!"

"Ya think?" replied Orion, grinning.

Palladin saluted Malloy and headed for the chopper. Looking back at Orion he said, "I'd ask you to hang out, but the Skipper thinks you're getting tied down. I definitely got to meet this filly who tamed the hearts of the craziest man alive."

Orion replied, "What do you mean, by hearts?"

"You've got two, one on your sleeve, and one up your ass." Palladin then started the rotors and threw a salute towards Orion.

Orion couldn't help but admire the situation. Look at this devious bastard, Malloy, using Bobby Palladin in his job to hide the transfer of the two women. The Captain thinks of everything.

As quickly as Bobby Palladin pulled up in the chopper, he vanished across the horizon. Best chopper pilot I've seen. I wish I were half the pilot he was, admired Orion.

He proceeded to help Malloy transfer the two still very incoherent young girls to Malloy's van.

"Where the fuck did you get this one from?" asked Malloy. "Can't you just keep things simple?"

"Hey, you told me to make sure this guy Pearson's, daughter has no idea her father is behind her abduction. Well Captain, the other girl would have told police about a kidnapping, assault and the killing of those two dirt-bag-pimping drug dealers." Orion explained further, "It would have caused a statewide alert and compromised the mission."

Malloy looked at him, shook his head a little, and said, "Very good, Lieutenant. Always thinking ahead."

"I regret to tell you that maybe our little princess here might of caught a glimpse of my lovely ugly mug."

"What?" groaned Malloy. "Did this other girl see you too?"

"Negative," replied Orion, "Got her from behind with a sleeper hold." Malloy was worried. "This is why I told you never, ever do it alone. I keep telling you this, John! Orion, you're getting sloppy since you left the team."

Orion gave Malloy a squinty stare. "I'd only trust the men from my fire team," he responded sarcastically.

"How much do you think she'll remember? Kendra used to be a very bright young lady".

Orion looked at Malloy, puzzled, and asked, "Yo Skipper! Who the hell is she to you? She's not related, is she?"

"Kind of. Me and her father go way back to NAM. Let's just say, Lieutenant, I owe her father my life."

Orion automatically nodded in agreement. "I think I've kind of been there myself," and bowed his head in reverence towards Malloy.

Malloy checked to make sure the two girls were strapped in securely and safely, and both were still unconscious, blindfolded and handcuffed. Only now they were cuffed to a fortified restraining bar along the back seat.

Malloy closed the door to his van as a stretch limo pulled up fast. Orion immediately reached for his sidearm, but as he cleared his holster Malloy put up his hand to stop him.

"Put that fuckin' thing away," Malloy scolded.

As the limousine came to a stop, both the driver and passenger doors opened. From the driver's side out stepped a very beautiful woman, looking like she worked on Wall Street. She was dressed in stylish and respectable attire. A second later, out stepped a man in an Armani suit, refined.

As he turned to face both them, Orion saw through the man's aviator sunglasses and recognized Ex Master Chief Petty Officer Michael Trudeaux. Trudeaux was also part of Orion's unit between the late '90s until Orion gave up his commission in 2005.

"Still a trigger happy son of a bitch, Lt.? You still wear your heart on your sleeve? How've you been, Johnny?" the refined man asked.

Orion looked at him and said, "Tell me you work for the Skipper, too. Trudy, you're too smart for him."

Malloy interrupted, "FUCK BOTH OF YOU PUSSIES," and walked up to the woman. "Sorry for the French, Claire."

She smiled at Malloy. "Your redefined vocabulary does not bother me." She reiterated, "Not one fuckin' bit."

Malloy shook his head laughingly. "Well, Miss Vanderkamp, you have an extra young lady in the van, same predicament as Kendra. Please just proceed to the institute and I'll explain everything to Dr. Pearson when I get there later." Without any hesitation, Claire climbed into the driver's side of Malloy's van. She headed east and disappeared into the distance as the three Ex-Navy Commando's gathered at the front of Orion's van.

"Like I was saying before I was rudely interrupted, you work for the Skipper?"

"No, not at all!" replied Trudy. "I do little odds and ends for his good friend, Dr. Jeff Pearson." He went on, "Dr. Pearson helped me get into law school here with Captain's help."

Orion laughed out loud. "From shooting a Ma Deuce 50 caliber to an ambulance chaser. If that ain't fucked up!"

Malloy cut in, "Hey Orion, don't laugh. With the bad habits you pick up, you might need him one day."

Trudeaux handed Captain Malloy a manila envelope. He pulled a double-edged dagger from his boot and opened it. Extracting a single sheet of paper, he skimmed it, then folded it up and put it away. He then handed the envelope to Orion and said, "Here's the twenty grand I promised you, and the doctor has given you another twenty grand bonus on top of that."

Orion looked at Malloy, very confused, and asked, "What's going on, Captain?"

Malloy looked first at Trudeaux, then turned to Orion. "I told Jeff all about you, Lieutenant, and he would like to meet the man who rescued his little girl." Orion responded right away, "I don't have time for this, Captain. I'm having a special dinner tonight with my girlfriend and my whole weekend is at her disposal."

Trudeaux interrupted, "Lt., take my word for it. This is one extraordinary scientist."

Malloy cut in, "He's having a big shindig out at his estate tonight at 1800 hours. Bring your lady along. I'd like to meet the girl who captured John Patrick Orion's heart. You know, the one you wear on your sleeve. There will be a lot of big shot dignitaries, and Johnny, I guarantee she'll be impressed."

"I'll run it past her, but if we come, it's in the Roadrunner."

Malloy responded, "Let me know by 1620 hours so you're on the invite list."

"Will do. Aye, aye, Skipper."

With the conversation ended, Trudy went to the rear of the limousine and opened it for Malloy. "After you, Your Majesty."

Malloy started to climb in and said, "You're pushing it, Mikey."

Trudy shut the door and gave Malloy his middle finger while heading for the driver seat." Just before getting into the limo he turned to Orion. "Bring your sorry-looking ass there, brother."

"We'll see. I promised her a night alone, but anything's possible." Both men entered their vehicles and drove off.

Time: 1345 hours.
****

Time: 1555 hours.

Former Navy Lieutenant John Orion arrived at his warehouse and pulled in right next to his souped-up 1969 Plymouth Roadrunner. Exiting the van, he reached into the back and grabbed his cache bag and approached the Roadrunner. He unlocked the passenger door and placed his Sig Sauer 45 in the glove box, with its holster. Under his leather jacket he fished out his combat knife, unzipped the cache bag and deposited it. Then he retrieved the smaller version, a S.E.A.L pup knife, and opened the trunk, reaching in to grab a shotgun bag with a Mossberg in it. He unzipped it and put in the pup.

Orion shut the trunk, grabbed the bag and headed for his special bookcase. All this damn driving has made me hungry. He reached for his trouser belt and grabbed his cell phone, pressing number 2 on the speed dial. It rang immediately.

Lanny Cromwell was just manhandling a really big frying pan out of her cupboard when her favorite ring tone sang, "I'll Stop the World and Melt with You." It was Orion, and she eagerly answered. "Hey baby, what do you have, a sixth sense? I was just about to start cooking."

After a short silence Orion replied, "Lanny, I am going to throw something your way."

She interrupted, "Johnny, come hook or crook. You better be here at seven like you promised. Don't you dare tell me something has come up."

Orion replied softly, "Baby, you haven't started dinner yet, have you?"

"I was just about to, John Patrick Orion. I will hunt you down if you tell me you're not going to make it."

"I know I promised we would stay in for dinner tonight, but I ran into an old friend and he invited us to a big rich gala out in the Hamptons. Lots of big shot dignitaries there. Please don't be pissed, sweetheart. If you don't want to go, we won't. It's just that I haven't seen him since I left the Navy five years ago."

After a three second silence he said, "Okay Lanny, you're right. This is our night together. I'll just call my friend and let him know we decline."

Lanny screamed into the phone, "Oh, don't you dare! Big shot dignitaries? Well, you're showing me off tonight, Orion. I have the perfect dress, it's just the thing. Of course I want to go, especially after seeing nothing but blood and guts all month at Winthrop Hospital. I deserve this, baby. What shoes shall I wear? I think I'll put on Chanel perfume."

Orion cut in, "Yes darling, just be ready at 1630 hours. I mean 4:30. I'm going to pick up my tux at my mom's and I'll shower there to kill time. Baby, it's a real long drive, so be ready."

She started saying, "Maybe I should wear my satin Vera Wang."

"Just be ready, Lady Beatrice," he said, hanging up quickly. His two pet wolves were at his side. "Women, can't live with them, and can't live without them," he said while grabbing a bag of dry dog food. He mixed in two cans and watched as they grubbed it down.

"Slow down, you eat like a pack of wolves!" he laughed. "Well, at least two. Now I'm going to go clean up whatever mess you made and I got to go." He patted each affectionately. "Now guard the shop and eat anybody who comes in except for old man Walter, 'cause he feeds you when I'm not here." Both animals wagged their tails. They loved their master, and he trained them so well. If anybody broke in, they knew to be silent, crawl and sneak up on any intruder. Orion hugged these two extraordinary pets and jumped in the black Roadrunner. He pulled out of the warehouse and the iron door began to shut.

Time: 1608 hours.

****

Time: 1610 hours.

Malloy's cell phone jingled "Closer to home" by Grand Funk Railroad. "Skipper, it's me. We'll be a tiny bit late, but we're coming."

Malloy replied, "Is your lady friend annoyed with you?"

"I practically had to twist her arm. You owe me, Skipper."

Malloy replied, "Both of you will have the time of your life. It will be a day, or should I say night, that you'll never forget."

"Got to go, Skipper. See ya at the party."

Orion was 20 minutes late picking up Lanny. It didn't matter, because Lanny still took 15 more minutes than usual. It was worth the wait. She was beautiful and elegant . . . Orion couldn't keep from staring. He knew this was the girl he wanted to finally settle down with. Fortunately, Lanny wanted this also. Orion, of course, was a tiny bit shy and hadn't yet expressed it to her, but this weekend he planned to let Lanny know for sure.

"Lanny, honey, you are going to stop rocket ships the way you look tonight, baby," he gasped.

Lanny looked at him. "You really clean up nice, Johnny. I'm used to you in that horrible looking military type stuff. That is one sharp-looking tuxedo."

"This suit is my favorite. It's a Christian Dior," He said proudly. "I've got only two other suits and they're Giorgio Armani, and Dolce & Gabbana." He grimaced and added, "Cost me a fortune, so don't be ripping my clothes off later."

Lanny laughed. "Just drive, cowboy."

Time: 1650 hours.

****

Sixty miles off the coast of New Jersey, a Liberian freighter paralleled the shores of the United States.

Time: 1650 hours. November 26, 2010.

4 FUTURE SCIENTOLOGY

Time: 1910 hours.

"Holy shit," Orion said in amazement. "Look at all those fancy limos, sports car, and Rolls Royces!" As he and Lanny pulled into the estate driveway, Orion's thundering motor could be heard 1000 feet to the back of the house where the luxurious pool shimmered. The valet opened the passenger door. "Good evening, Ma'am, may I assist you?"

"Oh, thank you very much, but I'm okay."

Orion stepped out of the driver's side and spoke to the valet, "Yo, my laptop better be in there when I come back."

At the front door stood Captain James Malloy and next to him was Dr. Jeffrey Pearson.

As Orion finished his comment to the valet, Lanny scolded him. "Johnny, behave yourself." Looking at the valet she explained, "Don't mind him, I forgot my old man's leash."

With that, the valet closed the door and drove off . . . when all the sudden a blinking set of lights went off, accompanied by a blaring siren. Orion ran to the driver's door and opened it. "Sorry about that, Honcho, forgot to turn off the security."

The Maitre d' came bolting. "Excuse me, sir, are your names on the list?" Orion replies sarcastically, "Well, they better be. I didn't drive fuckin' three hours and fifteen minutes to jerk off."

As the Maitre d' summoned security, Dr. Pearson intervened. "Easy, Ludlow, they are special guests of mine."

Orion cracked a mile-wide smile. "Hear that, Lud Dick, we're special." Malloy walked up. "Know your place, Lieutenant."

Orion lowered his head and excused himself. "Sorry sir; got carried away."

Malloy eyed him for one second, then walked up to Lanny and spoke reverently, "Ah, you must be the beautiful young lady my old Lieutenant has told me about."

Lanny put on a little school girl smile and replied, "Thank you very much." Orion made introductions. "Captain James Malloy, this here is Lanny Cromwell." He turned to his girlfriend. "Lanny, this old coot was my Commanding Officer in the Navy."

"I'm very pleased to meet you. Johnny has mentioned you lots of times." Doctor Pearson interjected, "Shall we join the other guests inside?"

The entrance was grand, and exquisite sounds from an expert orchestra wafted from the rear of a great big hall in the back of the house — "Bolero" by Ravel.

As they walked in, Pearson said to Lanny, "May I borrow John from you for a minute?"

"You may, but I want him back right away. He's mine for this weekend."

"I need him just for a second," Pearson reassured her.

Jim Malloy offered his arm. "Care to dance with this old sailor?"

Lanny replied, "I would love to, James, and I don't find you old. Shall we?"

Malloy headed for the ballroom, which made a gymnasium look like a bathroom.

Watching as the two slipped just out of ear reach, Dr. Pearson told Orion, "I don't know how I could ever repay you for bringing my little girl back to me alive."

Orion sarcastically answered, "Yo Doc! Kendra is only 19-years-old and she's strung out bad. I see all your well-to-do digs, and why would a girl who has everything want to become a piece of street trash? Hate to say it, Doc, but the buck stops with you."

Pearson covered his brow slightly with his left hand. "Oh! Believe me, John, I do blame myself. It's just I've been caught up in my research projects, and I've completely neglected her. I'll never, ever put my work above my daughter again. You see, John, when I lost my wife Arlene, I went on a crusade to conquer all cancer known to this earth. Arlene died of breast cancer six years ago. From that time on I've buried myself in work."

Orion interrupted, "I didn't know what kind of person I was going to meet when I first pulled into this fancy mansion, but Jeff, any man that does what you do for his fellow human beings is my friend for life. And because I'm your friend, make a deal with me. Pearson, keep your attention focused on Kendra, or next time I'll kick your ass!"

Both men shook hands and patted each other on the shoulder.

"C'mon, Doc, let's get lit. You're buying." Orion laughingly pulled on Pearson's lapel and led him.

"John, I never ever drink."

Orion shrugged his shoulders. "You're just like my Lanny. She never drinks either; must be some kind of sickness going around. Guess you're going to have to find a cure for that, too!"

"Grab yourself a drink and meet me in the ballroom," responded Pearson. "I'll introduce you around."

"Be there in a flash." Orion moved to his right where the waiters entered with fresh champagne. For fun he grabbed a fluted glass of bubbly, not that he cared much for it, and entered the adjoining room. Standing at the edge of the bar was none other than Bobby Palladin.

Beating Orion to the punch line he said, "Hide the silverware, there's a pirate in the house." Both men grinned and Bobby continued, "I met your girlfriend when she was dancing with Skipper." He paused for a second and added, "Not   bad   Lt,   not   bad   at   all."

"Thanks, Master Chief. Man, it's good to see you, Bobby."

Before Bobby could answer the bartender approached the two friends and Orion beckoned him. "To hell with champagne. Can I get a Sam Adams? Also, let me have a shot of Jack Daniels."

"I'm sorry sir, but we only have two shot cocktail glasses."

Orion replied, "That will do.'

"Hope you aren't driving, Lt.," commented Palladin.

Orion jumped right in his face. "Do I look that irresponsible? Bobby, I'm still the same guy from five years ago. Lanny doesn't drink, so she carries my sorry ass around."

Palladin reiterated, "Just checking. I'm always looking from above, as you said, for that sorry ass of yours."

Orion answered, "Besides, I'm going to propose to that gorgeous girl and pray she says yes to this sorry sailor.

"Hey, congrats," answered Palladin. "Finally, this buccaneer is gonna settle down."

"Ya'll bet your sorry ass." Both men burst out laughing at the inside joke. When Palladin was first assigned to his unit, Orion always made fun of Palladin's southern accent.

Palladin looked up at the clock and said, "C'mon, ten minutes to show time."

Orion, befuddled, said, "What show"?

"Dr. Pearson has a bunch of stockholders and investors here tonight to advertise his research. It seems he's had some big breakthroughs with that there all nano-type technology."

Orion blurted out, "Nano what?"

"I don't much know at all about that scientific stuff, but I hear it's about the microscopic stuff with cell regeneration."

Feeling somewhat amazed, Orion responded, "Oh yeah, I've heard about this study. Supposedly they were experimenting with micro-circuitry with live human cells." He snickered, "I'd better bring an extra drink. "Probably going to be boring." Summoning the bartender, he commanded, "Barkeep, give me one more for the matinee."

Grabbing his drink and Bobby, Orion headed for the ballroom and ran right into Pearson at the entrance. "Professor, does your orchestra take requests?"

Dr. Pearson replied, "Not my orchestra. But if you go up to the conductor and ask, 'Maestro Faison, could you play this?' he might say yes."

The former S.E.A.L. headed to the orchestra pit. The conductor was just finishing a waltz when Orion yelled up to him, "Maestro, do you take requests?" The conductor, without a twitch, asked Orion, "What do you want to hear?"

"A Kiss from a Rose, by Seal."

"Right after this piece," the maestro answered.

"Thank you, Maestro Faison."

Orion headed over to Lanny, who was sitting with Captain Malloy and a lot of military brass looking types. He recognized the Sixth Fleet Top Admiral of S.E.A.L. Team Two. Walking right up he spoke. "These musicians seem to know how to play almost anything. C'mon baby, the song is just finishing and the next request is ours."

Lanny took Orion's hand and entered the ballroom floor. Every eye in the house turned suddenly to witness the two lovebirds.

"What song are we dancing to?"

Orion smiled and replied, "The one from our first night dancing."

Lanny got nervous. "They play classical music. Your telling me they just know it out of the blue?"

As she finished talking the orchestra started the medley.

Holding Lanny gently in his arms he moved slowly across the ballroom floor. About 20 seconds into the song they clearly heard Seal singing the song from the P.A. speakers. Orion and Lanny look over at the same time to behold the real-life Seal singing next to the orchestra pit.

"Oh my God Johnny, that's really Seal! John Patrick Orion, I Love you!" "Baby, I had nothing to do with that," he laughed. "But I love you, too."

The whole evening's entourage gasped as Johnny and Lanny passionately embraced while they danced. As the song slowly came to an end, Orion looked over at the Captain's table and saw Mike Trudeaux arriving.

The song ended to giant applause for the couple. Dr. Pearson suddenly appeared from the other side of the mansion and spoke to the crowd.

"Ladies and Gentlemen, if I may have your undivided attention." A deep silence descended on the grand ballroom.

"In about ten minutes I hope to see everyone seated in the building

Citadel next door to the house. You may bring your drinks with you and we have set up a small bar for your convenience in the auditorium."

Orion yelled, "Way to go, Doc!"

Pearson continued, "The presentation will start in twenty minutes. Hope to see you then." As he headed out towards the back of the ballroom, the servants began opening one of the two 20 foot doors. Pearson called to the ushers, "Please accompany our guests and make them feel comfortable and relaxed before the show. Have the Military Attaché seated in front, by the main column. Have our science division next to them. I'm going now to help Claire finish setting up." With that, Pearson disappeared out the back door.

Lanny asked Orion, "What's going on, Johnny? What presentation is Dr. Pearson talking about?"

"I think this is about the research with nano-technology that Dr. Pearson has been working with. You know, working with human cells and that microscopic bullshit to help cure disease. We'll just stay here, baby. We don't have to watch all that hoopla crap."

Lanny's face showed disgust. "First of all, Johnny Patrick Orion, it would be rude and insulting to not show up. Second of all, if you haven't noticed, I'm an emergency nurse and I see helpless people dying of horrible diseases every day. Now you will escort me to the very front of the good doctor's auditorium and you will stop with those childish wisecracks. Understand?"

Orion covered his head. "Sorry baby, it must be the booze." He offered his arm to Lanny and slowly they walked towards those humongous doors. As they left Malloy's table, Orion noticed Trudeaux, Palladin and Malloy in hysterics. Walking past part of his old team, he picked up his left hand and pointed the middle finger towards them.

Right away out of Lanny's mouth came, "I saw that, and another thing. Enough with the stinking booze tonight. You know I can't stand that stuff." Then stopping abruptly she put her face in the front of Orion's and said, "Love you, Johnny".

"Love you too, baby doll." They kissed for about 5 seconds and started walking again. Lanny lifted up her left hand and gave the trio her own middle finger, without Orion noticing. The whole table broke out in uncontrollable laughter.

Palladin stood and said laughingly, "Love you too, kiss, kiss, kiss, pucker, pucker, pucker. I can't believe that tigress has tamed our infamous sandman." Trudeaux laughed and responded in a low baritone voice, "Sorry baby, it must be the booze. I wouldn't believe it if I didn't hear it with my own ears!" Malloy also stood and told Palladin and Trudy, "Give the guy a break. Both of you should be so lucky to have somebody like her."

Both Palladin and Trudeaux stopped laughing immediately and put on serious faces. At the same time, they shaped their right hands like a gun and pointed at their skulls, saying "BANG." The laughter got hysterical again.

Malloy continued, "Come on, you cowards, the presentation is going to start soon."

With that, everyone at the table, including the military attaché, stood and proceeded toward the giant doors. The S.E.A.L. Team Two Liaison, Vice Admiral Fischer, slowed down to have a word with Malloy.

Fischer asked, "So he's the famous sandman I've heard all about. Malloy, he was your boy. Why did they give him that name?"

Malloy looked the Admiral squarely in the eye. "He would be the first to sneak into enemy encampments and destroy everyone and everything in his path. The rest of his team would scrawl sandman all over after wiping out the enemy." Malloy continued, "I trained Orion myself. He excelled above anybody I ever trained before. Sir, when I tell you he is the best, I mean it."

Malloy stopped for a second then continued proudly, "I'm saying the best."

The admiral looked astonished. "Then why did he decide to leave the team?"

"His dad died six years ago. Three months later his mother, Rosa, had a stroke and has been confined to a wheel chair. Admiral, the team lost a real good man who loves his country more than anything, but he loves his mom even more."

"Shame," said the Admiral. "We sure could use him now."

As they walked out the ballroom toward the Citadel, Admiral Fischer introduced Malloy to the military brass accompanying him. "Jim, this is General Arlen Douglas, head of the Army's Medical Research and Development." General Douglas acknowledged, "Please to meet you, Captain. Fischer talks a lot about you."

"All lies, sir, I'm innocent," responded Malloy.

As the military entourage continued down the short path to another giant building, General Douglas beckoned to Malloy. "I understand you served with Fischer in Vietnam."

"Yes, I did, sir. That's how we met Commander Jeffrey Pearson. The Admiral was a Captain then and I was a Lieutenant. Captain Fischer back then was in charge of our amphibious base in Pelou north of Saigon. Want to hear the story?"

"Absolutely," replied General Douglas.

"One day we came under artillery fire from the V.C and Captain Fischer was hit with shrapnel right in his torso. We mayday'd command and they sent a chopper up to get us out to a hospital ship in Cam Ran Bay."

Admiral Fischer interrupted abruptly. "I wouldn't be here if it wasn't for Dr. Pearson. He saved my ass that day and five months later saved Malloy's. Enough of this jungle talk. Let's go inside and enjoy ourselves."

An usher swept the entourage through the doors and said, "Enjoy your evening."

The auditorium was set up beautifully, like a giant movie theater. The first 20 rows were parallel and straight from the stage. The seating arrangement curved perpendicular to those seats. It reminded Orion of the Ryman auditorium in Nashville where he visited a couple years ago.

They were led to the front rows and Malloy spotted Orion and Lanny sitting center of the stage.

"Captain Malloy, sit next to me and Johnny," invited Lanny.

Malloy gratefully responded, "I've love to, Miss Cromwell. Don't look so bored, lieutenant, you might learn something to stimulate that stubborn brain of yours."

Orion shrugged. "Whatever!"

"That's exactly what I told him. See, Johnny?" agreed Lanny.

Orion put his left hand to his forehead and exclaimed, "Yeah, yeah, yeah." He looked around to find the place was getting packed and noticed his girlfriend's innocent and gleeful smile. Why does this sweet and gentle girl want anything to do with me? he wondered for the umpteenth time.

"You look real happy, baby. I'm glad."

With puppy dog eyes Lanny replied, "Your friends are so nice. They make me feel like family. James, Trudy, and Bobby — you're lucky to have some great friends."

Orion smiled and agreed. "I'd die for them".

"Well then, Lieutenant Orion," Lanny joked, "I've finally found the man I've always been looking for."

Just then the stage lighting toned down and the curtain opened slowly. The crowd automatically fell silent. From the right side of the curtains, Claire Vanderkamp walked toward the podium front and center. Commanding the microphone she announced, "Ladies and gentlemen and distinguished guests, we welcome you tonight to our corporate presentation. We will share with our stockholders and constituents the vital progress and research that Pearson Global Technologies has pioneered."

The crowd enthusiastically applauded.

"The past year has been exciting. Our research team, led by Professor Jeffrey Pearson, has stumbled on amazing scientific discoveries. I'm proud to announce that our institute has put our several scientific laboratories and robotic science departments to good use. To tell you about the progress, I present to you the founder of our institute. Ladies and Gentlemen, Professor Jeffrey Pearson."

The crowd stood and repeated the thunderous applause.

"Ladies and gentlemen, and of course our fellow stockholders, please be seated. After all, you're all paying for this." The crowd rumbled with good humor. "I'm kidding, of course," added Pearson with a smile. "Just in the past year alone, we've made scientific breakthroughs that are beyond imagination. With these breakthroughs we hope to impact the future of mankind and completely eradicate deadliest of diseases on the planet."

More applause erupted, along with a very loud whistle coming from the vicinity of Orion's seat. Lanny nudged him.

"Our research teams have combined nano-technology, human cell regeneration, and robotic science all into one equation. We are starting to master the regeneration of human cells through mitosis and microscopic robot engineering to stimulate the growth process. Just imagine, ladies and gentlemen, the stimulation of cells not only to regenerate them, but to aid them through micro-computers. Further imagine nano probes teaching the brain to destroy deadly dangerous organisms in our bodies. These tiny microscopic machines assist with what the human body cannot accomplish on its own. Who would want this?"

Lanny bursts out, "I would, Professor Pearson." The crowd gave a pleasing chuckle, and it was Orion's turn to nudge back.

"Of course you would, Miss Cromwell. I found out tonight, ladies and gentlemen, that Miss Cromwell works at a very prestigious hospital as an emergency nurse. Just imagine intravenously injecting what we call Super Nano-Microbes into human bodies and electrically and neurologically healing them while stimulating production of antibodies and cellular reconstruction. The outcomes could be endless." The crowd applauded.

Dr. Pearson beamed. "We've filmed one of our experiments to share the extraordinary results of our research."

With that, the room darkened as an enormous screen lowered from the ceiling to the stage floor. The voice of Claire Vanderkamp opened the prologue. "Here at Pearson Global Technologies we dedicate ourselves to top quality research and development in pursuit of excellence. Our goal? To achieve a better quality of life throughout the world for all mankind."

The film showed Dr. Pearson and other scientists around a lab table, with Dr. Pearson narrating the demonstration. "This bunny rabbit has been diagnosed with liver cancer, and in order to save its life we've introduced our super-nano microbes to its body. We've first extracted a cancerous culture from the diseased liver and put it under an Electron microscope." The film showed the deadly organisms in a Petri dish under microscopic enhancement. The doctor grabbed what looked like a harness and attached it to the rabbit.

"We secure the Electromagnetic Accelerator to the host subject to supercharge the super nano probes and microcircuits, accomplished through an injection of the technology. We first introduce a mixture of the regenerating microbes and glucose liquid intravenously." The professor continued, "To do so, we strap the harness around the body of the test subject. The remainder of the microscopic probes are introduced to the host via the harness. On the underside are tiny syringes containing the robotic nano microbes. The Accelerator is powered by one small nuclear battery which shall remain top secret to protect our corporation's security and intellectual property. The accelerator produces an unbelievable amount of magnetic current, so powerful it surpasses any known magnetic detector. Within five minutes, the harness syringes automatically release the second half of the concoction. The accelerator targets the source of disease before the deadly organisms have time to react."

Lanny's mouth opened wide in amazement. All Orion noticed were the purple L.E.D lights that flickered on and off, much like the lights in his Roadrunner.

Professor Pearson continued. "We've set the accelerator for only five minutes because a longer duration would hamper removal. The magnetic field, you see, creates an indescribable force field and would very likely overcharge the microscopic nano probes. We aren't certain, but assume an overdose may then kill the host subject." The film then showed the harness powering down.

Dr. Pearson removed the harness from the rabbit. Almost instantly the animal jumped nearly the length of the operating room.

Everyone on the auditorium was in complete awe of the presentation and of Dr. Pearson. He elaborated, "The rabbit's jump is just a nervous reaction we believe is caused by the incredible magnetic force."

On the film a scientist retrieved the rabbit and returned it to the table. Orion yelled out, "Yo bunny rabbit, I'd jump across the room if someone tried to magnetize my balls." The whole auditorium burst out in hilarious laughter. Lanny glared at Orion with disgust and scolded him, "I'm warning you Johnny, stop the shit now." Orion cowered down and said, "Okay, okay, okay. I'm sorry, it won't happen again."

As Orion and everybody in the auditorium settled down, the demonstration continued. The doctor pushed a fat syringe into the liver for a another Petri dish culture. As the doctor pulled out the syringe, the rabbit jumped across the room again.

Lanny immediately turned to Orion and held her finger right up to his face. "Don't even think about it," she hissed.

Orion cowered again and made a zipper movement across his mouth. Lanny nodded in approval.

Dr. Pearson proceeded to examine the contents of the Petri dish under the microscope.

As the results appeared on the screen, the auditorium erupted in awe. There is no sign at all of the cancer.

"Wait one minute, ladies and gentlemen," said a reluctant Professor Pearson. The cheering of the crowd was so overwhelming that Professor Pearson had to move closer to the microphone in order to be heard.

He cried out, "Please, can I have your attention?"

The crowd began to settle down. Pearson spoke discreetly, "I understand your jubilant reaction, but there was one setback in the experiment."

The audience responded with looks of bewilderment.

"Almost a week after this demonstration, the test subject started showing signs of acute Parkinson's disease. After that, our research teams began a more precise calibration of both types of super nano microbes. We still have more kinks to work out, but are very close to achieving total success. Recently, I and my colleague have completed a belt and harness attached to a suit — the Electromagnetic Accelerator. My colleague, Professor Kamal Darfuir, one of the most renowned scientists of our era, has made nerve end modifications to both the microscopic nano microbes."

The professor paused to give the audience time to digest the complexities of his research.

"The intricate circuitry alone for one super nano probe takes at least thirty days to complete. These nano super microbes are manufactured in a white room with technicians dressed in masks and special suits to prevent contamination. From there, they are stored in a deep freezer until they are ready for deployment. Until we get it completely right, we will have to use small lab animals. We are so close to using it on a human host, but until then, we are regulated by Congress, the Justice Department, the AMA and the FDA to operate within strict guidelines.

"I bet they want a blood sample and your first born, too!" shouted Johnny, who hated red tape and was unable to restrain himself.

Lanny pinched the daylights out of his pectoral muscle as the crowd murmured agreement.

"Ladies and gentlemen," continued the doctor, "Pearson Global Technology is entering an age of discovery far beyond man's imagination. With the support of our stockholders and distinguished investors, I can guarantee strength in profits and prosperity. Within six months' time, we'll be ready for a human test subject. After N.A.S.A. verifies our research and findings, they will sign on with complete approval. Until then, ladies and gentlemen, enjoy your evening in the ballroom."

Pearson walked to the back of the stage as the giant screen ascended and the curtains closed. The audience applauded thunderously, then began exiting the auditorium and heading back to the main house.

As Orion started up the path he whispered to Lanny, "Baby, you really don't buy all that mumbo jumbo, do ya? I don't really believe that this will save all mankind."

Lanny frowned with disapproval and responded, "Of course I do. Johnny, don't have such a closed mind. From what I see, it's just a start. Have faith in your fellow man."

Orion snapped back, "I've seen what my fellow man can do, and he destroys everything for his own benefit, Lanny. I don't want to get started about it. This is our night, baby."

"Okay, Johnny." She reached up and kissed him. When they walked ten feet she got in the last word. "But you are wrong, as usual. Discussion over."

"What, I don't have no say in the matter?"

"No."

Knowing Lanny's tone of voice, Orion shut up and kept walking.

Their entourage entered the mansion and located their reserved table. The military heads quietly began bickering amongst themselves. The four main top brass consisted of Vice Admiral Thomas Fischer, General Arlen Douglas, General Franklin Castorino (U.S.A.F.), and Lt. Colonel Marcus Henderson (U.S Army). They each lent their voice to a robust assessment of the presentation. "I don't know if the boys on the Hill are going to be on board, or if they are too chicken shit to get their hands dirty with this one. I like what I see, but too many officials are afraid of stepping up to the plate and swinging for the fences," remarked General Castorino.

General Douglas concurred. "Yes, Franklin, but what if N.A.S.A. approves this in the next six months? Do we tell our superiors we weren't sure, so we scrubbed the appropriation funds because we didn't know how to take charge?"

General Douglas' Liaison Officer, the Lt. Colonel, cut in. "Well, I tell you what. We make them think on the Hill that there is only a small remedial quirk that will be eradicated. We then hold the funds in an Escrow Account marked: Time to be Determined."

Hearing this, Malloy whispered to Orion, "Look at this shit. Even the High Command is still passing the fuckin' buck."

Orion answered, "Let the Marx brothers play fuck fuck with each other. We're here to have a good time, Skipper." He suggested that he, Lanny, and his old team go up to the dock.

Malloy agreed, "Good idea, Lieutenant. Jeffrey has his yacht parked there."

The comrades once again headed out those colossal doors in the back of the ballroom. Approaching the canal, they come across seven immense yachts.

Malloy pointed to the sailing schooner in the middle and said, "It's Pearson's."

More of a ship than a yacht, all of them thought at the same time.

As they climbed onto the gangway, Bobby Palladin exclaimed, "Nice to have fuckin' money, huh?"

Malloy said reassuring, "He's earned every nickel and dime of it."

While they climbed onboard, Dr. Pearson and a short man come from the forecastle and spotted them.

"Ah," remarked Dr. Pearson, "Friends seem to have found their way to my little dingy."

Palladin joked, "Where do you park your airplane on this carrier?"

As Dr. Pearson and the short man walked into view, they noticed the man was of Middle Eastern descent. Pearson welcomed everybody and introduced the man as Professor Kamal Darfuir.

Orion and Palladin whispered to each other at the same time, "This guy's a hadjee."

Trudeaux overheard and responded, "Yo Lieutenant, and you too, Chief. This man is the kindest man I've ever met. Excuse me, Dr. Camel, I'd like for you to meet my unit buddies from the Navy."

The professor replied candidly, "Mr. Trudy, it's pronounced Kamal. Plus my last name is Darfuir," he told Trudeaux. "No reason to apologize, Mr. Trudy." Just as Trudeaux tried to speak, Dr. Pearson interrupted, "Dr. Darfuir, we must lock the harness up before it gets too late and we forget."

Pearson turned his attention to Lanny and asked, "Miss Cromwell, would you be interested in seeing the electromagnetic device we've been working on?

Lanny looked at Orion and gave him the 'do you mind if I go?' look.

"Go ahead, sweetheart. I'm not interested in some wacky doggy leash. I'm going to sit here with my buddies and have one beer."

As she and the two scientists crossed the gangway to the dock, she scolded Orion, "One beer and one beer only."

"Yes, Your Highness."

Professor Pearson and Dr. Darfuir led Lanny back to the citadel and to a door behind the stage. Pearson took the keys out of his pocket and opened the passage leading down the hall to an elevator. To summon the elevator, a retinal eye scanner awaited on the left, requiring him to peer into it. Dr. Darfuir did the same and was scanned on the opposite side. Instantly the elevator started its assent from somewhere below and whispered to a halt at their feet. The door slid open slowly as a voice over the intercom said: "Identify yourself."

Dr. Pearson complied. "Dr. Jeffrey Pearson."

The voice on the intercom responded, "Voice identification recognized." The door shut and they descended for at least 20 seconds before the elevator came to stop. "Research Laboratory," blurted the voice from the intercom, and the doors opened.

Lanny stepped out and couldn't believe what she saw. Multiple millions of dollars must have gone into the building of this facility. Electron microscopes were everywhere. Lanny noticed the top-of-the-line surgical instruments that weren't available even in the hospital where she worked. There were Xray machines, Cat Scans, and M.R.I. cubicles. The facility was sparkling clean.

The professor led the way to an area that dropped down in a circular glass enclosure. It was like a TV show where all the medical students looked down to witness an operation in the pit. But the pit Lanny peered into had an operating table with thick metal restraints. The table was also chained to the floor, even though the table bottom was embedded in concrete.

Dr. Darfuir unlocked a door leading down to the pit and the table. "Come in, Miss Cromwell, nothing to be afraid of."

Dr. Pearson reassured her, "This will be the table that makes history many months from now. Just think, Miss Cromwell, of the countless people who will no longer suffer from disease and disparity. I pray to Almighty God that we are successful in our noble endeavor."

Lanny replied with a sweet voice, "I have faith in you, professor. Please don't think ill of Johnny's demeanor. He's seen too much of the dark side of life." Pearson softly told her, "There is great good in this world, but there is a very great evil, also." Pearson elaborated, "Perhaps John Orion is the Equalizer in this world to rid it of filth and keep our way of life from being destroyed. Somehow, I think deep down inside he's fighting his own demons. Let me show you something." He reached over to a big metallic box next to the table. The professor pulled from the box what appeared to the untrained eye to be a soft metallic harness with straps of a weird looking metal attached all the way from a collar with some funny looking shoulder pads.

Lanny inquisitively asked Dr. Pearson, "If you say this is an incredibly powerful magnetic device, wouldn't it be useless because it's metal?"

Both scientists snickered for a moment, and then Dr. Darfuir broke in to ask, "May I, professor?"

Pearson gave a quick nod of approval.

"Miss Cromwell, what metal do you know of that is not magnetic?"

Lanny immediately and decisively answered, "Aluminum."

"Correct," said Darfuir. "But this aluminum is high grade centrifuge, the kind used in nuclear fission containment. We've just gone one step better and combined our super nano robotic microbes with the alloy. When the belt and harness are applied, a special suit made of neoprene and more super nano robotic microbes are first put onto the human host to sequester the sudden pressure from the magnetic force. Hence, we won't have another rabbit jumping across the room."

Lanny requested, "Dr. Pearson, do you think it all possible I could be here when it comes to play?"

"Well, since are you an emergency room nurse, maybe that could be arranged."

As they headed back to the elevator, Lanny commented, "I wish Johnny was excited as I am, professor."

I think he'll eventually show more compassion for the dedication that goes into this work," Pearson assured her. "I have a sense that there's more to John Orion than both of us think we know."

The elevator door shut and headed up to the Citadel. As the trio approached Dr. Pearson's schooner, the sound of the ex teammates carrying on in a drunken comedy reached their ears. The boisterous pals were bowling with the beer bottles.

Lanny spotted what must have been a case of consumed beer, if not more. Orion had cut off the rope tied to a docking buoy that was a little larger than a basketball. Just as Lanny was about to yell at him, Orion rolled the "ball" at the beer bottles. They crashed everywhere.

She screamed at top of her lungs, "John Patrick Orion," then hesitated for one second and continued, "I said one beer, not one barrel."

Orion turned around and squinted through glassy eyes. He looked like a toddler caught with his hand in the cookie jar. "Uh oh" he blurted, trying foolishly to hide a beer bottle behind his back.

Trudeaux and Palladin started laughing and making fun. "Can Lieutenant come out to play?" asked Palladin as he jumped up, assuming Trudy would catch him in his arms. Trudeaux didn't realize this until the last second, and both wound up going overboard into the canal.

Everyone rushed to the side to see if they were all right.

"Maybe now you'll grow up for a change and be more responsible," mocked Lanny.

They both yelled back from the water, "Never!"

As Lanny turned around to retrieve her man, she spotted Pearson, Darfuir, and Malloy, who just got back on the boat. They were laughing. She hesitated, but a second later burst out laughing with them.

Pearson, still laughing, approached Orion and Lanny. "Both of you will stay in the guest house tonight. I'm going to bring our whole entourage out sailing; this way you won't have to make that long drive back. I won't take no for an answer."

Lanny with her puppy dog eyes said, "Thank you, Professor Pearson. You are a good friend."

With that, Pearson asked Dr. Darfuir, "Kamal, can you take our lovebirds up to the main house and ask one of the bodyguards to escort them to the guest house? Have fresh and casual clothes brought to them tomorrow morning at 0630 hours. John and Lanny, I'll have suitable night pajamas sent to both of you."

Orion blurted out drunkenly, "Who says we're wearing clothes?"

Lanny face showed her embarrassment. "Pajamas will be appreciated. Thank you again, professor."

Pearson told them, "You both remind me of Arlene and me before our daughter Kendra was born."

From out of nowhere Orion pulled away from Lanny and puked all over the lawn.

Professor Pearson then elaborated, "Except for the drinking, of course." Lanny apologetically said, "Sorry again, professor." She grabbed hold of Orion and followed Dr. Darfuir.

Pearson acknowledged with, "Good night, Miss Cromwell, or should I say the future Mrs. Orion."

Orion and Lanny kept walking, holding each other even closer than before. Pearson watched as all three of his friends disappeared into the distance.

Time: 2330 hours.
****

Time: 1655 hours (6 and half hours earlier) on the Liberian Cargo Freighter, Alladin, 65 miles off the coast of New Jersey's main shipyards. November 26, 2010.

The wheelhouse on the bridge of the Liberian freighter rang out with two gun shots. A man wearing a Palestinian bandana had a 9mm Baretta to the head of the ship's helmsman while his hands were on the tiller wheel. On the deck at their feet was the body of Captain Andrew Stoffos, Commander of the vessel. Terrorists hiding out in one of the containers emerged and were in the process of commandeering the ship.

Time: 1700 hours on the nose.

JOHN PETER FERRIS

5 SACRIFICIAL LAMB

Aboard the Cargo Freighter Alladin, al-Qaeda terrorists from the Hezbollah faction had taken control of every inch of the vessel. The Captain, Andrew Stoffas, was just murdered by a gun-toting terrorist, leaving behind a wife and four baby girls who would now have to fend for themselves.

Another terrorist entered the bridge, speaking to the terrorist holding the gun to the Helmsman head. "Amal, we have taken control of the ship. Time to radio contact Shaleem that it's safe to proceed."

Two other crew members with their hands on top of their heads had faces of dire concern. Amal Haafaal Baraash was the leader of the pirates and was wanted in four countries around the world. Baraash was on every no-fly list on the planet. He questioned the two helpless crew members. "Which one of you is the radio operator?"

The taller of the crewman nodded his head and said, "That would be me."

In that instance, Baraash pointed his Baretta at the other crew member's head and pulled the trigger. Blood splattered from him onto the radio operator. His body fell within six feet of the slain Captain.

Baraash told the radio operator, "I am now captain of this ship. If you don't want to acquire the same fate as your comrades, you will follow my orders without hesitation. Is that clear?"

"Yes," complied the Operator.

Baraash repeated, "Yes what?"

The operator said nervously, "Yes, Captain."

Baraash laughed and said to the other terrorist, "Who says I didn't possess leadership qualities?"

The other terrorist, Bolaan Mohammed, replied, "The ones who did are all dead." Both of them laughed.

Baraash asked the radio operator his name. The frightened man replied,

"Armand Varadios." Baraash looked at Armand and handed him a slip of paper with radio frequency numbers written on it. "Armand, you will dial these numbers on your frequency panels and when we make contact you will repeat everything I tell you. Is that clear?"

Armand replied, "Yes, Captain."

Baraash then asked the helmsman his name.

"Francisco Tomasso, Captain."

Laughingly Baraash said, "See what a little courtesy gets you. Now Francisco, reduce ship's speed by six knots and set us in a course 60 degrees Southwest 10 minutes, then in five minutes change course to 35 degrees north by five minutes and reduce speed to one knot. Understood?"

Francisco replied, "Yes Captain."

Baraash checked his watch and saw it said 1720 hours. He told Armand to sit down in front of the radio. "When you make contact you will say, 'Red fish calling Falcon, come in Falcon.' You will do this until we make contact. When we make contact, I will tell you what to say then."

Baraash checked outside the window of the bridge. He saw his men standing over the fourteen crew members laying face down on the deck. Two of his terrorist compatriots had their AK-47s trained on them.

Baraash told Mohammed, "Have two of our men sweep the ship for any stragglers we might have missed. Come back and report to me."

Mohammed reassured Baraash, "I've already taken the initiative and it is being done as we speak."

Baraash responded, "Prepare to remove the package for transport to the submarine."

Mohammed laughed and said, "Should we put a big ribbon on it?" Baraash candidly replied, "Sure, if it will get us our five million dollars any faster."

As Mohammed left the bridge, Baraash went over to Armand and ordered him to start broadcasting the message. Three minutes passed when over the radio came, "Red fish, this is falcon. We are receiving you to come in. Over." Baraash then instructed Armand to say, "Falcon, this is red fish. Have had a great fishing trip and the boat is loaded." Armand complied and broadcast the message.

Over the radio came, "Red fish this is Falcon, now arriving."

Just as the message completed Mohammed burst into the wheelhouse smiling. "Amal," he said, out of breath, "Submarine surfacing on the port side." A commotion stirred on the lower deck where the crew was being held prisoner.

Baraash stuck his head out the door and saw a high performance racing boat pulling up. The terrorists on the lower deck jabbered in panic. Baraash called out to reassure his men, "Don't worry, this is part of the plan. Get ready to lower the package to the submarine. Don't worry about the boat.

Just move your asses. We've only got fifteen minutes before they send the Coast Guard." Baraash followed up with concern, "They are probably looking at their radar right now and wondering why two vessels have suddenly stopped moving. Now hurry up, I want to be on a beach in some tropical island this same time tomorrow."

He went back inside the bridge and told Mohammed, "I'm going out to make sure there are no problems with the loading. Stay here and keep your eyes on these two. I'll come for you when it's time to leave."

Baraash closed the door of the bridge and headed down to greet the submarine pulling up port side of the ship. When Baraash looked out and saw the sub only fifty yards away, he told one of his men alongside the railing, "Go up to the bridge and tell Mohammed to come to full stop."

With that, the terrorist headed to the wheelhouse. On the deck of what looked to be an old Cold War Russian sub, three men of Middle Eastern descent started throwing mooring lines to Baraash's men on the deck of the Alladin. Also standing on the deck of the sub was a man dressed in an outdated Russian Captain's uniform. Next to him was an incredibly, gorgeous looking woman with raven black hair.

Baraash yelled down to her, "Shaleem, we probably only have 15 minutes at the most to get the package, get everyone aboard, and get underway before the American Coast Guard is upon us."

As soon as he finished speaking, hydraulic doors opened on the deck of the sub. A diamond steel-plated platform rose from the deck below and came to a full stop in front of the three men who just previously had thrown the mooring lines. The man in the Captain's uniform yelled to him, "We have anticipated that problem beforehand, as you can see."

Baraash replied, "I like the way you operate, Captain Vladimir Koslovski. Always ready to the last detail."

"I'm Chechnyan. We've always have had to be one step ahead of our adversaries." Cpt. Koslovski then screamed up to Baraash's men, "Make sure those fuckin' lines are tight. We don't need our two parting gifts to the Americans at the bottom of the ocean."

The cargo container that Baraash and his men had hidden since they snuck out of Libya now produced four men. They emerged on a litter with two men in the front and two in the back. In the middle was a crate about two feet in height by four feet in length with Iranian markings on it.

On the Alladin's deck by the side railing was a loading boom with block and tackle suspended from it. Hanging from the block and tackle was a rectangular steel platform. The men laid the litter on the platform, then hooked four chains from each corner, and then attached them to the hook and the block and tackle.

As soon as the last chain was attached, Baraash yelled to his man who was operating the boom, "Lift and lower the crate to the platform on the sub, Hassan."

His man Hassan picked up the crate, and swung it out and carefully lowered it to the submarine. Soon as the crate was on the sub platform, three men unhooked and lowered it to the deck below. As the hydraulic doors closed, the speed boat came alongside the sub.

Baraash yelled to the driver of the boat, "Shamir, stay here until you catch sight of the Coast Guard approaching. I'm giving Mohammed a locked briefcase with coded messages in it. Soon as you catch sight of them, speed out of here as fast as you can and go north. They will probably catch you in about 20 minutes. By then, we will be long gone. When they figure out they have no reason to hold you, our lawyers will force them to release you. Khaleef Abdullah Musheen will then tell you where to proceed."

The ravened-haired woman who had been silent this whole time suddenly lifted her head and closed her eyes. She put the tips of her fingers from her right hand to her forehead and blurted out, "The Americans are deploying a large ship to intercept us; we must go now!"

With that, Baraash ran up to the wheelhouse and went inside. Five seconds later two shots rang out. From out of the wheelhouse, Baraash and Mohammed came running. Baraash yelled to his man Hassan, "Finish the task at hand and let's go, now!"

Hassan looked at the three men with their AK-47's and nodded his head. The three blasted away at the helpless men lying on the deck. Baraash told Mohammed to jump in the boat with Shamir and hold onto the briefcase at all costs. "The case is locked, so the Americans will think we are hiding something from them. They will think they've discovered secrets, when all there is is gibberish and nonsense."

With that Baraash left the deck of the Alladin and climbed down the conning tower of the submarine. Mohammed climbed down onto the speed boat from the makeshift gangway his crew concocted for transfer and pushed it into the ocean. He quietly sat down in the boat and clung to the briefcase.

The two men sat for about fifteen minutes when a Coast Guard helicopter came flying over fifty feet up. Shamir automatically started the engine and sped out north. A Coast Guard cutter appeared in the distance, as well. From the cutter, a high speed rigid-hulled inflatable boat (RIB) was deployed and began to give chase.

As both helicopter and RIB start closing in after fifteen minutes, a sharpshooter pointed an AS: 50 caliber rifle at the engine compartment of the speed boat. Before he could fire, the speed boat exploded into thousands of pieces. The Commander of the Coast Guard Cutter, Lieutenant Commander Carl Brown, told his radio operator to summon the helo and to head back to the freighter, Alladin.

Ten minutes went by before Commander Brown glimpsed the Alladin coming into sight. The helicopter was already there circling the ship. The pilot of the Coast Guard helicopter radioed to Brown, "Commander, have sight of fourteen crewmen laying in pools of blood on main deck."

Lt. Commander had his radio man tell the pilot to back off to a distance while he set up a party to board the ship. But as the Cutter was within 600 yards astern of the Alladin, the ship also blew into pieces.

Commander Brown told his radioman, "Alert Command and let them know of our extenuating circumstances. Inform them we have a crime scene here and we've detected radioactivity in the area. Priority One Echo Tango. Do it now."

The Priority One Emergency Transmission was sent immediately to Norfolk Sixth Fleet Command in Norfolk, Virginia. The Fleet was put on full alert. As the alert came across to Norfolk, Admiral James Maguire was entering the amphibious base at Little Creek, Virginia. When he heard of it, he contacted Naval Intelligence and told them to keep him completely informed of any enemy chatter being picked up by American satellites.

Admiral Maguire then made a personal phone call to his friend and confidant, Admiral Thomas Fischer. After the phone rang three times, Admiral Fischer answered.

"Hey Jim, nothing to do on this beautiful Friday evening?"

Maguire hesitantly replied," "Tom, something has come up and I could use your expertise back here in Norfolk."

Admiral Fischer could tell by his close friend's voice that it was very serious.

"Jimmy, I'm here with Malloy on Long Island checking out a scientific presentation. I'll cancel and get out a flight right away."

Admiral Maguire stopped him with, "No, no, Tom, enjoy your evening." Get a flight out tomorrow morning as soon as you can, and Tom, do it discreetly. I'll see you when you get there."

Fischer replied, "Roger Wilco."

Maguire urgently said, "Also, Tom, we are at Priority Alpha One Romeo Xray."

"Understood," Fischer replied. "I'll be on a 0230 flight out of Calverton. Time: 1900 hours.

JOHN PETER FERRIS

6 METAMORPHOSIS

Time: 0530 hours. November 27, 2010

John Orion awoke to the sound of the alarm clock coming from his cell phone. Orion stood up and stretched his arms and legs, then fell forward to the floor in pushup position. Controlling his breathing, he silently cadenced out 100. Standing back up and he began stretching all over again. He then sat down on his derriere and did 200 sit-ups.

Orion stood up once again and stretched one more final time.

From under the blankets Lanny said, "Show off."

"You didn't complain when we did it three times last night. To keep my Lady Bee content, I must do this as a daily regimen."

Lanny popped out from underneath the covers. "Well, you better drop down and give us 500 more pushups and 1000 more sit-ups."

Orion snidely looked at Lanny. "Very funny. You should be in stand-up comedy. Lanny, I'm gonna go for a 15 minute run since, according to our new dress ensemble, we have boat sneakers to wear on the professor's yacht today."

Lanny, with a puzzled look, said, "How on earth could they have known our specific sizes?"

"Our clothes were taken away and came back dry cleaned and wrapped. Look for yourself, baby. There's my suit and your Vera Wang hanging up neatly close to the island in the kitchen. Boy, I could get use to this."

Orion headed out the door, and as he went to leave he yelled back to Lanny, "Luv ya, baby."

Shutting the door he began the same run he normally undertook at home.

Lanny grabbed her Louis Vuitton pocketbook and headed to the bathroom to shower and doll herself up. She was about to turn on the shower when the house phone rang in the kitchen. With one towel wrapped around her body and the other around her head she scurried to pick up.

"Hello," she said hurriedly.

On the other end a voice spoke out, "This is the main house just making a wakeup call, and we need your breakfast order."

Lanny replied, smiling, "How thoughtful. Saturday mornings we usually have bacon, eggs and toast."

The kitchen asked her, "How would you like your eggs?"

"Oh, scrambled is fine," replied Lanny.

"Would both you enjoy a carafe of coffee and glasses of orange juice with your meal?"

"Yes, thank you, and could we both have two glasses of whole milk with that."

"No problem, Miss Cromwell. We'll have it sent to you in about 15 minutes."

"Thank you very much." Lanny went back to the shower, then emerged to hear Orion entering the guest house. She exited the bathroom looking puzzled and said, "I know I had a curling iron in here. I'm too young to start getting this forgetful."

Orion turned away with that 'uh oh' look and with his back turned replied, "Baby, you probably took it out when you were home. I'll buy you a better one when we get back."

"Don't be silly, Johnny. I love the one I have at home. Breakfast will be here in about 10 minutes. Hmmm, I'm almost positive I put the curling iron in my bag. Oh well, at least I have my hair dryer."

Orion cuts in, "That's the way, honey. You'd look good even if you had to wear burlap."

Lanny kissed him. "That's my man."

Orion walked in to the bedroom and wiped the back of his hand across his forehead, whispering silently, "Shit, that was close."

As Lanny began drying her hair, Orion pushed gently past her in the bathroom and dropped his undershorts. He climbed into the shower and asked Lanny outside the shower curtain, "Sure you're clean enough? Want to go again?"

Lanny laughed, and shutting bathroom door, said, "Take a cold shower there, sailor, and cool down."

Orion shook his head with a flat feeling of rejection and turned on the shower. Five minutes later a buzzer went off on the intercom at the front door.

Lanny went to the front door and looked at the intercom, noticing six buttons with writing on them. Spotting the one that said 'front door' she pushed the button.

"Hello," she said. "May I help you?"

The Intercom voiced back, "It's the kitchen, Miss Cromwell. We have your breakfast."

"Oh, thank you. Let me open the door." A man in kitchen white clothes handed her a bag with a half gallon of milk and a half gallon of Tropicana orange juice. He walked in carrying a very large tray that had a plastic cover over it with small ropes going under the tray up to the handle. He set it down on the island in the kitchen and told Lanny, "I hope you both enjoy the meal."

"Thank you, I'm sure we will."

She untied the ropes from the handle and lifted up the tray revealing two plates with bacon and perfectly scrambled eggs. In between them were two platters, one with a carafe of coffee and the other with toast and a side dish of home fries.

Orion, having finished his shower, opened the door and inhaled the smell of fresh coffee. Looking over into the kitchen he spotted Lanny setting up the tableware. She grabbed two sets of silverware and placed them next to each plate. Then she unwrapped the linen and cotton cloths.

"Johnny, the coffee smells just like the coffee your mother makes."

Orion took a whiff from across the room and replied, "It sure does, baby." "Well, let's see if the food is just as good as Mama Rosa's."

Orion interrupted abruptly, "That'll be the day."

Lanny nodded her head, acknowledging the truth to that statement. "Come on, let's dig in. I'm so excited! it's my first time on a yacht."

Orion answered that it was his first time, too.

Lanny looked surprised and commented, "All that time in the Navy and you've never been on a yacht?"

Orion answered with a big smile, "Baby, all the ships and boats in the Navy are a bunch of tin cans that are overcrowded with a bunch of noisy guns. This will be a first time for me too, sweetheart."

Lanny exclaimed as she ate her meal, "The food is not as good as Mama Rosa's but, it is really good, none the less."

Orion took a couple of bites and agreed, "Ain't bad, ain't bad at all. Still, not the way my mom spices it up."

The couple dug into the delicious cuisine prepared just for them. Lanny always enjoyed a tall glass of milk with every one of her meals. Orion, from being with her all this time, made it part of this daily regiment, as well.

Lanny finished and brought her plate and silverware over to the sink and started washing them. The phone suddenly rang. It was Professor Pearson checking to see if they were up and ready.

"Hello, Murphy's Funeral Home. You kill 'em, we chill 'em."

Lanny gave Orion that 'cut it out' look again.

On the other end Dr. Pearson respond laughingly, "Did you eat well, Johnny?"

"It was delicious, professor. Me and Lanny appreciate all you're doing for us."

"Very good, Lieutenant. We single up all lines at 0730 hours. I've just got off the phone with Captain Malloy. He, Bobby, and Trudy said they'll see us on deck."

"Affirmative, we'll see you on board." He hung up and said to Lanny, "Honey, I'll be right back. I have to get some gear from the Roadrunner. Do you ever get seasick, because if you do I have some Dramamine."

"No, I'll be fine. Just go and do what you have to do. I should be ready in about 20 minutes."

Orion closed the door behind him and walked along the path to the main parking lot of the citadel. He saw the parking lot was the size of a small airfield. Right in the front by the security cubicle sat the Roadrunner with about 30 other cars next to it. He approached the cubicle and asked the guard for the keys.

"I'm not going anywhere, I just need to get some things for our little voyage," he explained.

"No problem, Mr. Orion. Your car keys are right here."

Orion opened his trunk and retrieved an extra gym bag that he stored for different purposes. Opening his tactical cache bag he pulled out a repelling rope, carabineers, Kevlar repelling gloves and a framing hammer. From the trunk he also grabbed an extra fire extinguisher and a three-minute bottle breather with mouth regulator. He closed the trunk and opened the passenger door. From the glove compartment, he threw his Sig Sauer and three pairs of handcuffs into the Gym bag.

Orion was about to take the cuffs back out of the bag when he got a weird premonition and said, "Can't hurt, this will probably not be needed here, but I've been wrong before." He threw the cuffs back into the bag.

Giving his keys back to the guard in the cubicle, he threw the strap of the bag over his shoulder and headed back to the guest house, stepping over the threshold to take a gander at his girlfriend. He was in awe. She didn't wear too much make-up because she definitely didn't need it, and her gorgeous jet black hair made her brown puppy dog eyes glisten in the light.

"God, I am a lucky man," Orion thought to himself.

Lanny, seemingly still annoyed, said, "I can't believe I can't remember what I did with my curling iron."

Orion immediately interrupted. "You're the most beautiful woman on the planet. You look fantastic, baby. We'll find it when we go home."

Lanny walked up to Orion and put her left arm around his waist. "You always know what to say to me, Johnny. Now let's go sailing, sailor."

Time: 0715 hours.

Orion and Lanny made their way past the Citadel. When they reached the dock, they noticed deck hands loading provisions for the outing. On the bow of the yacht, Galaxy, was a platform with a Zodiac raft and attached small outboard motor.

Malloy was there loading emergency provisions just in case of a disaster. When they reached the sixty foot schooner they saw Dr. Kamal Darfuir raising the shipping lane banners. He went to the main sail and pulled on a slip knot string, the one that releases the American flag.

Professor Pearson came out of the cabin below, yelling out jokingly, "All ashore that's going shore." He spotted Orion. "Still got your sea legs, Lieutenant?"

Orion gave him a sarcastic look. "Shit, I hope I remember how to swim." Everybody on deck broke out in laughter.

Orion looked to the starboard side and saw Claire Vanderkamp over next to the Helmsman's chair. As they entered the main deck, Claire walked right up to Lanny and said, "I was busy last night when I saw you both come in. Hi Lanny, my name is Claire. I love the way you wear your hair."

Lanny replied in a giddy schoolgirl voice, "Thank you, Claire. You have the most gorgeous blonde hair I've ever seen."

The two women hit it off right from the start and Lanny walked away with her new friend without her introducing Orion to her.

Orion and Malloy looked at each other and broke out laughing.

"What am I, wood? Fuckin' women. What do you expect?" said Orion. Dr. Pearson yelled to his crew, "Single up and prepare to get underway." From the dock the Harbor Master released the bow and stern lines from the Bollards. The inboard engine's RPMs revved up and the schooner started turning to port (the left) and made a 180 degree move to head down the canal. Pearson told his first mate to sound the horn so the other vessels in the Harbor were alerted to their departure. He then went over to the first mate and said, "Take us out, Manuel, slow and steady and stay within the 5 mph wake speed." As Pearson approached his guests, he invited them to make themselves comfortable, especially since it would take a little over a half an hour to make the edge of the canal.

"The wind has picked up substantially and we are definitely going to have great time sailing," he informed them.

Malloy came up from inside, where the galley was, and had with him a large thermos filled with coffee. He handed the thermos to Trudeaux and said he'd be right back because he was going to retrieve the Styrofoam cups.

As the Schooner Galaxy came around a bend in the canal, everyone noticed large amounts of smoke coming from another waterfront mansion on the canal. It was surreal and totally unexpected. Suddenly, blood curdling screams came from children in the distance.

Shocked, Lanny put her hands in a prayer position and laid them on her chin and exclaimed, "Oh my dear God, those are babies screaming!"

Professor Pearson told his first mate, Manuel, "Bring us alongside and bring the Galaxy to their mooring slip." Orion, Palladin, Trudeaux, and

45

Malloy were already at the Zodiac.

Orion, with his gym bag, went to untie the ropes that tethered the boat to the platform. "Fuck this," he said, reaching into his bag stowed in the Zodiac. He pulled out his combat knife, cutting the ropes like butter with the razor sharp blade.

The four ex Navy S.E.A.L.s in perfect synchronicity grabbed handles from the raft and pulled it until it went over the side. All four men jumped into the water onto the Zodiac; Palladin, the coxswains mate, lowered the outboard propeller and started the motor.

Orion yelled to Pearson aboard the Galaxy, "Get me a bunch of blankets and toss them here." Dr. Darfuir in a flash went down into cabin of the Galaxy and returned with four thick cotton blankets. He reached over the railing and threw them right to Orion's arms.

Palladin gunned the motor full throttle and headed for shore. They arrived at docking space near the mansion.

As they pulled up Malloy noticed a small Boston Whaler parked slightly hidden from view. The four men looked up to behold the left side of the house engulfed with flames. Looking to the right top bedroom window, they saw a young teenage girl holding a toddler with smoke billowing heavily out the window. Behind her, another young girl was trying to stick her head out, desperately needing air.

Orion looked at his three comrades. "Gotta go. Watch your asses, there's stolen booty in that boat. I think somebody is gonna try to make a fast get away." With that, he reached into his bag and pulled out repelling lines neatly wrapped. He also pulled out his Sig Sauer and handed it to Malloy.

Orion quickly dumped the rest of the bag out onto the ground. Once again they heard frightening, blood curdling screams coming from the children. The Galaxy was now only 200 feet from the dock. Lanny peered to see her boyfriend put the rope to his shoulder. She watched him dunk two blankets in the water. Orion draped them over the same shoulder as the fire started spreading faster due to the wind. He grabbed the framing hammer, fire extinguisher and three carabineers and loaded them back into his bag.

Bursting into a fiery run, Orion headed to the 10 foot sliding glass doors facing him from the house.

Malloy was 25 feet behind him with the 45 Sig Sauer in firing position. Palladin flanked Malloy to the right and Trudy flanked to the left.

Bobby had his service Glock 19 in a prone firing position. Trudy stayed back about 40 feet behind a garden shed in the yard.

Orion entered the doors and experienced a nearly insurmountable burst of heat. As fast as he could with the soaked blanket affixed over him, he flew up the blazing stairs. At the top he crouched down as low as he could and crawled to the bedroom full of children.

Meanwhile, outside Malloy took his middle and index fingers and pointed to his eyes, taking only the index finger and making a circular motion going to the right. Palladin knew to head in that direction and carefully, but quickly, began to move.

Trudeaux pointed his 40 caliber Sig Sauer just in front of Bobby.

Back upstairs Orion entered the bedroom to see the youngest girl lying on the floor. The teenaged girl was holding her baby brother in her arms, frightened to death. Orion, with all his strength, picked up a small recliner and threw it through the bedroom window. The sound of the chair coming through the glass could be heard for at least a mile.

Outside to the right of the house appeared a man holding a woman in a headlock, cowardly forcing her in front of him. The man robbing the house had a revolver to the head of the woman.

Bobby took careful aim and fired, instantly hitting the dirtbag with a head shot. As the lifeless body fell to the ground, his partner in crime appeared with the barrel of his gun trained on Palladin.

A shot rang out. Trudeaux, with his training, already had a fix on the other dirt bag and killed him center mass of the torso.

Palladin tried to comfort the woman, who had been beaten up badly. She screamed out in anguish, "My babies, they're still in the house! Please, you've got to save them." Palladin picked her up because she could barely walk and headed a safe distance from the front of the dock.

Trudy checked the bodies of both dirtbags to make sure they were dead. He joined Malloy at the back of the house.

By now, the right side of the house was engulfed with flames. Parts of the front of the house were caving in. But just as everyone outside appeared to think all was lost, Orion appeared in the front of the window spraying the fire extinguisher about the room until it emptied. He dropped the container and immediately grabbed the girl passed out on the floor and covered her, styling a makeshift bag from the soaking blanket. He gauged holes on the edges of the blanket with his knife. He banged his framing hammer into the header above the window.

Orion quickly drove the knife like a nail through the sheetrock until only the handle was visible. He took a large carabiner and clipped it around the right side of his belt. Then he took the rope with the little girl in it and threaded it like a needle until she was completely enclosed. He draped the rope to the knife handle above the window.

Orion ran the rope through the carabiner on his belt. He picked up the little girl who was now tied securely in the blanket, and gently lowered her 25 feet to the ground below.

While this was going on, the Galaxy's crew moored the ship to the dock. Professor Pearson and Lanny witnessed all that was going on while the ship was docking, and came running at a full gallop towards Orion, who was still lowering the little girl to Malloy and Trudy.

When the child finally descended safely, Malloy pulled on the rope around the top of the blanket and freed her.

As soon as she was out, Orion pulled his makeshift litter back up to the bedroom, which was now even more smoke-filled. The girl holding her brother was crying hysterically. "Don't worry, sweetheart, you and your baby brother are going for a ride just like your little sister did. Okay, trust me sweetheart."

Orion, seeing the fire rushing even faster, put her and the toddler in together. Orion had them both wrapped tight in the blanket and lifted them as he put the rope once again around the handle of the knife. Being very careful as he felt the hot air starting to burn the skin on his back, he lowered the children safely to the ground.

Lanny was now crying and screaming to the man she loved, "Johnny, get out now, baby, please baby, hurry!"

When Orion retrieved the makeshift litter, he cut the rope from the blanket and put the remaining carabiner around a brass bar on one of the two little girl's beds. Orion took the rope out of the carabiner on his belt and put it through the one he fastened to the bar on the bed, then put the rope back on the carabiner on his belt. Only this time, he tied it solidly with a sheet bend knot to the carabiner itself. He drug the somewhat heavy bed and snagged it up against the wall of the window.

Orion climbed out on the ledge window and affixed the rope for the final time to the knife handle. He made sure the line was taut and began his descent. When the mother realized her children were safe, her mind cleared enough to say,, "I pray he hurries up. Those bastards killed my husband and planted a bunch of propane tanks in the house."

Palladin automatically ran towards the house yelling, "GET BACK, GET BACK, EVERYBODY GET BACK, THOSE SCUMBAGS PLANTED PROPANE TANKS IN THE HOUSE!"

The men instantly grabbed Lanny, Claire, and the children and moved them far away from the house.

Orion descended ten feet when he heard Lanny's desperate voice. "Baby, hurry please, they booby trapped the house!"

Just as he was two feet from the ground a humongous explosion blasted out the house throwing Orion back at least fifteen feet. Pieces of glass, metal, wood, and debris flew everywhere. The mansion was now a giant inferno with walls slowly caving in throughout the structure.

As the scattered group slowly regained their composure, Lanny spotted Orion lying on the ground, twisted sideways and bleeding. She screamed in anguish, "JOHNNY. OH MY GOD, NO PLEASE NO, NO, NO!" and ran to him, crying uncontrollably.

Professor Pearson and Dr. Darfuir were right behind her running with a serious sense of purpose. Around Orion, his ex team mates knew that he was in dire straits. Pearson screamed to Manuel on the dock to retrieve his medical bag. "Make sure you bring the sulfur patches, and Manny, bring the vials of morphine."

Orion's breathing was erratic and he went into shock. Dr. Darfuir immediately grabbed the two dry remaining blankets and placed one over Orion.

Manuel practically flew across the black lawn and handed Pearson a very large black valence. Pearson lifted the front of Orion's burned and tattered shirt to discover he was bleeding profusely. Instantly he ripped open four sulfur patches and applied them to the wounds.

Orion, barely conscious, moaning and in terrible pain said, "Lanny, Lanny, I love you." His eyes shut from exhaustion.

Lanny pleaded with the two doctors, knowing that the man she loved more than anything was close to death. Pearson said to her, "We are too far from any hospital to treat these extensive wounds." Tears came from his eyes and with the look of helplessness he said, "I would give my own life if it would save his."

Right at that moment a Suffolk Police helicopter arrived directly overhead. Around the front of the house Sheriff's deputies pulled up in three cars. Dr. Darfuir walked over to the professor and said, "If anybody is a prime candidate for the ICARUS Device, it would be this poor, dying, heroic soul."

Lanny, overhearing what Professor Darfuir just said to Pearson, pleaded, "Please, Professor, the belt harness is the only chance he's got." Pearson responded to her and Darfuir, "It's not ready, and it may even kill him." He put his head down and started processing the pros and cons.

Lanny, kneeling on the floor, put her arm around Orion's neck and reached down to kiss him with tears falling on his face. Crying hysterically, she spoke to his unconscious body, "Please don't leave me, Johnny. I can't live without you."

During this chaos, Palladin had called to have the helicopter land on the back lawn. As the chopper descended, Pearson said to Doctor Darfuir, "Let's get him quickly back to the laboratory underneath the citadel. Have all trauma and surgery teams to operations center right now. Tell everyone we are initiating Project ICARUS."

Professor Darfuir called the institute only four miles away and had everything put on Red Alert.

With the chopper now landed, Malloy, Trudeaux, and Palladin placed Orion on the last blanket and each grabbed a corner to carry him the way they were all taught in their training. When they get him in the chopper, the police medical technician in the back administered oxygen.

Palladin knew the pilot and told him, "Franky, this is my old team leader. He'll never make it if we go to the hospital in Brookhaven. My doctor friend here has his own surgical and trauma unit four clicks east of here. Throttle up, Franky, he ain't got much time."

As the Citadel started to appear in the distance, Pearson told the pilot about the three landing pads forty feet apart from the back of the building. As the chopper descended Lanny noticed about fourteen surgical doctors and nurses standing by to receive the patient. When the chopper landed, the team ran a gurney to the side door of the helicopter. The doctor opened the door and swiftly they grabbed Orion out of Lanny's arms.

Professor Pearson looked at Lanny reassuringly and said, "Lanny, I can't let you in. I know you're a well-trained surgical nurse, but you know the rules. No personal loved ones. You may watch from the observation gallery above the heavy aluminum operating table."

Lanny, still crying, tried to keep her composure. "I understand, professor, but please do everything possible and bring my Johnny back to me."

Pearson answered with a lump in his throat, "I think a prayer to the man upstairs from you would give our boy a chance."

"That I'll do with all my heart."

Pearson left Lanny and rushed to join the scientists, all the best in all fields of medicine, robotics, nano technology, magnetic science, and biological structural mechanics.

Lanny entered the observation gallery and saw their friends, Trudy and Bobby, looking down into the pit nervously. Lanny started to really break down and looked like she was about to fall to the floor. Bobby came over and comforted her.

Palladin said, "That down there lying on that funny looking table is the toughest man alive I know. Oh, he's not going to leave his Lady Bee."

Through her crying, Lanny was able to give a smile and replied, "You guys are the best friends we could ever have."

Trudy walked up and put his arm around her shoulder. "And we always will be."

Lanny looked around. "Where did Jimmy go?"

Trudeaux said he went to make arrangements to have Mama Rosa rushed here. He wanted to make sure she didn't freak out and have another stroke like she did six years before.

At that moment Dr. Pearson and Dr. Darfuir entered the operating room in full scrubs and surgical masks. All that was visible was the top of their surgical caps. The room around the gallery started to darken, but the area around the immediate operating vicinity became lit with purple.

Dr. Pearson blurted out, "Put filament goggles on now!" The whole surgical team donned the goggles in sync. Dr. Pearson explained the procedure as he was actually performing it. Everyone in the area heard, "Clear and extract all foreign matter from wounds. Make sure all airways to the lungs are not compressed."

When this was done, he instructed, "Secrete biological nonrobotic nano micro into the lining of the intestinal tract. Once bleeding is brought under control, prepare host subject with embolic composite neoprene body suit.'

The team hustled to save Orion's life.

Dr. Pearson continued, "Fit host subject's head, hand and foot gear. Place the Ultra Violet spectrum goggles to our host before initiating Project ICARUS. Now, with help from the Almighty, let's save this young man's life."

They operated for seemed like an eternity to Lanny, but in reality it was only 20 minutes. Different men and women in three different types of scrubs entered and left, back and forth, throughout the entire operation. Those in maroon brought in all different types of medical looking devices. Oddly, the ones dressed in purple brought in weird mechanical and strange electrical components.

All throughout the operation the monitor hooked to Orion's heartbeat added to the noise and could be heard over a speaker in the gallery, as well as the operating room. Lanny, being an emergency room nurse, knew from the sounds of the beat that Orion was incredibly weak.

As time went by the medical crews worked feverishly and expertly with one conviction, and that was to save John Orion's life. Ten additional minutes passed when the audible diminishing of his heartbeat and pulse rate occurred. Lanny cupped her left hand over her mouth and started to cry even harder.

At that time, Malloy entered the gallery and saw Lanny breaking down. He walked up and comfortably held her, saying, "John's no quitter, so don't you quit him."

Lanny turns her head and sobbed into Malloy's shoulder. "I'll never give up on him!" This increased her crying to new levels.

Then all of a sudden, Professor Pearson spoke. "Bring in the Electron Generator and prepare host subject with embolic composite neoprene body suit."

To the back of the room, two doors opened with a purple strobe light spinning atop the ceiling. Five men dressed in what seemed to be white-lined decontamination suits entered, pushing the weirdest looking machine imaginable. On the top of this machine was the same box that the professor had shown Lanny the night before. But on the top of that was a small box with funny looking propellers, indicating radioactivity.

On the other side of the room walked in a man with what seemed to be a weird looking wet suit complete with a balaclava head piece. This was draped on a hanger with what appeared to be diving foot gear pinned to the suit. Professor Darfuir and the team in purple began to don the dying Lieutenant with the gear.

Palladin, with a look of bewilderment, said to Captain Malloy, "What the fuck are they going to do, drown him? Jesus, what the fuck are they doing to Johnny?"

Malloy's replied, "Calm down, Chief Palladin. If I thought they were trying to hurt our boy, I'd be down there already."

Pearson spoke. "All nonessential personnel evacuate the cubicle now. Except for Dr. Darfuir, everyone but our purple scrubs leave the room."

Orion was dressed in the black suit from head to toe. Before they put the head gear on him they placed weird looking purple sun glasses over his eyes and banded them to the back of his head. They donned the balaclava-looking head cowl over his head and Velcro'd it to the suit.

Darfuir reached into the big box and came out with the ICARUS harness and belt. He and Pearson first attached the collar that was attached to the belt with two straps in the front and two straps in the back. From the belt, itself, one strap was attached to smaller belt just above the kneecap on the thigh. There was also a strap leading down the back. The other leg received the exact same treatment.

But on the side of the main belt around the waist, Dr. Darfuir opened a compartment and went to the small box. He placed the box on the tray next to Orion. Dr. Darfuir donned a lead apron and a special helmet that looked like something used for welding. He put on thick gloves and opened the box as everyone moved to the other side of the room. He then grabbed tongs and pulled out a square compact battery, inserting it into the open compartment on Orion's belt. Then he closed and locked it with an odd looking key.

Pearson said, "Okay, let's attach the Electron Generator, set timer and evacuate to the observation gallery."

With that, Darfuir attached the thick cable from the machine to another compartment opening in the belt. Pearson injected the regenerating super nano biological microbes with the glucose solution into Orion's rolled up left arm. Meanwhile their top assistant, Carl Livingston, set the timer for five minutes.

Pearson urged, "C'mon, c'mon we have to be out of here now." Quite by accident Livingston set the timer at fifteen minutes instead of five. All three scientists ran from the cubicle room without noticing.

Up in the observation gallery the rest of the crowd assembled to pray their years of hard work would pay off and save this man's life.

The ICARUS Device emitted light as the purple L.E.D strobe light spun faster and faster. All over Orion's body were tiny particles of purple light colliding and the opposite, repelling, the particles. After two minutes, Orion's head started to move from side to side. His gloved fingers also responded, as did his feet.

With the cubicle amplified to a microphone, Orion's still unconscious brain began calling for his girlfriend. "Lanny, Lanny, get the children back, hurry, danger."

All of a sudden, his body became rigid and he simply stared into space. As Pearson, Darfuir, and Livingston entered the observation gallery, they checked the big clock on the wall in the gallery. It had been four minutes and ten seconds since they started the sequence.

Lanny said to Professor Pearson, "Doctor, he was just moving and calling to me. I think it's working."

Pearson and Darfuir both smiled with delight, but Pearson told Lanny, "Just keep your fingers crossed. We still have to examine him when the device powers down."

As he said that he looked at the clock and saw it was past the five minute mark. Nervously he said, "Something's wrong. Why hasn't the device shut off?" Pearson, Darfuir, and Livingston immediately headed back down to the cubicle. As they left, Orion's body started to move erratically. He clenched his teeth with his mouth open. It's now eleven minutes into the sequence.

The three scientists ran into the room and Pearson noticed a "three minutes to shut off" period. He yelled to Darfuir, "I have to shut down the generator before it kills him."

But as he went to shut the machine down, an invisible force picked him up a foot in the air and dropped him on the other side of the room.

There was now one minute to shut off time, and millions of particles of purple lights swarmed all over Orion's body. Orion screamed out, "Lanny!" as the generator finally came to a full stop.

Professor Pearson shouted out angrily, "What the hell just happened?" He looked at Livingston, knowing Livingston set the timer, and threatened, "I'll have your balls in a sling if you've killed this boy."

Just then Orion, still unconscious, started saying, "Lanny, Lanny." His words were garbled but yet, looking at him, it was obvious he was breathing normally and comfortably.

Dr. Darfuir yelled out in excitement, "Professor, we've done it! The device really works!"

In that instance, Lanny, Malloy, and Trudy ran from the observation deck and hurried down to Orion.

Meanwhile, Pearson tried to remove the belt and harness and immediately was thrown back by a force field. Dr. Darfuir tried it himself and was also thrown. Both scientists shared a similar thought: We have no way of examining him; seems the microbes have intelligently created an indestructible containment field to keep any threat away from them. God forbid if they have complete control over the host.

Lanny burst into the room yelling, "Johnny, I'm here baby." She ran straight to him and Pearson yelled for her stop. "No Lanny, no!" But to their surprise she made it all the way to Orion with nothing happening. She lifted his unconscious head, kissed him and said, "Don't you ever do that again to me, John Patrick Orion. You know damn well you can't go anywhere without my permission."

Still unconscious, Orion started groaning like he had the worst hangover in the world.

Pearson said as Malloy, Palladin, and Trudeaux entered the room, "Lanny, we just tried to release the power cord from the belt, and an incredible force picked us up and threw us across the room. We need you to unfasten the cord so we can make sure he's perfectly okay."

Lanny, grabbed the cord and pulled it out easily. She looked at the two scientists and said, "You two are being ridiculous. Here, I'll show you." She then removed the harness and the rest of the ICARUS Device and laid it back in its box. She then picked up the box, walked to the other side of the room, and slowly put it down while Dr. Pearson and Darfuir went to examine Orion. While her back was turned, this time both of them tried and were stopped from touching him within one foot of his body. Lanny turned around and immediately saw what was going on.

Everybody in the room is in awe of what just happened. Lanny, with no regard for herself, walked right up to Orion . . . and nothing happened. With happy tears falling from her eyes she told the two scientists that she, alone, would examine the man she loved. "Something weird has happened to my Johnny, but I thank both of you with the bottom of my heart that you've fulfilled your promise and returned him to me." She grabbed Orion's left wrist with the tips of her fingers and thumb, then looked at her watch and began taking his pulse. 68 and normal.

She then grabbed the automated blood pressure machine on the table and affixed the cuff to Orion's left arm. "Hmmmm, blood pressure is normal, 132 over 78. He should be awake. What's going on?"

Lanny pulled off the balaclava cowl and put it on the tray next to him. She removed the purple colored glasses, lifted his closed right eye lid and jumped back in amazement. "What the hell happened? His corneas are purple with blinking tiny orange lights that you can just barely make out."

She instantly broke out in tears again. "He should be awake. Why isn't he awake?"

Malloy came over to comfort her and was immediately stopped by the force field.

Lanny asked Professor Pearson to bring in a bed for her, because she would not leave his side until he woke.

"Anything you want, you will have," assured Pearson.

Lanny asked for a sleeping pill and an iPod so she could listen to "I remember" by Madonna. The song memorialized her first kiss with Orion.

Five minutes later two orderlies entered the room and opened a large foldout bed, placing it as close as they could to Orion. The orderlies then made the bed with sheets and a fluffy blanket and were about to leave when Lanny asked them for an extra blanket.

One orderly came back and knocked before entering. "May I come in, Miss?"

Lanny opened the door to take the additional fluffy blanket. "Thank you very much."

The orderly informed her, "Professor Pearson told me to give you these two pills and this glass of spring water."

Lanny swallowed the pills. Approaching her boyfriend she draped the blanket gently over him. "Please come back to me, my love."

She leaned over and kissed him, then pressed play and actually smiled when their favorite song aired. She then snuggled next to him, pulling the blanket over her shoulders and grabbing Orion by his right hand. She fell gently to sleep, exhausted.

Time: 2100 hours.

****

Time: 2235 hours.

Lanny awoke to Orion's eyes blaring out the mystical purple light, but this time even brighter. Lanny gently put the banded sunglasses back on him, kissing him with concern. She slowly drifted back to sleep.

Time: 2245 hours.

7 RESURRECTION

Time: 0610 hours. November 28, 2010.

"Lanny, Lanny, Lanny, wake up. Jeez, what a friggin' hangover I got."
John Orion, unaware of the drama during the past nine hours, tried to wake
his girlfriend from a deep sleep.

"Lan, c'mon, I'm hungry as hell. Will you move that hot looking ass of
yours and make me breakfast?"

Lanny slowly moved her exhausted body and incoherently began to
answer Orion, when she suddenly remembered he was previously
comatose. "Oh my God, oh my God, oh my God! You've come back to
me!" Lanny started crying tears of joy and practically wrestled Orion to her
folding bed.

Orion looked puzzled, but grinned. "What do you mean, 'come back to
you.' Why the hell am I wearing this wet suit? Did we try something kinky
last night?"

Lanny shook her head in happy disbelief. "And you're still the same
horse's ass that I love so much."

The iPod still hummed Madonna's music.

Orion, still in a state of bewilderment, asked, "Honey, I know we both
love Madonna, but can someone turn that damn thing off before I go
crazy? Seems to me like too much of a good thing you should only indulge
in once and a while."

A knock on the cubicle door startled him. "Go away. Unless you've got
breakfast, don't come in."

On the other side of the door Professor Pearson replied, "John I don't
have breakfast but it is imperative I speak with you."

Orion jumped up only to find himself landing ten feet away, right in
front of the cubicle door. Stunned, he opened the door. "Sorry, Doc, I
wouldn't have misspoken if I knew it was you."

Through the door came Pearson and Dr. Darfuir. Orion, trying to make himself presentable, started fixing his hair. He noticed the sunglasses banded to the back of his head and reached behind to pull them off.

Pearson, Darfuir, and Lanny each had mouths opened wide with awe.

Both of Orion's corneas were a mystical shade of purple. Faint tiny orange light orbited in each eye, much like an electron in an atom.

"Hey you all are looking at me like you've seen a ghost."

Pearson slowly walked up and hesitated, then reached out to touch him. This time there was no force field to stop him. He instructed Orion to walk with him to a mirror above an aluminum push cart.

Looking curiously the whole time at the professor, Orion shifted his gaze to the mirror. "Holy mother of God, what happened to my eyes?" Scared as hell, he flinched and pushed on the cart, sending it flying. Across the room it crumpled like a crushed beer can.

Lanny immediately ran into his arms. "Johnny, don't be scared, Dr. Pearson saved your life last night. Don't you remember anything, baby?"

Orion looked back at Lanny and closed his eyes. "This is all a dream, Orion. Wake the fuck up. Your eyes are blue; your eyes are blue; when you wake up, your eyes will be blue."

He slowly opened his eyes, looking straight into the mirror. His eyes were blue.

The two scientists and Lanny couldn't believe what they just saw.

Right away Dr. Darfuir said to Pearson, "The nano microbes must be listening to his nervous system and doing what the brain's cortex is telling it to do."

Orion then realized he was not in a dream. He pled with Professor Pearson and his colleague to help him understand what was happening to him. The two scientists painstakingly begin to explain the events that led up to the saving of his life . . . and his current dilemma. Over the next hour they also explained that they violated the strict guidelines of the American Medical Association by using the device on a human. They debriefed him about the life-threatening circumstances and their decision to act.

Just as the two scientists finished Orion asked, "How are those babies? Did they make it?"

"They wouldn't have stood a chance if it wasn't for your quick thinking and bravery," Pearson replied. He reiterated, "Except for a little smoke inhalation and some cuts and bruises, the children are just doing fine."

With the cubicle door wide open, Orion's teammates Malloy, Trudy, and Palladin barged in.

Malloy laughingly proclaimed, "That wasn't bravery. He just likes being the main dish at a barbecue."

Bobby walked over to Orion and commented, "You gave us one hell of a scare last night, Lt. I don't know how they did it and I don't care, but I love you, brother."

They both hugged, which caused Palladin to grimace in pain. Orion immediately let go and with a scared look said, "Bobby, I'm sorry! I don't know what's happening to me. I might be turning into some kind of freak."

Dr. Darfuir interrupted, "No, John. We think the super nano microbes in your body have done their job beyond anyone's comprehension. Your mind and your body will slowly acclimate to whatever adjustments the microbes, computer and robotic tissues cause as they adhere to your being. We are going to have to take tests and monitor all results."

Pearson interrupted, "In the meantime, John, you get some rest with your lady. Your body has gone through a tremendous amount of stress. So Lanny, make sure our patient here rests and recuperates with no interruptions. Now I have to come up with some cockamamie story to tell the media about what's going on."

Time: 0910 hours.

Outside the institute, the press began to assemble and prepped their cameramen and audio assistants for Professor Pearson's broadcast to the public.

Malloy exhaled and said, peering out the lobby doors, "Look at this fuckin' circus. What are you gonna say, Jeffrey?"

Pearson replied, "I don't know, but I have until 1100 hours to release a statement. My main problem is what happens if my corporation decides to penalize me for jeopardizing the whole nano tech industry? After all, I used and abused strict government protocol. Congress could shut down everything and that would set us back to the Dark Ages."

He took a few seconds to collect his thoughts. "Don't get me wrong, Jim; I'd do it all over again in an instant. On top of that, the military attaché from the Pentagon and probably those farm boys from Langley will be sticking their noses up our asses so far that we won't be able to walk. What would you do if you were me?"

Malloy pondered for about a minute and then blared out, "Jeff, nobody really knows what the hell went on here last night except your project team and us. You simply tell the press that a man arrived at your triage center with multiple wounds from the explosion and will need constant around the clock nursing and rehabilitation. Our team of professionals have worked hard and fearlessly to save John Orion's life. If you think about it, there's no reason to tell anyone anything else. Only a well trusted group— us— need to know all the details. You're not really lying; you're just holding back information."

Pearson smiled and responded candidly, "Tell me, are all you S.E.A.L.s this sneaky?"

Malloy grinned, "Just the smart ones who will do whatever it takes to accomplish the mission. Let's get everyone on board our covert ship and get back to making John and Lanny's life their own."

Malloy went to the waiting room on the east wing of the institute. There he noticed Walter, the caretaker for Orion's dogs. This very nice black man was somehow related to Billy Stokes, Orion's best friend growing up. Stokey — the nickname given to him by the team — had joined the Navy with Orion and they later on went on to B.U.D.S. training together.

William Conrad Stokes was killed in action as he stole a chopper with Malloy when they were told to stand down. He went in and rescued Orion and his fire team. When Stokes was in the Landing Zone, an enemy sniper got him just before takeoff. Lieutenant Orion then commandeered the chopper and flew his team to safety.

Stokes was awarded the Navy Cross posthumously even though he disobeyed orders. However, Malloy was given a choice to be demoted and stuck at a cushy desk job, or resign his commission and keep his rank as Captain. Malloy immediately resigned his commission.

Orion was completely devastated and was never the same again. Four months later his father died of a massive heart attack. Three months after that his mother suffered a stroke. That's when Orion had enough and resigned his commission from the organization he loved so much.

No one really knew how Orion hooked up with Walter, but just the same, they were also very close.

Malloy also spotted Orion's mother, Rosalinda Orion. She was in her wheelchair trying to get information about her son from the receptionist, angry because she was getting nowhere.

Malloy slowly snuck up behind her and said, "Lady, are you giving our receptionist a hard time?"

Mama Rosa replied, "I know that you're behind me, James Malloy. Now come over here and give me a hug."

Malloy appeared in front of her. "Mama Rosa, I could never fool you. Now I know how Johnny Boy learned to sneak up good enough to fool a cobra."

Mama Rosa's faced became frightened Malloy could tell she was about to burst into tears.

"He's fine," reassured Malloy. "Maybe a little bruised and battered, but he's got the resilience of his father, Gordon Thomas Orion, and the loving soul that he inherited from some old broad named Rosalinda Estrella."

Just then Claire Vanderkamp came through the triage doors and said to Malloy, "James, a man is demanding to see Johnny. I told him if Captain Malloy authorizes it, he can see him. I promised to return and let him know."

She angrily pointed to the door, and with everyone looking said, "You can plainly see he's been tailing me the whole way."

There stood Kyle Duffy, the youngest member of Orion's fire team. He was only 20 years old when he got that assignment. His father was Irish and his mother Taiwanese, and he graduated B.U.D.S. at age 18 and went on to capture a high ranking Taliban Warlord just as Lt. J.G. William Conrad Stokes was killed in action. He was only 20 years old at the time when he made the capture.

Trudeaux recognized him first. "Hey, it's Duffy San!"

Malloy calmed Claire down and explained who Duffy was.

Claire asked inquisitively, "Why did he keep following me everywhere I went?"

Palladin answered quickly, "Well, first look how hot you are. Second, he's in the intelligence business. He's taught to never let the objective get away. Looks like he's good at what he does."

Malloy interrupted, "Claire, tell him he can come in now."

But Claire was looking straight into Palladin's eyes and gave him a devilish smile.

Malloy restated, "You can tell him to come in at any time, Claire."

Claire replied, already walking towards the doors, "I'm on it, James." Trudeaux talked over Palladin's shoulder, "I've been trying to hit on that for the last six months and she goes ga ga over you because you tell her she's hot. I thought I knew how to infiltrate, but I guess not!"

Bobby smirked.

Trudeaux walked away remarking snidely, "Okay Palladin, you might of hooked her, but now let us see you get it in the boat."

Mama Rosa yelled out to Malloy, "Jimmy, I need to see my son. Can you take me to him, or what?"

Malloy scurried over and knelt in front of her wheelchair. "Dr. Pearson, I'm sure, wouldn't object. Just stay here a minute while I confirm it with him."

Kyle Duffy walked up at that moment and asked Malloy, "Skipper, I came as soon as I saw on the news. Is he going to be okay?"

Malloy, with his hands on the back of Mama Rosa's wheelchair, replied, "He'll be fine, Duff. This here is the Lieutenant's mom. Please keep Mama Rosa company while I go see if the doctor will let her in to see her boy."

"It would be my pleasure," said Duffy.

Time: 1017 hours.

Malloy found the professor surrounded by his entire project team that assisted the night before. The professor was instructing his colleagues that they all would meet in the auditorium theater in the Citadel at 1200 hours. Pearson also told them not to talk to the press or anybody who was not connected to Project ICARUS.

Professor Pearson then walked up to Malloy. "Well, I've got our project team on board. They know the complications if anything about what happened last night gets out." He reiterated, "Jim, we need Bobby, Michael,

Claire, and anybody of significance in his life there also."

Malloy replied candidly, "Good, Jeffrey, because his mother Rosalinda is demanding to see him now. We have to fill her in a little discreetly, a little bit at a time. She's like a lioness watching over her cub."

Professor Pearson responded reassuringly, "Good, I'm glad she's here. If anything, this might help keep Orion calm as we attempt to examine him. Jim, it's imperative that we get the data, because he may seem alright now . . . but there may be hidden dangers inside his metabolism that could kill him. So take me to the woman who raised this unbelievably brave and heroic man."

Malloy escorted the professor to the triage center located in the East wing of the building. As they approached Mama Rosa, Malloy looked at the lobby doors and the reporters outside. There a small frail black woman in a heavy dark blue overcoat stared worriedly through the doors.

Malloy recognized Millicent Stokes, the mother of their comrade Billy Stokes who was killed in action while rescuing Orion and his fire team in Afghanistan. He immediately told the door guard to let her in and hurried toward her.

The guard opened the door, let her in, and shut it immediately.

Malloy greeted her with, "Millie, it's been a real long time. How have you been?"

She replied desperately, "Captain James Malloy, stop bullshitting this ole gal. Tell me how my son's brother is doing."

Malloy smiled and replied, "He's had somewhat of a rough night, but the doctors are very optimistic that he'll make full recovery."

Suddenly from across the room came, "Millie, is that you? Oh, Johnny will be so glad to see his other Mama." Mama Rosa rolled her wheelchair as fast as she could to greet her long-time friend.

They meet in the middle of the room amidst camera flashes coming from outside the lobby doors. Mama Rosa looked towards the doors, then looked at Millie. "Damn bunch of vultures. They only care about making their stories and could care less about people's feelings or privacy."

Millie asked, "What about Johnny? It's all over the TV and newspapers. They say that he had to be air lifted here because he was hurt real bad. They also said he saved the lives of three very young children while their house was on fire."

Mama Rosa nervously replied, "Millie, I probably know as much you because I just got here myself."

Professor Pearson and Captain Malloy suddenly appeared in the waiting room. Malloy led the professor over to Orion's mother so he could explain her son's situation.

Malloy leaned down in front of Mama Rosa's wheelchair. "Rosalinda, this is Johnny's doctor. He'll explain whatever you want to know about

Johnny's condition. Dr. Pearson, this is Rosalinda Orion, Lieutenant Orion's mother." Mama Rosa blurted out, "God bless, you professor! I don't know how I could ever repay you for saving my baby's life. Can I please see my son now?" Pearson reassured, "Mrs. Orion, right now he's asleep down stairs with Lanny keeping an eye on him. But at 1130 hours we are going to wake him up for a post-op examination. At that time immediate family and friends will be able to see him. John's body needs total rest from the trauma and stress his nervous system endured."

Mama Rosa's eyes welled with tears of both relief and frustration. She wanted to see her boy pronto.

Dr. Pearson reassured her, "Mrs. Orion, our boy is doing fine. In twenty minutes I'll head outside to make my statement to the press. Afterwards, I'll have Miss Vanderkamp escort everybody to the Lieutenant's room. Till then, I'll indulge your patience, Mrs. Orion."

Mama Rosa answered sternly, "Please, enough with the Mrs. Orion shit. Call me Mama Rosa, everybody else does."

Pearson replied jovially, "That I will, Mama Rosa." The professor departed to a TV makeup artist to prepare for his media statement.

Millie Stokes headed back over to Mama Rosa's side. "Well, I'm glad to hear that poor Johnny is still with that sweet girl Lanny. What a difference from that shallow, lying sneaky girl, Theresa, who took advantage of his trusting, loving heart." She added, "Besides, she had an enormous ass."

Mama sighed with relief. "You're right there, Millie. Lanny loves him for that trusting, gullible soul of his. That other thing he used to love was a coiled-up viper ready to strike. I knew my boy would finally see right through her."

As they discussed Orion's previous love interest, both women thanked God he had finally seen how materialistic she truly was. And praise be, just a couple of months later fate intervened and he accidentally crossed paths with Lanny. Since then, it definitely had been a match made in heaven.

Orion hadn't been to Mama Stokes house in almost a year because of his devotion to the beautiful, kind-hearted woman he fell in love with. On numerous occasions he'd bragged about the Stokes clan— Mama Stokes and her fallen son who had become his irreplaceable best friend and brother.

Lanny, on the other hand, was a devoted registered surgical nurse studying for her M-CATS to become a surgical technician. Talk about opposite attraction; this was one for the books.

When their paths crossed the first time, she was fiery with rage at two belligerent bigots picking on a gay man by shoving the poor soul to the ground and kicking him. Orion watched this woman punch a 230 pound man to the ground while his fellow bigot poised to attack her. Orion intervened and dispatched them appropriately.

He admired her conviction to defend someone who could not defend himself. He usually witnessed others willing to simply ignore the cruelty, but this time he saw someone who was more than willing to act on the behalf of the helpless. From that day on the couple shared one another's convictions and decent philosophies on life.

Interestingly, Lanny had complete trust in her fellow human being while Orion, from his viewpoint, saw the evil side of man's corruptibility and would never expose his guard under any circumstance. Lanny was just the opposite. It put balance in their relationship, her strengths covering his weaknesses and vice versa.

Mama Rosa and Mama Millie were both glad that John Patrick Orion was pussy whipped. They also knew he was a determined and unstoppable force and the only one of his kind. It took a strong, vibrant woman to tame him.

At this moment Mama Rosa saw a very pretty blonde girl dressed in a fancy businesswoman's suit and skirt leading Professor Pearson and Dr. Darfuir to the lobby doors along with executives from the corporation's Legal department.

Professor Pearson walked through the lobby doors held open by the institute's security guards. Surrounded by a multitude of cameras and microphones, he braced himself for the onslaught. A very attractive reporter from Channel 12, Lydia Chevron, aggressively put herself and her microphone within two feet of the professor.

"Dr. Pearson, can you tell our viewers about how your day of recreation and relaxation turned into a life and death situation?"

Pearson complied, asking, "And what is your name, young lady?"

Lydia answered politely, "Lydia Chevron, Channel 12 News."

Pearson elaborated, "Yesterday as our sailing party was underway to have a day of open ocean navigation and seamanship, we came around the Southeast bend and all onboard heard screams of children in the distance. Once we negotiated the turn, we noticed smoke billowing from the Carmichael's residence. My friend and colleague James Malloy, a retired Navy Captain, immediately deployed a Zodiac rescue raft that was moored to the bow of my Schooner, the Galaxy. Captain Malloy with crew mates from his former command proceeded to reach the docking slip to the residence and assess the emergency."

The reporter interrupted brazenly. "Why was the crew equipped with automatic handguns if it was just an ordinary day of sailing?"

This annoyed Professor Pearson. "First of all, Robert Palladin is a Suffolk County Police Officer. Secondly, Michael Trudeaux is employed by my corporation as a bodyguard and legal consultant. As for John Orion, he's a Licensed Private Investigator in the State of New York. All things taken into consideration, if these men were not armed, those children would have been at the mercy of two ruthless killers."

Miss Chevron apologetically replied, "I'm sorry, Professor Pearson. I didn't mean to sound insolent and we are all proud of these extraordinary heroes. Please go on."

Pearson explained every detail except the extensive nature of Orion's wounds, leading them to believe the only reason Orion was air lifted was because they didn't want to take any chances.

"What is the condition of John Orion presently?" Lydia asked.

"John Orion is listed as serious with trauma wounds from the explosion, but within weeks, maybe months, he should make a complete recovery. Now, I have very important matters to attend to, so if you need additional information you can talk later to our triage unit if and when they are not busy."

The professor quickly scurried back through the lobby doors, cameras and microphones on his tail. One of the security guards locked it behind him. Time: 1125 hours.

Professor Pearson approached Mama Rosa and Millie Stokes who were seated next to Captain Malloy and his former teammates. "Now let us go join Lanny down in the observatory and wake up the extraordinary former S.E.A.L."

Captain Malloy quickly corrected the doctor, "Jeffrey, once a S.E.A.L. always a S.E.A.L."

Pearson grinned wide. "Oh yes, the Lieutenant surely convinces me of that."

Claire Vanderkamp walked right up to Bobby Palladin and hooked her arm around his. "Hey handsome, will you escort me to our friend?"

Palladin looked her right in the eyes. "You better believe it, gorgeous." Trudeaux face-palmed and said, "You've gotta be kidding!" and gave Bobby a look of disbelief.

When they reached the elevator, Dr. Darfuir was there to meet them. He and Profession Pearson put their eyes to the eye scanner and the doors immediately opened. Automatically, the voice over the intercom spoke: "Identify yourself."

"Jeffrey Pearson."

The intercom responded, "Voice recognized."

The elevator began its descent to the secret laboratory below. Mama Rosa exclaimed, "What's with all this James Bond type of stuff?"

Malloy comforted her. "Only the best for your son, Rosalinda. We want to make sure Johnny gets complete recuperation without any disturbances."

He shot the professor a look of 'was that the right way to put it?'

Professor Pearson gave Malloy a quick look of approval.

The elevator came to a full stop and the doors opened. Professor Pearson asked all of Orion's family and friends follow him across the vast complex of the underground institute. The professor finally came to a large door at the other end of the laboratory. He gently knocked.

"Lanny, it's Professor Pearson. I've got John's mother and friends here to visit him."

Lanny immediately opened the door with glee and rushed over to Mama Rosa. "Mama, oh God, it's good to see you! Johnny's going to be so glad to know you are here."

Lanny and Mama Rosa hugged as if they were mother and daughter. Lanny looked up to see Millicent Stokes lovingly smiling at her.

"Oh Mama Stokes, you're here too! I can't wait to see Johnny's face." Lanny was overwhelmed and couldn't help but cry. Millie hugged her reassuringly. "Our boy has definitely found the perfect girl for himself. Now stop your crying, child. We don't want to be too emotional in front of him."

They all entered the main operating and technological room. Orion was lying on the special aluminum table, the same one on which he had been operated upon the night before. His eyes were closed, but he looked lost in thought and slowly moved his head.

From the box where Dr. Darfuir laid the belt and harness came a small rumbling.

Lanny commented to Professor Pearson, "It started vibrating and making those sounds as soon as he closed his eyes and went to sleep. I didn't know if I should have called you right away or not."

Professor Pearson moved cautiously towards the ICARUS. Everyone in the room became completely disoriented and confused. The professor carefully opened the lid to see the device illuminating that strange purple light. The device was also defying gravity and hovered slowly to the top of the strange box which contained it.

Out of nowhere, Orion suddenly spoke. "The guardian component is calling to my body for regeneration configuration. They must again process new and primary sequences to reestablish nutrient sustenance for my body."

Everyone jumped as Orion continued.

"I must reset the Electron Generator once more, but this time at only one quarter of composite energy cycle. This must be done for five eight-hour periods. You must separate from the guardian component for exactly one hour between regeneration."

Mama Rosa looked as though she was about to have a heart attack.

"Mama, I'm fine," spoke Orion. "Me and the docs here are working on this new scientific kind of crap, isn't that right, Professor?"

Pearson, with a sigh of relief, blurted out, "Ah yeah, John, that's exactly what we're doing. So where did your, um, your guardian receptacle say to hook the device back up?"

Orion corrected him. "The guardian component told me within the next hour."

Professor Pearson again questioned, "Are you positive the computer told you this?"

Orion suddenly sat up on the table and smilingly responded, "Of that I am positive, Professor."

Mama looked annoyed and scolded her son, "John Patrick Orion, are you trying to give your poor Latino mother a full blown heart attack? Why are you wearing those awful looking goggle things on your head?"

Lanny cut in. "Mama, the reason is simple. The ultra violet lamps in the treatment would damage his eyes if he didn't wear the goggles. Am I correct, Dr. Pearson and Dr. Darfuir?"

Right away Dr. Darfuir agreed, "That is correct Miss Cromwell. The ultra violet rays can do a significant amount of damage to the retina and corneas of the eyes. So, Mrs. Orion, we are taking every precaution to ensure John's safety."

Mama Rosa inquired, "How long are you going to be all the way out here at the end of Long Island?"

That's when Professor Pearson realized he had to tell her Orion was in for an extensive stay. "Mama Rosa, Johnny here went through debilitating trauma and it will take quite a lot of time and therapy before he can be released. I know John takes care of you and supplies a home caretaker for you, so we're going to move you out here to the main house. That way, you'll have all the help you require while our boy here heals from his injuries. Rosa, is this all right with you?"

Mama Rosa's expression exploded with delight, which was suddenly replaced by a frond. "But I'll be so far away from my friends who I play cards with, and I'll miss them badly."

Pearson reassured her that all accommodations would be made on her behalf.

Lanny came over to Rosa and said, "Me and my younger sister Lauren will help you with the move and make sure the house is well locked up and secured."

Professor Pearson, with a stern voice, told Lanny, "Miss Cromwell, you are now employed by Pearson Global Technologies Corporation. Our staff will let Winthrop Memorial know of your move to our medical team."

Lanny, looking into Dr. Pearson's face, saw how serious he was. "Thank you, Professor."

Pearson informed her that she and Orion were also moving into the main house. "For now, Lanny, I recommend you get yourself acquainted with everybody in the main house, because there are a lot of caretakers all about the mansion."

Then Professor Pearson turned his attention to Orion. "John I'll let you spend another fifteen minutes with everyone, but I'll be back with Dr. Darfuir to start the procedure you so desperately need."

Pearson and Darfuir departed the room.

Orion looked at both his mom and girlfriend and asked, "Are both of you all right with these drastic changes in our lives, because if you're not, I'll talk to the professor. Mama, I'm sorry to put you through this. I know we were just getting settled in Rockville Centre, but that's been the story of my life. Everything is given to me, then quickly taken away. I don't know what God has in store next, but I feel the need everyone in this room to be part of what he, or she, has got in store for us."

Malloy walked over to his buddy and replied, "Having been your Commanding Officer all this time, I'm ordering all personnel in this room to be stuck with your sorry ass for good."

Palladin, Trudeaux, and Duffy all yelled at the same time, "HOO-YAAH, CAPTAIN".

Malloy looked at the women and scolded, "I didn't hear you."

All four ladies smiled and replied, "HOO-YAAH."

At that moment a tear rippled down Orion's right cheek. "I damn sure wish Billy, Lars, and Benny were here too," he noted.

Millie Stokes kissed him on the forehead. "Oh Johnny, I know he's here. No doubt about it. My William is here."

Duffy approached Orion and said, "Lieutenant, I was able to get hold of Lars. He's some sort of ski instructor in Colorado, but he said he'll be flying out ASAP. As for the Wizard, your guess is as good as mine."

Lanny, being confused, asked Kyle, "Who's the Wizard?"

Orion and all the members of his team started with excerpts from the motion picture, Wizard of Oz.

"Wizard, you want to see the Wizard?" proclaimed Trudeaux.

"Nobody gets to see the Wizard," Palladin added laughingly.

Duffy contributed to the fray. "Anybody check the cat houses in the green light district of the Emerald City?"

Lanny got pissed off. "Should of known better than to ask the Sesame Street dropouts a serious question."

Orion calmed her with, "Baby, that was the name Billy gave him because he was an unbelievable escape artist, magician, and an expert on chemical agents. He'd get out of handcuffs or disappear with smoke screens from stuff he concocted himself. And he'd get into places nobody else could. If anyone deserves the designation of Wizard, it would be Benjamin Kraemer."

Claire asked, "Johnny, do you remember his last known address, because our corporation's investigators will probably be able to get in touch with him."

Malloy interrupted her, "Claire, if Benny doesn't want to be found, nobody on the face of this earth can find him. I have a friend in the Israeli Defense Force. He's a Captain named Joshua Golon. I'll ask if he's heard from him. They go back a while too. Now let's get out of here so the professor can start getting our Lieutenant prepped for his treatment."

The group gave Orion their goodbyes, complete with kisses from the matriarchs, and left.

Lanny stayed behind and asked, "Baby, do you want me to stay, because I really don't want to let you out of my sight. I'm so scared with all the weird and unexplainable things that are happening to you. I love you, Johnny, and I can't bear thought of losing you."

Orion grabbed her and pulled her close. "I'm not going anywhere, Lanny ,and I also can't bear the thought of losing you, either."

They passionately kissed for at least a minute. When they broke from their embrace, Orion said, "Baby, I'm going to be here for the next nine hours in treatment with Dr. Pearson and Dr. Darfuir. They are having a meeting in ten minutes in Citadel. Do me a favor. Start getting my mom settled in. Afterwards, do what you have to do to make our accommodations more comfortable. I'm going to be here for the next forty five hours. After that, we'll be able to spend some quality time together. I won't be able to concentrate on my rehabilitation if I know you're not okay. So are you all right, sweetheart? I need to ask you something that's very important later when I'm all finished."

Lanny interrupted, "Johnny, ask me now. I'm right here."

Orion shook his head. "No it must be when I'm in a relaxed state of mind." Lanny looked at him inquisitively, "By hook or crook."

Orion smiled. "By hook or crook, Lanny."

She kissed him and headed for the elevator where everyone waited for her.

The entourage ascended to the main floor thirty feet above. As they reached their destination, the doors opened to the hallway leading to the front of the theater where the rest of the Project ICARUS team had already settled. Dr. Pearson had two orderlies help Mama Rosa and Mama Millie over to the main house where a hearty lunch awaited them. Pearson assured the matriarchs that Lanny and Claire would join them shortly after the meeting.

Then Pearson gave explicit orders that no one, not even the President of the United States, was allowed in until the meeting had concluded.

The professor walked through the doors of the theater's auditorium and up to the podium in the center front of the stage. He began with, "Ladies and gentlemen, it seems that I have put everyone in this room in dire straits and jeopardized our corporation's reputation. Disregarding all laws of protocol made to protect people of this country, I used a human host in order to save a man's life. I knew all too well that I was doing needed approval of the AMA. But this man became a very personal friend to me before the incident and I acted to save him."

The gathering was silent, all eyes on the doctor, who continued.

"I now have put at risk the very being of this corporation's existence. People from all over the world are employed with our company. Until now, we've stood always for integrity, and thankfully the man who became our unwillingly candidate for the device has made a miraculous recovery. We now must conduct every necessary test to chart every unbelievable change of molecular structure his body is experiencing."

Dr. Pearson paused. Then seriously, very seriously, he informed them, "If this situation was to get out beyond these corridors, the military, C.I.A. farm boys, and God forbid who knows who would descend upon us like locusts. All of us would wind up on the chopping block. That's why last night I asked if everyone was on board. We may just have come across the greatest find since the power of flight. Until we know that we have completely crossed this momentous bridge, this is TOP SECRET to only the trusted people in this room."

Every face nodded in silent consent.

"All Project ICARUS teams are to meet me in the observation promenade above the operating cubicle," continued Dr. Pearson. "At that time, you will observe the procedure that will be introduced to John Orion. From there, Dr. Darfuir and I will assign tasks to the specialists. Okay, let's go, folks. I'll meet the medical team in five minutes."

The Project staff rose and headed for the secret entrance to the laboratory. Once the last one departed the auditorium, Pearson confronted Lanny and Claire.

"Good, now you young ladies know the scoop. I hate to do this to all of Johnny's loved ones, but you'll be assigned bodyguards if and when Malloy or any of his team is not available."

"Bodyguards!" exclaimed Lanny.

"I know it's an inconvenience, but imagine what Orion could, and would, do if something happened to any of you girls. Don't worry, nobody knows anything, but I will not take chances."

Claire immediately replied, "We understand, Dr. Pearson, and Lanny and I don't mind the least bit."

Pearson elaborated, "Miss Cromwell, you are now in the employ of the Pearson Global Technologies. So you must dress as Miss Vanderkamp does, with the same professional style and distinction. Miss Vanderkamp, I'm sure, will help you with your attire."

Lanny raised an eyebrow, realizing her professional life and her wardrobe had just kicked up a notch.

Dr. Pearson added, "In other words, Lanny, you and Claire take care of the two senior citizens in the house, but go out and have some girl time.

God knows both of you have earned it."

Both Claire and Lanny approached him from either side, grabbed his arms, and kissed him on his cheeks.

Dr. Darfuir cut into the room and announced, "We love you two, but we have an extraordinary Lieutenant we must attend to."

Claire grabbed Lanny. "C'mon girlfriend, let's do what the doctor ordered." They both walked out the doors of the main entrance of the Citadel with a tall bodyguard ten feet right behind them.

The two professors headed for the laboratory and back to Project ICARUS, both of them in awe of the medical breakthroughs in store ahead for them.

Time: 1240 hours.

Along the New Jersey shore, a periscope peered out from the top of the surf twelve miles out from the shore. A shrimp boat slowly chugged along the outside of the harbor in roughly the same spot. The shrimp boat cut its engine and came to a full stop.

Time: 1930 hours. November 2, 2010.

JOHN PETER FERRIS

8 CONSORTIUM OF EVIL

Time: 1930 hours. November 26, 2010.

The night was frigid cold. A submarine's conning tower came into view of a 28 foot shrimp boat that had just cut its engine. Both vessels were twelve miles out from the Jersey shore.

The shrimp boat's first mate threw the anchor at the bow. The hatch of the conning tower suddenly opened and three crew members immediately set up to receive lines from the shrimp boat.

Captain Vladmir Koslovski disembarked down the conning tower's ladder. Amal Haafaal Baraash was right behind him. The submarine stopped and the crew of the shrimp boat threw three lines to the submarine.

The shrimp boat Captain ordered his men to release the winch lock on the cable of the boom. He instructed them to unlock the mooring blocks to the boom and swing it into place above the submarine's forward deck.

The captain of the shrimp boat, Meadiav Bosloff, served with Koslovski during the Chechnya Rebellion. Captain Koslovski yelled over to his comrade, "Meadiav, move as quickly as possible. We don't want to be spotted from the air."

Bosloff replied, "Vladmir, just have the parcel on the deck ready to be transferred." As soon as he finished talking the sub crew stepped back and the hydraulic doors opened, revealing the crate with Iranian markings on it.

Now the boom operator on the shrimp boat adjusted the boom directly over the crate. From the deck of the shrimp boat two crew members grabbed a sixteen foot aluminum stage used as a gangway on which passengers could cross.

The first crew member tied a line to the front of the stage. He threw it to a crew member on the sub, who pulled on the line to make it taut. The crew member on the shrimp boat walked it into place and secured his end of the stage to a bait chopping table anchored to the deck.

The crew member of the submarine lashed the other end to the sub's deck mooring chocks with cleats.

Baraash summoned the raven-haired beauty, Shaleem Khodeef, and saw to it that she safely made her way to the shrimp boat. As she walked across, Amal Baraash said to her, "Be very careful, Your Holiness. We have now brought you to the land of the people who killed your father, his Lordship Omal Hussein Khodeef."

With a tear appearing in her left eye, she replied to Baraash, "I don't know why you need me here, Amal. I would rather serve Allah on Arabian soil than that of the murderers of my father, the Khaleef."

Baraash, with an evil smile, answered, "Your Highness, without the gift that Allah has bestowed on you, we would never achieve retribution against the infidels who spit on the teachings of Mohammed the Holy."

As the princess made it to the other side of the makeshift gangway, she turned. "Amal, aren't you sure it's also because of the Power of the Scared Talisman, that reveals only to me things that only I can interpret?"

She opened her Kashmir overcoat to reveal a beautiful Amulet chained around her neck. The metal taking up most of the base of the jewel was a gem like no other, not quite as shiny as chromium, but close enough. In the center was a giant blood red ruby. Legend had it, and many believed, it was a gift to Hodesha, Mohammed's wife, supposedly given to her back in 632 A.D. when Mohammed ascended into Heaven.

Baraash's crew got one gander of the talisman and instantly dropped to their knees and bowed.

Captain Koslovski screamed out in anger, "WHAT THE FUCK IS THIS? We have to get the fuck out of here, and now you decide to hold mass. Yo Amal, money or no money, get these Hadjees to fuckin' move or they'll swim to shore."

Baraash instantly spoke, "Karuus, Tarig, and Maleesh, you are jeopardizing our Holy Cause. Either move now or I will kill you myself, and may the sharks shit you from their bowels."

All three men jump back into working like they never stopped.

The Princess Shaleem yelled out, scolding Captain Koslovski. "Where do you think you come from, threatening my people for your own personal gain?"

Koslovski demanded of Baraash, "Keep that crazy Arab witch away from me." Suddenly Koslovski's face became very pale and he doubled over in pain.

Baraash yelled to the Princess as her grip tightened on the amulet, "Forgive him, your Highness. He did not think before he spoke."

Shaleem let go of the talisman and broke her own concentration.

"Make this perfectly clear, Amal," she said. "If I see this is not for the greater good of the Muslim people, I will return to Iraq to take my place amongst my beloved countrymen."

Baraash pleaded with her, explaining, "Your Holiness, I was your father's highest consul and loyal friend, and I am only carrying out his sovereign wishes. What I do is to only protect the good people of Islam."

Shaleem headed for the crew's cabin down below.

The boom operator swung the crate to the stern of the shrimp boat. As he began lowering the crate to the deck of the boat, the Chechnya Captain came over and whispered to Baraash, "Be very careful of her. If she was to discover that Lamarra is still alive, all we've done would be for nothing."

Baraash reassured Koslovski, "Don't worry. Lamarra is kept under guard that she thinks it is for her own protection. The acting Khaleef, Abdulah Musheen, has her with him in the Mosque in Hoboken, New Jersey. Now, only worry about your next assignment," he cautioned, adding, "There is a refueling tanker at the coordinates in your manifest and navigational charts. Make sure you follow instructions to the precise longitude and latitude specified. The Americans have found a distinct amount of high grade of yellow cake uranium in a disclosed secret area of the Veruga region of the Congo. We don't know where this is, but we know where they are transporting it. We have assembled a sizable army to hijack it without the Americans even knowing we are aware of its existence. So get out of here as fast as you can and meet up with the tanker at the assigned rendezvous point."

Baraash yelled for his other seven men on the submarine to quickly board Captain Bosloff's shrimp boat. As the last man crossed the gangway, one of Koslovski's crew untied the lines lashed to the sub's deck. Captain Bosloff's crew brought the stage back on board the shrimp boat. The crew brought up the anchor immediately and the hydraulic doors closed on the submarine.

Both engines started at the same time on the vessels. Just as Captain Koslovski was about to close the hatch of the sub, he yelled to his old comrade, "Meadiav, watch your ass and I'll see you in Barbados next week."

Bosloff's yelled back, "Don't worry about me, Vladmir. I've already got plans for our retirement. Das vadanya, comrade." With that Captain Koslovski closed the hatch and the submarine commenced to dive.

The shrimp boat now loaded with its deadly cargo headed for Harbor Marina twelve miles in.

Time: 1948 hours. November 26, 2010.

****

Time: 2112 hours.

Two vehicles entered the docking area of Port Elizabeth, New Jersey. The first was a dark-tinted Crown Victoria, deep black like those of most law enforcement agencies throughout the United States. Behind the car was a twenty foot box truck with a loading lift gate at its rear. The Crown Victoria first pulled up to the security entrance of the Marina.

The guard walked up with a puzzled look on his face. The driver of the Crown Victoria rolled down the power window and flashed a New Jersey State Police Detective's badge.

The guard asked the two men, dressed in policeman's plain clothes attire, "Something wrong on the pier, Officers?"

The man on the passenger side replied, "Hope not. Just checking on a shrimp boat that's coming in. We're here to make sure the only thing coming off that boat is shrimp and nothing else."

The security guard smiled and responded, "I'm glad to see somebody is on their toes around here. Is the truck with you?"

"Just a precaution, in case we have to confiscate any contraband or anything that violates our State's ordinances. If that's the case, we have authority to confiscate the boat."

The security guard scratched the top of his head. "How you gonna put the boat in the truck?"

Both detectives laughed and the detective on the passenger side explained, "No, that's the Marine Patrol's jurisdiction. The truck is only there for illegal goods or contraband."

The security guard asked the driver, "Want me to lock the gate and follow you back, just in case."

The passenger detective blurted out, "No, not necessary. Our backup teams are just outside the gate. They are only one mile up the road waiting for just a peep from us. So don't worry, just act like everything is normal. If anything seems out of the ordinary, we'll definitely call for your assistance."

The security guard asked the driver, "Maybe I should have my gun drawn, just in case."

The driver looked concerned, but his partner spoke up, "You know, I think that would be an excellent idea. Sometimes our backup lags behind."

The driver's mouth opened wider as his partner continued, "Do me a favor though."

"And what is that?" the security guard asked.

"Put a complete lockdown on the Marina for at least two hours. This way, if we apprehend some scumbags, we'll have the time to completely process them."

"I know what you mean; these fuckin' illegals get away with too much as it is. Anything else you need me to do?"

"Matter of fact, stay hidden just until we leave so we know they don't have accomplices waiting somewhere in the bushes to take us out."

The security guard said proudly, "Nobody will ever know that I'm even here."

"Good," said the driver as he looked straight ahead and stepped on the gas.

They moved about sixty feet in the Crown Victoria when the driver commented to his partner, "Bella, what in the fuck is wrong with you? 'I think that's a great idea,' and 'Keep your weapon drawn.' What, have you lost your mind? This fuckin' asshole is going to get suspicious and we'll be in Rahway State Prison just in time for breakfast."

His partner replied, "Parnov, how can he be suspicious when the moron is hiding in the woods? Settle down, this guy believes that we are more Secret Service than fuckin' pigs. Plus, the good thing is that he will have the harbor locked down for two hours as we climb under our blankets."

Little did the security guard know that the two phony cops were wanted Serbian war criminals working with the cleric priest, Abdullah Musheen. Musheen had been financing his operation of terror with the dowry of wealth that had been automatically put into effect from the reading of the will of the Khaleef Omal Hussein Khodeef. All had been left to his daughter, Shaleem Khodeef.

One of Khodeef's demands was to make sure certain allotments went to keep the Holy Laws of Islam alive for the worthiness of their blessings. Because the princess was never brought into the ways of the Khaleef's repertoire, he assigned his assistants, Abdullah Musheen and Amal Haafaal Baraash, to be the guardians of her complete rule. The only problem was that, unknown to the Princess Shaleem, Abdullah Musheen and his nephew had her father killed and made it look like the American military was completely to blame. This was about the same time the Iranian students stormed and took over the American Embassy in Tehran.

Even though Abdullah was of Yemenis descent, he still had favor from the Khodeef's royal family. This royal family had been kept secret from the West for over a century. Their bloodline, some said, dated back to Mohammed, himself. No one could really know for sure, for such a thing could not be authenticated, but why hide their existence all this time from the West? Even when Saddam Hussein came to power, his own Bath Party did not know of its existence.

Now Abdullah Musheen had put together a terror organization of consorts from Yemen, Libya, Chechnya, Serbia and Somalia—his own consortium of evil. The Khaleef's wealth was immeasurable beyond belief. The Princess every now and then contacted her accountant, but she was unaware of anything nefarious because the accountant was being paid off by Abdullah Musheen.

Musheen hired the phony detectives Parnov Bistra and Bella Steflenik because they were in the Serbian Secret Police when the atrocities were going on in Montenegro, in the former Yugoslavia. Both of them were trained in linguistics and lost their Serbian accent in favor of a New York accent.

Parnov and Bella pulled up along the docking slip as the crew of the shrimp boat piloted in. The truck following them swerved in order to back up to the stern of the shrimp boat.

Baraash and his crewmen from the Alladin were already setting up to transfer the crate. Parnov and Bella both opened the doors to their fake police vehicle and exited. Slowly they walked towards the boat.

Baraash yelled from the boat, "Bella, I see you you've received the special armored police cruiser I had ordered for you."

Parnov looked at his partner Bella and commented, "Bella you never told me this car was armored." Bella shrugged his shoulders. "This is the first I'm hearing of it too."

Then Bella asked Baraash, "Why the need for armor? We are hiding the car away till next Wednesday."

Baraash smiled and yelled down into the lower cabin of the shrimp boat. "Hassan, bring the Princess up. It is now safe to transfer her to the safety of the car."

With that the Princess appeared right behind Hassan Khaldif, the nephew of Omar and Mustaffa Khaldif.

Baraash said to Shaleem, "I'm sorry, Highness, of the terrible smell of the wharf."

Shaleem instantly replied, "Nonsense, Amal. Ever since I was a little girl, my father would always take me sailing on his yachts. I love the smell of the sea. Now I am tired and sleepy, so do whatever you have to do so I can finally rest in a comfortable bed."

The three men of Amal Baraash's crew who had killed the helpless sailors aboard the cargo ship Alladin started moving the sixteen foot aluminum stage in place so everyone could depart the boat. The two phony detectives finally got a closer look at Shaleem and saw how unbelievably beautiful she really was. She looked just like another Eva Longoria with the most captivating eyes any of them ever seen.

Parnov whispered to his partner Bella, "What I wouldn't do to fuck that one."

Bella quietly replied, "So would I, but be very careful what you say. These Hadjees take all this royal shit seriously. They'll cut your balls off and force them down your throat if you disgrace anyone of her stature."

Parnov looked down at the crotch of his pants. "FUCK THAT. The quicker we transport this bitch, the better."

Captain Meadiav Bosloff appeared from the starboard side of the boat and called over to Baraash. "Amal, I need my airline ticket for Africa. My flight leaves Newark at 0600 hours tomorrow morning."

Amal answered Bosloff, "My driver in the truck, Kadash, has it. He will first transport the package to our warehouse in Kearney. From there we have made arrangements for you to be driven to a hotel suite near the airport. It's a real long flight to the country of Zambia, but don't worry, you'll be flying first class." Baraash cried out to his other crewmen, "Tariq and Karuus, open the lift gate so we can transfer the package to the truck." Then he turned his attention to the driver of the truck. "Ahkmed, wait for Maleesh to tell you when to back up. We don't need any accidents. Once we are out of the marina, we are home free. Now hurry before we are detected."

As Baraash's crew got on with the transfer, Hassan led the princess across the gangway towards the car and then opened the right rear passenger door. "After you, Your Highness," Hassan bowed.

Shaleem got in but seemed nervous with the two men in the front.

The crew member, Maleesh, began operating the boom aboard the shrimp boat. As he lifted the crate, he yelled to the driver Ahkmed Kadash to back the truck up slowly. Just before Ahkmed's rear tires were about to touch the wooden planking of the dock he yelled for him to stop.

With the truck stopped, Maleesh told Tariq and the other crewmen to bring the lift gate up all the way. Maleesh swung the boom over right above the platform of the gate. Maleesh told the other crewmen, Karuus, to open the back door to the truck.

Once the door was open, chains and harness strappings were visible inside. There was also one other man inside the truck waiting. He had a hydraulic walking dolly that quickly brought the forks all the way out onto the lift gate.

Maleesh gently brought the crate down onto the forks of the dolly. The man pulled the dolly handle and brought the crate into the truck. Maleesh quickly put the boom back into its locking chocks and set the steel rod to secure it.

Captain Bosloff instantly locked the main doors to the cabin and wheel perch. Baraash had his other cohorts immediately get in the back of the truck. Captain Bosloff jumped in the passenger side of the truck and waited to follow the Crown Victoria out of the Marina.

Baraash pushed the aluminum gangway into the water and ran to the rear driver's side of the car.

Bosloff immediately opened the passenger window of the truck and said, "Why the fuck did you do that for?" Just as he opened the door, he told Bosloff, "I've set charges in it for to go off in two hours. We'll leave no trace that we were here."

Then Bosloff gave Baraash the thumbs up and said, "You're sure you're not Chechnya?"

Amal Baraash gave a sinister smile and got into the Crown Victoria. He told the driver, "Let's go, Parnov, I need a good stiff drink after this." The phony police cruiser headed for the main gate with the truck carrying the deadly cargo not far behind.

Time: 2204 hours.

The two vehicles were just about to reach the gate when that same Security guard appeared at the opening. Amal Baraash instantly groped a gym bag for his Baretta 92-F. Bella saw this and told Baraash to leave the gun alone and that he would handle the situation.

Shaleem automatically put on a face of disgust and said, "Are we down to killing innocent people for our cause? This man probably has a wife and children. It's the American government that we are at war with you said, Amal." Bella, with a forceful voice, cut in, "Nobody's killing anybody. Just don't say a word and go with my lead."

As they come to a stop, the guard noticed a man and a woman now also in the car. The security guard leaned down to talk to the phony detectives.

"Where did you get these two from? Must be illegal, huh?" he inquired.

Bella replied very quickly, "You hit right on the nail there. We caught them and another couple of these towel-head fucks hiding in the boat's forward hold; got the fuckin' Captain in the truck. We're confiscating the boat. Ah, what's your name?"

The security guard answered right away. "Larry Monroe, there, officer. Should I call I.C.E. and inform them of our situation?"

Bella shook his head. "No, no, no. I need you to now lock the gates and let no one in unless they can prove they're Homeland Security, like us. Mr. Monroe, I have your full name now. So if you definitely want to be promoted to Sergeant, don't let anybody near that shrimp boat. Guard it like you're guarding your kids."

Larry, with a big shit eating grin, said, "They definitely don't stand a chance in hell."

Bella replied, "Well, I know we got the right man for the job. Just keep all of our evidence locked up. We'll be back as soon as we have all the prisoners processed."

Larry saluted him and responded, "Ten Four."

Bella gave Larry a look that a proud father would give his son and replied, "Hold the fort, Sergeant."

Parnov pressed the knob to the power window and started snickering. As they get about a half a mile down the road, Parnov broke out in hysterical laughter and said, "Ten Four, hold the fort, Sergeant." He broke to catch some air and continued, "Guard it like your brats. Right man for the job; Oh, this is too much! 'FUCKIN' TOWEL HEADS."

Parnov thought for a second and apologetically said to Amal Baraash, "I hope I'm not offending you, Amal, but you got to admit that was an Academy Award winning performance."

Baraash immediately replied, "So you think this is funny? You Serbian wannabe."

Parnov shook his head and told Amal Baraash, "Amal, I swear I was only kidding. Please don't hold this against me. I'll prove to you that we are comrades."

Baraash with a snickering grin replied, "I cannot forgive you."

Then he paused and said, "I cannot forgive you because that was the fuckin' funniest performance I have ever seen."

"Yours just now wasn't bad either," replied Parnov.

The three terrorist broke out in hysterical laughter. In the backseat, the princess turned and laid her right cheek on her shoulder, a small tear coming from her eyes. She wiped her cheek and closed her eyes to search in her inner soul.

Time: 2212 hours.
****

Time: 2351 hours.

One hour and 50 minutes later at a guest house in East Hampton, New York, a retired Lieutenant was carefully peeling the Vera Wang dress off the woman he loved. He looked at her incredibly beautiful body now in thong panties that matched her satin black bra. She was dressed in five inch black velvet stilettos with diamond sequins draping their outlines with class. They both made love feverishly like the world may end tomorrow. Finally, both lovers exhausted, they fell off to sleep. They have a very tough and important sailing trip into destiny.

Time: 0206 hours. November 27, 2010.

JOHN PETER FERRIS

9 JOURNEY INTO THE VOID

Time: 2100 hours. November 28, 2010.

Below the main floor of a mansion, an elite team of the scientists and technicians were steadily at work, monitoring a man whose life the night before was in dire straits of not surviving.

The Pearson Technology Complex consisted of a main house, a theater auditorium, and three huge guest and servant's quarters, all two hundred yards from the Citadel. The Citadel was the nerve center of the entire complex. Only known to Professor Pearson and Professor Darfuir was an intricate number of concrete and steel bunkers and passageways thirty feet down.

Each corridor was blocked off by huge titanium and carbon composite doors. At the entrance to each door were eye and handprint recognition scanners. At the present time, only the professors and few handpicked scientists were able to gain entry. Claire Vanderkamp, who Pearson thought of as another daughter, was the only non-technician able to gain entry to all of them.

Outside behind the three guest houses was a high tree line going back about one mile. Behind that was a secret airfield with four humongous aviation hangers. Captain Malloy, using his expertise, had instructed Jeffrey Pearson on the construction of the entire complex. The four runways accommodated the arrival and take off of each type of airplane and jet. Only Malloy, Vanderkamp, Darfuir, and, of course, Dr. Pearson, knew what was inside the giant hangers a far distance from the main house.

The Navy Department, having business with Pearson Global Technologies, only knew of their contracts with the corporation. Professor Pearson wanted to get other branches of the military on board. Until all designated projects were in their final stages, everything was kept TOP SECRET. As of last night's fiasco, Project ICARUS was TOP, TOP

SECRET. The foundation of the Corporation now rested with a number of well-chosen professionals to protect and expand the global dynasty.

It was just about the eight hour mark to shut down the Electron Generator attached like an umbilical cord to the ICARUS device. This time Pearson had the generator set to shut down automatically at the precise second. As the digital clock counted down to zero, the Electron Generator audibly came to a full stop.

Dr. Darfuir, with a little hesitation, slowly reached for the umbilical cord attached to the Guardian Component, finally breathing a sigh of relief when he made contact. "Oh, thank God. I thought we might have a repeat of what happened yesterday."

Just then Claire's voice wafted over the observation area's intercom. "James, its Claire. I have Lanny with me. How is Johnny doing? My girlfriend has been biting on bullets for the last fifteen minutes."

Pearson pushed the transmit button on the intercom and replied, "Claire, you and Lanny may come down just for a quick visit, but be aware our boy here is asleep and needs complete rest."

Claire asked, "I thought Captain Malloy was in the observation gallery. Is our security chief still in the complex?"

"No honey, he received an urgent phone call from Vice Admiral Fischer about a half hour ago and bolted out of here. I pray everything is alright."

Claire, with a reassuring voice, responded, "Professor, I'm sure James will fill you in if anything is wrong. See you in a minute. Lanny and I are on our way down."

Meanwhile, Dr. Darfuir was attaching an electrical line from the main computer to the guardian component, and another one to a wired cradle cap around Orion's head. He pulled over an E.K.G. monitor and set it for a pulmonary reading. He fed data into the hard drive of the computer. When he got what he wanted, he downloaded it to store all vitals to a flash drive.

The soft bell of the elevator sounded and the door slid open. Lanny and Claire walked out and across the laboratory to the operation room on the other side of the medical unit. They arrived at the operation door and Claire pushed the transmit button on the intercom. A buzzing noise erupted, but Carl Livingston opened the door immediately and welcomed the two ladies.

"Hello Miss Cromwell and Miss Vanderkamp, come right in," Carl said with a smile.

Lanny automatically headed toward Orion and Dr. Darfuir, who was starting to open the chest area of the special suit her boyfriend was wearing. "How's my man doing, professor? Is he awake?" Lanny whispered.

Dr. Darfuir shook his head. "No, my dear, but the data indicates something extraordinary has happened to John. The epithelial tissue all over his body has regenerated and restructured his molecular density beyond belief. The funny thing about it, though, is that his brain cortex can mimic, copy, and duplicate what he sees fit for his epidermis."

Lanny's eyes grew wide as she struggled to process the enormous changes her beloved was undergoing.

"Right now he's in a relaxed state of flux," continued Dr. Darfuir. "The super microbes inside him give him the ability to accept and teach himself to adhere to his new body."

Lanny, with a face of dire concern, blurted out, "What do you mean, new body? You're telling me Johnny's not human anymore?"

Professor Pearson, who was up in the observation gallery, quickly cut in, "No, Lanny, he's very human, but the data feedback is telling us that yesterday's incident probably did a whole lot more than just heal his injuries."

Lanny looked up into the gallery from where Professor Pearson spoke from a microphone. Puzzled, she said, "I'm scared, Professor. Johnny's my whole world."

Pearson quickly assured, "Lanny, you and John are now practically my children. Believe me, I will do everything in my power to protect both of you from anybody or anything that would try to hurt either one of you. Ask my other child, Claire, and she'll tell you."

Claire began explaining to Lanny that six years ago her mother was treated for breast cancer at the same facility Dr. Pearson's wife, Arlene, was being treated. Her mother and the professor's wife became very close friends and Claire watched both of them go through horrible pain and suffering. Claire's mother died three months before Arlene. She had no family at all. Her father had died the victim of a tragic drunk driving car accident when she was only eight years old.

Lanny teared up. "We'll, I'm your sister now. Get used to me being around." She peered up in to the gallery and asked Dr. Pearson, "Professor, what are you doing up there? Come down here so I can give you the biggest hug you've ever gotten."

Professor Pearson smiled and replied, "Perhaps I will in a little while. Right now I've got too much on my mind."

Claire immediately with concern yelled up to him, "Papa, what's wrong?" Pearson, with a slight tear in his left eye replied, "I just had to sign the papers to have your sister Kendra put in a closed and secure rehabilitation facility. I also found out that the scum who was holding her had her so hooked on heroin that it's going to be a living hell to bring her back."

The women heard him sob, "Those fuckin' animals also gave her Gonorrhea."

Claire and Lanny ran out the door together and sprinted up the stairs to the Gallery. Both hugged him frantically.

Lanny said to the professor reassuringly, "I'm your oldest daughter now, plus I am one of the best surgical nurses of any emergency room there is. I have seen on a day to day basis what that drug does to people. I know now what I have to do to straighten Kendra up so she flies right." She looked directly at Pearson and continued.

"She will never be one of those poor souls who loses the battle." Her words were a comfort. Professor Pearson nodded his head and spoke to both his girls, "Why did he (God) send me these beautiful angels?"

Both women looked each other and smiled, echoing at the same time, "You mean SHE sent me beautiful angels."

Pearson grinned and looked to the ceiling. "Well, thank you, ma'am." Lanny kissed him on the cheek and reassured him, "Papa, you, me, and Claire are going out to the facility once Kendra has done her to week dry out. We have to treat this like a horrible accident, and we're going to let her know that we love her and really need her in our lives. Now professor, let's work on your son getting better."

Pearson looked at Lanny in amazement. "I hope John Orion knows what an amazing young woman he has."

Lanny with a real devilish grin replied, "Oh he does. I remind him of it every day."

Professor Pearson quickly thought back to Friday night at the presentation, and answered with, "Ah yes, that you do."

The three of them laughed together, enjoying the moment.

Down on the operations floor, Dr. Darfuir and the rest of the team laughed along.

Lanny looked over on the table toward her man and saw a big shit eating grin on him too. Lanny clenched her teeth and exploded, "WHY YOU UNDER HANDED SNEAK!" She sprinted back down the stairs like a rabbit.

The professor and Claire were both befuddled and wondered what in the world was wrong with her. They decided to follow Lanny down to operations.

Lanny entered the room and immediately acted like she was about to break down. "Oh, Dr. Darfuir, are you sure he's going to be alright? I don't know what I would do without him," she said in a helpless baby voice. Then she squinted her nose and curled her lips, pronouncing to the professor and Claire as they entered the room, "When I'm in a state like this, I like to show off my nice breasts to calm me down."

Right then and there Orion's comatose face started squinting uneasily. Lanny walked right up to middle of the room and yelled as she grabbed her breasts, "Who among you wants to see my breasts?" Two of the older technicians on the floor immediately dropped their trays.

Then Lanny walked right over to Orion and said, "I know you're awake, you phony horse's ass. Stop the shit now, Johnny".

All of a sudden across the intercom, Orion's voice spoke, "Baby, I'm only sort of awake. I can hear everything that you say, but from the time I was disconnected from the Electron Generator, my body can't move from this constant state of flux. I must finish the whole process to make sure all the super nano microbes are fully stable along with the robotics".

Professor Pearson looked at Orion in complete amazement and asked, "John, how are you able to talk through the intercom unit?"

Orion replied, "I seem to be able to interact with everything on this subterranean enclosure that is connected to the high velocity computer I'm attached to. Even what I'm doing now is expending energy, so I must return to a state of concentration. Professor, the memory chips will collect all data for you at the end of each cycle. By the end of the next cycle, you will be able to retrieve everything from this cycle on the memory discs."

Orion's voice was fading, but he added, "Now Lanny, promise me you won't show anybody your breasts?"

Everyone in operations broke out in hilarious laughter. Lanny, with a happy sigh of relief, bent over and kissed him on the lips. "They are only there for you to look upon, you big lug. I'll be back in eight hours to kiss you good morning. I guess that's 0600 hours. See Johnny, I'm catching on. C'mon Claire, I promised Mama Rosa I'd check in with her and Millie before I went to bed." Lanny and Claire headed toward the two professors and kissed them goodnight on the cheek. They walked across the subterranean complex to the elevator.

Time: 2150 hours. November 28, 2010.
****

Time: 0500 hours. November 29, 2010.

Purple lights illuminated from all around John Patrick Orion's body. He levitated ten inches above the table on which he was resting. The twenty-four memory compact discs connected to the main hard drive of the super computer all began spinning at the same time.

Carl Livingston, Chief Logistics Scientist, automatically went to a separate laptop on his studies desk and called over to the main house, where everybody was fast asleep. Inside Dr. Pearson's bedroom suite, his laptop buzzed with a flickering purple light next to the eye cam. He jumped out of bed and headed across the room to his 60-inch flat screen television. Touching the remote control brought Carl Livingston into view on the big screen.

Pearson sleepily asked, "What's the emergency, Carl?" He looked at the time on the screen and noted 0506 hours.

Livingston replied, "Check this out, professor." He lifted his laptop off his desk and let the eye cam explain it for him.

The back of the professor's neck gave him a weird chill. Pearson instructed Carl with urgency, "Tell Professor Darfuir to meet me in operations NOW!"

Still in his pajamas, the professor grabbed his lounging robe and headed for the secret entrance to the subterranean complex below. He entered his study and spun the large globe counter clockwise and inserted a pen in the top of it when it stopped. He turned the special pen clockwise. A giant bookcase in the study rolled to the right, stopping at a door woven of titanium and carbon composite.

Pearson placed his right hand on the recognition scanner and the door slid upward and disappeared into the ceiling. Another door slid to the right and the professor walked into the elevator. Automatically the intercom demanded, "Identify yourself."

"Dr. Jeffrey Pearson," he replied.

The intercom responded, "Voice recognized."

The elevator descended to the subterranean complex below, its door opening so that a very excited and concerned professor could sprint through another titanium carbon composite door.

This time Pearson had to use both hand and eye scanner recognition. As that door opened he ran down another corridor that finally led out to the Operations Room. A little out of breath, he opened the final door and entered.

What he beheld was Orion still levitating ten inches above the table, but with a much darker purple light illuminating around his whole body. Around his head appeared the same tiny orange light circulating at a high super rate of speed, so fast that Pearson could just barely make it out.

The professor looked at the main hard drive and could not believe all indicators were spinning in a strict sequence with the rest of the twenty four. He figured, just for the hell of it, perhaps Orion could communicate with him. Bewildered, he asked, "John, it's Dr. Pearson. Are you able to communicate with me?"

Orion's body remained in a levitated state, but over the intercom he spoke, "Yes professor, I have no problem hearing you at all. Don't be startled by what you are seeing. The small entities of new life have combined themselves with my molecular bio-structure and are like infant babies adapting to the first breath of life." His voice sounded quite normal, and he continued.

"In other words, Professor, you have introduced a symbiont life form in various abundance. Instead of sharing my host body, it has done something surprising. The symbionts have conjoined with my body's complete molecular structure — biological and robotic super nano microbes. This really means congratulations are in order, for now, Professor, you have a brand new type of life in the known universe."

Dr. Pearson reluctantly asked, "John, do you know if you're still traverse and able to know the difference between robotic and biological life?"

Orion steadily replied, "Yes, I sure do. We are but one entity, and both life paths share each other's life force. Professor, please understand, we are now entering a void, something only the Mighty Creator can understand." Orion sensed the doctor's confusion, and clarified.

"The entities, before they were able to conjoin with my body, told me it was difficult at first, but teardrops from another human being's DNA made it easier to accept a host that showed nothing but compassion for all life forms. That's when they decided to conjoin us and completely trust us to be just one type of human being. With the help of the Electron Generator, which powers the ICARUS Device, I called the guardian component and it has given my being a power I have not been able yet to comprehend. Yet I realize I will probably know much more when the full replenishing cycle is finally complete."

Orion paused, waiting for Pearson to absorb the details before concluding, "Doc, I really don't know yet the extent of the power I possess."

Pearson gave Orion a pat on his shoulder while he levitated. "I'm with you all the way with your journey," he reassured. "That makes you my son now, John. No one will ever hurt my boy. I brought you back into this world, but they will have to kill me first if they were to do you harm."

Pearson asked one more question. "John, when you told me they would only have had combined themselves to you because of another one's DNA, whose DNA were they talking about?"

Orion, even in a catatonic state, was able produce a giant smile and said, "It was Lanny. When she was crying over me, her teardrops fell into my tear ducts." He pleaded with Pearson, "Professor, please don't let her know. I'll never get a minute's peace with her."

Pearson burst out laughing and told him, "I know what you mean, and I promise, Lieutenant. Now I'll make sure after Lanny and Claire visit you at six o'clock after your rejuvenation process is complete."

The professor looked at the other two technicians on duty. "When Miss Cromwell and Miss Vanderkamp leave, only names that Dr. Darfuir includes on watch may stay."

Professor Pearson walked out of the room and ran into an out of breath Dr. Darfuir.

"Jeffrey, I came as soon as I could. Is everything okay with Johnny?" Pearson replied, "Come, old friend, let's get a cup of coffee and some breakfast. We have a lot to go over and discuss."

Time: 0555 hours. November 29, 2010.

Second Generation Cycle complete in five minutes.

JOHN PETER FERRIS

10 MESS WITH MOTHER NATURE

Time: 0915 hours. November 29, 2010.

In the cafeteria room inside the complex where the triage and trauma units were located, two girls entered the dining area. Lanny Cromwell and her new best friend, Claire Vanderkamp, removed their winter coats and hung them up on the coat racks in the entrance to the facility.

Earlier Professor Pearson contacted them and said he'd meet for breakfast. He told them that all the project's personnel must be there.

The girls had earlier visited Orion in the laboratory. He was resting peacefully after his second generation cycle.

Professor Darfuir told the girls that his team had momentarily taken off his special composite suit in order to wash his body and give Johnny's skin a chance to breath. Darfuir told Lanny that the terrible wounds sustained in the explosion had completely healed; not even a scar was visible on Orion's body. He said they had tried to shave him, but the force field that protected him generated as soon as the razor was within six inches of his face.

The professor comforted Lanny by telling her that her boyfriend was not in any danger. In fact, he told her that after his prognosis, he couldn't believe the data readouts about Johnny's physical condition, which was superb, but still in flux. He reassured her that after the next 27 hours they would be more informed. He told the two girls to go and get ready for breakfast, and he would see them in the cafeteria at 0930 hours.

Lanny and Claire pushed their trays across the metal shelving of the serving area just as others from the project team made their way in. Professor Pearson suddenly appeared at the entrance and immediately made his way up to the girls. Grabbing a tray, he slid it on the shelving at his waistline.

"Girls, what do you think I should have this fine morning?" Pearson asked, looking at all the food behind the counter. He spoke to a woman in front of him. "Margaret, any surprises for us this morning? What do you recommend?" Margaret replied, "Well professor, there is French cinnamon toast, Eggs Benedict, and quiche with spinach."

The professor pondered for a couple of seconds. "Okay, beautiful, I'll have the Eggs Benedict because I know there's Hollandaise sauce somewhere down this line."

Margaret gave a big smile. "Right you are, sir. The sauce is at the end by the napkins and silverware."

Lanny looked bewildered. "Hi Margaret, my name is Lanny, and I think I'm going to play it safe and go for the French toast."

Claire quickly spoke up, "Same for me, Margaret. Nothing fancy this morning."

They proceeded to grab coffee, orange juice, and any fresh fruit on display in the serving line.

The professor led his two adopted daughters to the largest table in the cafeteria. As they sat down and began to eat, the professor told them, "I spoke to Mama Rosa twenty minutes ago, and told her that both of you were going to take her to her house in Rockville Center. Claire, use one of the corporate limos and help her retrieve some of her belongings. I'll have some of the staff follow you in a small box truck, so Lanny may also retrieve some of her and the Lieutenant's items."

"You are so thoughtful, Papa," commented Claire.

"Agreed," added Lanny. "Thank you."

"Well, just to let you know, we have an important staff meeting in the Citadel auditorium. The meeting convenes at 1015 hours, so girls, it looks like you both have a very busy day ahead."

At that very moment Michael Trudeaux entered the cafeteria. He walked right up to the professor and whispered in his ear, "I just got some terrific news from my Law School professors."

Pearson looks up at him. "Well, let's have it, Trudy."

Trudy paused for a second and shared, "I passed. I actually passed!" Pearson exclaimed, "Do you think I would have helped finance your schooling if I didn't think you could?"

Trudy acknowledged the professor. "Thank you sir, and I mean that from the bottom of my heart."

"C'mon son, sit down here and have breakfast with us."

"Okay, boss, I'll be right back. I can smell that spinach quiche from here." As Trudy made his way to the serving area, Claire threw in a little snide remark. "I thought real men don't eat quiche."

Lanny with a look a surprise remarked to Claire, "Oh c'mon Claire, he's a real sweetheart. Johnny, on the other hand, tells me he's a real tough customer."

Claire with a little giggle replied, "I'm only kidding, Lanny. I know he's a sweetheart, but he used to do the same thing to me a couple of years ago. If he didn't try so hard at picking me up, I'd probably be his girlfriend right now. I don't know what it is, but I really got a thing for Bobby. You're right, big sister; I promise I'll be nicer from now on."

The professor cut in. "What's wrong with quiche? I eat quiche all the time."

Both girls start laughing and assured the professor, "Nothing wrong with quiche."

Trudy came back with his breakfast on his tray and started to sit down. "What's so funny, girls?"

Claire got up and walked over to Trudy, leaned down, and kissed him on the cheek. "Nothing, Mikey. I'm really very proud of you."

Trudy smiled. "Thanks, Claire. That means a lot to me, coming from you." Lanny interrupted. "The same goes for the rest of us, Mikey. We are all very proud of you."

Claire finished her food and looked up at the clock, noticing that it was 0948 hours. She commented to Professor Pearson, in a business like tone, "Professor, I'm heading over to the Citadel to set up for our project meeting." The doctor replied, "Very good, Miss Vanderkamp. You'll find my logistical report inside the podium cabinet on the stage."

With a very serious face she responded, "Sir, I'll have them ready for your presentation right away."

Claire then stood and said to Lanny, "Come with me, Miss Cromwell. I could really use your help in the Citadel."

Lanny, with a bewildered face, rose and followed Claire out of the cafeteria. When they get into the corridor, she asked, "What the hell just went on there?"

Claire explained, "Honey, Papa runs a worldwide corporation. He had me trained for my position by having professionals teach me business etiquette and courtesy. Our corporation's look and stature demands excellence in every aspect that we project." She added, "You'll get used to it, older sister. Look at all the gorgeous clothes we get to wear."

Lanny pinched the shoulders of Claire's Eve Saint Laurent suit and said jokingly, "I love what you wear, little sister. Do you think I can get something like this in an amber color?"

Claire laughed. "That's the ticket, Lanny. Me and you are going to hit Saks Fifth Avenue tomorrow."

Both girls continued towards the Citadel with their high heels clicking in unison down the corridor. Three minutes later, as the girls entered the theater auditorium, they saw Dr. Darfuir running in from behind the back of the curtains on stage. Claire yelled to him as they approached, "Professor, we didn't see you at breakfast. Is everything all right?"

Smiling with happiness he replied, "Nothing could be better. I just got off the phone with my sister, Lamarra, from New Jersey. I'm going to meet her in Manhattan Tuesday evening for a dinner and a show."

Claire smiled. "Oh, that's wonderful, professor. It's about time you get some R and R away from the complex. I wish I could meet your sister. You've talked so much about her."

Dr. Darfuir replied, "Perhaps we'll arrange something like that in the near future. She's only been in this country for four months. Being from Iraq, she must get used to the American way of life. This country has probably put a weird sense of cultural acclimation on her."

Lanny asked, "Where is she staying now, professor?"

At that moment Claire's cellphone started ringing. Claire excused herself for a minute because Bobby Palladin was calling her from his work.

Lanny asked again as Claire walked away for some privacy, "Professor Darfuir, is your sister nearby?"

"My sister is teaching Holy Prayer with others from her congregation in Hoboken, New Jersey. The Cleric who resides over the Mosque, Abdullah Musheen, had summoned her there to teach the children of the congregation Islam's holy ways. Lamarra is an expert in the teachings of the Five Pillars of Islam. So when I see her Tuesday, I will extend to her an invitation to our facility."

Lanny smiled. "I'm looking forward to meeting her."

Claire hung up and returned, saying to the professor, "I'm sorry for the interruption, Kamal. I've been anxiously waiting for Bobby to call for a while."

Dr. Darfuir laughed. "Ah, young love. I completely understand, my dear. I was once young and in love myself."

Claire started to blush. "Professor, you've got it all wrong. I just met Bobby."

This time Lanny interrupted. "Yeah, yeah, yeah, we understand, little sister. C'mon, we've got to hurry; the meeting is in fifteen minutes."

The professor headed up to the projection booth in the theater. Claire and Lanny went directly behind the curtains on the stage. Claire reached into the podium's cabinet and retrieved the professor's notes and glimpsed at the findings. Shaking her head she said, "Good thing I go over these, because I don't think he could make heads or tails of this himself."

Lanny smiled. "Isn't that why we're here, Miss Vanderkamp?"

Claire replied, "Yes, Miss Cromwell. That's exactly why we are here." She stopped for a minute, then told Lanny, "I'll be right back, Lan. I have to fix Papa's notes. I'll have it in a Word document in about five minutes. In the meantime, there's a vending machine area backstage if you're hungry or thirsty."

Lanny replied, "Go right ahead, Claire. I've got to use the little girl's room, anyway."

Both women proceeded with the tasks at hand.

Meanwhile, the project team assembled in the auditorium. Professor Darfuir, having set up the computer presentation, descended to the main theater of the auditorium. Arriving backstage, he pushed the button to open the curtains. It was now 1011 hours and just about everyone was seated.

Professor Pearson entered the auditorium with Michael Trudeaux. Trudy took a seat in the front row, while the professor climbed the stairs to the stage. He turned on a switch from the podium and started speaking into the microphone. "Testing one, two, testing one, two, three." He asked the crowd, "Am I talking loudly enough for everyone to hear?"

The crowd answered with "Yes" and "We hear you."

Claire came from behind him and handed Pearson his research notes. Lanny appeared out of the backstage door with Professor Darfuir. They both sat down next to Trudeaux.

Professor Pearson and Claire mumbled a few things to each other, and Claire descended the stairs to sit next to her best friend.

Dr. Pearson said as she reached the bottom of the stairs, "Thank you once again, Miss Vanderkamp. Okay now. Good morning, everyone, I hope you all enjoyed your breakfast. The last twenty four hours have been compelling, to say the least. By some freak accident we have stumbled upon an amazing scientific discovery and are working toward a plausible explanation. Before us are a multitude of steps through which we must navigate for the positive future of all mankind." He paused and referred to his notes.

"First, for all our new colleagues, we gladly welcome you to our research facility. We will try to bring you up to date on the basic continuity of what we are trying to accomplish. All of us are working hard to take the nano-technology field of medicine to the next level. We have done a tremendous amount of research and experimentation. People forty or fifty years ago would never believe how far we have advanced."

The audience agreed with scattered applause.

"Our technology," continued Pearson, "Is the miniaturization of biological and robotic cells. Most of them are more minute than the atom itself. Now we are going to present much of our current research. I think much it will be self-explanatory."

Professor Pearson pushed two remote toggle switches on the podium next to his right leg. The lights automatically dimmed, and the computer projected onto the screen. A narrator explained the graphic of an atom and then displayed the nucleus with a proton and a neutron inside the atom with an electron orbiting outside the nucleus. The film went on to highlight today's feats of nano-technology, a field which grew through experimentation. The induction of cells with microscopic stimulation occurred in several distinct ways. In one instance, though, they used elements from the periodic table to accomplish their goal.

The presentation showcased a scientist from a renowned computer company, who combined two of the elements to make a delivery system which moved throughout the body. The two elements were samarium and cobalt. With an electro magnet the scientist was able to direct the microscopic robot to a precise part of the body for exploration. It reminded some of the senior participants of the movie from the early sixties, Fantastic Voyage, except this was more plausible.

In another instance, they used honeybee venom known as melatonin and delivered it to a cancerous tumor by encircling the melatonin with a combination of carbon and fluorine to be cast around the bee venom, itself. By putting a protective coating around the two combined elements, they were able to introduce it into the bloodstream. Programming the tiny microchip that combined in the two elements, they sent the melatonin safely and directly to the diseased tumor. This was done without causing cellular damage to any part of the human body.

By this time most of the basic research made more sense to Lanny. As the film ended, Professor Pearson turned on the lights in the theater. From that point on, he explained something much more astonishing than they could have expected as his dialogue turned to a geological expedition he and Professor Darfuir had undertaken four and a half years ago.

Their journey to a hidden part inside the Republic of Congo took them to an area so remote, no one even knew about it. It was located in the Verunga region of the country, where both mountains and dense thick jungle coexisted. The professor had been told of a strange metallic substance found there at the turn of the twentieth century. He heard stories the indigenous tribes of the region, who thought they were cursed because anyone returning from this area was struck down with horrible sickness and disease.

In February 2006, they went on an expedition to the area to determine the facts. After two months in the jungle, they came upon the same indigenous tribe, and some of the ancestors of those affected by horrible sickness agreed to take them to area where it all originated. When they came upon the area, none of the tribal people would go on further. They called the area black JUJU and believed in an evil presence lived about the premises.

The expedition team moved on just a little further before coming to the edge of the jungle. A giant mountain now faced them. As Professor Pearson looked up the southern side of the mountain, he saw a cave opening about a quarter mile up. The team of scientists approached the cave, their Geiger counters ticking away. The professor, taking preventative measures, set up camp and used a magna phone satellite communications device to have his corporation immediately send out the necessary radiation equipment to him. The equipment would not arrive till the next morning. It would also have to be air dropped because there was no way to land an aircraft.

A most mysterious thing occurred when darkness came that night. An eerie glowing purple light illuminated from inside the cave. The next morning, an hour after daybreak, a Hercules C-130 dropped the equipment right on target.

The two professors and another scientist entered the cave an hour later to find out the place fully enriched with ground elements necessary to produce uranium. By looking at the inner walls of the cave, they could see it was created by a violent, but small, meteor strike. As they moved in deeper they saw the same mysterious purple glow ahead. After finally reaching the back of the cave, they witnessed portions of the meteorite sprawled everywhere, perhaps at least three tons of it.

Leaving the cave, Professor Pearson made arrangements with the ruling president of the country to buy that specified part of the mountain. For the last four years the corporation mined nearly all the enriched earth of uranium ore. All but a very tiny amount of the meteor was still present at the site. As a matter of fact, the last of the meteorite rock was being loaded and carried 50 miles through the jungle to Lake Tanganika for its journey to Mombasa, Kenya. From there it would be loaded on a C-5 Galaxy transport cargo air carrier to the United States.

This was all happening this Tuesday morning. Along with the rest of the meteorite rock was also two tons of the enriched uranium earth. The Corporation had carved out a secret road through the jungle to reach Lake Tanganika. From there, a loading barge would travel northeast with a caravan of armored personnel carriers waiting at the northern tip of the lake. From there, they would travel east to Lake Victoria and reload the cargo to another barge for its trip to Kenya. Then armored personnel carriers would transport it safely across to Mombasa.

They didn't fly it out of Nairobi because al-Qaeda was known to have spies in the area.

The professor went on to explain how the purple glow would stop when removed from a two mile distance from the radiation. He also explained that the metal used in the ICARUS Device was that of the strange metal. He then informed everyone that all the nano super microbes were made with the metal. The processor explained that he gave the strange new metal the name chorominium, after the meteor, which they dubbed the Choromin Meteorite. He let the whole project team know of the dire consequences if this information leaked out to the world.

Every soul in the room took the professor's caution very seriously, not only because of their jobs, but because of the love they had for the two noble scientists. Even after Carl Livingston made that grave mistake

Saturday afternoon with the botched timing of the Electron Generator, the professor sat him down and told him he had also made similar slip ups in the past. He encouraged Carl by reassuring him that the way one learns not to make future mistakes is to keep one's dedication on track.

Professor Pearson truly was a magnificent and kind man.

He looked quickly at the clock and told the Project team, "Okay, ladies and gentlemen, time is of the essence, so we'll conclude our meeting for the day. All teams head back to the operations lab and continue the ongoing strategy."

Everyone stood and made their way out of the Citadel. The Professor saw the look of amazement on Lanny and Claire's faces. As he approached them, Michael Trudeaux said to the professor, "Somehow, I kinda knew you were doing more than just playing with little buggy thingamajigs."

The professor laughed. "Jim Malloy has known everything that's been going on for the past three years, himself. I can tell by the integrity of the people with whom he surrounds himself that our secret is safer than ever. So Claire, take Lanny and our two prestigious old gals in the main house and accomplish your mission."

"Yes, Papa, I mean Professor Pearson," she replied.

Pearson told Trudy, "Michael, you drive the limo. This way I know they're in more than capable hands."

"Aye Aye, sir."

Claire called up to the main house and told Mama Rosa and Mama Millie to start getting ready. They were heading out west across Long Island.

Time: 1117 hours. November 29, 2010.

11 JUNGLE JUBILEE

Time: 1400 hours. EST New York Time. Time: 2200 hours. Nairobi, Kenya. November 28, 2010.

A Delta Trans-Atlantic flight had just landed in the capital city of Nairobi, Kenya. Getting off the flight was Captain Meadiav Bosloff and Ahkmed Kadash. The two al-Qaeda operatives made their way down the plane's departing ramp to be greeted by a Somalian national. His name was Tuncha Sabissa, an ex-pirate who decided to move up to terrorist.

Waiting outside the airport's main gate was a Land Rover all-terrain vehicle with two Hutu tribal bodyguards inside. They were there to escort Bosloff and Kadash southeast to a rendezvous point between Nairobi and Mombasa. This would be the designated target area where they planned to hijack the shipment of uranium ore from the Caravan.

Tuncha yelled up to Kadash, "Ahkmed, good to see you. Who is the friend with you?"

Kadash replied, "He is here on the orders of my Uncle Abdullah to assist in the operation. Captain Bosloff, this is my friend and collaborator in this Holy endeavor of ours. His name is Tuncha."

Bosloff extended his hand. "Pleased to meet you, Tuncha. Just call me Meadiav."

Tuncha replied, "Both of you must be exhausted from the long flight from the United States. So let's get into the Land Rover and travel to our base camp sixty five miles southeast of here."

Bosloff told Tuncha, "I sure hope you've got something cold to drink for the ride. I'm already starting to fry in this unbelievable heat."

Tuncha laughed. "You better get a quick bottle of Coca Cola inside, because from now on you'll mostly be drinking water. I do hope you understand we are now only forty miles from the Equator."

Captain Bosloff with a big frown said, "Oh, lovely. Okay, I'll be right back. I definitely need a Coke."

The Captain went with Kadash to check in with the officials. They both made their way to baggage claim and waited for their bags to arrive. Five minutes passed before they noticed their luggage, two black bags, coming through the conveyor storage.

Grabbing the bags, they headed for customs check-in. There they stated their reason for coming into the country, and both got their passports stamped. Once they got beyond the main terminal gate, Bosloff immediately stormed the vending machine and bought four bottles of Coke. He stowed two in his bag and handed one to Ahkmed.

"Here, drink this," Bosloff said. "This is our last taste of civilization for a while."

Ahkmed grabbed the bottle and opened it. "Thank you, Captain. Let's get moving. It's a long drive through the jungle. The brush in this country is rough." Both men walked outside to find the Land Rover pulling alongside to pick them up.

When the Land Rover stopped, Tuncha opened the passenger door and motioned for the two men to get in. As they drove off, Tuncha suggested, "Try to get some sleep on our journey. For it is night time in the jungle. I must let you know we will be traveling slowly. This is because night time in the jungle means all the predators are on the hunt. We keep a very close eye out for danger at all times. Please don't be too alarmed. My two comrades here are very well armed."

Captain Bosloff replied, "How can I fuckin' get to sleep now after you tell me this shit?" He looked out into the eerie dark night as long trip began.

Time: 2230 hours Nairobi Time; 1330 hours EST New York Time.

Time: 0105 hours. Nairobi Time. November 29, 2010.

After a bumpy and uncomfortable ride through the African bush, the five terrorists finally reached their base camp. Bosloff looked out of the truck and saw nine feet tall thick, thorny bushes wrapped in a giant circle around the compound. The bushes were from the Acacia tree and the brush was from the existing terrain.

Tuncha told Bosloff and Kadash that the tribal people call this make shift fortress a "boma." The villagers would construct large thickets to deter lions and other predators from entering their villages. This boma was constructed for the sole purpose of fooling the caravan into thinking that a nomadic tribe had settled in for a short time.

Inside the boma were one hundred and fifty well-armed Hutu tribal warriors. On the other side of the boma, just sixty feet into the thick jungle, sixty more men of the tribe dug in and made trenches. Here they were setting up for a parallel ambush. They also had two M-106 recoilless rifles trained on the center of the road that the Caravan would be taking. The rifles were up high and hidden three hundred yards back into the mountain that opened up into the jungle.

The Hutu warriors inside the boma were equipped with AK-47's, RPK's, 80mm mortars, RPG's, and American made M-19 30 Caliber machine guns. Outside the boma were mostly indigenous tribesmen who spoke a strange dialect of Swahili. They were set back into the jungle because the Hutu terrorists made them believe strange white men were coming to destroy their village.

Sixty five Hutu tribesmen were set up only fifty yards from the center of the road. They were only equipped with AK-47's and RPK's, so as not to accidentally put artillery fire down in the wrong position.

They only used 80mm mortar rounds from inside the boma. It was the same if they tried to run forward — they had four tribesmen with RPG's. Same scenario if they tried to escape to the rear.

Abdullah Musheen had given the orders to kill everyone and make sure no one was left alive. The plan was that after the assault was carried out, they would take the hijacked ore north along the coast into Somalia, to the capital of Mogadishu. From there they would have it flown to the west coast port city of Monrovia, Liberia. There they would load the uranium ore aboard the same submarine that Captain Koslovski commanded.

Only Abdullah Musheen and Koslovski knew where the uranium ore went from there to be enriched. Abdullah wanted to be dead sure nobody knew anything they didn't need to know, just in case the operation went south. This way he, Koslovski, Baraash, Omar and Mustaffa Khadif could never be implicated in the crime. Everyone else would just be an expenditure of their evil cause.

Time: 0120 hours. Nairobi Time.

Bosloff and Kadash, after seeing the boma area and ambush set-up, were led to an area inside the boma to finally get some much needed sleep. Just before the two separated, Kadash reminded Bosloff that he had to call Musheen on their satellite magna phone. Musheen had told them that at 1000 hours Bosloff had to report that everything was in place and ready to go. Captain Bosloff acknowledged Ahkmed and they turned in for the night.

Time: 0130 hours. Nairobi Time. November 29, 2010.
****

Time: 0700 hours. November 29, 2010.

Captain Meadiav Bosloff was awoken by the sound of a male lion roaring in the distance. He looked up to see men moving about all over the boma. He got a whiff of some strange smelling food coming out of the boiling pot hanging over the fire outside. Getting out of his cot, he walked over to the three men taking servings from the pot.

He said to one Hutu warrior who was already eating, "You don't mind if I help myself to some grub, do yah?"

"Go ahead knock yourself out. There's plenty there to fill your belly." Bosloff grabbed a funny looking piece of wood, fashioned it into makeshift ladle, and helped himself. He noticed the stew had a funny taste, but with the herbs and spices added he didn't think it was bad at all.

After about ten minutes of enjoying his meal, Bosloff asked the tribesman, "What kind of meat was in that? Was it zebra or something fancy like antelope?" The Hutu warrior replied, "No, it's bush meat."

Bosloff, bewildered, asked the Tribesman, "What the hell is bush meat?" The Hutu warrior laughingly answered, "Its monkey; lots of protein. Tastes pretty good too, huh?"

Bosloff immediately ran into the jungle and threw up the food he just ate. He traveled for about two minutes when he entered a clearing close to the mountain. All of a sudden to the right of him appeared a five hundred pound male lion, two hundred feet right in front. Fear traveled through his entire body and he started slowly backing up. The lion easily picked up on his fear, charging with his front canine teeth fixed to kill.

Just as the lion got within fifteen feet of him, Tuncha stepped out of the bush and fired a Browning automatic rifle straight at the beast. The momentum of the now dead lion knocked Bosloff to the ground. He tried to get up, then realized the lion was a lot heavier than he thought.

Tuncha laughed hysterically. "You had to see your face. Did you shit your pants? You asshole, this is lion country. Hyena, leopard, and wild dogs won't hesitate to rip you apart. Don't ever leave the safety of the boma unarmed." Bosloff lowered his head. "Thanks, Tuncha, for saving my life. Believe me, I'm going to now on sleep with my rifle all the time."

Tuncha came over and with an intense voice said, "The jungle is a very serious place. You drop your guard, even for a second, you are dead. Even at night we have had starving lions to try to penetrate the boma just to get some food. You watch me and you will learn."

Bosloff replied reassuringly, "I won't be here long enough to be taught;. The sooner we reach Mogadishu, the better."

Just as Bosloff finished talking three armored personnel carriers pulled up alongside both men. The man behind the 50 caliber machine gun called out, "Tuncha, where do you want us to hide these APC's? I don't think there's a room in the boma for them."

Tuncha pointed towards the mountain. "Lawana, bring two of them over by the M-106s and cover them with brush. Then we'll use your armored personnel carrier to carry out reconnaissance. Park it just about thirty feet into the brush for now. Then I'll meet you inside the boma."

Tuncha Sabissa took Captain Bosloff back to the safety of the boma. As they both were about to enter, Bosloff asked Tuncha, "I thought you said they were night predators."

Tuncha smiled. "When you're hungry, day, night, what's the difference?"

Then Basloff laughed. "This is a very strange place to live, but I got to admit it's more beautiful than anyone could imagine."

Tuncha agreed. "It sort of grows on ya."

Bosloff replied jokingly, "Yeah, as long as you don't wind up as lion shit." Both men entered the compound and Tuncha told the Captain, "I'll try and find some food that you will be able to keep down." Tuncha Sabissa then took Bosloff around and filled him in on the plan that Abdullah Musheen had laid out for the terrorists.

Time: 0745 hours. Nairobi Time: November 29, 2010.

****

Time: 2345 hours. EST New York Time. November 28, 2010.

Outside a warehouse in Kearney, New Jersey, two tractor trailers pulled up by the roll-up steel doors. On the side of the two trailers were the Pathmark's logos. As the roll-up doors began to open, out of the passenger side door exited a man with a limp, who walked to the entrance. Mustaffa Khaldif was waiting there to greet him.

"Rashaad, welcome, comrade. I see you had no problem finding our Mr. Shaveski." Farkon Shaveski was an arms dealer out of Serbia. Shaveski, a Croation industrial steel manufacturer, had changed professions at the very beginning of the Serbian uprising. With his ties to rifle and other weapon manufacturers, he was able to make a considerable profit off the deaths of the innocent.

When the Serbian Army capitulated later to the N.A.T.O peace keeping forces, Shaveski, with tons of weapons and other ordinances, fled to Libya in exile. He had his appearance changed with the help of Abdullah Musheen's ill-gotten wealth and changed his name to Garret Sharansky. This made it easy to move about the globe.

Since his exile, Shaveski was been able to build industrial complex in Libya and Algeria. He made state-of-the-art weapons for anyone meeting his price, paying off the ruling factions of both countries. Most of his business came from al-Qaeda, itself. By hiding his manufacturing plants in the two countries, he was able to operate with impunity.

Rashaad Saleem answered, "Mustaffa, it was no problem. He was in that Denny's Restaurant waiting for us just like you said. We all ate breakfast together and he took us to some humongous warehouse, ten miles west of Camden. Even though I was blindfolded, I could tell it was only five minutes away from where we left the restaurant. ALLAH be praised, he even had surface-to-air missiles there."

Mustaffa sarcastically replied," Believe me when I tell you, Rashaad. He is charging us more that he should, that fuckin' Croat prick. The package price alone for our plan in Nairobi was fifteen million . He wanted nine million for the Loach Little Bird helicopter that was built in the '80s. Since he had his face changed with plastic surgery, I think his greed has changed him even more."

As the door finally opened, Mustaffa motioned for both trucks to enter. He pointed them to park next to a large number of fifty gallon steel drums. A door from a small vestibule in the back opened and out stepped Omar Khaldif.

"Open those truck doors now. I want to make sure that Serbian fuck gave us everything specified," Khaldif commanded.

Rashad quickly yelled out to Omar, "I went over everything you gave me on the list carefully. I made sure everything was there before I gave him the other half of the money."

Omar, with a sinister smile, replied, "Not everything, my comrade." With that, Omar entered the back of the truck and wiggled past the armored personnel carrier and dozens of crates of munitions and other unique weapons. One particular crate stood out from the rest. The markings said 'Water Filtration Units.' Omar grabbed a flat crowbar and pried it open. Inside, under Styrofoam peanuts, were two funny looking containment devices.

"Ah, at last," Omar Khaldif exclaimed in ecstasy. "These are the components of our salvation from the imperialists of America. We shall bring them to their knees for all the suffering our people have endured, Insha'Allah." He had the men from the trucks carefully move the components to his office inside the vestibule. He yelled for them to start spray painting the tractors brown, and the trailer a dull silver gray. On the other side of the warehouse were men welding and doing mechanical work on three 24 foot box trucks. Mustaffa yelled over to his men laboring on the hydraulic platforms, "Make sure they work perfectly. By Tuesday morning I need to make a trial run to ensure there are no mistakes." Mustaffa then joined his brother Omar in his office.

Time: 0125 hours. November 29, 2010.

****

Time: 1335 hours. November 29, 2010. United States Naval Base. Norfolk, Virginia. Naval Intelligence Command.

Having received an urgent phone call from Vice Admiral Thomas Fisher at 2030 hours the day before, former S.E.A.L. Captain James Malloy was in a very secretive conference with his ex-Commanding Officer. A knock came from outside the door of the office. Malloy opened the door and in walked the Commanding Officer from the Amphibious base at Little Creek, Virginia.

Time: 1345 hours. November 29, 2010.

12 THE SATELLITE BLUES

Time: 1345 hours. November 29, 2010.

Admiral James Maguire had just entered a conference room in the building complex of United States Naval Intelligence in Norfolk, Virginia.

"Hi Jim, come on in. I'd like to introduce you to my friend and ex-S.E.A.L. Team Captain James Malloy," said Vice Admiral Fisher.

Malloy put out his right hand and said to Admiral Maguire, "It's an honor, sir."

Maguire grabbed Malloy's handshake and replied, "No, the honor is all mine, my friend. You are well known to all the S.E.A.L. community. Tommy here tells me you could probably help us in this dilemma that has reared its ugly head."

Malloy said, "Anything to help the Navy. I would still consider it my duty and my job, sir. Just because I'm no longer on active duty doesn't mean the uniform came off."

The Admiral, with a proud smile on his face, pulled out a variety of satellite photos and recording devices from his briefcase. As he laid down the first photo he explained, "This photo was captured by one of our own spy satellites. The photo shows the Alladin cargo freighter on fire and listing fifteen degrees on its port side." Maguire elaborated, "Our satellite captured this photo at 1900 hours on November 26th. Two hours before, our radar picked up a reading that a large vessel was covering the same coordinates for thirty five minutes straight. We automatically put our Pegasus satellite to work taking pictures at fifteen minute intervals."

Maguire placed one photo next to the other. "We got this one at exactly 1700 hours. If you look real close at the area of the bridge, you will see two men of Arabian descent holding the wheelhouse crew hostage. We are taking this incident very seriously because it happened inside the perimeters of the United States." He laid down the next photo opposite the other.

"Fifteen minutes later we captured this one of the entire crew being forced to lay face down with their hands behind their heads."

Then with a grave face, Maguire laid down the next satellite photo. "This one was shot a half hour from the first. Looks what's docked alongside her." Fisher and Malloy's eyes bugged out of their heads as they beheld an old Russian submarine made back in the late '60s or early as the '70s, moored to the Alladin.

Malloy exclaimed, "How the hell did this one get past our Vanguard buoys?"

Vice Admiral Fisher replied, "We really don't have a clue how they did, but they did, and now we really have some bigger problems figuring what they are planning to do."

Maguire positioned another photo next to the previous ones. "Now look at this. On the forward gun deck, notice what's there instead of their heavy 47mm deck gun." All three of them studied the photo and saw the crate with the Iranian markings on it.

Vice Admiral Fisher, with a worried look, said, "Where the hell was this freighter's place of origin?"

Maguire answered, "It took on its cargo in Monrovia, Algeria."

Malloy opened his mouth with astonishment

Fisher continued, "Here the sub is ready to deploy. We are lucky we got this one just in the nick of time. Look who is about to close the conning tower hatch before they get underway."

Both Fisher and Malloy looked down at the photo and immediately recognized who it was. Simultaneously they blurted out, "Amal Baraash."

Malloy looked up with dire concern. "Now we definitely have an enormous problem. This guy was responsible for a teammate getting killed in Afghanistan. The C.I.A. were totally convinced that he was a friendly collaborator. After giving up enemy sites and positions a couple of times, he set a trap for American forces to attack an area designated to have top Taliban commanders there. I kind of suspected he was an enemy operative and didn't trust the fuckin' viper, but I and the Marine Commandant, Colonel David Caldwell, were told to give him the utmost cooperation. I sent in my best man for the job, along with his fire team, only to find out that they had been setup." Malloy took a breath, his countenance darkening with the memory as he continued.

""When I and my Sea Hawk helicopter pilot heard their cry for a Q.R.F. emergency extraction, we were told to stand down. The C.I.A. didn't want it known that they had fucked up big time. So I and one of my Junior Officers commandeered a Sea Hawk chopper that had just been refueled. Admiral, if it weren't for my Junior Officer, my men would have been at the mercy of those fuckin' snakes. He was killed for his heroism, but the C.I.A. was allowed to sweep their fuck up under the rug. You definitely have to let me in on this one, sir. My whole team wants this fuckin' coward."

Maguire and Fisher looked at each other with determination.

Admiral Fisher said, "That's what we were hoping you would say, Jimmy. Now that I, too, know it's Baraash, we are going to hunt this slime prick down." Maguire cut in, "We have another problem, we think, on top of that one. Before the Alladin sank, there were small traces of radioactivity in the vicinity." Malloy asked Admiral Maguire with concern, "Do you think they got a W.M.D. into the country, sir?"

The Admiral replied, "I pray to God that they didn't, but you know perfectly well we have to assume they did."

Admiral Maguire pulled two more photos from his briefcase. "These were taken by Coast Guard surveillance cameras aboard the helicopter that was chasing a speed boat from Alladin. One photo shows the speedboat exploding as the chopper reached the hijacked freighter."

Malloy right away said, "They blew up the freighter so as not to leave any clues behind, but the speedboat was just a diversion to keep the Coast Guard busy while the hijackers made their escape in the submarine."

Maguire reiterated to Malloy, "I came to the same conclusion and put out a reconnaissance sweep with submarine hunter aircraft and more than a dozen sonar equipped warships towards the coastal shore. We've come up empty. But on a routine fly over of one of the shipping lanes five hundred miles out to sea, our submarine hunter on a pass over recon spotted this one submarine probably charging its battery conduits while surfacing. Look carefully at the marking on it in this photo captured by the hunter."

Maguire grabbed the one visibly showing the crate on its deck. "Compare both of them, and BINGO, it's the same exact submarine. We couldn't do anything because it was in areas beyond our jurisdiction. I told Norfolk Command to have the hunter come about and follow it for a while to see where it was headed. After a short time it was detected and submerged deep and quiet enough for us to lose its signature, but in that short time our Navigational Command said the present course would take it to the vicinity of Cape Verde. So we know they're heading back to Africa." Maguire paused to let the information sink in, then went on.

"I advised Command from that point to carefully watch with Sixth Fleet sub hunters to see if later the bastards decided to make a surprise return trip."

The three men proceeded to plan a strategy to spread out several different operators in hopes they would catch a slip up and discover whatever the enemy terrorists were up to.

Admiral Maguire reached into his briefcase and pulled out a couple more photos along with an audio recording device. He arranged it all on the table, then pointed to a man in the photo. "Our Intelligence took these pictures with a camera we hid in an airport in Nairobi, Kenya. We also had a hidden microphone placed by the vending machines in the lobby."

With his finger on the picture, Maquire told Malloy and Admiral Fisher, "This man we identified as a Serbian war criminal wanted by the European community so he could be brought to trial in The Hague. The black man next to him, well, we have no idea who he is. To me, I would say he's another Somalian out for terrorist money. Let me play you the tape we have of them conversing by the Coke machine."

Admiral Maguire pressed the play button.

"Here drink this. This is our last taste of civilization for a while."

Thank you, Captain. Let's get moving. It's a long drive through the jungle. The brush in this country is rough.

Maguire pushed the stop button.

The Admiral elaborated, "Why are these two scumbags heading out into the jungles of Kenya?"

Just then, Malloy remembered there was a shipment of Pearson's corporation's enriched uranium earth being secretly transferred cross Kenya to the port city of Mombasa. Malloy told Admiral Maguire and Fisher that as security chief for his new company, he knew what was going on.

"I know positively that no one is aware of the route the caravan was taking. Even the Nuclear Regulatory Committee doesn't know the plan at hand. They just inspect it when it arrives in the states under our heavy guard."

Vice Admiral Fischer told Malloy, "Jimmy, maybe you should check this in with your boss as soon as possible. Captain, it's better to be safe than sorry. Jimmy, keep us informed. Just in case, we have back-up from our amphibious base at Diego Garcia in the Indian Ocean. By the way, how's your boy, Orion, doing? What a proud representative of the teams we got there. Hear he saved three small children from a house fire burning around them."

Malloy replied proudly, "He's got a lot of recuperation ahead of him, but he's the toughest S.E.A.L. I've ever trained. I have all the confidence in the world he'll come back even better than before."

The three men continued going over different maps and photos from the past to see if there was something they might have missed.

Time: 1415 hours. E.S.T. November 29, 2010.

13 ASSIGNMENT AFRICA

Time: 0720 hours. Democratic Republic of the Congo. 0020 hours. E.S.T. November 29, 2010.

At the edge of the mountain were three mining sleds completely filled with the enriched earth containing uranium ore. A man of German descent yelled out to his hired Tutsi tribal members to get ready to hook up the sleds of the armored personnel carriers. His name was Hans Von Dietrich.

James Malloy hired him as Security Chief for the African Mining excursions. Von Dietrich once was a Master Sergeant in the GSG-9 special forces of the German Army. Malloy and Orion became very close personal friends with him.

Von Dietrich and his men used to carry out joint war games with Malloy's S.E.A.L. Unit, Sgt. Major Cowan's S.A.S. British Special Forces, and some of the mysterious Gurrkya Guerillas of Nepal. Malloy hired him because of his uncanny way of detecting trouble before it even started.

As an A.P.C. backed up to a mining cart, one of Hans armed guards pushed up to Von Dietrich holding a fax message from Global Technologies on Long Island. The guard, Gunnar Mientz, announced, "This just came over the wire from operations, Chief Malloy. It was sent two and half hours ago, but Bonsa, our communication operator didn't think it was important enough to bring it to you."

Von Dietrich unfolded the message: All is well, proceed to the Rendezvous Point A beginning at 0800 hours your time. Malloy.

Von Dietrich smiled and said to Gunnar, "Don't worry, Corporal. I told Bonsa he could spend some quality time with his wife back at their village. But I'm glad to see that my number one man here is on his toes." Gunnar smiled as Von Dietrich continued.

"Okay, Gunnar, get everybody ready. We head for the lake in exactly thirty five minutes. Make sure the choerominium is stored away from the uranium ore. We definitely don't need that purple glowing light giving away our position."

Gunnar took off to make sure the rest of the convoy would be ready.

Hans headed to the satellite magna phone and held up the portable dish while unhooking the battery. He then went to his personal Humvee and hooked up the main drive unit to a box unit on the floor. On top of the truck was a set-up post on which to attach the dish.

Another one of Von Dietrich's GSG-9 Army buddies, Klaus Steubern, pushed up next to Von Dietrich's Humvee. Klaus drove a fully armored half-tract vehicle with a M-2 50 caliber machine gun. It was also equipped with the side mounted 80mm mortar launch capability.

Klaus yelled over to Hans, "Don't worry, Master Sergeant. I've got your six with this here baby."

Hans laugh out loud. "Yeah, but who's gonna babysit your ass when you're watching mine?"

Gunnar Mientz walked up. "Don't look at me! I guess you're fucked."

The three men met between the two vehicles. Gunnar laughingly said, "Only kidding, my brother. Anybody tries anything, I've got an Israeli Matador anti-tank weapon. Operations Chief Malloy really knows his shit."

Hans hugged both of his ex-GSG-9 buddies. "Yo, once we've completed our mission to Mombasa, we'll head down to Pretoria to get smashed with bunch of hot looking South African girls. After three months out here in this God forsaken bush, I think we all need to get laid."

Klaus handed a black flask of Jack Daniels to his buddies. Hans took two huge chugs and handed it to Gunnar. "Just take a few swigs now. Once we get going, no more drinking till the cargo is safely aboard the United States merchant ship."

Klaus grabbed the flask from Gunnar and took two hefty swigs. "South Africa, here we come."

The three men went off to help bring down all the bivouac tents and get them loaded. Von Dietrich informed everybody of their position in the convoy. Most of the mine workers would be in the first two Land Rovers in the lead of the caravan. They had the special containment suits to handle most of the enriched earth, even though the threat of radiation poisoning had decreased. Professor Pearson still wanted to take precautions.

Gunnar Mientz would travel in the second Land Rover equipped with a Beowulf assault rifle which could shoot 50 caliber rounds semi and automatic. He was rear backup for two of his team in the first Land Rover. The first Land Rover had two of Von Dietrich's men equipped with M-16 assault rifles with M-203 and 40 mm grenade launchers. Following them were two of the three armored personnel carriers.

Behind them was Von Dietrich's armored Humvee carrying the remaining four hundred pounds of chorominium. The chorominium was kept in a lead composite titanium-carbon reinforced box. This was to make sure the unknown mineral would not give off that eerie purple glow, even though the enriched uranium earth wasn't giving off that much radioactivity. No one wanted to take that chance.

To open the box, one had to know the digital code. The only two who had access were Pearson and Malloy. If any tampering or jimmying of the lid occurred, five pounds of RDX high explosive would detonate the box. Once the box was shut with the mineral inside it automatically armed itself.

Even Hans Von Dietrich didn't know the code. He knew his job was to safely transport everything to Mombasa, Kenya. After that, it was Malloy's problem.

Behind Von Dietrich's Humvee was the other armored personnel carrier. Following at the very rear was Klaus Steubern with the very heavily armed half-track. The only hindrance was that the three armored personnel carriers had one mining cart with the uranium ore attached. The armored personnel carriers all had M-60 light machine guns with them, plus they carried M-249 saws attack assault rifles.

One thing that really worried Von Dietrich was an assault from the air. But if any tanks were detected, they had Matador anti-tank weapons.

It was now turning 0800 hours. Von Dietrich motioned Gunnar in the front to deploy into the makeshift road. As they left, several Tutsi tribesman's covered the entrance to the encampment with brush and foliage from the surrounding area. The convoy now headed east towards Lake Tanganyika.

Time: 0805 hours. Congo November 29, 2010.
****

Time: 0905 Nairobi Time.

Captain Meadiav Bosloff and his Somalian cohort, Tuncha Sabissa, checked on their hired Hutu warriors who were digging foxholes and trenches two hundred feet outside to the Boma.

From center of the narrow road thirty feet from the entrance, ten load bearers unloaded ammunition from an old canvas-covered truck. Inside the crates were the rockets for the RPG-7s, 80mm motors for the launchers and hundreds of 7.62 x 51 ammo for the AK-47s.

Two more trucks showed up to be unloaded, as well. They carried the more potent and powerful rounds for the RPK's, M-19 30 caliber machine guns, and for the big M-106 recoil rifles.

Ahkmed Kadash told Tucha Sabissa's right hand man, Lawanna, to bring all the armor piercing rounds of the M-106's up to the area where the two rifles were hidden.

Bosloff seemed to be very impressed by the way the Hutu warriors camouflaged their foxhole back in the jungle. Then, as he looked up, he saw nothing but the strange indigenous people from back in the jungle converging on the camp, which scared him half to death. With a broken, raspy voice he called to Sabissa, "Tu, Tu, Tuncha, we've got company. Get over here quick."

Tuncha strolled over to Bosloff. "Don't worry, Meadiav, they are here to join us."

The strange tribesmen came out of the jungle like a giant nest of Army ants. All of them either carried spears and shields or were equipped with bows and arrows. Tuncha saw a very elderly warrior all painted up and wearing strange looking tribal dress. The man's name was Sulpa Juna, chief of the Supawani tribe. This was the same tribe that Professor Pearson and Professor Darfuir came upon four years before in the Republic of the Congo. Tuncha Sabissa went to the old warrior and spoke a strange form of Swahili. Immediately Sulpa Juna's face gave off a look of dismay and betrayal.

Tuncha had unknowingly just stirred up a hot and angry killer bee hive. What was a tribe that came from the most remote part of the jungle of the Verunga region doing so far from their home? Being the cowardly scoundrel that he was, Tuncha and his comrade-in-terror, Lawanna Kosi, had traveled to the Congo on a tip from Amal Baraash. Baraash asked them to gather up a recon-Safari party and try and find the source of an enriched uranium earth that Abdullah Musheen spoke of.

Several coincidences had converged into the perfect scenario, gaining the terrorists knowledge about the uranium ore. It all began innocently, for without knowing the consequences Lamarra Baraash had started a chain of events. She had spoken with her brother Kamal from America. Kamal told her of her exciting adventure with his colleague, Jeffrey Pearson, via the computer laptop he gave her. Little did Lamarra know that Abdullah Musheen had tapped into her computer and identified every conversation she received regarding the enriched earth containing uranium ore.

With the wheels of his evil brain turning, Musheen conjured up a diabolical plan to try and find the source of the dangerous mineral.

Lawanna Kosi, when he was younger, had travelled to that same remote part of the Congo. He and his poaching party had accidentally stumbled upon the Supawani tribe hunting for bush meat and elephant ivory. Kosi knew of their strange dialect of Swahili. Sulpa Juna asked the party of travelers if they were there to kill the animals of the jungle. Lawanna had lied his way out of that predicament. He told them they were working for the United States and said they were trying to make census count of endangered species of animals.

Sulpa Juna told him of his meeting with Professor Pearson and wanted to know if they worked for him. Of course to save their own cowardly necks, they said they did. Kosi tried to get the chief to tell him where the site of the place where his people were dying from the strange disease.

That's when Sulpa Juna drew the line and told him of his solemn promise to Professor Pearson to never reveal its location ever again.

This loyalty was earned. Professor Pearson had treated Sulpa's villagers, saving them from horrible diseases like Cholera, Typhoid Fever and Dysentery, just to name a few. He had also taught a lot of the Shaman witch doctors ways of extracting modern variants of medicine from the botanical wonders all around them. Sulpa Juna loved the man because he also saved the life of his daughter, Sajani. Since then, his daughter had blessed him with a grandson.

So Lawanna Kosi had to depart the jungle with only the knowledge of the existence of the uranium. Later in Nairobi, he was recruited into Tuncha Sabissa's network of terror. Kosi had told Tuncha of this expedition of his and later conveyed the information to Amal Baraash. Baraash told Abdullah Musheen. Musheen put two and two together, accidentally stumbling on the link between Lamarra's conversation with her brother and Lawanna's accidental surprise encounter with the Supawani people.

Musheen continued to weave his evil plan. He was going to create two diabolical acts of terror around the same time frame. Each would be carried out on two different continents to create chaos amongst the masses. If one failed, most likely the other would be successful.

Tuncha, now speaking with Sulpa Juna, made him believe that the men carrying the evil dirt from the mountain were stealing it from Professor Pearson. Tuncha told the Chief that these men were also going to come back afterwards and kill everybody in the village. He also warned that if these men were successful, they would also kill the professor.

Sulpa Juna sprang into action. He had over a thousand warriors with him. Using their war canoes, they paddled across Lake Tanganyka and went across land to Lake Victoria, then paddled their way to Kenya. This was the first time the Supawani people left the safety of the jungle in one hundred and fifty years.

Sulpa Juna asked Tuncha where he would like his warriors to be positioned for the assault. Tuncha, thinking that they really didn't need them, told Sulpa to stay back almost three quarters of a mile into the jungle. Tuncha took out a portable air horn and turned it on, bracing himself for the shrilling sound. All of Sulpa Juna's warriors became frightened by ear piercing blast. Tuncha had told Sulpa Juna that as soon as he gave the signal, the warriors should attack. Sulpa was made to think that Professor Pearson made the strange horn noise to alert the warriors that he was in trouble. So Sulpa called to his warriors and they all headed far back into the jungle.

Tuncha walked up to Ahkmed Kadash and Lawanna Kosi. "This will be like taking candy from a baby." The three al-Qaeda terrorist's got busy getting everything ready for the big assault tomorrow.

Tuncha saw it was almost time to check in with Abdullah on the satellite magna phone. He proceeded towards the Boma to hook up the dish and battery for Bosloff's transmission. It was now 0953 hours.

Tuncha headed over to one of the load bearers and asked him to get the white Captain. Two minutes later, Bosloff approached Tuncha as he had just unfolded the Satellite dish.

Captain Bosloff pulled his wallet out of his back pocket and retrieved what looked like a credit card, complete with a magnetic strip on the back. Bosloff inserted the card sideways into the keypad, which automatically pulled the card in. On the thirty two inch screen in front of him appeared text that instructed "Enter password". He punched in the code that Baraash had given back on the wharf in New Jersey.

The pixels on the screen came together and all of a sudden there appeared a man wearing a PLO bandana on his head and a mask covering his face from the bridge of his nose down to the bottom of his chin. His voice underneath the mask was further disguised with a tone scrambler.

But Bosloff and Kadash knew all the time it was Abdullah Musheen. Abdullah started with, "Comrade, how goes the expedition?"

Bosloff replied, "Everything goes well, your Excellency. Our Safari is ready to cage the lions. I'm sending you all of our expedition excerpts in the cryptic-scrambler, as you asked."

"Excellent. Have all supplies been delivered as specified?"

Bosloff answered, "Everything but the T-55 package; I would feel better if it were here."

Abdullah assured Bosloff, "Don't worry, Captain. I already know it will arrive in the cover of darkness. This is so it will not attract unnecessary attention. By 2100 hours tomorrow, you will contact me the same way. If anything goes wrong, you are to destroy the satellite magna phone. So if I do not hear from you at this time I will presume you have not captured our lion quarry."

Captain Bosloff confidently told him, "Don't worry, your Excellency, we have followed your instructions to the letter. I will definitely be transmitting good news tomorrow night."

With that Musheen cut off his end of the talk and the picture on the screen went blank.

Time: 1005 hours. Nairobi Time.

****

Time: 0900 hours. Five minutes before, Congo Time.

The magna phone picked up a beeping sound in Hans Von Dietrich's Humvee. Von Dietrich told his driver to stop right where they were. He opened his laptop and pushed the SET button. On the screen he saw a man with a PLO bandana on his head, talking. Von Dietrich turned a dial on the roof of his Humvee and the picture and voice became much clearer.

He listened in on the transmission between the man on the screen and whoever was on the other end. Once he heard the entire conversation, he immediately entered a secret code to his magna phone. Finishing the set-up on the Satellite dish, he called East Hampton, New York.

Time: 1911 hours. Republic of Congo. New York Time: 0111 hours.

JOHN PETER FERRIS

14 THE CALL TO ARMS

Time: 0111 EST New York Time.

Inside a bedroom on the back end of the main house, a purple light blinked on and off erratically. Former Senior Chief Petty Officer Michael Trudeaux turned on the table lamp next to his bed. Trudeaux knew the purple light only activated if someone had used the secret code on the other end. Entering his identification pin number and pushing the set button caused Hans Von Dietrich's face to appear on the screen. Trudeaux wiped his tired eyes. "Hansy, What's going on? It's one o'clock in the morning here."

Von Dietrich replied with a smile, "What's the matter, you old French fuck, too much civilian life making you soft? Or am I interrupting a date with one of you barnyard animals?"

Trudy sarcastically answered, "You should see, you fuckin' Kraut. I just gave your sister my Vienna Schnitzel."

Both old friends burst out laughing.

"Seriously, Hansy, something has gotta be wrong for you to be calling at this time."

Von Dietrich with a face awash in concern replied, "Mikey, where's Malloy? I think we've got real big problems. I'm gonna send you a transmission I accidentally intercepted. I want to see if the Captain can make heads or tails of it."

Trudeaux replied, "The Captain is right now on his way back from Norfolk. Hook up your scrambler to the magna phone and transmit everything you got, buddy. I'm going to bring it to the professor for his examination."

Hansy reached into his briefcase in the Humvee and pulled out a scrambling device that encrypted all information; only the super computer at the company could decode it. Von Dietrich inset the female end of his tethered attachment to the thirty two inch laptop terminal. Binary codes of ones and zeros begin to flutter across the screen. His laptop screen began its sequence spin and then came to a halt. Safe to proceed, it flashed.

Hansy pushed the send button and the printer in Trudeaux's bedroom began spitting out paper. The compact disc spun and another purple light appeared on the screen. Downloading.

Trudeaux told Von Dietrich he was going to go wake up Professor Pearson and get him over to the main computer. He also let him know that as soon as he examined the data, he'd be back to him right away. "Continue on schedule until further notice," he told Hansy.

Trudeaux dressed as quickly as he could and tied his shoes.

Grabbing the line phone on the night table next to his bed, Professor Pearson shook away sleep as a purple light blinked. "What's going on, Michael? It must be something very important to wake me at this hour."

Trudeaux with a sound of determination replied, "It is, Professor. Hansy just contacted me as he was leaving the meteorite site. He picked up a transmission nearby that looks like an al-Qaeda broadcast. That listening device that the Skipper installed into all of the magna phones sure came in handy this time."

Pearson, now fully awake, asked, "Did Hansy transfer the data to our mainframe?"

"Yes he did, professor. Is there some way we can get in touch with the Skipper? He won't be arriving into New York till 0630 hours this morning."

"If it's al-Qaeda, we must not hesitate," answered Pearson. "We'll take the initiative utilizing who we have available for the time being. Meet me in the Captain's security office, where we can tap into the main computer."

"That's a roger, Sir."

The professor called his partner Professor Darfuir and told him to meet with them also, then dressed hastily. He scurried out of his bedroom heading downstairs towards the entrance lobby of the main house. To his surprise, he saw Bobby Palladin kissing his daughter Claire goodnight as he was about to leave.

Bobby, with a bashful voice, said, "I'm sorry, Professor, if I awoke you."

The professor with a smile responded, "Don't worry, son. Besides, I'm glad you're here. Claire, can both of you follow me to Captain Malloy's office?"

Claire squinted her brow. "Is there something wrong, Papa?"

Pearson with a face full of worry told her, "At the moment, I really don't know. Just follow me to the security office and I think then we'll both find out." Bobby and Claire followed the professor to the far eastern part of the main house. When they arrived, Claire walked up to the hand and eye scanners and activated them with her palm and eye print. As the door opened, Dr. Darfuir and Trudy arrived right behind them.

Trudeaux handed Professor Pearson a flash drive loaded with information from the data burner that was printing out the Von Dietrich intercept. Pearson inserted the flash drive into the computer on Malloy's desk. After the group watched the five minute talk between the terrorists on the screen, Pearson shut off the software and stored the flash drive in Malloy's top drawer.

Claire, with a very annoyed look on her face, said," The satellite positioning coordinates tell us the transmission was located somewhere between Lake Victoria and Mombasa, Kenya. I went over the secret routes the convoy planned to take with the Captain four days ago. The Captain and I are the only ones, besides Hansy and Bonsa, who know of the routes. Either we're interpreting the message from the wrong perspective or somehow al-Qaeda has learned of the mineral shipment."

Right then and there Professor Pearson cut in. "Well, there is no doubt what measures we now have to take. We definitely have to send some kind of reinforcements for Hansy, Gunnar and Klaus."

Bobby Palladin interrupted the Professor. "I don't know what it is, but I think I recognize the voice of the operative we do not see."

Trudy, with a look of awareness, commented, "You know, come to think of it, Bobby, I think ya'll be right. I know I recognize that voice from somewhere. I just can't place it right now."

Pearson pound his fist on Malloy's desk. "That's good enough for me. We have to send a backup team right now. The flight alone takes fourteen to fifteen hours tops. For right now though, Trudy, take three of our security staff to the Galaxy and prepare for a flight to Nairobi."

Palladin cut in, "Yo, Professor, I'm off this week. I'm not letting anybody from my old team face those al-Qaeda terrorists by his lonesome. I'm also going. Just get us hooked up with some good assault weapons and we're ready to roll."

Pearson told Trudeaux to take Bobby to the private aviation hangers on the far side of the Citadel complex. There inside the hanger awaited an assortment of state-of-the-art weapons from all over the world. Also, inside the hanger was a Spooky C-130 Hercules gunship equipped with a 25mm Gatlin gun, a 105mm Howitzer, and a 47mm 5 inch. Extra equipment included a forward looking, infrared (FLIR) capability.

Next to the C-130 was a K-C 135 refueling aircraft. The hangar adjacent to the one holding the Spooky also had aircraft and weapons. This hangar, though, contained a C-5 Galaxy transport and cargo carrier, and also a K-C refueling aircraft. Along with the two planes were two Seahawks and two Super Cobra helicopter gunships. Most of the high Caliber ammunition for them was stored in a vault concrete basement under the hangar itself.

Malloy with all his connections in the military had been stocking up the storage areas for the last three years for the security of the corporation.

Every door was so reinforced that even a JDAM bunker busting bomb wouldn't be able to penetrate it.

Trudeaux and Palladin went in to the hangar with the Spooky. There Trudeaux grabbed a Beowulf assault rifle that could fire 50 caliber rounds semi and automatic. To Palladin's surprise, he spotted a state of the art Cheytech Model 200 that fired a 408 ballistic round faster than a 50 caliber round. It even had a ballistic computer to trajectory speed and wind velocity.

Palladin had heard of this beautiful rifle from his friend, Colour Sergeant Patrick Tinsdale, of the British S.A.S unit. Tinsdale's Commanding Officer, Major Percival Nelson, was looking for a rifle that had the punch of a 50 caliber weapon. He also needed a more lightweight and more round capacity assault rifle. The major chose the Cheytech in consideration of its ground observation designation.

Palladin grabbed the weapon and held it like he was getting ready to play a classic vintage guitar. He started to rig his rack sack for parachute deployment. The coils of secondary line he rolled and hooked to a small carabineer attached to his primary chute. Usually he would pack 250 rounds of 5.56 Nato ammo in the rack. Along with the 408 ballistic rounds, he only packed an extra 200 caliber rounds to make more room for grenades and additional canisters.

Trudeaux loved the punch of the 50 caliber from Accuracy International. Known as the A.S. 50, it had a floating titanium barrel. It was one of the best weapons on the market next to the Beowulf in his rack sack. The rounds for the Beowulf 50 were much shorter than the ones for the A.S. 50. He packed the rounds for the A.S. 50 on a drop sled and also set up a space on the sled for a RBS-70 Anti-Aircraft weapon.

As they were getting ready to deploy, three men that Malloy hired months ago entered the hangar. All three of them grabbed for the M-110 Knights assault rifle. It was great weapon that could shoot a 7.62x51 round. Might as well, for it was the weapon of choice by most al-Qaeda Operatives. Because it shoots the same round as the AK-47, the operators would take them from dead American soldiers. Plus, the rifle was much smoother and accurate than any weapon they'd ever shot.

But the enemy mostly used the AK-47 because they were cheaper and more abundant.

Trudeaux told Palladin that the three men were ex-Army Airborne. Bobby, knowing that Airborne Army were well trained and established fighting men, felt a little more secure about the mission. He watched as they helped each other with their rigs and chutes. It reminded him of many years before when he trained to become a Navy S.E.A.L.

Just as all five of the men started walking out to the Tarmac, Professor Pearson entered the hangar with Claire Vanderkamp. Pearson walked over to Palladin and whispered to him, "My little girl here is begging me to stop you from going. She's very worried and tells me that she's scared you won't return. Bobby, she is almost in tears, son."

Palladin told the professor, "Let me talk to Claire for a second. I'll calm her down." He walked over and grabbed her in his arms. "Baby I'm going to be fine. This is probably nothing at all, but in my Unit we all watch each other's back. With me not there, Mikey wouldn't know who to trust."

Claire, with tears coming from both eyes, said, "Bobby, can't you wait till Captain Malloy gets here this morning?"

He smiled gently. "When good people are in trouble, it's my job and my duty to protect them from those who would do harm to them. Claire, I'm coming back, especially knowing how much you mean to me, baby."

They kissed feverishly, then Bobby pulled away. "I'm going to be gone for a couple of days at the most. So keep Lanny busy, and I'll be back before you know I'm even gone."

They start walking out to the Tarmac. Trudeaux looked to the right side of him and saw a ground controller leading the Galaxy C-5 with his waving lights towards the start of the runway. There were three aviation fuel trucks just at the edge of the tarmac.

From the same hangar as the Galaxy, the KC-10 started taxiing out right behind the Galaxy. A black Land Rover pulled right up on the tarmac and out stepped a man in his early 60s. With him was a well-groomed man in his early 40s.

The giant semi-vertical back door of the Galaxy started opening. When the door finished opening, a man in a g-flight suit walked down the ramp to greet them. His name was Joe Coffey. After sixteen years as an Ordinance Flight Engineer and Jump Tender for the Air Force, Coffey went Reserve for his last four. He was a personal friend of General Franklin Castorino. Coffey had told General just before his last re-enlistment that he needed to be closer to his wife and kids. He said he would quit before his twenty years were up before he would lose his wife, Kate. So the General, knowing Jeffrey Pearson and his government contracts with the Air Force, asked if he would hire him for his experience and commitment to his country. Professor Pearson called and hired Coffey right on the spot.

Since then, he and the professor had become really great friends. This would be Coffey's first Jump Tender and Weapons Ordinance deployment since Pearson hired him six months ago.

The man in his 60s was retired Air Force Colonel Carl Bingham. With him was his copilot and friend, retired Air Force Major David Banks. Pearson went way back to his Vietnam days with Colonel Bingham. Back then, though, he was Captain Carl Bingham. Pearson hired Major Banks on Bingham's recommendation.

The three men converged on each other as Coffey stepped off the loading ramp onto the Tarmac. Bingham put his hand out to shake Coffey's and said, "Good to see you, Joey. Do you know why we are flying to Mombasa way ahead of schedule?"

Coffey replied, "I'm in the dark just like you, Colonel. You're gonna have to ask the professor yourself, but I'll tell you one thing. the flight plan says the route is South by Southeast, 3' degrees South latitude by 40' degrees Southeast longitude, and we know that's the general area for Mombasa."

The professor, Bobby, Claire, and Trudy came up upon the three conversing men. The professor, overhearing their conversation, filled them in on the recent events. He told them when Malloy finally arrived from Norfolk, he'd contact them via satellite. He let them know he was sending up the refueling KC-10 to ensure a nonstop flight. He also lets them know that as soon as he got Captain Malloy's recommendation, he'd forward all information to them immediately.

Professor Pearson introduced the small Q.R.F. team to the flight team. The three Airborne soldiers were ex-CWO Mike Maguiness, ex-Staff Sergeant Calvin Thomas, and ex-Sergeant Carlos Alvarez. They were also hired by Malloy because of their experience in Africa. Thomas spoke fluent Swahili, as did Alvarez. Maguiness was jump master and a well-trained paratrooper in almost any terrain. Malloy was also impressed at his prowess in Korean Sangee knife fighting. The only knife fighters who were better, he thought, were Orion and himself.

The three were very well supported, especially for this job. Michael Trudeaux, ex-Senior Chief Petty Officer, was jump master on this excursion. He started going over the itinerary with everybody when another of the corporation's Land Rovers pulled up.

From out of the driver's side came another member of the Flight crew named Liam Faraday. He was an ex-Lieutenant Commander, U.S. Navy. Faraday used to fly Super Tomcats for the Navy before they were discontinued. He had just finished his twenty when his buddy, Jim Malloy, came to him with a job proposal for Pearson Global Technologies. With the money that was offered, Faraday jumped on it and did not re-up his commission. On this flight, Faraday was Navigator and Radio Intercept Officer.

The professor told Joe Coffey to first load the Land Rover packed with provisions, then load the drop sled with RBS-70 and high caliber ammunition. Pearson reassured the pilot Carl Bingham that the KC-10 would be at the secret coordinates as scheduled.

Palladin told the other Jump Team members to double check their oxygen and stabilizers along with their chutes, and also to make sure the line rope to their ruck sacks were secure.

The two fuel trucks, having finished fueling the C-5 Galaxy, returned to the fuel depot and left the other to finish his load of the KC-10. As the two empty trucks disappeared behind the hangars, two more made their way onto the tarmac to finish refueling the KC-10.

Palladin came from out of the Galaxy, annoyed and said to Trudy, "I just looked in the Rover. There's mostly M.R.E.'s in the back. Why can't the Skipper ever lighten up with fuckin' protocol?"

Trudeaux and Pearson both start laughing and Trudy replied, "That's our fuckin' Skipper. He will never let up or give in. C'mon, Bobby, I gotta eat the same shit like you do."

Claire came up to Palladin laughing and said, "Sure you can't change your mind and stay here with me? I'll make you a dinner you'll never forget." Palladin slyly smiled and replied, "Nice try, baby, but I'm still going. I'll take you up on the offer when I get back, honey".

She pointed her finger at him. "You just make it back here in one piece, Robert Alouishes Palladin."

Bobby grabbed her real quick and gave her a kiss. With a whispering voice he told her, "Baby, don't use my middle name."

Just then the four propellers start throttling up and Trudeaux yelled over to Palladin, laughing hysterically, "C'mon, Alouishes, time to deploy."

Bobby stared into the air. "Now you see why? Oh God! The whole team is gonna ride me now. Okay, honey, gotta go. Love you!"

Palladin ran up the ramp as the door started closing.

Trudeaux said, "Alouishes? What do we call you now, Ally?"

As the door was just about to shut came the expletive, "Oh! FUCK YOU! Trudy's a fuckin' girl's name, anyway."

The giant engines of the C-5 Galaxy roared as they taxied for the runway. The giant aircraft started down the runway and the booster rocket turbines flashed flames. The Galaxy was airborne.

Professor Pearson, seeing his adopted daughter with tears in her eyes, came over and hugged his little girl. "He'll be fine, sweetheart."

Claire looked up at him. "I know, Papa, but I'm still scared. It seems everybody I love in my life, God takes away from me."

Pearson hugged her a little tighter. "I don't think this time, my princess. With these last few days and turns of events, I think God will protect your fragile soul and everyone you love."

Time: 0202 hours. EST New York Time.

15 LEFT IN THE CLOUDS

Time: 0400 hours. New York Time. November 30, 2010.

From the control tower of the secret airport in the Citadel Complex came a transmission from a Gulfstream Lear jet coming in for a landing. "Tower, is this Flight 65 from Norfolk awaiting instructions to land."

The control tower's Lead Air Traffic Controller answered, "We've got you on radar, Flight 65. The winds are 15 knots, so suggest that you start your descent now. Maintain present course of one five nine. We are now activating the lights on runway three."

The pilot replied, "That's a copy, tower; now reducing airspeed and maintaining course one five nine."

The tower relayed a message from Professor Pearson. "Flight 65, please relay message to Captain Malloy to report to his security staff upon landing. The liaison Range Rover will be waiting for him when he touches down."

"That's a copy, tower. Will tell Captain Malloy."

"We have visual, Flight 65. You're all cleared to land."

"That's a Roger, tower. Now bringing her in at 70 knots and gradually reducing airspeed."

The tower replied, "That's a copy, Flight 65. Welcome home."

The Lear jet pilot adjusted his flaps for the landing and started gradually pulling back the throttle, coming in nice and soft as his landing gear locked in for touchdown. The Lear jet jumped a tiny bit as the wheels hit the runway. Captain Malloy looked out the starboard front window and saw a Land Rover pulling up to the edge of the tarmac. The jet began its taxi while James Malloy grabbed the photos and papers that were scattered out in various sequences on his echelon table. He made sure they were all in order and walked slowly to the port side of the aircraft to de-plane.

Finally the Lear jet came to a complete halt and a green light illuminated right above the entrance door. Captain Malloy first knocked on the cockpit door and heard the pilot tell him to enter. Malloy opened the door. "Steve, bring the plane in for a quick go over, just in case. Don't worry. I know you've got to be tired after the last two days. Just park her in the hangar and go home and get some sleep."

The pilot with a look of relief said, "Thanks, Jim. I'll get back to you later on tonight."

Malloy closed the cockpit door and headed down the steps for his ride to the security office. The Land Rover left the edge of the tarmac and followed a narrow road carved into the mile and a half stretch of woods. As the car came out the other side of the woods, Malloy noticed a melee going at the entrance gate of the complex. Malloy instantly told his driver to head there so he could check out the disturbance.

As they come to the gate, Malloy noticed somebody he hasn't seen since his forced retirement. The man at the gate giving the guard a hard time was none other than Orion's Second Officer In Command, ex-Lieutenant J.G. Lars Olsen. He was a giant of a man standing six foot five and weighing two hundred and seventy pounds. Plus, he was all muscle and his body strength was unbelievable.

The Land Rover pulled up and stopped. Malloy yelled over to the Security guard at the gate, "What seems to be the trouble, Artie?"

The guard with a terrified look on his face replied, "This giant behemoth here is telling me he's going to break me in half if it I don't let him into see Mr. Orion. Don't worry, Mr. Malloy. More security is on their way to remove him from the premises."

Malloy burst out laughing. "I really don't think they can, Artie. Call them back and tell them everything is okay. Lieutenant Olsen here is one of Mr. Orion's best friends." He looked over to Lars. "Kind of early to be arriving at this hour, hey Lieutenant?"

Lars shook his head. "Not at all, Skipper. I'm a pilot for Delta Airlines. This was the first available flight to Macarthur that I could catch soon as I got the news about Johnny. So I'm here. How's my old partner fairing?"

Malloy put his fingers to his chin. "Get in the Rover, Lars. I'll fill you in on the way to the main facility."

Lieutenant Olsen grabbed his large cargo bag with two fingers and threw it in the back of the Land Rover. He got in the back seat of the passenger cab and they headed off to the medical and security building.

Captain Malloy gave Lars a quick rundown of the events leading up to the present, but soon as they rounded the corner Malloy noticed teams of scientists and technicians arriving in a panicked hurry. He noticed Lanny with a look of concern on her face.

Malloy immediately jumped out of the Land Rover and hustled over to Lanny, asking why everyone was rushing in at this unconventional hour. As Lanny turned to answer him, she spotted a very big man who come up next to him. Staring in amazement, she finally found the words to answer Malloy.

"I really don't know, James, but the main alarm just went off for the operations unit for you know where." Then recalling her talks with Orion, she remembered and said, "You must be Lars. Johnny told me how big of a man you are."

Malloy cut in. "Lars, this is John's girlfriend, Lanny Cromwell. C'mon you two, let's get inside and downstairs now."

They followed the Captain to his private elevator down to the operations center. Approaching the elevator, Lanny started shaking with fear for her man. As the door opened, Malloy reassured her, "Hang in there, sweetheart. It might just be a power shut-off to the back-up computer."

Before the elevators moved, the voice from the loudspeakers demanded, "Identify yourself."

Captain responded, "James Malloy."

The voice replied, "Voice recognized." The elevator began its descent to the operations center below.

When the elevator door opened, Lanny, like an Olympic sprinter, headed for her man's room.

Lars looked at Malloy. "Wow, Johnny has got himself a real pretty one there, huh Skipper?"

Malloy nodded and agreed, "She's also got brains besides her beauty." They walked over and found that Lanny had left the door wide open. That eerie purple light was everywhere. As they crossed the threshold, both men witnessed Orion floating vertically in the air almost two feet from the ground. The finger tips from both of his hands were touching his temples. He seemed to be in a transcendental state.

The ICARUS Device was still on him but no longer connected to the accelerator. Even with the sunglasses on, they could see the eerie light coming from his.

Lanny in a fright yelled to Orion, "Baby, are you okay? You're freaking me out!"

Right then and there Orion slowly drifted down to the floor and opened his eyes. "I'm sorry, baby. I forget nobody is used to see me doing these things." He removed his strapped-on sunglasses to reveal his purple corneas.

Lanny went to him and immediately wrapped her right arm around the side of his waist. He gently grabbed her back and gave her a quick kiss. As he looked around, he spotted his old buddy, Lars, who had eyes bugging out of his head and a mouth that was wide open.

"What the FUCK just happened here? You were floating around the room like a ghost, and on top of that your friggin' eyes are purple!"

With that Orion closed his eyes and concentrated. He opened them again to reveal a normal blue.

Olsen fell back against the wall.

Professor Pearson, who had seen what had been going on the whole time, walked in. "Lieutenant, can you tell us why the emergency alarm was set off? Also don't you still have five more hours of regeneration?"

Orion's face turned serious. "Sorry, professor, but the super microbes in me just picked up data from the mainframe that was earlier recorded in the Skipper's office. The transmission from the terrorist to the another in Kenya made me trip the emergency alarm. I was able to decode the encrypted binary sequences that were hidden amongst the screen's timetable and the digital numbers next to them." He paused so they could process this information, then continued.

"I also recognized the other al-Qaeda operative. We've tried in the past to capture him, and I'll never forget that voice. He's the Serbian war criminal, Meadiav Bosloff. The World Court wants him and his other buddy, Vladmir Koslovski, for genocide against the good people of Bosnia. They are Chechnyans who helped two more wanted criminals for the same thing, Parnov Bistra, and Bella Steflenik." Now his voice got deadly serious.

"If any of them are working together with the masked terrorist on the screen, we definitely have problems. Captain, Bobby and Trudy are walking right into a trap. The main computer also relayed to me the professor's deployment of Bobby and Trudy with three others to make a Fire Team. From what I picked up on the encrypted message, they are being set up for a parallel ambush somewhere between Nairobi and Mombasa. We have to get word to Hansy and his team right away."

Malloy looked at his watch and at the twelve clocks on the wall, searching for the one that said Nairobi. He shook his head in dismay. "Shit. Our communication satellites, the one we call Rigel One, won't be over them for another four hours. On top of that, our photocell and reconnaissance satellite, Bellatrix, follows three hours after that."

Professor Pearson walked over to Malloy. "Jim, I didn't know what to do. We weren't even expecting you till at least 0630 hours this morning." The professor's head bowed with disgust. "Jimmy, I'm praying I did the right thing. I just might have killed them all."

Without anyone noticing, Claire Vanderkamp was just about to step into the room and overheard her father and the Captain talking. She started crying uncontrollably, "Oh no . . . Bobby! Somebody do something! I should have stopped him from going."

Leaning up against the wall, she suddenly slipped down as her high heels went out from underneath her. In a Flash, Orion glided past everyone and picked her up with one hand, gently cradling her in his arms. Her eyes and mouth opened wide in amazement as he assured her, "Claire, Bobby and

Mikey are my true brothers. Do you think I'm gonna let anything happen to them?"

With tears streaming steadily from both eyes she replied, "What can you do, Johnny? The Galaxy is probably almost across the Atlantic by now." Professor Pearson and everyone from the Project ICARUS team were all gathered in the hall. The professor with a look of shame said to her, "I'm so sorry, sweetheart. Maybe I should've waited for the Captain. I know I don't have his expertise in these matters. I just know that I had to try and stop these terrorists from getting their hands on the uranium."

Malloy scolded the professor. "What are you talking about, Jeff? You did all and more than you could. You expedited the situation perfectly. Now let's regroup. We still have the Spooky in the hangar."

Pearson looked at his security team. "Call the fuel depot and tell them to start fueling the C-130 and KC-135. I'll get Steve Cocharan out of bed and back here to fly the KC-135 refueler. Since he's the only pilot we have, we're going have to decide which aircraft we start loading with assault weapons." Claire looked at them. "Papa, I'm a pilot. I can fly the Lear jet."

Right there on the spot Lars Olson yelled out, "Yo Yo Yo. Did everybody here forget I can fly anything? I don't give a flying FUCK. I'll fly the Spooky. Just get another pilot here to fly the KC-135 and the skipper knows damn well I'd be going along."

Malloy give a devilish smile. "Claire, don't worry. The Galaxy is only 2 ½ hours into its flight. Just to cross the Atlantic takes 9 ½ hours. From there, it's still another five to six hours to the East coast of Africa."

Orion interrupted everyone. "Well, what are we waiting for? They still have to slow down a bit to refuel, don't they?"

Professor Pearson immediately cut him off. "Wait one minute there, Lieutenant. You're forgetting that you still have five more hours of the regeneration cycle."

Lanny added, "Johnny, the professor is right. Didn't you tell us it was crucial for you to regenerate?"

Orion looked at to the professor. "When were you going to tell me that the aircraft on this complex are equipped with hookups for the Electron Generator?" Pearson, with a look of surprise, replied, "How the hell in the world could you know about that?"

With a sarcastic smirk on his face Orion answered, "Professor, please. Any data in the Main computer is now stored in the robotic super microbes throughout my body."

The professor made a plea. "John, I would have told you if I thought it was pertinent to your rehabilitation and physical therapy. The magnetron units in the planes were only put there just in case we were able to use it in an emergency during nano-tech surgery. We don't even know it will be useful; they were put there as a precautionary measure."

Orion cut him off. "Well, there you go. By accident we have now a use for it at last. Now let's bring the Electron Generator out to the Spooky. We're just wasting more time talking about it. There's lots of people I love who are just about to be caught in a death trap and we are the only means of preventing it." Pearson reluctantly nodded. "You're right, Lieutenant. Technicians, let's get the Electron Generator out to one to our cargo flatbeds. Like Mr. Orion said, time is of the essence."

The technicians and security personnel start getting everything ready to move the generator to the freight elevator. The professor saw Dr. Darfuir get off the main elevator and updated him about the current circumstances. He told Darfuir that he'd have to stay in the security office and monitor everything that went on.

Then Pearson went over to Lanny and Claire and painfully told them they were to stay at the Citadel with Professor Darfuir. Claire tried to make a point that even though she's never flown anything as big as C-130 Hercules, now would be a good time to learn from Lieutenant Olsen.

Just as her father was about to tell her no, Lars told the professor, "She has a point, Professor. It would not be a bad idea to have a backup pilot in case of emergency."

Lanny, with an angry look on her face, grabbed her younger sister by the arm. "You're my little sister and it's too dangerous. Please Claire, listen to me and don't go."

Claire gave Lanny a kiss on her cheek. "I love you, big sister, but if Johnny was in the same predicament as Bobby, I know I would never be able to stop you from going, either."

Lanny hugged her little sister and told her to be very careful. Then she turned all her attention to Orion. The couple let everybody walk ahead of them. Lanny looked at her man and said, "As for you, John Patrick Orion, bring everybody home safe because I can't live without you. Being off the Electron Generator, will that cause any problems for you?"

"As long as I'm hooked back up to the guardian component and the generator within one hour, I'll be fine."

Lanny took his left hand and led him to the main elevator. They got on with everyone else and ascended to the main floor. As they approached their destination, Orion asked if Trudeaux's team had equipped themselves with communications gear on their Biv-Packs.

Malloy informed Orion that they did, and that there were four more in the hangar's gear locker.

Orion asked the professor if there was a shower facility in the Spooky's hangar, because he was starting to reek of smelly sweat. The special titanium carbon carbonite suit he wore had been talking a toll on him even though the inside lining was made of neoprene synthetic rubber.

The professor assured him there was a shower in the hangar used by the flight crew, but urged Orion to shower fast so they could get him connected to the electron generator as soon as possible.

As they reached the outer door of the Citadel, Lanny and Dr. Darfuir said goodbye to their comrades and headed upstairs to the security office.

Pearson told Claire that she'd have to change into a flight suit and utility boots to fly in the cockpit. He laughed when he told her he hoped he had one that would fit her petite little body.

Orion rode in one Land Rover with just Lars and Captain Malloy., while Professor Pearson, Claire, and two security guards went in another. On the way to the hangar, Lars asked the Captain if the entire girl population in New York was as hot as Lanny and Claire.

Orion told his Buddy that they sure were, but you had to put up with their BITCHINESS. The driver with the rest of them started laughing.

Malloy looked at his watch and saw it was 0440 hours. He told Orion to hurry and shower because they needed a window of opportunity to catch up with the C-5 Galaxy.

As they entered the other sides of the woods, they saw both the C-130 Spooky and the KC-135 on the edge of the tarmac being prepped and fueled for the long flight. When they arrived at the entrance of the hangar, Orion sprinted at an incredible speed for the shower room.

Lars began to feel uneasy and asked his old Captain if his buddy was now a super human robot.

Malloy shared with his second-in-command the previous events leading up to the present. Lars was completely flabbergasted. As he and Captain Malloy donned their B.D.U.'s (battle dress uniforms), Orion came flying back, again at an incredible speed. He looked all refreshed and clean, and was back in his special suit with the ICARUS device activated.

Professor Pearson pulled up in the Land Rover and told Orion that the electron generator was hooked up to the magnetron, instructing him to hop in the Land Rover because he only had ten minutes left to be back in his regeneration cycle.

Malloy told Orion not to worry — they would check his gear and chute. Professor Pearson stepped on the gas even before Orion could shut the door. Orion started laughing. "I can hover and glide almost as fast as this thing. Calm down, professor. You know I owe you my life."

Pearson looked at Orion with concern and scolded him. "John, be very careful. We still don't know what kind of effects your body will feel after you do whatever amazing feats that you do. Please try to refrain from using your powers until we have come back from our mission. We need to monitor your body in a scientific manner to find your limits and capacities."

Orion bobbed his head. "Okay, you're the Doc. Besides, I'll be in a trance for the next five hours, anyway."

As the Land Rover stopped at the end of the loading ramp door of the

C-130, two technicians waited to hook the ICARUS device to the generator. When Orion and Pearson walked into the back of the plane, they noticed a table secured to the bulkhead of the starboard front of the Spooky.

Orion looked on both sides of the rear of the plane and saw two Mini-Guns. He asked the flight sergeant, "Are those Dillon Aeros?"

The flight engineer replied, "They sure are. They shoot three thousand rounds per minute. Just imagine 3000 7.62 caliber rounds coming at you in that time slot. Plus, the tracer imaging helps to acquire the target more easily and accurately."

Orion laughed as he lay down on the cushioned table. "Maybe I should take one down with me when I make jump."

The flight engineer shook his head. "Wouldn't be a bad idea, if only they weren't bolted to the slide ramps. Besides, they need a power source to hook up to. You would need a battery pack, and plus, with the weight alone you wouldn't be able to carry it around."

Orion put on the banded purple sunglasses. "Well, one can dream, right?" He smiled and shuffled through the music on his iPod, asking the flight engineer if there was a place to charge it.

The Flight Engineer Sergeant Michael Calloway grabbed a small tethered electrical line connected to a power supply box on the bulkhead, and Orion plugged it in. Calloway told him, "You're all set, sir. Just press the play button and you're ready to go."

Malloy told Orion to put in earplugs because he and Lars really needed to sleep.

Orion snickered and said to Lars, "Get a load of our pussy, Captain. How many times during training did we go without sleep? Can dish it out but can't take it."

Captain smirked and replied, "Just put it your ear piece, you insubordinate fuck."

Over the plane's intercom spoke Professor Pearson. "Okay back there, strap in. We're ready for take-off."

In the cockpit, Lars commanded the pilot's seat and Professor Pearson stood behind Claire in the radio and navigator's chair. Lars showed Claire all the controls on the instrument panels. He pushed the throttle levers forward slightly and the plane started moving towards Runaway One. He showed Claire the booster rocket switch and told her he'd let her know when to hit it.

When they reached the start of the runway, Lars pushed the throttle forward another two notches and the C-130 began taxiing down the runway. The airspeed indicators started climbing 10 knots, 20 knots, 30 knots, 40 knots, 50 knots, 60 knots, and as soon as it reached 70 knots, he shouted, "Now Claire!"

The booster rockets blasted out from underneath the fuselage and the

C-130 gunship was airborne.

Time: 0507 hours. November 30, 2010. Nairobi Time: 1307 hours.

Professor Pearson in the cockpit of the C-130 Spooky gunship tried to get the corporation's C-5 Galaxy aircraft to answer his radio transmissions. The professor knew to be careful so anybody listening in to his broadcast would not detect the nature of his business. He didn't want the United States government to know unless it looked like they wouldn't make it in time. The professor figured if they discovered that any part of Project ICARUS has been implemented, his company's future would suffer the dire consequences.

Since the C-130 was lighter and traveled faster, he hoped they would reduce the three hour distance between them. Any possible E2-C Hawkeye Surveillance aircraft within a thousand miles would be able to listen in with ease. So the professor tried every twenty minutes to establish contact. He told Lars and Claire that if he couldn't raise the Galaxy in the next seven hours, he'd have no choice but to let the military know of the plot to steal the ore from the convoy.

Claire, hearing that, began to get upset all over again. Lars let her know of the enormous firepower that the gunship could inflict on the enemy. The two-man Howitzer crew could take out any tank and the five inch gun plus the 25mm Gatling gun would sweep up the rest.

Claire, being a young 24 year old woman, should have been impressed. But Lars could tell she still wasn't satisfied.

Three hours ahead of the C-130 gunship, the C-5 Galaxy's Navigator and Radio Operator tried to make a transmission back towards the United States. Faraday looked annoyed with the instrument panel and radio gear. He rubbed the top of his brow with his left hand. "I don't know what's going on today, but something feels out of whack."

The pilot Carl Bingham ask Liam, "Why, what seems to be the problem"? Faraday answered, "I don't know. I just can't seem to make heads or tails of it. In all my years of flying jets and planes, this is the first time I've seen this kind of weird shit happening."

Carl looked at his copilot David Banks. "You ever run across this problem in all your time flying?"

Banks looked at both his crew. "Come to think of it, one and one time only. Years ago, I was four hundred miles from Baghram's Air Base in Afghanistan when my RIO complained of the same circumstances. I had to fly under the clouds exposing my aircraft to any type of ground forces. Thank God, we were able to make our way in without any problems after we spotted the air field. We found out later that a huge solar flare from the sun the day before had disrupted everything in its path. Every single satellite around the world fucked up. I hope that's not the problem now, especially on this dangerous mission." Carl replied, "Ah, it's probably just static electricity in the upper atmosphere. Liam, keep trying to raise Von Dietrich, anyway."

Faraday went back to working his console to restore communications. Time: 0807 hours. London Time. November 30, 2010. Time: 1207 hours. Congo Time. November 30, 2010.

The convoy of armored personnel carriers, a half tract armored reactive plated attack vehicle, an armored ground mobility vehicle, and four other jungle terrain Land Rovers finally reached the first destination point. They were on a flotilla of small and slow moving barges traveling to the Northern point of Lake Tanganyika.

As they moved across the unloading ramps to the shore, Hans Von Dietrich tried to make a transmission on his satellite magna phone. Figuring that maybe the Rigel One satellite was not yet in position, Von Dietrich stopped his transmission.

Once every vehicle had been unloaded on the shore, Von Dietrich double checked with everyone in the caravan to make sure that there were no problems. He called Klaus Steubern and Gunnar Mientz over for a quick conference.

"Gunnar, keep alert for anything out of the ordinary. Klaus, since you're covering our six you better watch your six, too. I don't know what it is, but I got a strange feeling again that something could be wrong. We've got two and a half hours before we reach the western side of Lake Victoria. We have another six and a half hours before we finally arrive in Kenya. It's a long and slow moving trip across the lake, so don't let your guard down even for even a second. Position all your guns towards the shore. Let's not take anything for granted." Klaus and Gunnar nodded, waiting for Von Dietrich to continue.

"I don't know why our communications are down. So I'll have to speculate on the precautions we take from here. Now take your positions in the convoy and let's move out."

Klaus and Gunnar head for their vehicles. Klaus jumped aboard the half tract and pulled the breech lever towards him to arm the fifty caliber Ma-Deuce. He told his driver to look for anything out of the ordinary. He also told his Ordinance man the same thing. The convoy set out again in the same order as they did when they first left the Congo.

Time: 1245 hours. Congo Time. Time: 1345 hours. Nairobi Time. November 30, 2010.

At the terrorist ambush site, the small army of evil was making preparations for a late night assault. Meadiav Bosloff was told in an encrypted code, hidden in Abdullah Musheen's broadcast the day before, that the convoy was to arrive in Mombasa between 0100 hours and 0200 hours Nairobi time. Having different spotters circling in a perimeter ten miles around the Boma camp, Bosloff and Sabissa told them to report in as soon as they caught any glimpse of the convoy.

All of a sudden a Loach Littlebird helicopter flew over the camp. Everybody scrambled towards their weapons. Ahkmed Kadash took out a Bullhorn and yelled, "Do not fire upon the chopper. This is our air cover."

A lot of Hutu warriors didn't understand English, so Kadash handed the Bullhorn to Tuncha Sabissa and told him to make them understand.

Tuncha spoke in their language and the warriors started disarming.

The fully-armed helicopter landed in a large area at least a mile from the Boma. Meadiav called to Lawanna Kosi to grab one of the Jeeps so they could retrieve the pilot and being him back to camp.

Kosi pulled up alongside Bosloff, who jumped in. They headed off to the landing zone and drove about two minutes into the brush, coming upon a clearing that they actually made for the helicopter. When they pulled up, an angry looking man was standing next to the helicopter holding a Baretta F-92 hand gun.

Meadiav recognized the man as an old comrade named Demetri Roskin. He also was in the attacks by the Serbian forces in Montenegro and was an accomplished attack helicopter pilot. The jeep pulled up twenty five feet from the Loach and Roskin realized that it was his buddy Bosloff coming to greet him. Roskin, with a bewildered frown, asked Bosloff, "What the fuck is going on? I've been trying to get you on my radio for the last fifteen minutes. Don't tell me you turned it off, Meadiav. I know you know better than that."

Bosloff with a puzzled face replied, "You've got to be kidding. We've been waiting for your call. Come with me back to camp and we'll figure out what is going wrong."

Demetri got in and they headed back to the Boma. As they were driving, Roskin told his cohorts that he'd been having trouble with communications for some time. As soon as he was airborne from Nairobi's airport, he called them on the frequency that Kadash gave him the day before.

When they entered the camp they saw Tuncha Sabissa holding the receiver to the magna phone and shaking his head in frustration. As they pulled up, Lawanna got out and went straight over to Tuncha, asking, "What seems to be the problem, Tuncha?"

Tuncha answered in disgust, "I can't get through to anybody. It's not possible that anyone receiving my transmission would not reply back. I think we should all take battle positions in the meantime. Unless I can raise our communications, we can't take the chance of a surprise attack."

Roskin said to Tuncha, "I don't give a rat's ass what you do. I'm fuckin' hungry and I need to take a piss. If you think I'm going back to the chopper just when I get here, you're seriously mistaken."

Tuncha stared with a hateful look right at him. Before any argument broke out, Bosloff stood between the two. "Please, we are all comrades in this Holy Jihad. Demetri, go get yourself something to eat inside the Boma. Tuncha, we have men spread out in a ten mile radius. We will definitely be forewarned in time to get Demetri back to the chopper. Now Demetri and Tuncha, shake hands and Demetri go get some food."

The men shook hands reluctantly, and Roskin went to relieve himself in the bushes.

Ten minutes later, Bosloff and Sabissa walked into the Boma and saw Demetri Roskin eating next to the same men that gave Bosloff the bush meat. Just as Bosloff went to warm him, Tuncha says, "Let him enjoy his meal. I really don't need to be chasing him into the jungle like I did with you."

Tuncha and Bosloff agree to leave the Boma for the time being.

Time: 1415 hours. Nairobi. November 30, 2010. Time: 1500 hours. London Time.

After five hours into their flight, and not being able to raise Carl Bingham on the radio, Professor Pearson decided to try and get through to his RIGEL One satellite via a special magna phone in a large case in the back of the C-130 Spooky. He looked at the air pressure indicator for the area behind the Cockpit and made sure it was safely inside. He opened the cockpit door and saw only the Flight and Weapons crew awake.

Pearson looked to see that the time on the Electron Accelerator had finally completed Orion's regeneration cycle.

Malloy and Olsen were both snoring.

Pearson slowly reached it to unhook the ICARUS device from the Magnetron Accelerator. He went over to a big case about four feet by three feet and opened it. Inside was another satellite magna phone, but the antenna dish was made of a mixture of titanium, carbon carbonite, and the chorominium metal. It was all melted and pressurized to make an alloy of impenetrable composition. Both the Rigel One Satellite and the Bellatrix Satellite were made of the same element. This provided a shield that automatically surrounded the satellite when small meteorites or solar radiation became a danger to the components in the satellite itself.

The professor pushed the code into the keypad and on the screen came a message that an incredible amount of solar radiation was outside the satellites. As he read the data, Pearson saw that all over the earth communications were completely shut down.

"Holy Neptune," he exclaimed.

Right then and there, Malloy, Orion, and Larson woke up and walked over quickly. Malloy asked, "What's going on, Jeffrey? Everything copacetic? You look worried."

The professor explained that the solar radiation in space had knocked out all communications around the world. He let them know that when they had gained some ground on the C-5 Galaxy, he'd be able to send instructions to the Rigel One satellite to open a small window on its exterior, so they'd be able to raise the plane. Pearson shared that the satellite computer told him the radiation was dissipating and within three hours he should really be able to make contact with Bingham.

Pearson finally let Orion know that the suit he was wearing was made of the same element as the shields of the two satellites.

Orion reminded the professor that he already knew all the data the super computer knew.

Professor Pearson asked Orion, "John, now that the regeneration cycle is completed, has your body adapted to all the nano microbes inside?"

"Everything that was introduced to my body has now become one with me. We are now just one entity. Little by little I'll test my new found abilities with, of course, the restraint that I promised you."

Professor Pearson with a smile of glee responded, "Thank you, son. Now you still need to rest after the ordeal you've been through."

Orion became complacent and laid back down on the make shift flight gurney.

Malloy stayed awake because now the circumstances called for the commanding officer to initiate all the commands to the strike teams. It was a good thing both refueling aircraft had VHF and VLF antennas.

Pearson knew that Malloy always wanted his mission aircraft to be able to fly non-stop for at least thirty six hours at a time. Radar was working fine around the earth. Except for a couple of dead zone areas, the outer shell of earth's atmosphere kept the deadly radiation at bay.

Professor Pearson and Captain Malloy knew the other aircraft might be having trouble contacting any airports. They knew that most of the satellites in space were protected with barrier shields in case of this very rare circumstance. Many airports around the world right now must be going crazy. On all Pearson Global Technologies' aircraft the fail-safe protocol was implemented. But now air-to-air transmission required at least 400 miles between aircraft to make contact. They wondered if Carl Bingham was having difficulty because it was time to hook-up with the KC-10 refueling aircraft.

Time: 1535 hours. London Time. November 30, 2010.

On the C-5 Galaxy Aircraft, now only two and a half hours ahead of the C-130 Spooky, Liam Faraday tried to contact the KC-10 for refueling. After another ten minutes, he switched over to the VLF antenna and began broadcasting. "One November Mike, this is Three Echo Romeo, do you read?" Faraday repeated the transmission six times when a beeping signal came over his radio and squelched, "This is One November, Mike. We read you loud and clear and have you on radar approaching your position at 0651 correcting course to 0612. We'll be coming up from your port side ETA five minutes."

Faraday with a sigh of relief responded, "One November Mike. Read you loud and clear, keeping course 0612 steady for your arrival."

All three men in the checkpoint smiled with jubilance and prepared for the arrival of the KC-10, knowing for security reasons they must not converse over the air. Both flight crews from both planes were wondering if there were any glitches in the mission due to the communications problem. They were still glad they had followed Captain Malloy's protocol and switched antennas.

Carl Bingham looked to the left side window in the cockpit and saw the KC-10 approaching gradually to refuel. The KC-10 maneuvered thirty feet above the Galaxy and moved a little forward into refueling position. From the back of the KC-10 came a tethered fuel line, which Bingham had to pull up to the Galaxy in order to meet his refueling cone with the fuel line itself. The nozzle was gradually inserted into the refueling cone, and the indicator lights showed the fuel tanks starting to fill up.

They held this position for twelve minutes until a green indicator light went on. The KC-10 retrieved the fuel line and transmitted to the Galaxy. "Three Echo Romeo, glad to oblige. Have a safe trip to Nairobi. Over."

Faraday responded, "Thanks for the drink, One November Mike. See you on the ground. Roger, Wilco, over and out."

The KC-10 veered off and disappeared into the clouds.

Now flying over Cameroon airspace, Faraday checked to see if the VHF antenna came back on line. Still not able to transmit or receive, Faraday went back to the VLF.

Time: 1710 hours. Rome Time. November 30, 2010. London Time: 1610 hours. November 30, 2010.

Flying above the Atlantic in the vicinity of Cape Verdi, Africa, the pilot of a C-130 Spooky picked up a garbled transmission from a submarine below. Just making it out vaguely, he heard, "Falcon calling Stingray, come in please."

Lars Olsen heard the same thing again and recognized the voice. He told the professor to go get Captain Malloy and bring him to the cockpit immediately. As the professor and the Captain come back into the cockpit, Malloy heard the voice on the radio just faintly. They lost radio contact immediately. Lars looked at the Captain. "I took a precaution and recorded the transmission, just in case. Listen to this, Skipper, and tell me if the voice sounds familiar."

Lars had Claire play back the broadcast and Malloy's eyes opened wide. He looked at the professor with concern.

"I'll be damned if that isn't Vladmir Koslovski. I'm starting to see a pattern with all the events in the last seventy two hours. When I was in Norfolk with Admiral Fisher and Admiral Maguire, they showed me satellite photos of Amal Baraash climbing down the conning tower of an old retired Russian sub. He's the same man Orion vowed to kill for the ambush in Afghanistan. We all want this piece of shit for the death of Billy Stokes, but do me one favor. Don't let Orion know yet. I need him focused on this mission and this mission alone."

The professor nodded in agreement.

Malloy continued, "If Baraash is involved with Koslovski and Bosloff, that definitely means al-Qaeda is behind the scheme. Jeffrey, in the meantime keep trying to raise Carl on the radio. We need to warn them somehow, without actually telling them what's going on."

Professor Pearson immediately started trying to gain contact with the Galaxy.

Time: 1630 hours. London Time. November 30, 2010. Time: 2200 hours. Nairobi Time. November 30, 2010.

After three hours of trying to contact their Security Chief Captain James Malloy, the VHF antenna started picking up a transmission as the C-5 Galaxy began flying over Uganda airspace. It was coming in very weak, but Carl Bingham recognized Professor Pearson's voice.

"Two Delta Sierra, this is Echo Romeo."

The broadcast started fading little by little and disappeared. Not knowing the C-130 Spooky was closing the distance between them, Carl Bingham, the pilot of the C-5 Galaxy, said to his co-pilot David Banks, "That's Jeffrey's voice we just heard. Two Sierra Delta is the call sign for the C-130. Do you think something's wrong there? It's hard to say with all the trouble we're having today. What do you think I should do, David?"

Banks looked at his friend. "I think we should let Mike Trudeaux in on this and see how he wants to go forward." He looked at Faraday with concern and said, "Liam, go get Trudeaux. Tell him it's of importance because we're starting to near the drop zone."

Faraday removed his headset and opened the door of the cockpit. He' was gone for a couple of minutes when the door opened again. First Faraday entered, then Trudeaux. Pilot Carl Bingham explained the incoming broadcast they had just received.

"Well Senior Chief, you've got the ball. It's your call. Are you going to deploy or wait and see if we can raise the professor over the radio?"

Trudeaux automatically responded, "Unless I hear otherwise, we do the drop as scheduled. I follow protocol when the mission could be this dangerous. If the C-130 is following, I have to make sure my fire team is prepared on the ground. Just to take a small precaution, we'll deploy three minutes ahead of schedule in order to do some recon on the ground. We'll probably land a click or two from the drop zone, but under the cover of darkness we should still be able to avoid detection."

Bingham let Trudeaux get ready, because they were only forty five minutes to the drop zone. Liam puts his headset back on and continued to try and make contact with the Spooky.

Time: 2220 hours. Nairobi Time. November 30, 2010.

On the ground just ten miles west of Nairobi, an armed convoy was pressing on to the port city of Mombasa. Klaus Steubern followed in the rear of the column and zigzagged slightly to make sure the terrain up ahead looked clear. The drivers of all the vehicles had their lights turned off and were wearing night vision goggles (NVGs).

Even with the cover of darkness, they still picked up the sounds of the APC's and the rest of the convoy. Because it was dark, they were only traveling at a slow pace of about twenty miles per hour.

Hans Von Dietrich knew at this speed they should arrive in Mombasa at 0130 hours Nairobi Time. He had his headset on hoping to be able to transmit or receive any messages. Because his mission was secret, he had no idea of the solar flare that had knocked out satellite communications. He also didn't know that an ambush awaited his convoy an hour and a half eastward.

Even though there was a full moon out, everything looked dark and eerie along the trail. In the background was the noise of lions killing some type of prey. The sound of their ferocious roars made everyone on the caravan feel despondent.

Von Dietrich softly said over the P.A speaker horn to keep on going and disregard the lions. He pulled alongside Gunnar's Land Rover and motioned to him to scout ahead, while they reduced speed a little bit.

Gunnar's driver stepped on the gas and the Land Rover pulled away from the convoy. They drove at about forty miles an hour and checked the perimeter two miles ahead. From there they stopped and waited for the convoy to catch up. This was a tactic to bring enemy to fire upon them. This way, if they were fired upon, the rest of the convoy had time to get into position for the skirmish. This strategy would be deployed all the way to Mombasa.

The next scouting expedition would be Von Dietrich's turn. If anything went wrong, they would split the column and cover each other's flank while Klaus Steubern circled them with the halftrack and a suppressing amount of fire to cover the convoy's escape. This was the protocol given to them by Malloy. Time: 2240 hours. November 30, 2010. Nairobi Time. Time: 2155 hours. Congo Time. November 30, 2010.

Aboard that C-130 Spooky Gunship helicopter, an ex-S.E.A.L. Captain was desperately trying to raise a QRF team, not knowing that a small army of al-Qaeda terrorists sat and waited in ambush.

Captain James Malloy looked at the coordinates on the radar screen. He noticed that they were only forty five minutes behind the C-5 Galaxy aircraft that had been dispatched on a rescue mission. Malloy felt a sense of urgency and told the professor to switch the communications antenna from VHF to VLF. Professor Pearson pressed the switch to engage the transfer of antennas and just like that over the radio was heard, "Three Echo Romeo, this is Two Delta Sierra. Do you copy? Three Echo Romeo. Over."

Everybody in the C-130 cockpit was relieved. Professor Pearson immediately answered into the mouthpiece of his headset. "Two Delta Sierra, this is Three Echo Romeo. I read you loud and clear. Over. Please standby for orders from Chief Security. Over."

Pearson handed the headset to Malloy, who donned it quickly and said, "Two Delta Sierra, please be advised. We've been picking up radio signals at coordinates three degrees south, by twenty five minutes, by thirty nine degrees, south by southeast, by fifteen minutes. Tell Fire Team designate to make drop three minutes before initial deployment. Is that a copy? Over."

Liam Faraday with a voice of joy, replied, "That's affirmative, Three Echo Romeo. Your team officer has already made the same exact scenario. Over. Please be advised, have already dined with One November, Mike. Over." Malloy nodded with pride. "We are closing in on your position, Two Delta Sierra. Will recon from above drop area in forty mikes (minutes) over."

Faraday replied, "That's a copy, Three Echo Romeo. Over and out." Faraday turned a dial switch on his console and talked to his flight engineer in the rear of the Galaxy. He told Joe Coffey to instruct Mike Trudeaux and his fire team to get ready. The time of deployment was twenty seven minutes away.

Coffey checked the drop sled to make sure the Ordinance was secure, along with the RBS-70 crate. The fire team started putting on their rigs and chutes. They hooked the Oxygen tank for their jump to the rigs on their stomachs, along with their stabilizers. Each team member helped double check each other's equipment for the jump.

Trudeaux had each member test the Comm. gear in their Biv-Packs to make sure all the communications channels were working perfectly. Trudeaux also tested the communication from his Biv-Pack to the Galaxy and the Spooky to ensure they were working perfectly. The Comm. in the cockpit was working inside the Galaxy, but they wouldn't know about the C-130 until it was in range of the drop zone.

Time: 2325 hours. Nairobi Time. November 30, 2010.

A red light had been on for three minutes above the cockpit door inside the cargo and deployment area of the back of the plane. All personnel had their oxygen masks on as the rear vertical ramp door of the Galaxy opened. Flight engineer Joe Coffey was waiting for the green light to deploy the drop sled first. The door finally came to a stop as the cold air rushed all over the rear of the plane.

The jump team began adjusting their stabilizers to the pressure. Another minute went by, then the Green Light went on in the front and aft of the Galaxy. Immediately, Joe Coffey pulled the release lever to send the drop sled in motion. As it left the plane, the others waited to follow. Fifteen seconds went by and the chute to the drop sled safely deployed.

The five member strike team went out in succession, with Trudeaux in the rear. Doing a H.A.L.O. jump at twenty thousand feet this time of night was very difficult. All the team members were now thanking God for NVGs which allowed their eyes to pierce the darkness.

As they were halfway down, the team encircled each other. Trudeaux waved a saluted hand at his chest first, then waved it towards a clearing on the ground. The team was able to see his signal with night vision, knowing that the hand signal meant Trudeaux was going first to deploy his chute.

From there the rest of the team followed him in.

At a thousand feet Trudeaux released his chute and the rest of the team followed suit in succession. Just before coming to the ground, each member pulled their release to drop their tethered ruck sack ahead of them. The Galaxy was going to circle once to ensure their communications were still working before heading for Nairobi Airport.

Trudeaux, once his chute was wrapped and secured, turned the switch dial by his left shoulder to communicate with the C-5 Galaxy. "Two Delta Sierra, This is One, Puma, Tango. Do you copy?"

Immediately, Faraday's voice came into Trudeaux's headset. "That's affirmative, One Puma Tango. We have picked up radio contact of convoy team two clicks south of your location. Over."

Trudeaux replied, "Check that Two, Delta, Sierra. You confirm two clicks due south of our location. Over."

Faraday responded, "That's affirmative, One Puma Tango. Over." Trudeaux left his last transmission with, "Copy Two Delta Sierra. Over and out." He turned the switch dial again next to his left shoulder and said, "Two Lima Xray, This is One, Puma. Tango, Do you copy?"

As he went to repeat the transmission, explosions were visible. Guns went off in the distance.

Maguiness, Alvarez and Thomas had just completed taking the RBS-70 out of the crate when all hell broke loose ahead of them. Automatically, the fire team grabbed all the ordinance and ammo they could carry and began sprinting towards the skirmish.

Maguiness and Alvarez were the first two of the team to shoulder carry the RBS-70 on the run. The team took turns switching off intermittently, close to the mile run.

Trudeaux looked at his watch and saw that the C-130 Spooky should be almost there. He waved for the team to keep going while he slowed down to an animal trot to try and raise the Gunship.

"Three Echo Romeo, This is One, Puma, Tango. Do you copy, Three

Echo Romeo? If you can hear this, Three Echo Romeo, please be advised that team Two Lima Xray is under attack. We are a click and a half from their position. Do you copy? Over."

Around the C-130 Spooky gunship, just entering the airspace above the convoy being ambushed, a radio transmission came into the cockpit. At first garbled, it became clearer as they approached. Over the radio, Malloy finally heard, Do you copy Three Echo Romeo? If you can hear this, Three Echo Romeo, please be advised that team Two Lima Xray is under attack. We are a click and a half from their position. Do you copy? Over.

Malloy instantly pressed the transmit button on the console and replied, "We read you loud and clear One Puma Tango. Our infrared has picked up Two Lima Xray's convoy and they have split their forces in a column. There are two vehicles on fire and they are pinned down in a parallel ambush now closing in on one click ahead of your current position. Over."

Trudeaux said, "You have the eyes, Three Echo Romeo, what's holding down their forward position? Over".

Malloy scanned the terrain with the F.L.I.R. positioning unit on the nose of the C-130 and got frustrated because he couldn't pick up the big gun or guns that had both columns pinned down. He relayed to Trudeaux, "We're not picking up visual on main gun."

All of a sudden from the corner of the nearby hill came a T-55 Russian-made tank. Malloy told the Howitzer crew in the back of the C-130 Gunship to lock onto the tank and open fire. Over the FLIR Screen came the second volley from the Howitzer, dead on its target. The crew in the back of the Gunship cheered as the tank burned brightly.

All the sudden, though, a transmission came in from Von Dietrich. "Three Echo Romeo, if that was just you, please be advised we are under heavy attack and there are two M-106 recoils rifles well hidden. Over."

Malloy turned the dial one more notch on the console and said, "We hear you, Two Lima Xray. Will give air cover for three more passes then must head for Nairobi Airport for landing. A strike team out of Diego Garcia on way with QRF team as we speak. Over."

Von Dietrich with a voice of desperation plead with Malloy, "Captain, please, they're all around us. I don't think we can hold out much longer. Gunnar is down and wounded and we can't get to him."

From the back of the plane a weird shaking began. Lars realized he could longer control the stick on the plane. It seemed to be maneuvering itself to a lower altitude and flew a smoother course right above the ambush.

Professor Pearson, seeing the altitude now at eight thousand feet, opened the door of the cockpit. Orion started to rise above his makeshift gurney with that eerie purple light, this time engulfing his entire body as he levitated horizontally.

Time: 2400 hours. Nairobi Time. December 1, 2010. Time: 2300 hours. Nairobi Time.

Vice Admiral Ford, receiving instructions from his friend and colleague Vice Admiral Fischer, gave the RED ALERT for a Quick Reactionary Force (QRF) to be deployed to certain coordinates. A C-47 jet engine Chinook was now on its way with a combination of Navy S.E.A.L.s and Force Recon Marines. The Amphibious Naval Base at Diego Garcia was a little more than five hundred miles away. Even though the solar radiation around the earth had begun dissipating, most communication satellites had not taken their shields offline.

The U.S. Naval Warship Carl Vinson left the Mauritius Key of Fort Louis in the Mauritius Islands, east of Madagascar. Admiral Ford had designated them as back up if anything went wrong. Admiral Ford was able to reach the Captain aboard the Carl Vinson because the military spy satellite, PEGASUS, came back on line.

Time: 2320 hours. November 30, Nairobi Time.

16 ENTER SANDMAN

Time: 0005 hours. December 1, 2010.

An eerie strange colored purple light illuminated from all the windows of a C-130 Spooky gunship flying eight thousand feet above an area where a convoy was being attacked by an army of al-Qaeda terrorists.

Professor Jeffrey Pearson left the cockpit of the C-130 and entered the rear of the plane to see ex-Navy Lieutenant John Orion levitating horizontally above his makeshift gurney. The high-rise, vertical ramp door of the plane began to slowly open. Cold air rushed all over the cabin.

Joe Coffey immediately fastened a tethered line to the professor's belt. Malloy entered the back of the plane to see Orion now levitating from horizontal to vertical. The strange shade of purple engulfed his whole body. Malloy yelled ever of the loudness of the wind in the cabin, "What the hell is going on, Lieutenant, and what do you think you are going to do?"

Orion had just been uncoupled from the magnetron line to the ICARUS Device and replied in a determined voice, "I'm going down to save my FUCKIN' team, Skipper. Are you coming, or you going to stay here and play with your Johnson? Don't even try and fuckin' stop me because nobody on the planet can."

Instantly Malloy started putting on the chute harness and replied, "We'll talk about this insubordination after the mission, you tyrant prick."

The door of the C-130 was now completely deployed. Pearson, with a look of concern, said to Orion, "Do you have any Idea what you're capable of doing, Lieutenant?"

Orion bowed his head down to him, reached into his pack and pulled out his iPod still lying on the gurney. "Professor, you've saved my life. I owe you more that any man could ever imagine. If I don't make it back, tell Lanny I love her more that life itself. Lars has control of the plane again. Once we jump, only make two more passes for air cover. Then get the fuck out of here. Me and the skipper are going to hook-up with Trudy and the team and try to save Hansy's team. I'm going to push this button on my iPod and the music that comes out of the speakers up here will be all over the place down there. I've picked up they have speakers all over their camp and was able to tap into them. We'll be using this as a diversion to be able to get to Gunnar. I know it's going to be loud, but at all costs let it play through." He paused, then answered the professor's question.

"I have no idea what I'm capable of doing. I guess we'll find out now." With that Orion pressed the play button and Metallica's "Enter Sandman" blared. He grit his teeth and made two fists, clenching them tight, then hovered slowly towards the door. Standing next to the Dillon Aero M-134, he motioned to Malloy to jump first.

Malloy, with a face of bewilderment, hesitated, but jumped from the plane. All of a sudden, Orion ripped the Dillon Aero from its bolted steel mounts and tucked it under his arm like he was holding a pillow. He put the power cord of the weapon to a compartment next to his battery pack and the gun lit up with power. "I'm going to need to borrow this. Any objections?"

Everybody in the rear of the plane was in shock and awe. Without saying a word they all shook their heads.

Orion responded, "Very good. Wish me luck." With that he floated right out of the plane and descended to the battlefield below.

As the door of the C-130 gunship closed, Joe Coffey exclaimed, "I'm not the only one who just saw that, am I?"

Professor Pearson, with his mouth wide open and his eyes in a daze, replied, "No, Joseph. We all just witnessed the same thing. All right, gentlemen, to your posts. Let's give them all the help we can." He went through the cockpit door where Lars and Claire were waiting to find out what was going on.

As Pearson sat down in the navigator's chair, Claire said, "Papa, the last time I saw that look on your face was when Johnny floated around the room." The professor gives his daughter a look of amazement. "Oh, he does a lot more than just float around a silly room. I'll get into that later. Right now, let's give our boys the air cover they need."

At a thousand feet, Malloy deployed this chute and looked up to see Orion coming from above. He was glowing that eerie purple light all over the place.

Orion pressed the dial on his Biv-pack with his right hand and said, "One Puma Tango. This is Two Indian Delta. Prepare yourselves. I'm bringing snakes out of the hole to your location."

Malloy noticed Orion still hadn't deployed his chute and that he was drifting right towards the middle of the enemy's encampment. As soon as Malloy reached the ground, he saw Trudeaux and the rest of his fire team coming over to him.

Trudeaux came running. "I knew it was you and Lieutenant as soon as I heard the song, but what the hell is he up to? This is totally against what we've been trained to do. He just told us he was bringing the insurgents our way. So I guest we'd better do as he wants. I don't know how he thinks he's going to flush that many men out of their cover."

Just as Orion was four hundred feet from the ground, he deployed his chute. Instantly the enemy encampment unloaded their fire upon him. Just like that, the aurora of light around him turned a more bluish purple and all the bullets and shrapnel around him was repelled by his force field. Thirty feet from the ground he released his chute so it completely flew away from him and immediately slowed down his descent like he was a balloon.

As he was two feet from the ground, he started hovering towards the enemy, opening fire with the Dillon Aero. Orion noticed he didn't need NVG's because he was able to pick up silhouettes without them. The ones he didn't hit were jumping out of their fox holes like they were on fire. They ran away from the front column where Gunnar laid in the middle of the path after being thrown from the vehicle, blasted from the M-106 Recoilless rifle.

Klaus Steubern, who was able to get out of his Half-Tract Reactive Armored Vehicle before it was hit, saw an opportunity to get Gunnar out of the line of fire. Dashing to his comrade, he pulled him behind a five-foot boulder by a tree.

As they were being fired upon, Howitzer shells started pounding the enemy positions. Twenty five millimeter shells were being sprayed all over the Bomas inner area. Two of the enemy's armored personnel carriers exploded, thanks to the five inch guns from the Spooky. Orion, just about out of rounds for the Dillon Aero, dropped behind an Acacia Tree for a second.

All of a sudden, Trudy, Malloy, Alvarez, Thomas, and Maguiness rose up out of the bushes in front of the retreating enemy and let all hell break loose. The terrorist began dropping like flies hit with insecticide.

As the firing was just about over, Orion's headset beeped. He turned his dial back one turn and heard, "Two Indian Delta, this is Three Echo Romeo, coming in for final pass then heading to Nairobi Airport. We are low on fuel and still have not been able to contact re-fueler. Over."

Orion pressed the transmit button on his comm. gear to his left shoulder. "That's a copy, Three Echo Romeo. If you please, can you pound position into the hill area underneath the tree line. Over."

Professor Pearson replied, "That's a copy, Two Indian Delta. Once we lead in Nairobi, we will get to you with extraction team. Over and out."

The C-130 was coming in and the hill was being pummeled beyond belief. As the smoke cleared, the sound of the C-130 faded in the distance.

As their fire team moved forward, a shrilling sound came from an air horn being shot all over the jungle. Nobody could see it at first, but everyone heard hundreds of the Supawani tribesmen howling their voices and coming down from their position about a mile back.

Orion, with a sense of super vision, saw them approach and motioned for the team to cross the road next to the burning Boma village. He told Malloy to aim the RBS-70 towards their left flank and wait for a flash. As soon as they spotted the flash, they were to target it and fire.

Malloy didn't understand his reasoning because they were using their only anti-aircraft weapon. However, after seeing the unbelievable powers his long-time friend had acquired, he choose to listen to him this time.

Orion started walking towards the sound of the warriors heading straight for them. His whole strike team looked in bewilderment, wondering why he was heading towards them with only a sidearm and combat knife. Still, they begin setting up again and spotted Klaus and Von Dietrich running towards them.

Klaus had Gunnar draped over his shoulder and back.

Hansy yelled out, "Hold your fire, hold your fire. It's me, Hans. Don't shoot."

They get behind one of the smoldering enemy personnel vehicles and waved for Malloy to come them. Malloy did a quick rush and made it behind the smoldering vehicle to see Gunnar's head wrapped in bandages and his shirt ripped wide open. Around his chest were bandages continuously wrapped around his body numerous amount of times. On the right side of his chest a straw stuck out of the bandage to his lung.

Tears came from Hansy's eyes as he said to Malloy, "Captain, Gunnar's lung has collapsed and he has a piece of small shrapnel imbedded to the right side of his head. The straw is good enough for now, but if we don't get him to a hospital within the next half hour he's definitely going to die."

Malloy told Hans, "We've got help on the way, Hansy. Try and get him over by us while I take a team ahead and knock out the few pockets of resistance."

Malloy motioned with his index finger pointing to his men, looked at Palladin and slapped his hand behind his head letting Bobby know he's talking to him. Malloy rushed to the left to flank where the enemy's guns were flashing. As he drew their fire, Palladin rushed to the right flank as the Captain drew their attention away from him.

Palladin pushed back five hundred feet into the jungle and came upon a giant looming tree that towered above the canopy. Bobby clambered up the tree to take the ground observation designated duty. He aimed his CheyTech 200 and surveilled the area where the weapons were flashing. From up above, he saw the Captain popping up and down, side to side, when two different flashes showed up twenty feet apart buried in loose camouflaged brush.

Bobby instantly placed both shots dead on. Both enemy combatants fell forward, hit. All of a sudden five more came running from their hiding places with fear all over their faces. They start screaming surrender and dropped their weapons, laying on the ground in the middle of the dirt road.

Meanwhile, behind the strike team a thousand Supawani tribal warriors converged within a hundred yards of them. All of a sudden, Orion started hovering five feet above the ground and told them to go back in their own language. They really didn't hear what he said and were freaking at the sight of the purple-glowing man defying gravity in front of them. One of them yelled something out to the others and hundreds of arrows and spears headed straight at Orion.

Orion put both palms toward them and concentrated, dropping the projectiles midair. They fired into the ground instead.

Every eye bugged out of their heads, and they instantly turned around and ran away screaming. Orion, having the knowledge from the super computer at Pearson Global Technologies, knew that these people were friends of Professor Pearson. He knew something was up when he realized the tribe was not indigenous to this region and came to fight with bows, arrows and spears. He knew they had to be duped, because only fools would try and go up against heavily armed machine guns and small artillery.

All of a sudden a helicopter buzzed from above the canopy. Appearing just above the trees was a Little Bird Loach helicopter armed to the teeth. It hovered while the two men inside looked over the devastation all around. The chopper sped off this time.

Palladin yelled to the team as he spotted it from his position in the tree, "Everyone cover now!" The Loach came in firing its 30 mm guns, spraying the area where the team had just been. The Loach did a one hundred and eighty degree turn and started firing its rockets, almost hitting the position of the team. Inside the helicopter, the Pilot Demetri Roskin laughed with his passenger, Meadiav Bosloff. Roskin wore night vision goggles. All of a sudden from the port side of the helicopter, a bullet slammed into the back passenger compartment. Roskin looked over to see an infrared image of a man set up high in the canopy. He flew right at him with an evil smile a mile wide. He started firing the guns right at him as Palladin tried to hide behind the tree.

Bosloff laughed with delight knowing the man now couldn't escape. Roskin laughed with him and came around the other side of the tree, getting ready to finish him off.

But from the jungle below, Orion jumped up to the Loach and plunked down on its landing sled. Roskin and Bosloff yelled at the same time, "WHAT THE FUCK?"

Orion opened the pilot's door and reached in, tossing Roskin to the jungle below. He entered and began flying the Loach towards a clearing near Gunnar.

Bosloff froze in his seat with fear. "What are you?"

Orion hearing his voice says, "Ah, Meadiav Bosloff. I should've known you'd be part of this." Orion backhanded him and knocked him out cold.

The Loach landed close to where the team was trying desperately to keep Gunnar alive. The blades turned at a low RPM. Orion dragged Bosloff out of the Loach with one hand and shouted over the helicopter's engine, "Skipper, look who we've got here."

Von Dietrich, still not believing what he was witnessed, recognized Orion's voice. With his eyes bugging out of his head, Von Dietrich responded, "Is that you, Yohan?"

Orion concentrated to turn the corneas of his eyes blue, then removed his sunglasses to reveal his eyes beneath the balaclava.

"Yeah Hansy, it's me. I've got no time to explain. Let's get Gunnar in the bird so we can get him to the hospital in Nairobi."

As Orion and Von Dietrich carried Gunnar towards the Loach, Bobby came out of the jungle dragging Demetri Roskin by his shirt collar. He pulled him over to the other prisoners and slammed him down in the dirt. He looked over to see Orion putting Gunnar in the Loach with Hansy.

Orion climbed into the pilot seat while Hansy held his comrade and best friend in his arms. As they began lift off, Orion switched on the side speaker of the chopper and said into mike, "Far Since." Everyone in the ground raised their fists and screamed, "HOOYAAH."

Palladin met Orion's eyes just before he left and saluted him as he flew towards Nairobi.

Orion only got two miles away when he heard from back of the chopper, "Yohan, is that really you, my friend?"

Orion, tearing up, replied, "Yeah, Gunnar it's your ole drinking buddy, Yohan. You just hang in there. We'll be at the hospital before you know it".

Communications had been restored all over the planet. Orion was able to contact with the Kenyan government officials and an ambulance was waiting at the airport along with Professor Pearson. Orion was still trying to make sense of everything. He was afraid that the love of his life would now consider him a freak.

Time: 0230 hours. Nairobi Time. December 1, 2010.

Above the burned-out compound of the enemy's failed attempt, a CH-47 Chinook hovered over the jungle. An elite force of Navy S.E.A.L.s and Force Recon Marines repelled to the jungle floor below. Aboard the CH-47B was Colonel David Caldwell, who wanted to come along to investigate the situation at hand.

Caldwell, having just communicated with his buddy and second in command four and half years ago, couldn't wait for the chopper to land. He and James Malloy had served together back in Afghanistan, when Malloy and Billy Stokes stole a Sea Hawk helicopter to rescue Orion's fire team. Caldwell was also upset at the way his friend Malloy was treated afterwards.

Colonel Caldwell was also there to await the Kenyan military's top brass to explain of the terrorist assault that took place in their country. They were on their way from Nairobi's hospital's intensive care unit. They left with Professor Pearson after he was told Gunnar had pulled through. The bleeding had been controlled, but little pieces of shrapnel imbedded in the right side of his torso still had to be removed.

Pearson, who had a government contract for moving uranium ore across Kenyan Territory, explained to General Bakumba Selee the circumstances that led to the rescue mission. He told the General he would have let him and his military in on it, but communications were out everywhere.

General Selee brought a convoy of his top elite soldiers with him towards the ambush site. When Orion landed at Nairobi Airport, he made sure that Lars and Claire put him on the C-130 gunship right away. It was being refueled as Pearson left with the ambulance towards Nairobi General. Now, almost to the ambush site, the General looked outside the Land Rover and spotted the C-130 gunship flying overhead going towards the west.

Bakumba said to Pearson, "How does that helicopter pilot of yours see in the dark with those dark purple sunglasses?"

Startled at the General's observation, the professor quickly replied, "Special night vision wear; company secret for now, but I'll make sure when the technology is available that your forces will be one of the one of the first to receive them."

The General smiled. "This is why my country does business with you, professor. You are a very generous man to my people."

The convoy entered the burned-out Boma village and ambush site. The General explained that this village was built by the Nomadic Massie people. They used it to keep their livestock of cattle safe from predators at night. Bakumba told the professor that they'll be able to rebuild when they return in four months for the beginning of the wet season.

As they pulled up, the professor saw his security chief talking to a full Bird Marine Colonel. He and the General got out of the Land Rover with Selee's top brass liaison in tow. Marines and S.E.A.L.s were leading the prisoners towards a canvassed military truck for their ride back to the Chinook.

From out of the jungle walked the Chief of the Supawani Tribe. Sulpa Juna had been watching the whole time and noticed the arrival of his friend, Professor Pearson. He and the Supawani people started appearing all around the burned out boma.

Pearson yelled immediately not to fire upon them.

The Marines and S.E.A.L.s couldn't believe how many of them there were. Malloy conveyed the same message for everyone to stand down.

The professor greeted Sulpa and asked what he is doing so far away from their home. Sulpa pointed to the two bound prisoners being led by two Marines and explained that Tuncha Sabissa and the man behind him had told him that evil people were going to attack this compound of the professor's friends, and would come back and kill his people in Congo. He told Pearson that with all the fire sticks going off, twenty five of his people had been killed. The professor let Sulpa Juna know that those two men deceived him and that they were the evil ones.

Sulpa, with tears in his eyes, told the professor that his sister's kid was one of the casualties in the assault. By his people's laws, they were entitled to administer justice.

Lawanna Kosi began screaming at the professor. "Don't let those savages take us. They've been known to torture their victims for hours at a time." General Bakumba Selee walked over to them and said to the professor, "I don't understand his dialect, but I've picked up a few words in Swahili. You must turn them over to him."

Pearson asked Malloy to turn the evil doers over to Sulpa Juna. Malloy looked at Colonel Caldwell, and Caldwell motioned for their release into to custody of the tribesmen. As they were lead them off into the jungle, the blood-curdling screams of Lawanna Kosi and Tuncha Sabissa echoed. The warriors took them deep into the jungle and stripped off all the prisoners' clothes, then bound them to a tree close to an area of swarming Ciafu army ants.

The tribesman cut off the eyelids of their prisoners and poured a sugar-like substance on the very top of their heads. One of the tribesmen made a hyena's mating call perfectly several times and left the men to their own evil fate.

Back at the ambush site, a messenger brought a message to Colonel Caldwell, who opened it and read: From Vice Admiral of Fifth Fleet Operations: please notify Security Chief James Malloy that at exactly 1730 hours New York time on November 30, terrorists believed to be al-Qaeda operatives have blown up three vehicles at the New Jersey entrance side of the Holland Tunnel. It is believed they might have brought WMDs into New York City. Please contact Vice Admiral Thomas Fischer in Norfolk, Virginia. Signed, Vice Admiral James Ford.

Malloy hurried over to the professor. "Jeffrey, we have to get back to New York right away. Somehow, I think this was a well-executed plan to keep us busy while al-Qaeda was carrying out another operation at the same time. Only, it looks like the one in New York looks succeeded."

Pearson looked at the message and told Malloy, "Come on, let's get back to the airport. The C-5 is being refueled as we speak. I'll phone in a flight plan to Bingham so we can get going right away. Is that okay with you, General Selee?"

"This is now a matter of our country's national security," Bakumba Selee replied. "We will help with Colonel Caldwell's extradition of the prisoners. We'll clean up with Colonel Caldwell. You have more pressing issues to deal with. I understand the one they call Bosloff is wanted for crimes against humanity. We'll make sure they are out of my country and on their way to The Hague."

Malloy told Caldwell that he'd be in touch and left in a security vehicle provided by General Selee for him and the professor. On the way to the airport in Nairobi, the professor asked Malloy for the casualty count. The Captain answered that there were two killed and fourteen wounded, two seriously.

The professor sighed in disgust. "Why do people create such turmoil and kill their fellow man? I'm repulsed that people in my employ had to be subjected to this horrible evil."

Captain Malloy tried to comfort his good friend. "Jeff, I would lay down all my weapons if I could. I'll take a quote from Lord Alfred Tennyson, 'Yours is not to reason why. Yours is just to do or die.' Until these evil vermin are eradicated from our planet, my guns stay locked and loaded."

The professor, not looking overly relieved, responded, "Well, at least I'm glad you've trained men like Orion, Mikey, and Bobby, who live for the greater good of our planet.

Time: 0315 hours. Nairobi Time. December 1st, 2010. Time: 1715 hours. New York Time. November 30, 2010.

Two hours earlier in the states of New Jersey, an evil plot was about to be implemented by a band of al-Qaeda terrorists.

17 THE EVIL INCARNATE

Time: 1715 hours. November 30, 2010: EST New York Time.

Coming from the Pulaski Skyway Bridge, three trucks and one passenger sedan slowly started rounding the curve to the entrance of the Holland Tunnel. It was now rush hour, and the checkpoints were extremely busy due to the heavy stop and go traffic.

Kassim Safir was in the first twenty foot box truck, just about to pull up. A police officer stopped him and walked up to the driver's side. "What's in the truck?"

Kassim handed him a clipboard of the manifest. "I've got broken pc units to be delivered to a Dell recycling plant in long Island City just outside of Queens."

As the cop looked carefully at the manifest, the K-9 unit walked around the truck. Another cop used a radiation detector, waving it thoroughly as he circled the truck. Behind the passenger sedan in front of him, Milan Safir became nervous and broke out in a sweat.

Inside the passenger sedan, the children sang the song they were practicing since they woke that day. Lamarra Balaash, sister of Kamal Darfuir, was eager to take the children to see the Lion King on Broadway. She was going to meet her brother in midtown for an early dinner with the children before going to the show.

The two officers waved to their colleague holding the manifest. Let him proceed, they signaled.

Kassim put the truck in first gear and slowly let off clutch. Looking at a monitor that had been installed in Kearney, he drove until a green light went on. He had already moved twenty two feet and immediately hit the toggle switch in front of him. The engine stalled as it rolled another thirteen feet and came to a halt.

The cop who just went over his manifest came running over as the

155

sedan behind him slammed on the brakes. The cop motioned to Kassim to roll down his window. "There's a carload of kids behind you. What, are you crazy?" Kassim, with a phony look of surprise, replied, "I'm sorry, officer she just stalled on me."

The cop with a stern look told him, "Well, get this thing out of here now. Otherwise I'll have you towed. NOW MOVE IT."

Kassim looked in his driver side mirror to see his brother Milan handing his manifest to another cop. He saw the cop with the Geiger counter yell to the cop with the manifest, "Don't let him move. I'm picking up high readings from inside the truck."

With that, Milan activated the remote control to the middle of his truck and the platform with deadly cargo lowered to the ground below. At the same time, the platform under Kassim's truck lowered. A robotic wheeled cart quickly moved forward under the car in front, just barely missing the under carriage of the vehicle. As soon as the cart was in motion, the platform immediately ascended back into place.

When it arrived at Kassim's truck, it rolled right onto the platform and stopped.

Kassim, this whole time, was trying to start the engine of his truck, but when he saw the red light go back again, he flipped the toggle switch the other way. His truck immediately turned over.

The cop by his truck tried to concentrate on him, and the truck behind the passenger vehicle yelled to Kassim, "All right now, MOVE THAT PIECE OF SHIT!"

Kassim waved to him in compliance and hit the gas.

The cop went up to the car with Lamarra and her girlfriend driving, politely telling her to drive on. The kids had now stopped singing and peeked out the rear window to see cops starting to surround the truck behind them. Lamarra's girlfriend Tiri tried to restart the stalled car as Kassim's truck was almost halfway through the tunnel. The car still didn't start and confusion broke out all around the car and the truck behind it.

The cop came back over as other police units began arriving at the entrance. While this is happening, Kassim's truck had already left the tunnel and was driving onto the West Side Highway along the East River.

Meanwhile at the entrance, seeing that the car was unable to start the cop began to shout to his colleagues to come over and help push it over to a parking lot. Just then, the cop from the K-9 unit came rushing from around the back of Milan's truck and screamed, "Cuff him and get the Bomb Squad here immediately! Buster just gave the signal that there's explosives in that truck." Milan Safir, looking bewildered, wondered to himself how that could be true. The plan didn't call for any explosives. He was thrown to the ground and immediately handcuffed.

Behind his truck, police officers came over and told Fashir (AKA Benny

Kraemer) to evacuate his truck right away. Benny said to the cops, "What's going on? I have to be in Long Island City in two hours."

One of the cops replied, "Well, that ain't gonna happen now. The dog just picked up the scent of explosives. Plus, our counter also picked up a high concentration of radiation in the truck in front of you."

Benny, with a worried look on his face, opened the door of the truck instead of doing what Kassim had instructed earlier.

Milan, cuffed and lying on the ground, looked up at who he thinks is Fashir Salaam and wondered why he didn't try and go around his truck. His brother Kassim explicitly told him to do this.

As he walked past Milan, the doors locked on in his truck and the windows rolled up. At the same time, though, he locked on the car engage and its windows rolled up, too. Both vehicles started making a loud and shrill beeping sound. The cops immediately started heading towards the women and children trapped in the car.

That's when Benny reached into his long overcoat and pulled out what appeared to be white ping pong balls. He threw them to the ground and a giant cloud of green smoke wafted everywhere. Benny put a putty-looking substance to the lock on the driver's door. After a tiny bang he immediately told the occupants to get out and run towards the wall on the left. As he pulled Lamarra from the car, he grabbed the last child and headed for the wall himself.

Just as they reached the wall, Benny yelled, "Everybody get down NOW." Two seconds later, the car and truck blew up simultaneously.

On the other side of the tunnel, Abdullah Musheen took his finger off the remote control button. From where he and Mustaffa Khaldif stood, the explosion was visible across the river. Abdullah, with an evil face, cried out, "DIE, JEW, DIE."

Mustaffa was puzzled. "What do you mean, Jew?"

Abdullah turns to his cohort. "Fashir might fool you and your brother, but I wasn't fooled for a second. Friday night, a secret camera in my office picked him up going through my computer. I watched him make a Judaen blessing as he tried to crack my encrypted code. I saw the frustration on his face."

Mustaffa listened, shocked.

"My cleaning lady almost surprised him and he had to get out of there before he was discovered," continued Abdullah. "Don't look so surprised, Mustaffa. We now have eliminated anyone who knew of the plutonium. Now let's go kill that ass kiss Kassim and get our packages."

Both of them climbed into a black Cadillac CTS and headed out to where they had told Kassim to bring the truck. Meanwhile, on the Jersey side of the tunnel all chaos had broken out. People laid dead and injured. Their moans were picked up and carried along as wind began blowing and the horrific scene unfolded.

Next to the two trucks in the rear of the recent convoy laid two police officers, burned beyond recognition. The poor German Shepard police dog tried to crawl towards his dead handler. The Transit Police booth was in shambles. Emergency Responders helped the injured who were also affected because they were behind the trucks.

Lamarra, shielding her body around the children, was covered in dust. Her friend, Tiri Palaat, was laying down holding her hand over a wounded little girl who had blood dripping from her upper leg. Lamarra was in tears and asked Tiri, "Where did Fashir go? He saved our lives. Oh, I pray to Allah that he is not dead."

TV Helicopters hovered overhead, while military and emergency service police units arrived on the awful scene. The Police units immediately began closing off the area with yellow police tape. EMT workers amidst sirens and flashing lights came over to Lamarra and the children and instantly placed the wounded child onto a gurney. A patrolman asked Lamarra to get the children and Tiri into the back of his police cruiser. He told them not to worry because they were going to follow the injured girl to the hospital.

The patrolman told Lamarra a detective would be talking to her and her girlfriend just as soon as he was done investigating the scene. Lamarra asked the patrolman to please look for their friend Fashir Salaam. She knew that he might still be alive because he was the one who saved them from the locked car.

The police officer assured her that they would do everything possible, and that the detective would fill them in at the hospital. They followed the ambulance through the Holland Tunnel and headed for St. Luke's Hospital on 10th Avenue close to Amsterdam Avenue.

Time: 1800 hours. November 30, 2010.

Back on the New Jersey side of the Holland Tunnel, the FBI and other Law Enforcement agencies searched for clues to find out who was behind this deadly attack. Helicopters swept the area looking for anything out of the ordinary.

A phone call suddenly came through on FBI Special Agent Barry Larkin's cellphone. He answered, "Special Agent Larkin."

"Yes, Special Agent Larkin, this is Lieutenant Stewart, New York City Police Transit Bureau. Our camera picked up a man of Middle Eastern descent fleeing the area when the smoke began to clear. He was next to the women and children who were pulled from the vehicle that exploded along with the two trucks at the scene. From what we are able to determine, it looks as though the two women knew the man who fled."

Agent Larkin asked, "Do you know what hospital they were taken to?" Lieutenant Stewart replied, "Yeah, they were taken to St. Luke's on 10th Avenue. I've got a Lieutenant James Ferris on his way there from the

Special Crimes Unit. He's part of Homeland Security."

Larkin said to Lieutenant Stewart, "Let Lieutenant Ferris know I'm on my way. Tell him to make sure no one, but no one, talks to the press. Stewart, make sure there's additional security put around the hospital. From what I see, somebody wanted them dead, also. Put out an APB on the man fleeing the scene."

Lieutenant Stewart replied, "Already on it, Agent Larkin. But do me a favor and tell Lieutenant Ferris to keep Captain Pendergrass in the loop."

"Will do, and if anything more comes from your end, let me know right away," Larkin replied.

"You got it."

Special Agent Larkin yelled to his partner, George Hopkins, to get into their black Lincoln SUV and head through the tunnel to Manhattan.

Time: 1840 hours. November 30, 2010 EST.

Inside the waiting room of the triage unit of St. Luke's Hospital, Lamarra Balaash's cellphone rang. It was her brother, Kamal Darfuir.

She started to cry in hysterics. "Kamal, somebody tried to kill me, Tiri and the children. I'm so scared, my brother. Little Setia was hit with fragments from the explosion. She is right now in the O.R. being operated on as we speak."

Dr. Darfuir said to his sister, "Lamarra, where are you? I'm here in the city. Tell me where you are."

Still crying she answered, "We're at St. Luke's on 10th Avenue by Amsterdam Avenue."

Professor Darfuir soothed her, "I'm on my way. Don't worry, sweetheart, your older brother will be there shortly. I love you."

Entering the hospital campus with police all over the perimeter, Lieutenant James Ferris of the Special Crimes Unit showed his badge and credentials to the Police Sergeant at the door. He made his way to the triage receptionist desk.

The nurse pointed to where Lamarra, Tiri and the other children sat. Lamarra looked up and saw a tall, strong looking man in a Brooks' Brothers suit walking up to her. He stood at an intimidating height of six foot four and showed her his gold Lieutenant's badge.

"Mrs. Balaash, I'm Lieutenant Ferris of the New York City Police Department. I know you are pretty shaken up right now, but may I sit and ask you a few questions?"

Lamarra nodded her head.

The Lieutenant put her at ease and conversed about the day's events. Lamarra told Lieutenant Ferris the details of everything she could remember since coming to the United States four months ago. She also told him her brother Kamal was on his way to the hospital.

After writing the information in his notepad, Ferris told her politely that he had to call into headquarters and let his commanding officer know all the details. Just as he stood up, Special Agents Larkin and Hopkins entered the waiting room and walked straight to him.

Special Agent Larkin told Ferris about a man of Middle Eastern descent who fled the scene of the explosion. Larkin stopped his conversation with Ferris and asked Lamarra, "Where is that piece of garbage who was with you? Tell us where he is. If you don't cooperate with us, we'll put you in a cage along with the rest of your towel head Taliban rats."

Lamarra instantly began to cry and Tiri comforted her.

Larkin continued, "What about you, Jihad Jane. Where is he?"

Lieutenant Ferris ran over and slammed Larkin into the wall, holding him a foot off the ground by his throat. "Who the fuck do you think you are. I'm tired of you racist son of bitches."

Larkin looked like he just wet his pants when his partner, George Hopkins, came over. "I'm sorry about my partner, Lieutenant. I have to put up with his bigot ass shit every day. Now Barry, apologize to the Lieutenant before he snaps that numbskull neck of yours."

Larkin gave a phony apology, fixed his tie and regained his breath.

The Lieutenant and Special Agent Hopkins traded information on the investigation. They both went over to Lamarra and Tiri and asked the children if they would like a soda or something to eat.

Hopkins asked, "Ms. Balaash, who knew of your trip tonight into the city besides this man, Fashir."

Tiri interrupted, "Many of the other women at the Mosque knew how much the children were dying to see the Lion King. We first had to get permission from our cleric. He made all the arrangements for our safety. A man named Kassim came to the Mosque about an hour before we left. That's when he told Fashir to follow them in another truck that was going to pick up school supplies for the children."

Ferris and Hopkins immediately looked at one another, then walked away to confer. Agent Hopkins said to Ferris, "That's funny. The manifest said they were carrying disposed computer boards. You thinking what I'm thinking?" Ferris nodded. "We need to get a hold of this so-called cleric right now." Hopkins pulled out his cellphone to call FBI Headquarters in New Jersey. He let them know what they had just found out.

Hopkins walked over to Lamarra. "Ms. Balaash, what is the name of your cleric in Hoboken."

Lamarra looked in a state of shock reluctantly told him, "Abdullah Musheen. But he is a kind man. He would never do anything to hurt the children."

Hopkins reassured her they just needed to ask him some questions. As Hopkins talked to her, Professor Darfuir walked into triage waiting area.

"Lamarra! Thank God all of you are alright. It took me forever to find out where they took you. How is little Setia?"

Lamarra stood while her brother rushed over and held her tight. He looked at the big policeman walking toward him. Lamarra introduced him to Lieutenant Ferris.

The professor asked Ferris for details. Ferris filled the professor in about the terrorist attack at the entrance to the Holland Tunnel. Special Agent Hopkins, after bringing sodas and candy bars to the kids, joined them.

Lamarra introduced her brother to the FBI Agent. Professor Darfuir let him know that he was the leading surgeon and scientist at Pearson Global Technologies.

Hopkins wondered if there was a connection because of the prominence of the corporation. He told Lieutenant Ferris he'd be back in a little after checking in with his New York office.

Lieutenant Ferris posted a police guard to keep the press away from Lamarra and Tiri. He found a secluded area where he could call his Watch Commander Captain Griff Pendergrass.

Time: 1930 hours. November 30, 2010 EST. Time: 0330 hours. London Time. December 1, 2010.

A C-130 gunship had left Nairobi Airport three hours before and was now entering the African country of Mali's airspace. The pilot was ex-RAF Major Reginald Townsend.

Pearson's Corporation had a Research and Development Institute in Nairobi and contacted Major Townsend who was there on vacation. Knowing that Lars Olsen needed to be relieved from all those hours in the air to Nairobi, Pearson was able to get Townsend onboard for the immediate flight back and offered him a raise and extra vacation time for his diligence.

Orion slept on his makeshift gurney while Lars and Claire were given sleeping berths made up of sleeping bags and rucksacks for pillows. Joe Coffey was asleep on top of two ammo crates with folded-up chutes as bedding.

His relief engineer, Arnie Barrow, saw a purple light coming from a large suitcase against the rear bulkhead of the plane. Barrow opened the case and inside found a secure satellite magna phone. He grabbed an aluminum rod from the case and opened it like a telescope, inserting it into a hole in the rear of control board. He clipped it on the unfolded dish and opened it.

Arnie reached into the top pocket in his flight suit and pulled out a special access card, inserting it into a slot next to a keypad. He punched in his access code and picked up the phone.

"Hello, Assistant Engineer Barrow speaking."

From the other end of the phone came, "Yes, Mr. Barrow. This is Miss

Cromwell, assistant to Dr. Pearson. May I speak with him?"

Barrow replied, "Oh, I'm sorry Miss Cromwell. He's with Captain Bingham back in Nairobi. I think they just departed Nairobi Airport about ten minutes ago."

Lanny asked if John Orion was with them.

Smiling, Arnie realized who she was. "Ah, you must be Lady Bee. Your man is sleeping right now. Do you think I should wake him?"

"Yes, Mr. Barrow, this is very important. Wake him."

Claire, hearing Lanny's name being spoken, jumped up from her slumber. "Mr. Barrow, I'll take that."

With that Arnie handed Claire the phone.

"What's up, sis? Johnny's out cold right now. Don't worry, everything came out all right."

"Hi sweetie. Oh thank God, I was getting worried. They just showed on Channel Four News that something was going on in Kenya and they would get back to the viewers as soon as more information was made available. But Claire, there was a terrorist attack by the Holland Tunnel today just about five thirty late afternoon."

Claire replied with concern, "Oh my God, what happened?"

Just as Lanny was about to explain, Orion and Lars both jumped up. Lanny informed Claire of the day's events from the area where the explosions occurred.

Claire's face showed she was spooked. She called over to Orion, "Johnny, here, speak to your girl. She's sounds like she needs to hear your voice."

Orion grabbed the phone. "Hey baby, I overheard everything you just told your little sister. The Skipper and the professor are on their way back."

"Oh my God, Johnny, it's so good to hear your voice!"

"Same here, baby. We'll be landing at the complex around 0700 hours tomorrow morning. All of us will have breakfast together then. I think we need some well-deserved sleep, anyway.

"You bet we do. I can't wait to see you!"

"I'm gonna alert the Skipper and the doc," continued Orion. "There's nothing we can do right now, Lanny. So get some sleep and I'll see you on the tarmac in the morning. Love you, girl."

"Love you too, sailor. Now you do the same."

With that Orion hung up and had Arnie call the C-5 Galaxy three hours behind them. He conferred with Malloy and they both decided to organize a strategy for when they were both on the ground.

Orion hung up as a painful memory consumed him. He began to recall the attack on the World Trade Center on September 11th and was now more pissed off than ever. The bastards once again attacked the city he was born in. Time: 0355 hours. London Time December 1, 2010. Time: 2100 hours. EST New York.

Back in New York, Special Agent Hopkins returned to the waiting room at St. Luke's Hospital to speak with Lieutenant James Ferris of the New York City Police Department. Holding a manila envelope in his left hand, he approached Ferris.

"Lieutenant, can I see you for a moment? I need to speak with you and also Professor Darfuir."

Both went with him to a secluded area just outside the waiting room. Near the entrance to the lobby, Hopkins spotted a waiting room with no one around. He motioned for them to have a seat there and handed Ferris a photograph of the exploded area of the entrance to the Holland Tunnel.

The picture showed Fashir running from the area while Lamarra tried to stand up.

Hopkins asked Professor Darfuir, "Do you have any idea who the man in this photo is, professor?"

Dr. Darfuir replied, "Never seen him before in my life."

Agent Hopkins told him, "Well, we've gone over the video tape just before the explosion, and if you look carefully, you'll see this man saved your sister, her friend, and the children. We're wondering why a terrorist would go all out to do this if he were involved. Our Agents went to the Mosque in Hoboken, only to find several offices with computer hook-ups, empty and barren. They took all computers and anything of significance with them. Whoever they are, they left in a real hurry. The Mosque doors were padlocked and a note on the floor read, "BE PREPARED TO DIE." No one from the Muslim community understands why the cleric just packed and left. Whoever he is, he's real good at what he does, because he had everybody fooled. Even your sister, Professor, thought this man was kind and thoughtful."

Hopkins handed over another photo of the area just before the explosion. "If you look at the face of the man in the truck that was ahead of the car and other trucks, you'll see he looks like he just stole a chicken from the hen house. Problem is, though, we found his body in a dumpster in the Bowery. He was shot with a 9mm automatic and it looks like an execution. Whoever this Abdullah Musheen is, he's so evil he'd even go to the lengths of killing innocent babies to carry out his plan."

Professor Darfuir looked carefully at the picture of Abdullah Musheen and registered it into his memory. This was the man who tried to kill his sister. Special Agent Hopkins explained that Musheen might have smuggled an atomic weapon of mass destruction into the city. They really don't know for sure, but if he did, they had to find him before he could set it off.

Time: 2140 hours. New York Time. November 30, 2010.
****

Time: 2200 hours. New York Time. November 30, 2010. STATE OF

163

EMERGENCY. United States Naval Base Norfolk, Virginia.

Inside the office of Admiral James Maguire a phone began to ring. On the other end was the Chief of Naval Operations, Fleet Admiral Mark Mancuso. He told Admiral James Maguire that the Sixth Fleet was on full alert and to implement the Operations Plan, RELEASE THE HOUNDS.

Maguire headed into the Operations center outside his office and told CDO Master Chief Collins to put out the alert. He instructed him to locate Vice Admiral Thomas Fischer and have him contact him immediately.

Time: 2220 hours. EST New York, November 30, 2010.

18 RELEASE THE HOUNDS

Time: 0655 hours. December 1, 2010, EST New York Time.

A C-130 Spooky gunship had just landed on a secret airship deep in the woods of East Hampton, New York. Out the rear of the plane walked John Orion, Lars Olsen and Claire Vanderkamp.

Lanny Cromwell approached them and Orion put his arms around her, kissing her with passion. Lanny went to Lars and kissed him on the cheek as he bent over so she could reach him. She grabbed her little adopted sister and hugged and kissed her, as well.

Lanny led them to an awaiting Cadillac SUV. Claire jumped in the front passenger side, because Lars would be very uncomfortable if he even tried to sit there. Orion told Claire that her papa was only two hours away from landing, as well. It seemed that Liam Faraday, who took over for the pilot Carl Bingham, was making good time across the Atlantic.

Orion looked at the driver's Daily News between him and Claire and asked if he could read it. The driver slipped it back, and Orion opened the pages to see the headlines. TERRORIST ATTACK TUNNEL. Orion studied the photo and couldn't believe who he saw in the picture.

He handed the paper to Lars. "Tell me, is that who I think it is?"

Lars brought the paper even closer to his face. "Holy shit, if that ain't the Wizard. What the hell is Benny doing there?"

Olsen immediately opened the paper to page three and continued reading. After about forty seconds he looked up at Orion. "Lieutenant, it says here the man in the photo running away had just saved the lives of women and children to the right side of the camera. We better keep this quiet until we get a chance to talk to the Skipper."

The Cadillac pulled up to the triage building and the entourage exited the vehicle. Both women excused themselves to use the ladies room while Lars and Orion headed for the building's cafeteria. As they entered, Orion saw his mother having breakfast at a table with Millie Stokes.

Rosalinda's face was suddenly filled with a look of joy as she saw her son enter the cafe. Orion happily walked over to his mother and leaned down to kiss her in her wheelchair.

"Hi Mama, what are you doing up so early?"

"I haven't seen you since Saturday and Lanny said it would be a good idea to surprise you."

Orion laughed. "Well, she was right, Mama, I've missed you too. That goes the same for you, Mama Millie."

Orion gave her a kiss hello and introduced Lars to both of them. Orion explained that he, Billy and Lars were the commissioned officers of their team. Lars also told them that after Billy's death and Malloy's punishment, they all decided to leave the team.

At that moment, Lanny and Claire entered the cafeteria. Orion told his mother and Millie they'd be right back after they ordered their breakfast.

As the group sat down with their food, a security guard came over to Claire and handed her a memo. Claire look at it with concern, folded it up and put it in her top left pocket. She told Orion that as soon as Captain Malloy landed, he had to call Vice Admiral Fischer. She also shared that the memo was marked as an Emergency, URGENT.

Orion told everybody to enjoy their meal, because it looked like it might be a very busy day.

Mama Rosa started telling stories of when Orion and Billy were growing up in Astoria Queens. Millicent Stokes added to the stories of the two inseparable boys. She recounted their wildest predicaments. Some of the stories made everyone laugh hysterically and others broke their hearts. All in all, it was obvious that Johnny and Billy were brothers forever.

After about forty minutes, Orion and Lanny told everyone to move to the main house so the weary travelers could shower and get ready for the C-5 Galaxy's arrival.

Time: 0725 hours. December 1, 2010. EST New York Time.

****

Time: 0810 hours. December 1st, 2010.

After a night of intense waiting during little Setia's operation, a doctor dressed in scrubs came out to talk with her mother, Tiri Palaat. Tiri had no insurance, but Professor Darfuir told them that the Corporation would pick up the bill.

The doctor introduced himself as Dr. David Chang, arterial and orthopedic surgeon of St. Luke's Hospital. He let her and the professor know that he had to remove several pieces of shrapnel from her left upper thigh and reconstruct an area of femoral artery that was badly injured. Even though she lost a lot of blood, they were able to save her in time.

Tiri cried tears of joy and hugged the doctor with all her might. In the midst of the happy commotion, Lieutenant Ferris woke up from the chair in the waiting room and joined them. Upon hearing the news, a smile of relief washed over his face. He shook the doctor's hand and let him know that he was told by his superiors that the city would pick up the tab.

Lamarra hugged her friend Tiri just as Professor Darfuir's cell phone began ringing in the pocket of his suit. On the other end was Claire Vanderkamp.

"Professor, this is Claire. We haven't heard from you this morning, so I decided to see if you were sick or something."

The professor relayed the horrible ordeal his sister and her friend had endured the day before.

Claire immediately began freaking out at the news and promised that her father would be told just as soon as he hit the tarmac. Sending him her love, she let him know that Captain Malloy would be in touch shortly.

Claire hung up and ran downstairs to let everyone know it was Professor Darfuir's sister and friends who were on the front page of the Daily News. She reported that the little girl survived her wounds and pulled through.

Inside the main living room, Orion's eyes began to turn purple as he got angry.

Time: 0830 hours. December 1, 2010. EST New York.
****

Time: 0902 hours. 32 minutes later New York Time.

The C-5 Galaxy owned by Pearson Global Technologies landed three minutes prior and taxied up to the tarmac for deboarding. The rear door of the Galaxy finally touched the tarmac's pavement. Stepping out first was David Banks, followed by Carl Bingham.

Claire Vanderkamp and Lanny Cromwell, now both dressed in business attire, walked from the waiting limousine to the back of the plane. Professor Pearson and Captain Malloy appeared. As they both stepped onto the tarmac, Claire handed a dossier to Captain Malloy.

"James, Vice Admiral Fischer's office faxed this memo over this morning at 0715 hours for you."

Malloy read the memo. "Thank you, Miss Vanderkamp. Now would you have everyone here assemble in my security office on the double, and if Orion gives you any guff, tell him I'll put my foot up his ass."

Claire and Lanny broke into laughter and she replied, "That I will, Captain."

"It's good to see you girls," added Malloy.

Lanny handed the professor his messages and said, "Professor, Dr. Darfuir is at St. Luke's Hospital with his sister Lamarra. You need to call him right away."

Claire handed Malloy the Daily News that Orion instructed her to give him. As Malloy climbed into the limo, he opened the paper to see someone had drawn a circle around a man glimpsing up at the camera. "What the hell, that's Benny."

He looked up and said to Lanny, "What's John got to say about all this?" Lanny replied, "He's just as much in the dark as you are, James. He just told us to hand you the paper."

Malloy told the driver to step on it and read the article as the limousine sped towards the security office. As he finished the article, he looked up and asked why Claire didn't get in the limo.

Lanny, with a smile, pointed over her shoulder to the limousine behind them. The professor and the Captain both said at the same time, "Oh." They could see Claire holding tightly to her man, Bobby Palladin.

As they came out from the other side of the woods, Malloy noticed green smoke all around the gate entrance to the complex.

"Oh shit, he's here now," observed Malloy.

The professor with a puzzled look on his face asked, "Who's here now, Jim?"

Malloy with a devilish smile replied, "You'll see for yourself." He told the driver to go to the main gate. When they pulled up, Malloy rolled down his window and asked the guard, "Pauly, what's going on?"

Pauly replied, "I don't know, sir. A cab from the city pulled up and this guy got out. As the cab left, this guy threw a bunch of ping pong balls to the ground, and all of this green smoke got all over the place. Don't worry sir, I stood and blocked the entrance. There's no way he could of gotten passed me."

Malloy with a shit-eating grin told him, "Good work, Pauly. Just keep an eye out for this guy, he may be trouble."

Malloy rolled up the window as a little bit of green smoke infiltrated the car. As the car reached the main building, the professor and Lanny wondered what he was laughing about. The car stopped at the back entrance to the building and Malloy jumped out and asked the driver for the keys. The Captain went to the back of the car and opened up the trunk.

"Wouldn't it have been easier to just ride in the front, Chief Kraemer? You haven't changed one fuckin' bit."

The former Chief Petty Officer of Malloy's unit climbed out of the trunk. Benny said to Malloy, "Well, how did you know it was me then, Skipper?" They both hugged like there was no tomorrow and everybody stared at them in amazement.

Michael Trudeaux yelled, "Well, if it ain't the wonderful Wizard of Ours." He opened the entrance door a little and yelled in, "Johnny, Bobby, Lars, look who's here! The Wizard has made another one of his grand entrances." Kyle, who arrived from Norfolk about twenty minutes before, was the first one out the door. He shouted over to Benny, "Worked just like you said it would, Chief."

Malloy said to Benny, "Should have known you are still teaching the kid that fuckin' magic crap."

Benny snidely replied, "It wasn't magic crap when I taught some of it to you, huh Skipper?"

Malloy responded, "Well, how do you think I knew you were in the trunk?" Malloy picked up the Daily News and pointed to the circled picture of Benny. "What kind of fuckin' magic is this, Chief Petty Officer Kraemer?"

Benny, smiling uneasily, replied, "Well, Skipper, you see . . ."

Malloy interrupted him. "You'll have plenty of time to explain yourself in about ten minutes. Right now, I've got to find out why Admiral Fischer needs to talk to me right away." He said to Claire, "Miss Vanderkamp, please lead these sorry-looking bunch of crybabies to my office in five minutes."

"Aye, Aye, Captain Malloy."

Malloy smiled at her and hustled upstairs to his security office. Maguiness, Thomas and Alvarez all collapsed on the couches in the waiting room. Everybody who just came back from Kenya was dying to take a nice hot shower.

Palladin, also dying for a shower, told them, "Don't worry, we'll be able to get out of these filthy threads in a little while. The captain would of let us do that already, but I think we're gonna be debriefed on something very vital."

In his office, Malloy finished pressing the buttons on his phone to Vice Admiral Fischer's office. "Hello Tommy, its Jim. I just received your memo. What's up?"

Admiral Fischer explained that Fleet Admiral Mark Mancuso had initiated OPERATION RELEASE THE HOUNDS to all special operations in the Sixth Fleet. Malloy knew this meant a lot of S.E.A.L.s and Force Recon Marines, in and out of the Navy Department, were able to conduct searches for al-Qaeda enemy personnel.

Admiral Fischer informed him that he and a contingent of Special Forces Operators were coming to New York. He asked Malloy for permission to land at their corporation's secret airfield. Malloy assured him there no problem and made out a flight plan for him and the tower on the complex.

Fischer told Malloy that they'll be leaving in twenty minutes and to start debriefing his men while he was on his way.

Malloy hung up and opened his door. "Everybody in here now, MOVE IT ON THE DOUBLE."

Maguiness asked Trudy, "Is he always like this?"

Trudeaux, putting his head down, replied, "Yeah, always. The prick never lets up, but all of us would follow him into Hell if he asked us."

Inside Malloy's office was a giant round table with sixteen chairs placed two feet apart from each other. Leaving his desk he ordered, "Park your asses down gentlemen. Orion and Olsen, you're my two officers. Orion, sit to my right. Olsen, you sit on my left. The rest of you just fuckin' sit."

Behind the table Malloy pulled up a sixty inch computer screen and called to Professor Pearson, "Jeffrey, we're ready for you now."

The professor entered the room with and Lanny and Claire holding folders of papers and photographs. Behind them Carl Livingston brought in a flash drive for the computer presentation.

Malloy informed them the professor would bring them all up to speed on the details of the last five days.

The professor pulled a remote control out of his white laboratory cloak and aimed it at the computer screen. A photograph of the Chorominium Meteorite appeared. The professor explained that this was the very first chunk of the amazing mineral that was discovered back in 2006. Since then, they were able to extract sixty tons of it altogether.

Professor Pearson said he believed it slammed into the earth via the asteroid that created Africa's Great Rift Valley millions of years ago. He went on to tell them that he and Dr. Darfuir had experimented with it by heating it, smashing it, exposing it to radioactivity, and other applications. It was ground breaking and nearly beyond the scope of their scientific knowledge.

Pearson told them the shields in all of the satellites of the corporation had this component, as they had discovered a way to heat the foreign mineral until it resembled liquid mercury. They could then combine additional heated minerals like titanium, carbon carbonite, tungsten, and other top secret elements to the chorominium. They quad-wove the finished substance into different objects.

The satellite shields had the strongest of the man-made substance. The team had also completed a scram jet with a fuselage wings and turbine engines made of the same indestructible element. They were only days away from testing it, along with the giant electromagnetic ramp to launch it. But the tragic events of John Orion's dilemma brought the top secret flight to a halt.

The professor went on to let them know the Orion's suit was constructed of the same material. Friday night, when Lanny Cromwell gave them their clothes, Malloy had the technicians measure his body size by his tailor-made Christian Dior tuxedo.

Malloy told all the warriors in the room that they needed to be mold-casted for their suits before showering after the debriefing. Everybody made sounds of disgust and Malloy told them to put their complaints in the suggestion box.

The professor looked at Lanny and Claire, who were to be fitted, too.

He said he'd explain later.

Orion smiled because he knew that the girls' beautifully endowed bodies would really be shown off.

The professor loaded the next photograph that showed the chorominium radiating a dark and eerie purple color when coming near enriched uranium 231 and 235. He explained that this shade of purple only reacted when the chorominium was electro-magnetically induced.

Everybody in the room looked immediately at Orion.

Orion nodded his head. "Yeah, yeah, yeah, yeah, I get it. The freak here should be able to find it. I guess I'm a volunteer then, huh, Skipper?"

Malloy replied, "That you are, Lieutenant. Professor, can we move onto the other slides before this crybaby starts to tantrum."

Everyone in the room, including Orion, cracked up.

Lanny put her hands on Orion's shoulders. "That's right, but if you think you're a freak, well, you're my damn freak, and nobody else's. Do you hear that, John Patrick Orion?"

Orion replied happily, "That I do, my Lady Bee."

The Captain jumped in. "Good, now shut up and listen, everybody, because we all know al-Qaeda means business. Vice Admiral Fischer will be arriving here with a contingent of operators just like yourselves. Only thing is, they're still under the Department of the Navy's thumb and you're not. Except you, Duffy. As far we're concerned, though, you are now our eyes and ears for our team."

Duffy replied to the Captain, "Sir, I still have until April, 2012 before my next reenlistment. I'd rather resign because of what they did to you. I want to be here with this team, no one else."

Malloy looked at him with a devilish smile. "You are, Kyle. Do you catch my drift?"

Duffy thought for a moment and replied, "Yes Skipper, I do know what you mean."

"Then quit being a little bitch and pay close attention, because your fuckin' boss is arriving here soon. I'm going to tell him that you're going up in one of our choppers because of your expertise in current Naval Operations." Malloy looked at Benny. "Okay, Chief Kraemer, somehow I think you know more of what is going on than us here regular people do."

Benny smiled and nodded, but his face became very serious. He relayed of all the circumstances that led up to the bombing of the entrance of the Holland Tunnel. He let them know of the two terrorist brothers, Omar and Mustaffa Khaldif, and how he was able to infiltrate into their organization and gain the confidence of other al-Qaeda operatives. He shared that he had never met the number one man because he was always too secretive.

He gave the group a couple minutes to digest this information, then told the Captain to get in touch with his old friend from the Mossad, Captain

Joshua Golon, and ask him to gain their confidence so as to lead them to their number one hard target.

Malloy instructed all of the men and women to report to the laboratory in the subterranean complex below the Citadel for their clearance processing (eye, palm print, and voice recognition identification) and then to proceed to body mold-casting for the creation of their special battle dress uniforms.

The whole crew, except for the professor, Malloy, Claire and Lanny, stayed behind. Malloy told the girls that as soon as the men were done being fitted, they'd be called.

Professor Pearson explained to Lanny and Claire why they were being fitted for the special battle suits. "Lanny, from what we see, you're the only one in the world that can get past that impenetrable force field should John need medical attention. I'm pretty sure Claire could too, but we can't take any chances. I've already read your dossier an you are an accomplished surgical nurse. On top of that, you will be now be going to flight school like your little sister here, and you will be able to fly everything from our smallest helicopter to our C-5 Galaxy Class, Cargo and Troop Transporter."

Lanny's face looked completely shocked, but willing. "Papa, you saved Johnny's life and put your whole livelihood on the line for me. From now on, I'm going to take every initiative given to me to make our corporation one that our world can be proud of."

She walked over to Claire and put her hands on her shoulders. "Besides, what are daughters for?"

The professor and Captain Malloy both smiled with approval. Malloy informed them that just to piss off the men, they were both now Lieutenant Commanders, meaning everyone had to follow any orders they gave.

Lanny and Claire look at each other and at the same time said. "Oh, we're gonna love this," said Claire.

All of them broke out into laughter.

The phone rang and Malloy answered. "Okay Carl, I'm sending the girls down now." He hung up and looked at them. "Well, do you need a special invitation? Get the hell out of here!"

Both girls clicked their high heels together and responded with, "Aye, Aye, Captain, sir." They saluted him, and he saluted back laughingly.

As they left the security office, Malloy looked through the teledex to find Captain Joshua Golon's phone number at the Israeli Defense Force. Pearson used the other phone to contact his partner, Dr. Kamal Darfuir.

Malloy began talking with his old friend in Israel at the same time Pearson began talking with Professor Darfuir.

On Malloy's line, Captain Golon said that for the past fourteen months they'd been trying to get their hands on a cleric leader who originated out of Yemen. He told him that his IDF agents had been picking up scattered bits and pieces of talk between someone in the United States and another who they believed to be Amal Baraash. Baraash was talking from a phone in Liberia, and whoever he was talking to came out of Hoboken, New Jersey.

Malloy confided in his friend all the details of the last five days. He let him know that Naval Intelligence had a Satellite photo of Baraash climbing into a conning tower of an old Russian submarine. Golon let Malloy know that the phone chatter they picked up from Baraash was on November 16th, eleven days before the assault on the Alladin.

They both realized that all the pieces were starting to fall into place. Malloy lets his old friend know that during the ambush in Kenya, two of his men from Germany were killed defending the uranium ore and that the team would be traveling to Dusseldorf, Germany for the funeral services. Malloy asked Captain Golon if he would meet him there with all of his Intelligence, so that they could devise a joint operation.

Golon said he'd make the necessary accommodations and call him on the third of December when he arrived in Germany.

They hung up. As Malloy turned to speak to the professor, Pearson handed his phone to Malloy with a look of worry. "It's Kamal on the phone. It was his sister Lamarra who Benjamin Kraemer saved at the Holland Tunnel." Malloy instantly took the phone from the professor. "Kamal, keep this to yourself, but the man who saved your sister was undercover for the Israeli Defense Force. Is anyone of high rank from the New York City Police Department with you?"

"Yes there's a very nice police Lieutenant who is keeping the press away."

Malloy asked him, "Now, how is your sister and everybody? Jeffrey told me you were going to meet her and a friend for a show."

Professor Darfuir said in a scared voice, "Captain, this man, Abdullah Musheen has killed a couple of people, along with trying to kill my sister, her friend Tiri, and the children with her. Tiri's daughter, Setia, almost lost her life if it weren't for the skilled surgeons here at St. Luke's."

Malloy cut him off. "Okay, Kamal, we're working on catching the son-of-a-bitch who did this, but is the Police Lieutenant available to talk right now?"

The professor told Malloy to hold on for a second and handed the phone to Lieutenant Ferris.

"Hello, Lieutenant Ferris speaking. Can I have your name?"

Malloy replied, "Yes, Lieutenant Ferris. This is Jim Malloy. I'm head of security for Pearson Global Technologies. Professor Darfuir is a friend and colleague of mine. I'm also an ex-Naval Intelligence Captain waiting for a conference with Vice Admiral Thomas Fischer. You can check with your department on this, but for right now put a real secure guard around them and whatever you do, don't release any information about their condition to anyone. I think if these bastards think they've killed everybody, so they'll slip up and make a mistake."

Ferris replied, "Captain Malloy, I'll inform my office, but have Admiral Fischer call Captain Pendergrass in Midtown as soon as possible."

"That I will, Lieutenant. Just tell my colleague we'll be on our way into the city as soon as we can."

Ferris reassured him and hung up.

Time: 1015 hours. EST New York.

The tune of "Popeye the Sailor Man" came over Orion's cellphone. Malloy told Orion to make sure everyone was dressed in time for the arrival of Vice Admiral Fischer. Everyone must be ready to leave at a moment's notice after his debriefing. He instructed Orion to let the team know.

19 SEARCH AND DESTROY

Time: 1145 hours. EST New York.

A C-130 Solo Hercules Aircraft had just landed on an airfield in East Hampton, New York. There to greet Vice Admiral Fischer and his men was his former S.E.A.L. Captain James Malloy.

Malloy waited at the edge of the tarmac with three armored Cadillac SUVs. They sped off to the security office where Orion and his men awaited them. They drove through the woods and across the giant parking lot to the main building and pulled up to see Orion in his special suit, minus the headgear and violet sunglasses.

Standing at attention in formation was Orion's team. They were all in green battle fatigues (BDUs) with their jump boots polished like mirrors. Even though they were no longer military personnel, they still showed their respect for the uniform.

When Admiral Fischer exited the vehicle, he was very impressed. "Okay men, at ease." He said to his second in command, Lieutenant Commander Donald Tremain, "Commander, acquaint yourself with Malloy's team while we set up a preliminary briefing upstairs in his office."

Time: 1200 hours. EST New York.

Meanwhile, two United Parcel Service tractor trailers were headed into Manhattan through the Lincoln Tunnel. Aboard were devices to make the plutonium 235 reach critical mass and explode a 100 kilo-ton charge in each. The trucks traveled to an area near 8th Avenue and West 57th Street where plutonium and HMX high explosive would be added to the mix.

The day before, five al-Qaeda operatives set many tiny explosives underground to blow up water mains near the United Nation's building, so the police would have no choice but to divert traffic closer to where the General Assembly was to meet that day at 4 o'clock EST. The water main charges were set up to blow at exactly 3:25 EST. This was to create chaos and put the Transportation Authority into a real mess right before rush hour. They would not know the water main was sabotaged deliberately.

The other United Parcel Service truck would be headed into the Theater District and was set to explode at exactly 1700 hours. This was to be the same time the Emir of Kuwait was addressing the General Assembly.

Abdullah Musheen wanted to see a hundred times more casualties than that of the World Trade Center, close to ten years before. Waiting close by were fanatical al-Qaeda suicide operatives armed with heavy machine guns and RPG 7's to create even more chaos right in front of Times Square. There were forty of them because Abdullah dubbed them his forty thieves, and he was Ali Baba. Except this time, the coward Ali Baba would be in the air in a flight back to Yemen. The trucks have just arrived on 57th Street from 8th Avenue.

Time: 1235 hours. EST New York.

Orion and his men, after acquainting themselves with Tremain's men, were now heading up to Malloy's Security Office for the debriefing. More chairs had been set up to accommodate the whole contingent's fighting force. They entered the office and Malloy told Orion that the seating arrangement would stay the same. He had Lieutenant Commander Tremain sit across from Orion and Lars Olsen to move over one spot.

Malloy asked Benny Kraemer to fill everybody in the room of his undercover operation in Hoboken. Benny got right to the point and let them know how he was able to infiltrate as a well-known al-Qaeda Operative.

After Benny finished, Vice Admiral Fischer let them know that after they received the name of Abdullah Musheen, Malloy had contacted Captain Joshua Golon for a dossier on this individual.

Malloy informed everybody that he learned Musheen was one of the top Commanders under Osama Bin Laden. He also let them know that Musheen's nephew, Amal Haafaal Baraash, was known to be part of whatever sinister plot they hatched.

Orion instantly clenched his teeth and quickly put on a pair of dark sunglasses. Everyone in the room wondered why, but Malloy drew their attention back to himself by saying, "Gentlemen, listen up here. Make no mistake about it. This man Baraash had the Central Intelligence Agency completely duped because he had given them information of the whereabouts of terror cells in Afghanistan and our forces were able to eliminate them. This was only a ruse. My men were lured into a trap and we were lucky that all but one of us escaped."

Orion, still not knowing the capability of his strength, pounded his fist on the table, and it crushed the top. The whole room couldn't believe what they just witnessed. Orion was wearing gloves and told everyone the gloves had steel liners in them. He apologized to Malloy, who shot Orion a look of complete understanding.

Malloy had Claire and Lanny hand out pictures of Baraash and the two Khaldif brothers. With the photographs were dossiers filled with Israeli Intelligence. Malloy let the whole operational team know that they would search the entire city by sea, air and land. However, he lied to Admiral Fischer's men and told them his corporation's weapons department had a device to locate weapon grade plutonium from the air. Malloy, though, was not completely lying, because Orion was that weapon.

He asked to use First Class Petty Officer Duffy in his search on one of the corporation's attack helicopters.

Admiral Fischer replied that there was no problem with that.

Malloy assigned air and ground units to all of the men and asked Admiral Fischer to coordinate his operation scenario with Captain Griff Pendergrass of the New York City Police Department.

Admiral Fischer said he'd contact Vice Admiral William Gortney to let Mayor Mark Blundenberg of New York advise his coalition and Police Commissioner Roy Kiley.

Fischer let the operations team know the C-130 Solo aircraft would coordinate the theater of operations from the air.

They set all of their transporter units of communication to the flight officer of the C-130 Solo Hercules so as to remain in contact with Orion's strike team helicopter. Malloy gave Claire the radio frequencies and visual coordinates. With the coordinates, Claire could give instructions to the Rigel One satellite. From there, the satellite would send all transmissions, audio and visual, back to the security office of Captain Malloy and also to the C-130 Solo. The same thing would coincide with the Bellatrix One satellite, as a backup measure.

Fischer and Malloy told their team leaders to expedite to Hangar Four and load provisions into two ground mobility vehicles (GMVs) for transport on the excursion to New York City. The GMVs would be loaded on a CH-47 Chinook jet engine helicopter.

The Chinook and the corporation's Blackhawk helicopter would fly to a secluded area of LaGuardia Airport. There they would merge with the New York City Police Department. They would conduct all of the search grids given by all their commanders. As soon as they received confirmation from Vice Admiral Fortney, they would proceed immediately.

As they were just about loaded at the hangar, Tremain asked Orion why he was wearing the black suit.

Orion explained it was an experimental battle dress uniform. The irony in it all was that the suit really WAS the ultimate in battle dress uniforms. Orion just wished his team's suits were already made. Carl Livingston told him they still needed twelve hours to complete. Still, Orion knew his men were the best ever to come out of Captain's Malloy training. None the less,

Orion kept thinking of Afghanistan.

Time: 1300 hours. December 1, 2010 EST.

Prompted by the Pentagon in Washington DC, the computer screen in Malloy's office came to life. On the screen was Vice-Admiral William E. Gortney, Assistant to the Chairman of Joint Chiefs of Staff, Fleet Admiral Mike Mullens. Admiral Gortney told Admiral Fischer that he'd been given the green light to expedite his mission. He explained that they would coordinate their efforts with Captain Griff Pendergrass of the New York City Police Department. Pendergrass and his units would be in constant contact with One Police Plaza's communication headquarters. There, Police Commissioner Roy Kiley would be in touch with all search units.

This was a nightmare in the making for Kiley because of the gridlock from the United Nations General Assembly. The first speaker to the Assembly began his speech at exactly 1600 hours EST. He was the diplomatic representative of the nation of Saudi Arabia, there to extend his country's cooperation with the global fight on terrorism.

At 1630 hours EST, the representative of the nation of United Arab Emirates would join in with a similar speech to show their county's support.

At 1700 hours EST, the Emir of Kuwait would personally thank the coalition forces that saved his country from the tyranny of Sadaam Hussein back in 1991. He was there also to reach out to all of the oil-producing countries of the World, asking them to help out in the crisis in the World's stock markets. Mayor Mark Blundenberg had told his police chiefs to make the General Assembly aware of the possible threat, but even the best police department in the world could be caught off guard by someone as evil as Abdullah Musheen. Time: 1310 hours. EST New York.

Time: 1325 hours.

Lifting off from the secret airfield in East Hampton, an entourage of the world's most dangerous and elite warriors headed to the same city that was attacked by terrorists ten years prior.

Vice-Admiral Fischer told the pilot of the C-130 Solo Hercules to take off and fly 35,000 feet above New York City in exactly forty five minutes. Captain Pendergrass of the New York City Police Department had already instructed Lieutenant James Ferris to move Professor Darfuir, his sister, and her friend Tiri to an undisclosed area of the city. From there, Dr. Darfuir would be taken to LaGuardia airport.

Professor Pearson, just before he left, gave Lanny and Claire specific instructions on what was to be done while they were in the city. He told them that Professor Darfuir would be put on one of the Corporation's Learjet's and flown back to the complex so he could monitor the operations and take care of essential things left for him and Carl Livingston to undertake.

After thirty minutes in the air, the control tower at LaGuardia gave permission for the two helicopters to land. From the east end of the airport, the Chinook and Blackhawk landed close to a hangar where a New York City Police Department police cruiser and a black Crown Victoria were waiting. Lieutenant Ferris exited the Crown Victoria with Professor Darfuir and walked over to Professor Pearson.

Pearson handed Dr. Darfuir a manila envelope and whispered in his ear for a minute. Dr. Darfuir climbed into the back of the police cruiser and was taken to an awaiting Learjet on the western runaway for smaller aircraft.

When the rear vertical door of the Chinook was finally lowered, two armored GMVs (Ground Mobility Vehicles) exited the chopper. Lieutenant Ferris introduced himself to Admiral Fischer and Captain Malloy. He told them to follow him in his Crown Victoria to his ground base of operations in Midtown.

He first handed Admiral Fischer the frequency codes for their air and ground forces. Malloy gave one copy to Lars who would be flying the Blackhawk. He gave the other to Marine Captain Earl Reardon, flying the Chinook with Lieutenant Mike Shasta. He told Admiral Fischer to call him as soon as he reached Captain Pendergrass' base of operation.

Malloy got into the copilot's side of the Blackhawk and they headed to the refueling area of the airport.

Meanwhile, throughout the city Commissioner Kiley's forces were already on the hunt with triple the amount of men, dogs and Geiger counters. Throughout the subways and depots, they combed every inch of New York City.

The Coast Guard and Harbor Patrols stopped every boat coming into the city. All available resources were being used and all entrances into the city were being checked thoroughly since the terror alert had heightened.

In a truck freight depot on West 57th Street, two unsuspecting United Parcel Service trucks waited their signal to leave the garage. Over both of the trailers on the trucks were giant tarps lined with lead fibers that shielded the radioactive signature. Once the trucks were set out to deploy, the tarps would be cut loose to cover the atomic weapons inside.

The depot was owned by a Yemenis shipping magnate. The first truck was to leave the depot at 1510 hours and head toward Times Square. The second was to leave at 1550 hours and head toward First Avenue, near the United Nations' building. The bomb in the truck going to Times Square would be armed at 1640 hours and detonate ten minutes after that. This would be ten minutes before the Emir of Kuwait made his speech in front of the General Assembly.

From there the blast radius should reach the second bomb and set it off. Abdullah Musheen made sure the second one, close to the United Nations' building, would be armed at 1645 hours to ensure at least one of the bombs did his evil bidding. The second bomb would be set off at exactly 1700 hours just as the Emir of Kuwait started delivering his speech.

Time: 1410 hours. EST New York.

Captain Malloy's cell phone vibrated in the left shirt pocket of his BDUs. On the other end was Vice Admiral Fischer telling Malloy to deploy and get airborne. Malloy signaled Lars from where he stood by circling his index finger above his head. The blades on the Blackhawk began to power up incrementally faster.

Malloy got back into the co-pilot's side of the chopper and activated the frequency to the CH-47 Chinook to give Captain Reardon his coordinate's grid. After he finished, he told Orion that if even the slightest bit of detection came to him, to let them know immediately.

Orion told Malloy that hospitals and nuclear power plants would also release a signature to him.

Malloy let Orion know the New York City Police Department was already covering that scenario and would be covering a grid starting from Tenth Avenue by the West Side Highway until they reached Midtown. The CH-47 Chinook would be covering the grid that started at the Queensbourgh Bridge to Midtown, also.

Other police and FBI choppers would be covering the outskirts and small deserted project areas that were abandoned. The Coast Guard would be covering the waterways and bridges.

Malloy reminded them that they would be dealing with that snake Baraash, once again.

Time: 1445 hours. EST New York.
****

Time: 1510 hours. EST New York.

A United Parcel Service Trailer truck left a trucking depot on West 57th Street and headed towards Times Square. Inside with the deadly cargo were Amal Baraash and 27 other heavily armed suicide terrorists. Baraash wanted his name to forever be known as the one who carried out the attack against the West.

Already driving close in the proximity of the Theater District were two Ford Explorers with six heavily armed suicide terrorists in each. So as not to draw attention, many were dressed as women, their beards and moustaches completely shaven. Plus, they wore wigs and make up.

They made sure they stayed away from each other's SUV until the tractor trailer appeared in the square. Abdullah Musheen told Baraash that he would personally tell Osama Bin Laden it was he who gave his life for the people of Islam.

As all this transpired, Abdullah Musheen was just about to land in Yemen.

At 1510 hours all of Manhattan was a busy and bustling metropolis.

Street vendors and pitchmen busily endeavored to unload their wares to the passing crowds. New York City businessmen took their afternoon breaks in coffee joints and taverns. The subways and railway lines prepared for an afternoon rush trying to get home to the suburbs and the calm of their daily lives.

In front of the United Nations' building, limousines with diplomatic flags pulled up for the General Assembly meeting with dignitaries from all over the world. This day, the President of the United States decided to make an unannounced visit and his office called ahead to let them know. Air Force One would be landing at JFK International Airport at 1600 hours. EST New York Time.

Police Commissioner Roy Kiley was not happy one bit. He tried to let the President's Press Secretary know that there was a possible threat of a WMD in the city. The President responded that if there was definite proof, he'd automatically turn the plane around and head back to Washington DC. Since there was no definite proof, he would not let terrorists dictate where and when he went.

The head of the Department of Transportation told Commissioner Kiley that there had just been a report of a very bad water main leak near Second Avenue around the block from the United Nations' building. Roy Kiley in his office at One Police Plaza looked up at his ceiling. "WHY ME, GOT ANYTHING ELSE TO THROW MY WAY?" He told his Transportation Secretary to divert traffic around the break, even though it was closer to the United Nations building, and not to let any traffic interfere with the President's arrival. Just at that moment, Mayor Mark Blundenberg entered into his office.

Time: 1530 hours. EST New York.
****

Time: 1550 hours. EST New York.

The second United Parcel Service tractor trailer left the depot at West 57th Street and headed across town towards the United Nations building. At the same time, Mayor Mark Blundenberg conferenced with his Police Commissioner and two of his Police Chiefs. He asked them if every possible precaution had been taken for the surprise visit from the President.

Police Chief Michael Chang asked Commissioner Kiley, "Roy, what's this I hear about a para-military team from Island? Are they law enforcement? I hope they are, because we don't need a bunch of trigger-happy mercenaries shooting up our city."

Roy Kiley smashed his left first to this desk and angrily replied, "Listen Chief Chang, if you think I'm not looking out for the welfare of this city I love, you come to me first and say so. This job is stressful enough without having my chiefs turn on me."

The other police chief from Manhattan South cut in and fired back, "Oh sure, Roy. All the pressure is on you. You didn't have the Governor call your office and chew you out asking if you're able to run your precincts. I'm under enough pressure myself from the bombing at the Holland Tunnel."

That's when Mayor Blundenberg intervened. "Casey, I told the Governor that I run the city, not him. We shouldn't be trying to bite each other's heads off. Chief Dunton, Vice Admiral Gortney called me himself to ask to have this ex-S.E.A.L. Captain's men scout the city for a nuclear threat."

Chief Casey Dunton held out his hand to Kiley, who grabbed it to reiterated his confidence in him.

Commissioner Kiley said, "C'mon guys, let's head down to Operations. We have Navy S.E.A.L.s in the city. Something is definitely up."

All the officials left Kiley's office with distraught faces. They headed for the tactical room on the ground floor of One Police Plaza.

Time 1620 hours. EST New York.
****

Time: 1630 hours. EST New York.

People heading for the entrance to the subways looked up and saw a Blackhawk helicopter flying above them. Bewildered faces wondered at the military presence this time of day.

Flying above Radio City Music Hall, Malloy asked Orion, "Nothing still, John?"

Orion shook his head. "No, Skipper. I have a funny feeling that scumbag is not far off. Just have Lars keep to the grid. Snakes always pop their heads out of the hole when it gets hot."

The CH-47 Chinook flew over the Avenue of The Americas and spotted a massive backup of traffic, pretty close to a standstill. Captain Reardon, the pilot, told his co-pilot Lieutenant Mike Shasta to contact Lieutenant Commander Tremain on the ground. Reardon wanted to know if anybody had located anything out of the ordinary.

Civilians were puzzled that such a big helicopter was patrolling the skies so close to the United Nations building.

Lieutenant Shasta, having just broken communications with Commander Tremain, told Reardon that the commander said nothing as of yet and to stay to the grid.

Captain Reardon's face showed frustration and anxiety. Being the Marine he was, he pushed on. On the other side of the grid, a United Parcel Service tractor trailer turned from Sixth Avenue and headed towards Times Square.

Time: 1637 hours. EST New York.
****

Time: 1640 hours. EST New York.

A United Parcel Service tractor trailer stopped right across the giant screen atop the Triangular Island at the center of Times Square. The driver got out and began running down the street. A police officer, seeing this, gave chase while calling it in.

The back door of the truck opened and men with machine guns and rocket-propelled grenades jumped out of the back of the truck. Two Ford Explorers containing heavily armed terrorists pulled up adjacent from each side of the Square. Some of them, dressed as women, instantly fired on the crowd.

Amal Baraash, having just armed and set the timer for ten minutes, appeared at the back of the truck's door with a megaphone. "GOOD PEOPLE OF NEW YORK, WE'RE HERE TO SEE WHAT BROWN CAN DO FOR YOU". With an evil laugh he fired his AK-47 towards people fleeing in horror.

The police officer who just gave chase came back around the corner with the driver of the truck in handcuffs. As he realized what was going on, two cowardly terrorists shot him on the spot.

Meanwhile, in the Midtown base of police operations the main switchboard to the public lit up like the Fourth of July. The calls streamed in reporting men with machine guns killing people left and right in the streets. Captain Pendergrass yelled across the squad room, "Rhodes, get ahold of Ferris and tell him it's Times Square. Fleming, Cochran, and Barnett, grab the M-4's; this sounds like the big one. Notify SWAT immediately."

Captain Pendergrass had the shakes from the amount of adrenalin coursing through his body and fumbled with his tactical vest and body armor as he headed out the precinct's door.

Word had now reached One Police Plaza and a full blown dragnet aimed for the heart of the city. Malloy, hearing the alert from ground communications, let Orion and the team know of the assault in Times Square.

Orion, overhearing the many different calls for help from different parts of the city, stood up and began hovering above the floor of the Blackhawk. He glowed that dark eerie purple all over his body.

Two police-assault helicopters arrived just before the Blackhawk veered and turned onto 7th Avenue. They immediately started to fire back at the terrorists scattered about the whole square.

Benny was now in a state of shock as he looked at Orion defying gravity. With his eyes popping out of his head, he said to his old friend, "This trick I do not know. When you find time, Jonathan, you must teach this to me."

Orion laughed. "You got it, buddy, only if I can still remember it."

They saw in the foreground from the air that it looked like the police were starting to pin them down. They soon discovered that the terrorist were dressed as women and had taken positions from the outer four corners of the Square. They simultaneously fired their RPG-7s and the grenades hit both choppers. The explosion sent the choppers into the side of the Cavalcades, raining debris and fire down amongst the frightened people.

Orion, seeing this, had his body illuminated with the glow of purple that began to even envelop the Blackhawk itself.

As the Blackhawk arrived, so did the SWAT and Emergency Services. Amal Baraash, having just pulled the lead tarp off the bomb, jumped into a swivel chair mounted with a M-2 50 caliber machine gun.

Everyone in the Blackhawk wondered why the glow was so powerful now. People from the streets, including the arriving SWAT team, were mesmerized by a man floating to the ground in a smooth glide.

Immediately the al-Qaeda terrorists turned their attention from the landing Blackhawk to Orion. Twenty of them opened fire with AK-47s and SKSs, aiming right at Orion as his feet hit the ground.

Orion went into a trance and grabbed the middle of the Lincoln Town car in front of him, tumbling it end over end like a rotisserie chicken in a washing machine. It slammed into some of them and crushed into the building behind them. The rest sailed fifteen feet in the air, knocked unconscious.

Orion hovered six feet in the air and swooped in on Baraash who was firing at the Blackhawk and Police Tactical Truck. As soon as Orion approached the bastard, a 50 caliber was turned on him. Orion slowly hovered in while the force field repelled the projectiles like rice.

Seeing now who was in front of him, Orion backhanded Baraash, knocking him out cold and breaking his jaw.

SWAT and the rest of the police quickly subdued the remainder of the terrorists, as Orion's fire team jumped into the back of the truck.

Orion looked up at Benny because he was the one trained as an EOD (Explosive Ordinance Disposal) technician in what they call SPECIALS. Chief Kraemer knew the rest of the team went to China Lake for EOD training. He was the only one who knew of Nuclear Devices Armed for Critical Mass. The timer on the device had just read one minute and fifty eight seconds and counting. The Wizard pulled out his para-tool and quickly opened the containment area that joined the HMX high explosive to the chamber of plutonium that had been activated for critical mass.

Right at that moment, Malloy yelled to Orion, "Lieutenant, another UPS truck has just been abandoned by First Avenue right by the United Nations building."

Orion slapped Benny on the shoulder. "Benny Boy, what do ya think?" Benny, pulling a small canister of CO-2 from his pocket, replied, "Piece of cake, Johnny. Do what you gotta do. I'll handle this from here. God be with you." With that, Orion grabbed Baraash by his throat and floated with him out of the back of the truck. Another police helicopter had just landed with its blades starting to slow when Orion swooped down with Baraash. "Sorry, Buddy, but I got no time to explain. I need to borrow this for a second."

The pilot, frozen with fear, just put out his palm to silently say, "She's all yours".

As Baraash started coming around, Orion, with little effort, tapped him unconscious again and lifted off as the people around the Square start screaming with cheers. Little to anyone's knowledge, television cameras caught the whole unbelievable rescue of Orion and his team with the New York City Police Department. But It still wasn't over. Orion, applying full power to the engine of the Police chopper, landed amongst police and secret service men with their weapons drawn.

He opened the door of the chopper and hovered toward the back of the United Parcel Service truck. The irony was that the President's limo was right there as Orion landed holding Baraash by his throat. "Keep the President back and get him out of here. I have to try and disarm the nuclear bomb that's inside of this truck."

With that, Orion turned around in midair and ripped the door right off the truck and threw it to the ground.

Baraash again began to wake up only because Orion was sending particle charges to his adrenal glands. Baraash came to and found he was floating in midair with a man in a funny looking suit wearing a partial hood covering and sporting strange purple-colored sunglasses. He screamed out in terror, "By Allah, who the Hell are you?"

Orion growled, "Oh, you know who I am and Allah can't save your ass, Baraash." Orion threw him in front of the bomb that was set to go off in three minutes and forty seconds. "Now fuckin' disarm it or I'll torture you so bad that you'll wish you were dead."

Baraash slurred through his broken jaw, "Go ahead, I don't care, because, you see, I'll be killing all of you INFIDELS along with me."

Orion shook his head gave the terrorist another slight tap, and once more he fell unconscious. Orion grabbed Baraash and the bomb and swooped back towards the chopper. He ripped off the plate where the wires were connected between the ordinance of HMX, the mercury switch, and the plutonium that had already started to fuse.

Listening to the super nano probes with his brain, he realized he could freeze the mercury switch by concentrating while he touched it.

The President, in the meantime, had told his bodyguards to leave him alone and just stared in amazement at what was going in front of him.

Orion was able to break the circuit to the plutonium but he couldn't release his finger without still exploding the HMX. He then separated the centrifuged Aluminum casing of plutonium from the device and threw it to the floor of the street. Orion yelled over to the President, "Mr. President, that's the dangerous stuff, but you all will be alright now, so go on back to your job and keep our country safe. I now have to get rid of two pieces of shit our country can do without."

With that, Orion closed the door of the chopper and lifted off heading towards the water with his finger still between the switch and plastic explosive. They were in his left hand as he held the controller stick, while his right hand steadily moved the siklet control to maneuver towards the river. He stepped on the tail rotor pedal and the chopper picked up speed instantly.

Orion gradually pulled up on the controller lever in his left hand. Concentrating not to let go of the switch and HMX ordinance while handling the controller, Orion finally reached the river. As he was about three thousand yards out and four hundred feet above the water, Amal Baraash woke up once more behind Orion in the chopper.

Carefully concealing that he was awake, he contemplated the situation at hand and noticed the plastic explosive in Orion's left hand along with the controls that lifted the helicopter. He also saw the timer next to the mercury switch that read one minute, nineteen seconds and counting. Baraash grabbed hold of Orion's head cover and ripped it off. "I need to see the man who I will now kill for Allah."

As Orion turned to look him straight in the eyes, Baraash's face became white as a ghost. "You! How can this be? I killed you and your men back in the mountains of Afghanistan."

Orion's eyes burned with the eerie purple glow and he roared back, "Allah decided to resurrect us to get you."

Amal pulled a two edged dagger from his coat and tried to stab Orion, screaming, "ALLAH AKHBAR." Orion dropped both controls and the chopper immediately went into a deadly spin headed for the surface of the water. As the chopper tumbled, he lost control of the explosive as his back smashed out the passenger side of the chopper.

As Orion free fell from the aircraft, the timer inside with the now wide awake Baraash counted down 8, 7, 6, 5, 4, 3, 2, 1 . . . KABOOOOOOOM.

People watching from all over the waterfront flinched from the size of the explosion. Some felt the shockwave.

Out of nowhere, the Blackhawk appeared and began to search and pray that Orion was still alive. After two minutes, Orion's comrades donned faces glum with despair.

Bobby Palladin's eyes begin to show tears, when all of a sudden Orion floated in the side door of the Blackhawk. Soaking wet he laughed, "Do you think they'll think I bought the farm?"

Everybody cheered and laughed. Bobby and Trudy were closest to him and hugged him first, but Orion held up his hand to pause them. He suddenly started to shake and vibrate like a golden Retriever, and whole entire chopper is filled with spraying water.

Everybody started bitching and complaining when Orion said, "What the fuck's the matter with you? You're fuckin' S.E.A.L.S., ain't ya? You're supposed to get wet."

Orion noticed a face of concern coming from the Captain. Looking straight into the Captain's eyes he said, "Skipper, I swear I didn't kill him. I had no choice; he came at me with a knife."

Malloy, now knowing that Orion was telling the truth, replied, "That's all right, Lieutenant. He might have given us the whereabouts of the big one, but somehow I doubt it, anyway."

Malloy faced all of his men. "Don't you fuckin' let this get to your head, men, but congratulations are in order."

Lars Olsen piloting the Blackhawk yelled back to team, "Take it any way you can, guys, because that'll be probably be the only time you'll hear it from the Skipper. He had to try to bring up a lot of spit to get that out of him."

Benny yelled out, "Here, Here, Lieutenant."

Malloy faced forward. "FUCK ALL OF YOU."

The jubilant warriors broke out in hysterical laughter. Malloy told Olsen to head right to LaGuardia. The Corporation's Gulfstream Lear Jet was there waiting for them to take off immediately. He ordered Orion to lay down on one of the litters and put a blanket over his head, just in case security cameras were watching.

Lars contacted LaGuardia's tower to let them know they were about to enter their Airspace. LaGuardia's tower acknowledged and relayed a message from Vice Admiral Fischer that the CH47 Chinook was now leaving the heliport by FDR Drive and would rendezvous with them in twenty five minutes.

Malloy told the tower to let Admiral Fischer know they had to leave in a hurry and to relay the message when he arrived. Malloy instructed Lars to re-fuel the Blackhawk and have Benny co-pilot back to the airfield in East Hampton. He also told them not to say anything to the Admiral except that he would explain everything to him and only him when they brought the Chinook back to base.

As the Chopper touched down on the tarmac at LaGuardia, Orion told Malloy there was something he had to do with no questions asked when they landed in East Hampton. He explained he was going to take a little trip, but that he'd be right back in a couple of hours. A silence spread over the whole Chopper as it landed, as Orion's fire team kept it to themselves. But they knew exactly where he was going.

Time: 1830 hours. East New York.

****

Time: 1845 hours. East New York.

A Gulfsteam Lear Jet had just taken off from LaGuardia airport in New York City while a CH-47 Jet Engine Chinook landed with Vice Admiral on board. The Admiral, accompanied by his second in command, approached Lars Olsen and Benny Kraemer outside the Blackhawk. Lars told the Admiral that Captain Malloy left orders for him and the Lieutenant Commander to ride with them back to East Hampton.

Admiral Fisher looked at them and said while they were standing at attention, "You sure there's nothing else you're supposed to tell me there, Lieutenant Olsen? Both of you look like a cat that just swallowed the canary." Benny replied, "No, sir, the Skipper said he'll talk with you as soon as we land at the base."

With an aggravated look, Admiral Fischer responded, "Well, let's get a move on. My superiors are going to be up my ass before you know it."

Lars and Benny tried hard to keep a straight face. "AYE, AYE, SIR." They saluted him and he returned it with a smile. They all piled into the Blackhawk and Admiral Fischer instructed Benny to tell Reardon to follow in their wake. Both choppers began lift off and headed east.

Time: 1900 hours. East New York.

20 STRIKE UP THE COLORS

Time: 1930 hours. East New York.

Having just landed at the secret airfield in East Hampton, Pilot Carl Bingham announced to Orion, Palladin, Trudeaux, and Duffy they could depart the aircraft.

Their flight attendant, Valerie Queen, had been flirting with Michael Trudeaux the entire flight. She handed him her phone number and let him know she was working the flight that would take them to their destination tomorrow — Dusseldorf, Germany.

Trudeaux gave Valerie a quick kiss before departing the plane, but commented, "Valerie, I know this sounds a little stupid, but this jet will never make it on a non-stop flight to Germany."

Looking surprised she told him, "Oh, I'm sorry. That's right, you don't know. We have a much bigger jet in Hangar Three that you probably haven't seen yet. Miss Vanderkamp will be piloting us there. Captain Malloy, I'm sure, will inform you when it's time for wheels up."

As they headed across to the waiting Cadillac SUV, they saw both Lanny and Claire greeting them with happy faces.

Bobby commented to Trudy, "That strawberry blond is hotter than the engines on an F-18 Hornet. Hope you can handle her, Mikey."

Trudeaux blushed. "Don't worry about me, you two pussy-whipped assholes."

Orion laughed as he slapped Trudy on the back, "We'll give you a week before you're kissing that one's ass, too."

Spotting the men from 20 feet away, Lanny and Claire rushed in to their waiting arms.

Lanny searched Orion's eyes. "Johnny, I was so worried when we saw the police helicopter go down. It was an agony until our satellite picked you up flying to the Company's Blackhawk."

Orion stopped with a surprised look. "What? You saw the whole thing?" Lanny instantly grabbed his chin with her right hand. "Yes, baby, the whole thing. I'm so proud of all of you. The professor explained a lot to me and Claire. Don't worry, Johnny. Only the people on the base know of your amazing abilities."

She smiled and whispered in his ear, "Let's put them to the good use in the bedroom tonight."

Orion blushed. "Lanny, be careful what you say. I don't need guys riding me about 'you know what,' okay?"

Lanny, not thinking, replied, "Oh c'mon, Johnny, they must know how big you are. I'm sure all of you used the same shower in your barracks."

Orion immediately looked up to the sky and slapped his forehead. Everybody burst out in hysterical pandemonium.

Lanny, just realizing her error, put her hand over her mouth and spoke through her fingers, "I'm sorry, baby! Oops."

Orion grabbed and squeezed her tight and began laughing.

"This is why I love you so much, Dopey."

"Who you calling Dopey, Dopey."

Claire shouted, "Yo Johnny, sis, give it a break, will yah? It's been a rough day."

They all laughed and climbed into the Cadillac SUV which sped off to the main house on the complex.

Poor Kyle was thinking he needed some well-deserved sleep.

Orion instructed the driver to take him to his Roadrunner by the entrance of the gate. Bobby, knowing what he was up to, said, "Yo brother, it's almost eight o'clock. They won't let you in now, and besides, we're all going to go with you in the morning, anyway."

Lanny looked at Bobby and he put his index finger to his lips for a moment of silence. She glimpsed Orion's eyes beginning to show tears and pushed over closer to him in the seat, hugging him even tighter. Thank God Professor Pearson had made arrangements for the whole team to have privacy in the three guest houses for the night.

Meanwhile, Carl Bingham and Captain Malloy were taxiing the Lear Jet towards Hangar Four. As they approached the hangar, they noticed Professor Pearson inside the front of the entrance with a waiting Land Rover ATV. Bingham brought the Lear Jet to a full stop inside Hangar Three. The maintenance crew immediately went to work securing it.

Malloy and Bingham got in to the Land Rover and the driver headed for Hangar Four. As they approached the hangar, Professor Pearson pressed a code into his laptop and a roll-up door made up of titanium, carbon carbonite, tungsten, and trace amount of the chorominium began to open as they arrived. Malloy asked Bingham, "Carl, are you positively sure she's ready to pilot this baby?"

"I trained her myself in the simulator and she flies rings around me."

He looked at Professor Pearson. "You should be a proud dad, Jeffrey. Your little girl has come a long way in the last two years. Not only is she one of the best pilots I've ever seen, but she's also the most proficient secretary and computer technician analyst."

The professor with a big smile replied, "I sure am proud of her." Then he informed them, "As you look towards the back of the hangar, you'll see two unbelievable jet aircrafts made of top secret elements combined to exceed anything beyond one's imagination. The one Claire will fly tomorrow is a twenty four seater with all the comforts of a five star hotel. It is it armed with an undisclosed ordinance that would rival an A-10 Warthog Tank Killer. Also, because of the durability of the top secret elements, it has no problem reaching speeds of Mach-2 or better."

Malloy whistled in admiration.

"It really hasn't been tested yet. But next to it is an experimental scramjet said to reach speeds enough to escape into outer space. This jet, you could say, looks like a cross between the Concorde and a Klingon Warbird."

Bingham and Pearson were the only ones who knew what it might be capable of.

Malloy told the maintenance crew to have it fueled up for the cross Atlantic trip tomorrow. He gave one of them his laptop and told him to store it in the forward hold of the jet.

They men got back into the Land Rover and drove back out to meet the Admiral's arrival on the tarmac. As the door of Hangar Four completely shut, they spotted the CH-47 Chinook in the far distance coming in for a landing. Malloy told the driver to step on it so they could beat the Admiral to the tarmac. They made it just in time as the Chinook set down.

Malloy could see his buddy from a window towards the front of the chopper. Admiral Fischer look angry about something. The Chinook began its taxi to the tarmac and glided up to the waiting Land Rover. The Tower advised Admiral Fischer that the C-130 Solo Hercules Aircraft would be landing in twenty minutes. He told Captain Reardon to contact the Solo and let them know to be ready to deploy in an hour.

As the Chinook finally stopped, the rear vertical door opened and the second strike team came out to stretch their legs. Vice Admiral Fischer, along with Lieutenant Commander Tremain, walked down the ramp toward the waiting Malloy, Pearson, and Bingham.

Malloy instantly and instinctively said to Admiral Fischer, "I know what you're going to say, Tom, but before you jump into any conclusions, let's go over to my office and we'll fill you in on every detail."

Fischer with a voice of sincerity replied, "Don't pull any bullshit, Jimmy. You and I have never lied to each other before. I'm your friend, damn it, and I would do anything to protect you. For God's sake, we've saved each other's lives in combat."

Malloy asked, "What about your second in command here? Can you vouch for him too?"

Tremain's mouth opened with astonishment.

The Admiral cut in. "I sure can. When you see how much, you'll take that back."

Malloy, lowering his head in shame, replied, "Tom, I'm sorry, but the one I'm trying to protect is like a son to me."

Fischer said sarcastically, "No shit, Jimmy. What do you think, I'm a moron? It's Orion. They didn't put me in Naval Intelligence just for my good looks. C'mon, let's go to your office so we can figure a way to whitewash this with Command."

Professor Pearson, choking up, said to Admiral Fischer, "Thank you, Tommy. You don't know how much this means to me and that boy of ours." Admiral Fischer puts his hand on the professor's shoulder. "Jeffrey, I'm your friend, too. Promise from now on you'll keep me in the loop."

The professor gave Admiral Fischer his solemn word.

They went to the security office where Professor Pearson and Captain Malloy went over every detail of the last five days. Professor Pearson used a flash drive to show all the proceedings in the surgery and the project maneuvers that were used to save Lieutenant Orion's life.

Admiral Fischer was stunned and amazed at the powers Orion possessed. He agreed with them that only the people who should know of it must never reveal it to anyone on the planet.

Just as he finished speaking, they all turned around to see Lanny Cromwell in a flood of tears. She walked up to Admiral Fischer and wrapped her arms around him, crying, "Oh thank you, Admiral Fischer. I don't know what I would do if the government tried to take him away from me."

The Admiral replied reassuringly, "Over my dead body they will, sweetheart. Now you go and take care of that hero of ours. Nobody will find out about him."

Lanny through her happy tears said to all of them, "Well, I really came to ask if you gentlemen would like a cup of coffee or tea."

Lieutenant Commander Tremain replied, "We'd love to, but our plane is just about to land. The quicker we get in the air, the better it is that the trail disappears."

Malloy stood up and said to Tremain, "Sorry about what I said before, Commander. I should have put my trust in a fellow S.E.A.L., anyway."

"Don't worry Skipper, I'm sure we'll be working together in the future."

Malloy responded, "Oh, I'm certain of that," as he gave Admiral Fischer a look.

Fischer stood and hugged his old apprentice. "Just keep our boy safe, Jimmy." He looks straight at Lanny and said, "And our little girl, too."

Malloy saluted him. "Aye, aye, sir."

Admiral Fischer returned the salute and headed out the door.

Professor Pearson told Lanny that he and Captain Malloy would have that coffee now.

Malloy asked her to inform the kitchen that he'd like a shot of Chivas in his.

Lanny told him that he really shouldn't.

Malloy responded sarcastically, "Just follow orders, Lieutenant Commander Cromwell."

She smiled, but replied seriously, "I'm sorry, sir, it won't happen again." Professor Pearson stopped her and asked, "By the way, Lieutenant Commander, are the special suits completed for everyone?"

Lanny assured him, "All of them were finished an hour a half ago, including Hansy's, Gunnar's and Klaus'."

Pearson instructed her to go get some sleep, and to tell her sister not to stay up all night with Bobby, either.

"I will, Papa," Lanny promised. After she returned with the coffee, she headed back to Orion to get a good night's sleep.

The professor and his security chief began to plan a strategy for the coming days.

Time: 2200 hours. EST New York. December 1, 2010.

****

Time: 0530 hours. December 2, 2010.

John Orion awakened to the sound of the alarm clock coming from his cell phone. He stood and began stretching his arms and legs, then fell forward to floor in a push up position. Controlling his body with breathing exercises he silently cadenced out one thousand pushups. He swirled around and did two thousand sit ups.

He stood up once again, but this time he hovered above the room about ten inches and he started stretching for the final time before his run. Thank God the ceiling in the house was ten feet.

From under the blankets he heard Lanny giggling. "Show off," she teased.

Orion snapped back at her, "Well, Lady Bee, you didn't complain last night when we did it six times, did ya?"

Lanny Cromwell removed her covers and her hair looked like it had been tossed into a tumbleweed. Makeup and lipstick were all over the sheets. She exclaimed in delight, "And I'll never complain again! Wow!"

Orion came over and picked her up, cradling her in his arms. "I don't know what I would do without you, baby."

She laughed devilishly. "Well, I certainly hope you don't try doing what we did last night by yourself."

"I take back what I said once before — you suck at stand-up comedy." Lanny laughed uncontrollably as Orion threw her on to the bed.

With a frown he told her, "Well, smart ass, I'm going on my fifteen minute run, so if YOUR HIGHNESS could get dressed and cleaned up, that would be great. This time we're eating in the cafeteria with the team."

Lanny, still laughing, replied," Are you not supposed to address me as Sir, Lieutenant?"

Orion growled and slammed the door, muttering to himself, "Oh, I could kill the Skipper for this."

He began his run, but was doing fifty miles per hour. In the dark, traces of the strange purple light glowed as he sped around the complex. The kitchen workers, valets and science technicians already heading into the building stopped to watch the incredible feat with awe.

Palladin and Claire were walking arm in arm when Claire said to Bobby, "How come you do your run at five o'clock, a half hour ahead of Johnny?" "Well, doll, it's not like I can keep up with him. Does it look like he'll slow his pace so I can keep up?"

Claire answered, "Well, I'll ask him for you."

"Oh no you won't, baby."

Still holding on to his arm, she told him, "Oh, yes I will."

Bobby insisted again, "Oh, no you won't."

With a smug face she finally replied" Oh, yes I will, and you will do as you're ordered. Is that clear, Chief Petty Officer Palladin?"

Bobby took a deep breath and growled, 'Yes Ma'am, I mean, Sir."

Claire continued, "It is bad enough I'm sleeping with an enlisted man. The least he could do is appreciate his superior officer."

"You're really eating this up, aren't ya?"

Claire with another smug smile replied, "Every last morsel on my plate." They kept walking and Palladin muttered to himself, "Oh, I could kill the Skipper for this."

Malloy's habit was to make employees sign an oath and pact with Pearson Global Technologies. The contract stated that all employees will abide his chain of command. NO QUESTIONS ASKED. Palladin, having quit the police force for his six figure job with the corporation, knew he must comply with his contract.

Orion and all of the team had just signed the contract before Lanny's and Claire's promotion to Lieutenant Commander. Benny said he would sign his this morning in Captain Malloy's office.

As Benny and Kyle reached the door of the main building, they saw a purple streak disappear in the background. Nothing fazed the Wizard. The tricks he had up his sleeve no one knew about. Kyle, still staring out into the distance by the door, heard Benny say, "Are you going in or are you just a doorman for the day?"

Kyle replied, "Sorry, Chief. It's still amazing every time I see the things he can do."

Kraemer then said to Kyle, "Don't worry, son. We'll all soon be used to it. Now let's eat. I've got to be in the Skipper's office in an half an hour."

As they entered, Malloy greeted Kraemer at the door, "Benny, when you sign today, you'll be promoted to Senior Chief. You'll be holding the rank by yourself now. Trudy's been promoted to Ensign since I can't stand hearing him bitch about how all officers are scumbags. I know this isn't the Navy, but this is my command and I run it as I see fit. That fuckin' hick Palladin will be promoted to Master Chief to take the pressure off his girlfriend bossing him around."

Kyle started laughing. "She could just as well be a seaman recruit and she'd still boss him around."

Malloy and Benny joined in the joke, but Malloy told Kyle, "Kid, you're our eyes and ears now. I can't do anything until you get out in 2012, but secretly, for all the risk you're going to take, effective immediately you have a stealth contract with the corporation with the same six figure pay rank of a Senior Chief Petty Officer in our corporation. Eat and enjoy, because I want both of you in my office at 0700 hours, is that clear?"

Both replied, "Yes, sir." But Benny asked Malloy, "What about the Lieutenant, Skipper? If anybody deserves a promotion, it's definitely him." Malloy responded, "I tried to, but he told me to 'shove it up my ass' and the rank of Lieutenant is fine with him. Bet ya he wished he didn't say that when he found out Lady Bee had the rank of Lieutenant Commander."

They all laughed hysterically as Malloy left and went in.

Meanwhile, at the complex entrance, a dark black Crown Victoria pulled up at the gate with a New York City ambulance behind it. Professor Darfuir shows his face to Pauly, the security guard. Both vehicles headed for the hospital and triage unit of the complex.

The house phone in Orion and Lanny's guesthouse began to ring. A woman's voice on the other end said, "Sorry to bother you, Commander Cromwell, but Professor Pearson needs you in the triage building immediately." Lanny, not recognizing the voice asked, "Okay, but who am I speaking with?"

"Oh, I'm sorry, sir. I'm Ensign Valerie Queen."

"Okay, Ensign Queen, tell the professor I'm on my way."

Valerie replies, "Will do, sir."

Orion, being able to hear like a guard dog, started laughing and told Lanny that Trudy will soon be dating Valerie and had no idea that she is an Ensign.

Lanny completely ignored that. "Oh good, at least there's another female officer for me and my sister to hang with."

Orion slapped his forehead and exclaimed, "Oh God, I give up."

"Oh stop your shit, Johnny. I'll see you after I find out what the professor needs of me. Now go eat, Lieutenant, and I'll see you shortly."

Lanny and he both shut the door and climbed into the golf cart for the ride to the complex. Lanny dropped Orion off at the cafeteria and headed for the hospital area. She pulled up and hustled through the door.

Inside she spotted Professor Darfuir standing next to a woman who resembled him quite a bit. Next to them stood Police Lieutenant Ferris, next to a little girl laying down on a gurney with her left leg wrapped intensely with gauze bandages.

Professor Darfuir introduced Ferris to the chief surgical nurse of the hospital and asked Lanny to set up a heparin IV for little Setia Palaat. Lanny found out that this was the little girl wounded in the attack at the Tunnel.

Setia's mother asked Lanny if she could walk with them to Setia's room. Lanny told Tiri that it would be no problem, but that she must stay behind the curtain as the baby's bandages were changed.

Lanny stopped at the nurse's station and told her colleagues to bring to room 604 an IV with a mild child's dose of Heparin. They finally got the baby into the room, and a commotion was heard back at the nurse's station.

All of a sudden, Benny Kraemer burst into the room. He looked right at Tiri and spoke to her in Arabic. Tiri, at first, didn't recognize him because he had shaven his beard to disguise his fleeing the scene at the Holland Tunnel. But when she heard his voice, she immediately started hugging him, saying, "Fashir, we thought you might have been killed after you pulled us from the car."

Benny backed away from her for a second and started to explain. Before he could utter the words, Dr. Darfuir and his sister Lamarra entered the room. Kamal said to them both, "Lamarra, Tiri, his name is not Fashir. It's Benjamin Kraemer, who was undercover for the Israeli Defense Force. He's an ex-Navy S.E.A.L. who served under our Security Chief James Malloy."

Lamarra instantly said, "You are Judain, are you not?"

Benny replied, "Yes I am, Lamarra. Does that make a difference to you?" With tears in her eyes she ran at him, hugged him and said, "No, Fashir . . . I mean Benny. I love you for what you have done for us."

Tiri Palaat, who had become romantically involved with him, stared into his eyes as he gazed back at her. Scared as hell, he asked her, "What about you, Tiri? You know how much I love you and Setia."

Tiri slowly walked over to him and began kissing him passionately. She backed away for a second. "I love you also, Benjamin Kraemer," and began kissing him again.

Everybody in the hall and the room started clapping and cheering.

Lanny, in tears, regained her composure. "Everybody, this is a hospital.

Now get back to your posts, PRONTO. Kraemer, you have two minutes and then you are out of here, understood?"

Benny thankfully said, "Yes sir, and thank you Lieutenant Commander."

Lanny replied, "Go on, Benny, say hello quick. I still have to attend to her."

Tiri took him over to a smiling little girl who loved him.

Time: 0645 hours. EST New York.

****

Time: 0710 hours. EST New York.

Having just signed their employment contracts with Pearson Global Technologies, Benny and Kyle saluted Malloy and left his office. Malloy's desk buzzer started ringing immediately. He pressed the intercom button.

"What is it, Miss Vanderkamp?"

Claire replied, "Sir, Lieutenant Ferris of the New York Police Department is here to see you. He assured me it's not official business."

"Send him in, Commander." As he entered, Malloy greeted him at the door and said, "Ah, the voice over the phone yesterday. Please to meet you, Lieutenant. I'd like to personally thank you for all you've done for Kamal and his family. They told me how you reacted when that FBI asshole jumped in their face."

Ferris replied, "No problem at all, Captain Malloy. I can't stand fuckin' bigots as it is."

Malloy asked, "Care for a cigar? They're Cuban Cohiba."

Ferris waved his hand to say no.

Malloy offered, "How about a taste of a sixty-year-old prime single malt Scotch?"

Ferris' face lit up. "Start pouring. I'm an old Marine. I'll never refuse great tasting Scotch."

Malloy laughed. "Now that I know you're a Marine. . ." He opened his bottom desk draw and pulled out Real Scotch Whiskey, pouring it over rocks a third of the way up, then handing it to the Lieutenant.

Ferris took a mouthful and replied, "Wow, that's good."

Malloy agreed. "Only the best for fighting men."

Ferris raised his glass and said, "HOO, YAAH."

Malloy's face then turned serious. "We'll, what can I do for you, Lieutenant?"

Ferris explained that he was retiring in a month. He spoke with Dr. Darfuir and asked if their corporation could use someone like him in security.

Malloy assured him he'd love to have somebody on board as qualified as him, but he must first meet with Professor Pearson. Malloy went on to tell him it should be no problem, because he already has his approval and that of Professor Darfuir who is second in charge.

Malloy promised Lieutenant Ferris that he'd get back to him as soon as he and the team returned from a funeral in Germany. They both shook hands and Ferris knocked back the rest of his Scotch, then left.

Time: 0750 hours. EST New York.

A knock sounded on Malloy's door and he wondered why Claire hadn't buzzed him. "Who's there?"

Claire opened the door with a worried look on her face. "Captain, Trudy just called and told me Johnny jumped in the Roadrunner and peeled out of here like a bat out of hell."

Malloy jumped out of his chair. "Go to the hospital and get your older sister. I'll get everybody else. I know exactly where he's going."

Malloy immediately called Professor Pearson and told him to summon the motor pool and bring up two of the Cadillac SUVs. He started calling the rest of the team to be ready to go. Locking up his office, he headed down to meet with the professor and Lanny Cromwell. When he spotted her on the street, he told her not to worry, but everybody had to be there. When they pulled up to the gate, Pauly's face showed his concern. Malloy signaled to him that everything would okay as they left through the gate.

Time: 0800 hours.

****

Time: 0905 hours. EST New York.

A 1969 black Plymouth Roadrunner had just entered Calverton National Cemetery and was headed for Section Six. Orion had stopped to grab flowers and an American flag so that he could visit his lifelong friend and S.E.A.L. teammate, Lieutenant JG William Conrad Stokes. Tears rolled down his face as he came closer to his gravesite.

Orion noticed six other American Flags next to the one he put there back on Memorial Day. Stokes' stone read, LIEUTENANT JG WILLIAM CONRAD STOKES — BORN AUGUST 2, 1977 — DIED SEPTEMBER 14, 2006 — KILLED IN THE LINE OF DUTY — AWARDED THE NAVY CROSS FOR HIS BRAVERY IN RESCUING HIS COMRADES UNDER FIRE — U. S. NAVY S.E.A.L.

Orion got down on his knees and placed the flowers across his grave. He pulled up all the tattered flags and rolled them up gently. Then he put a picture of him with his arm over Billy's shoulder with the rest of the team surrounding them on both sides. Billy was holding a Trident and Orion a Flintlock Pistol. Behind all of them in the middle, Captain Malloy held an eagle above all of them.

Taping it right under the Stars and Stripes, Orion pushed the other end into the ground and then began to talk as he looked up.

"Well, partner. Shit, I don't know where to start. I tell yah one thing, me and the unit got that fuck who set us up. I know I shouldn't be glad that another human being is dead, but God forgive me, I'm glad he is. I don't know if the man upstairs told ya, but I almost bought the farm myself. I don't know why I'm still alive. I shouldn't be. God knows I shouldn't be. Once again they tried to kill the people in the city we were born in. I guess God helped us to stop them. I still don't know why they want to kill us. We never started anything with them. All we want to do is have barbecues in the summer. Play baseball and football with our kids. Enjoy Christmas and Chanukah with our loved ones. We never wanted anybody to go over and hurt people they love. I just don't understand it. I'm tired of watching little babies from Israel and Palestine dying because the elders can't give up just a little bit of land. Don't they understand in God's eyes they're both killers? I don't know how they look themselves in the mirror. Yo Billy. I finally met a real pretty, down-to-earth girl who's much smarter than me. Maybe you had something to do with it. You always watched over me. Maybe you talked the man upstairs into sparing my life and sending her to me. If ya did, Billy, I'm eternally grateful. OH GOD, I MISS YOU. WHY DID GOD TAKE YOU AWAY FROM ME?"

All of a sudden, Lanny's arm wrapped around Orion's head as he cried uncontrollably. She pulled up on him so he stood, and fully wrapped her arms around his chest.

Orion looked up and saw Malloy, Trudeaux, Claire, Bobby, Kyle, Kraemer, Olsen and Professor Pearson all surrounding him.

The professor said, "John, Lanny's tears prompted me to bring you back to life. Her tears were the ones that gave you life. Just think, you saved one of my daughters and brought another one to me. I will be forever eternally grateful to you for that, also." The team, one by one, planted a flag in front of Billy's grave.

Orion regained his composure and replied, "Shit. It was you guys putting these flags here all the time."

Benny spoke for them all. "It was our brother we lost that day on the mountain, too. If it wasn't for him and Skipper, we'd have flags on our own graves. Now we gotta get out of here. We're all over the news. The radio's claiming a super hero saved the city and all that bullshit right now. Now let's get back and pack, team. Until all this boils over, we're going to Germany to bury more of our comrades in arms. C'mon, Hansy is waiting."

They all jumped into the Cadillac SUV while Orion and Lanny hopped into the RoadRunner heading home.

Time: 0945 hours. EST New York.

21 THE VIKING AVENGER

Time: 1100 hours. EST New York.

Orion's Roadrunner came charging up to the gate and stopped to see Pauly still on duty. Pauly went to the driver's side to see Lanny driving instead of Orion.

"Lieutenant Commander Cromwell, how are you? I didn't know it was you who left before."

Lanny laughed, "It wasn't, Pauly. My boyfriend here was just a little upset."

Orion replied from the passenger side, "Sorry, Pauly, for burning up the parking lot before."

"No need, Lieutenant, it's about time there was a little excitement around here." Lanny asked, "Pauly, what are you still doing here? Your shift was over at eight." Pauly explained that he was worried when he saw both the Captain and the professor leaving as fast as they did. So he put in for overtime till 1200 hours.

"Hey can you do it all over again, Lt. Orion? I can use the overtime."

Lanny waved goodbye and hit the gas. She drove like Dale Earnhardt to the Citadel.

Orion loved the little wild child in his woman and started screaming, "Yahoo!" They pulled up and Lanny said, "All right, baby, I'm gonna lock the car this time so you don't take off again without telling me."

Orion peeked at her like a toddler who just had his favorite toy taken away.

Lanny gave him the look, and repeated, "I said OUT, LIEUTENANT."

Orion exited with a frown on his face.

Professor Darfuir spotted him and said, "John, come with me to the lab, son. I just need to do a quick diagnostic of your body."

Orion walked with the professor. "Did you see that, Doc? She yelled at me like a little baby. On top of that, she thinks God is a woman."

The professor laughed. "Yes, Lieutenant, but what if she's right?"

Orion shook his head. "Oh God, don't tell me she's got you believing it, too."

The professor grabbed Orion by the arm and reassured him, "Don't worry, John. They can't live with us and they can't live without us."

Orion nodded. "Yeah Doc, you're right; they can't."

Dr. Darfuir grinned at the irony.

They came to the elevator and the professor activated it with his palm print and eye print scan. They both entered and descended to the subterranean laboratory below. Time: 1130 hours. EST New York.

Time: 1300 hours. EST New York.

Gail Landeta had replaced Pauly at the entrance gate an hour before. She was in her booth when a Mercedes SUV pulled up to the front gate. Rolling down the window, Marilyn Carmichael revealed herself. Orion rescued her children from the fire on Saturday. All three children were in the backseat.

Being friends and neighbors for years, Gail recognized her instantly.

"Hi Gail, we've come to visit the man who saved my children's lives," announced Marilyn. "I should say, those men who saved all our lives. Please, can you ask Jeffrey if we can see them?"

"How are you doing, sweetie? How are the babies?"

Marilyn replied, "They're still shaken up about their F-A-T-H-E-R, if you know what I mean."

Gail replied, "Wait one second and I'll phone the professor for you." She spoke with the professor for about three minutes, then told Marilyn, "Sweetie, you know where the main building is, right?"

"Oh it's been about a year, but I remember."

Gail said, "Go on through, honey, and if you have a problem just ask anyone to help you, and they will." Into the back seat she waved and said, "Hi, guys!"

The kids responded, "Hi, Gail!"

She waved them all through and Marilyn drove off. Just as the car pulled away, a corporation ambulance arrived the gate. Gail approached the Ambulance as EMT driver, Stephen Terranova, rolled down his window.

"What's going on today, Stevie?" asked Gail.

Terranova replied, "We're transporting the professor's daughter to the rehab facility they've just opened, at Lieutenant Commander Vanderkamp's request."

"Okay, just one minute, Stevie. I'll let Claire know she's here."

Gail called Claire and after about two minutes told Terranova, "Claire just informed me to have you bring Kendra over to the triage and hospital wing."

Terranova told her okay and drove off to the hospital area.

Malloy told the team to be ready for a debriefing and to pick up their new special battle suits at 1400 hours at Hanger Four. At the back entrance to the triage and hospital area, a Mercedes SUV came to a stop. A security officer helped Ms. Carmichael bring her kids inside the hospital unit. First out was the thirteen year old girl, clutching her fourteen month old baby brother for dear life after the security officer unhooked the boy from his car seat and handed the baby to her.

Marilyn came around and pulled her four-year-old daughter from the back seat. Looking over at them were Palladin, Trudeaux and Olsen. The three headed over to greet Ms. Carmichael. As they approached, she looked up to see the man who shot the Killer who had been holding her at bay.

"Oh my God, it's you," Marilyn said tearfully. She froze up and almost dropped to her knees.

Bobby ran to catch her, pulling her close as she said with pent up emotion, "I keep remembering that awful day when those horrible men shot my husband to death. Dear God, they were going to leave my babies to burn in a booby-trapped house."

Bobby replied for her comfort, "We've gotta find a way to protect our families from evil creeps like them. Ms. Carmichael. But right now, your children need your strength. I know it's almost impossible, but I ask you to show your kids what their father would have wanted for them."

She looked up at him, regaining her composure. "I'm going to try, and for my sanity and my children's, I'm gonna do my best. I don't know how I can ever repay you and your three friends for saving our lives that day."

Trudeaux, who knew her a little from working there, responded, "Marilyn, the only thing we ask of you is to make sure they grow up and never become like the vermin that killed your man."

She looked at them all and announced, "I've should have known that since you're all friends of that lonely, beautiful soul, Jeffrey, it means that you carry on bravely, the way he does."

Palladin, Trudeaux and Olsen gave each other a look that said ,SHE DOES SHE NOT KNOW US? THANK GOD.

Lars, lying through his teeth, told Marilyn, "Yes, Miss Carmichael, we try to be a carbon copy of the professor." He felt a small kick to the back of his leg. Trudeaux gave him the look, Don't ham it up.

Malloy and Claire, watching everything from the security camera in his office, come down to greet the neighbor they knew so well. As they opened the door for her and the kids, Claire stepped forward. "Marilyn, I'm sorry about Eugene. How are you holding out?"

"Oh Claire, I can't believe what has happened, especially in a neighborhood full of the most decent people with children. I am truly grateful to your father, Claire, for opening his lake house for me and the kids to stay in until everything's rebuilt."

Malloy cut in. "Marilyn, we're family. I Remember Kendra babysitting for Tessie when she was just seven years old. I remember well, they shipped my unit to Afghanistan at that same point in time. Family takes care of family and you and your kids are always welcome to stay here anytime."

A little anxious because he always had the hots for Marilyn, Malloy acted more like an officer and gentleman than the U.S Navy-produced horn dog he really was. He grabbed baby Eugene from Tessie and told everyone to come in while they awaited the arrival of Professors Pearson and Darfuir.

Marilyn, a beautiful forty-seven-year-old, inadvertently caused Malloy, a fifty-six-year old, to unwittingly send off signals that he very much liked Marilyn.

Claire, picking up the vibes, pointed to Malloy when he wasn't looking and clued in Lars, Trudy, and Bobby. She, with a big shit-eating grin, pointed to both of them and criss-crossed her pointing fingers. Just as she almost finished, Marilyn turned and caught her in the act.

Marilyn gave Claire a funny face, a "mind your own business" sort of look.

The door shut with Claire, Bobby, Lars and Trudy still outside,

Claire, with a look of, 'I just got caught stealing cookies,' said, "Oh, that didn't go too well, did it?"

Palladin, being a smart ass, replied, "What a command decision if I've ever seen one. The commander here learns real well of how to use stealth and make sure she's unseen. Best of infiltration, there, Claire. I'd love to have you with us on a mission."

Lars and Trudy burst out laughing, but Claire whispered to her boyfriend, "Let's see how much infiltration you can do with me in bed tonight. Oh, that's right . . . None."

She then went back in the building.

Palladin, all blushing, said as she closed the door and could longer hear him "Ah, can't do anything, anyway. You'll be flying the jet. So there."

Unexpectedly, she opened the door and responded sarcastically, "I was hoping to have us join the Mile High Club tonight, but it looks like my headache is gonna last a week."

Palladin, knowing he put his foot in his mouth, cried out, "OH SHIT. A WHOLE FUCKIN' WEEK? DAMN IT! I'LL DIE BEFORE THEN!"

Lars and Trudy laughed even harder when the ambulance pulled to the curb.

Steven Terranova, a nurse and a very large, mean-looking bodyguard accompanied her. Opening the automatic doors to the left of the main door stood Lanny Cromwell, still in her nurse's uniform.

With Claire and the professor behind her, Lanny immediately introduced herself as the chief surgical nurse in charge of the new rehabilitation wing. Although she didn't mention it, it was an incredible source of pride that Lanny had talked the professor into opening it.

Because of the short time available before the team was to set off to funerals in Germany, Kendra had planned ahead for Kendra's care.

Kendra, seeing her father and sister Claire for the first time in almost a year, began crying uncontrollably. Claire was at Columbia University, just about to graduate from law school, when Kendra ran away nine months ago, so they had some catching up to do.

Professor Pearson hurried to his daughter as she slumped in her wheelchair. Kendra, finding it hard to speak through the tears, clutched a newspaper next to her bathrobe and pajamas. She handed her father the new edition of the New York Daily News. Pearson opened it to see the headline on the cover showing Orion glowing purple and hovering above the streets of Times Square. It read, Unknown Flying Avenger Appears From Above.

Pearson, befuddled, asked his daughter, "Sweetheart, why does this make you cry so much?"

Kendra shook her head and replied, "Not the cover, Daddy. Look at page four." Pearson immediately flipped to the page four and beheld: Slain Drug Dealers Den used as House of Death. The bodies of four missing teenage girls recovered under concrete floor in garage. The girls' DNA matches that of two runaways from New York and one from New Jersey. The fourth girl matches that of a runaway teen from Philadelphia. The drug ring's leader, Joaquin Moreno, was wanted in Honduras for prostitution and homicide for the same crimes as those in New York. No release of the victims' names was given because the next of kin were in the process of being notified. The Second Squad Homicide Detectives of the Eighth Precinct in the Bronx are still looking for Moreno and his cohort Julio Vasquez's killers. An additional member of the drug ring witnessed the event and said the killer or killers used tear gas and smoke grenades for their assault on the den. Whoever gained entry was probably trained in military tactics. The only thing that puzzles investigators is the use of a curling Iron and a truck battery to heat the back door knob to a fiery red touch. The third gang member who survived a knife attack to his femoral artery suffered third degree burns to his right hand trying to escape the killers. The police identified the gang member as that of Carlos Padia of the Bronx.

Pearson looked up, his complexion turning as white as a ghost.

Malloy walked towards him.

Lanny instantly grabbed the paper out of the professor's hand and asked him if everything was alright.

Pearson, with a look of relief, replied, "I think so. I need to sit down. My knees are wobbly and I'm feeling dizzy."

Lanny instantly wrapped her arms around the professor just as he started to fall. She screamed, "Somebody help me. Papa, what's the matter? I said SOMEBODY HELP ME, DAMN IT!"

In that instant, Orion appeared out of nowhere and caught both before they collapsed. He released Lanny and told her to get a wheelchair while he held the professor gently, but with amazing strength.

Lanny positioned a wheelchair, given to her from a quick thinking staff member, as Orion gently seated the man to whom he owed his life.

The professor gained his composure as Lanny opened the newspaper to page four and began reading. Her face started grimacing over the grizzly findings of the police in the Bronx. Kendra had clearly escaped death, thanks to Johnny.

As she got toward the end of the article, she murmured to herself, "CURLING IRON," and closed the paper. Then she knelt next to the professor while handing the paper to Claire.

Orion, with his amazing auditory senses, heard his girlfriend murmur and tried to distance himself from her. As he walked down the corridor of the hospital, he ran into Professor Darfuir pushing little Setia Palaat to the playroom for children with Benny and her mother Tiri behind him. Lamarra and the other children followed.

Professor Darfuir said in delight, "Ah, Lieutenant Orion. Let me introduce you to my sister and her friend Tiri."

At the same time, Malloy was escorting Marilyn Carmichael and her children to the playroom, as well. Marilyn looked up and froze as she spotted the man who rescued her children from the grips of death. The tears began to roll down her face and she expressed her words with a hoarse voice, "Lah…Lah…Lieutenant Orion, I, I, I don't know what to say or how to thank you."

Orion cut her off right away and wrapped his arms around her.

"I know, sweetheart, and you are very welcome. If you really want to thank somebody, thank that there man holding your little boy. He's the one who trained us to do what we did. I just thank God that we were in the right place at the right time."

Lanny, standing on the sidelines, looked proudly and lovingly at her man. Glancing at her watch she relayed to the team, "Ah, Captain Malloy, sir. It's 1345 hours. We're supposed to muster at 1400 hours in Hangar Four, is that not correct?" Malloy's eyes light up. "Thanks for the reminder, Lieutenant Commander Cromwell. Now everybody, get your asses over there now. Professor Pearson, Professor Darfuir, we'll be awaiting your arrival at 1415 hours if that's okay with you, sirs?"

From over in the corner, Professor Pearson regained his composure and was being helped to his feet by, of all people, his daughter Kendra.

"That'll be fine Jim. I'll be there in a little bit. Just need time to get all my girls acquainted with each other," said Pearson.

All of Malloy and Orion's team converged in the parking lot where a Cadillac SUV was waiting to transport them to Hangar Four.

Lanny told Orion that they were going over together in the Roadrunner, and that Claire, Professor Pearson and Professor Darfuir would be coming over in a security van. Orion waited with Marilyn and Tiri with their children while the professor and Dr. Darfuir talked with the three girls. Pearson was horrified to read how Orion dispatched the drug dealers and began to express his fears privately with Kamal Darfuir.

Kamal tried to reassure him that there was no reason to fear, for Orion had acted in Kendra's best interests while facing murderous drug dealers who would have otherwise taken her life.

On a brighter note, the professor was happy to see how well Kendra had taken to Lanny, which helped to settle his nerves down a bit. They all talked to Kendra and let her know that they were behind her recovery one hundred percent.

Kendra and her sisters hugged each other and Kendra was taken to her recovery room as they all headed for the exit. As they turned the corner, they saw Orion gently holding Marilyn's baby son in his arms.

Just before Pearson and Darfuir made the turn, Pearson was reminded of the unnerving way in which Orion handled the dealers. He said to Dr. Darfuir, "Kamal, I'm praying to GOD now that we haven't created the evil Frankenstein monster of Shelley's epic novel."

But the sight of Orion gently playing with the baby stopped them in their tracks. With awe they witnessed Orion's sweet and nurturing side.

Professor Darfuir, with a big shit-eating grin, said to his partner, "No, not at all this time, Jeffrey. It seems we've created the only being alive that will destroy the Frankenstein Monster."

Professor Pearson's face lit with joy. "Yes, as usual my dearest friend, I think you are correct. There is finally a guardian of men that all evil cannot escape. You are correct, my friend, that if it weren't for the destiny of my meeting with this incredible, caring human being, my daughter might have joined those unfortunate young girls that those demons killed and tortured. God has a strange way of showing his face."

Dr. Darfuir replied, "Yes, and it is a blessing that all of your girls have adopted your way of thinking."

Pearson laughed, "Do you want to be the one to argue with them? I'm not."

Both professors led Orion, Lanny and Claire out the door to their awaiting vehicles.

Lanny said to Pearson, "You okay, Papa? You had us all worried there for a minute."

"Yes, my dear. I'm an old man and old men like me get a little flustered time to time."

Orion shouted, "Yeah Doc, don't do that shit to me. Maybe you should have a drink with me to kinda relax your nerves."

Lanny's face is now really peeved and told her boyfriend, "Please think before you speak, Johnny; the last thing the professor needs is to go off on a drunken tirade with you and the boys."

The professor left Orion with a look of being happy, and Orion and Lanny drove off.

Lanny smiling, commented to Orion, "Baby, I love you, and I'm so proud of you. Thank God we're gonna have at least a little R and R together for the next week."

"Yeah Baby, I'm glad we'll have time to be together alone, at least a little while on this trip."

Lanny hesitated. "Yeah . . . but baby . . ."

Orion responded, "Yeah, what it is sweetheart?"

Suddenly she gave him a nasty face and replied, "Next time, go buy your own fuckin' curling iron. I had that one for three years and you used it for one of your damn missions. Next time, use your own. I let no one, I mean no one, touch my beauty tools and make up."

Orion lowered his head and cowered.

Lanny continued, "I understand you meant good, but ya still didn't have the balls to ask me for it."

As they drive on, Orion began to laugh like crazy.

Lanny reached over and gave him a quick kiss, then burst out laughing herself. As they pulled up to Hangar Four, Ensign Valerie Queen was already dressed in her special battle suit. It looked a lot like Orion's, but there was a strange patch over the heart. It looked like a twelve pointed star, but the points were more rounded than pointy. In the center of it, a picture of the atom with dozens of electrons circling the nucleus appeared.

Of all things, it was colored in that eerie shade of purple that Orion emitted. Instead of headgear, the top of the suit went around the neck and collar, leaving the face and hair to be seen.

Valerie handed Lanny her suit while she told Orion that the professors had designed a new and revised suit especially for him.

Orion and Lanny looked to the back of the hangar and spotted two gigantic tarps covering something very large. Orion took a seat to wait for the professors while little by little each one of the team came from the locker rooms.

Orion was very impressed with the new battle uniforms, and when Malloy appeared with two eagles on both sides of his collar that were very visible. There were also four stripes on each mortar board on his shoulders.

All of them were wearing special black gloves and jump boots.

Professor Pearson and Professor Darfuir finally arrived in another van and came over to Orion, handing him his special suit with a hidden cover over it.

Orion headed for the locker room while Lanny and Claire left for the women's side. Michael Trudeaux approached Valerie wearing single bars on his collar, and shoulder boards like her.

Valerie smiled. "Well, at least, we don't have to salute each other."

He replied, "Why in the world did you tell me the new jet was in Hangar Three?" She laughed. "I'm sorry, Mikey, but I remembered what Captain Malloy told me to be wary of something."

Trudy asked, "And what's that, doll?"

Valerie replied sarcastically, "Watch out, especially for the smooth-talking S.E.A.L.S. He said they're the nosiest assholes on the face of the earth."

Trudy put his hands to his hips. "What else did he tell you to be wary of?"

"Don't keep moaning over that guy on the spy camera. Just because he has a French name doesn't mean shit. Plus I really think he's into guys."

Trudy broke out in hysterical laughter. "Nah, you really don't turn me on, but just for laughs, lets act like we're having tawdry sex. No, matter of fact, let's just have tawdry sex."

Valerie threw him a kiss. "See, your Captain was right. We should watch out for you Goddamn S.E.A.L.s."

Boom. Cupid's arrow definitely hit its mark.

The team, over time, gave them the comic names of Gracie and George in honor of George Burns and Gracie Allen. They both complemented each other's thinking and were a match made in Heaven.

Trudy later on in his life would be the first man on the planet Jupiter, and he and Valerie would also be the first husband and wife together in a mission from NASA. For the present, they just met eighteen hours ago.

Trudeaux, being from New Orleans, liked women with a little adventure in them. Cajuns liked a woman who knows how to fight back with her wits; it is especially good when they beat ya, because, at least in his experience, they gave sympathy sex.

Ten more minutes ticked by and the clock turned 1415 hours. Everybody assembled except Orion. When he finally arrived, he made a grand entrance. As he walked up, he lifted off the ground while purple L.E.D. lights made strobe patterns around his waist. He wore a flat, but thick, coupling belt made of smaller components than that of the ICARUS device. The battery compartment was much smaller, as well, but could achieve the same power as its predecessor.

He had single bars on his collar, but double bars on his shoulder boards. His jump boots were black and came up halfway between his ankle and his kneecap. This time, he wasn't wearing a balaclava hood or those specially made sunglasses.

The two professors went over the computer's database and studied Orion's rejuvenation periods. They took all of this into account with every specification that the super computer designated. As a matter of fact, new specifications were added to the two new secret aircraft.

Orion's gloves extended to the middle of his forearms, where more tiny purple L.E.D. lights stroked in a sequence of patterns.

Orion told the men and women to get into formation from highest rank to the lowest. As they jockeyed for position, Orion shouted, "Platoon, attention." Everybody immediately stood firm and as stiff as a board.

Orion said loudly, "All present and accounted for, Captain."

Malloy proudly walked the rank to inspect everybody's battle dress uniforms, making sure all were completely squared away. He stopped short in front of Lars.

"Sorry about your inconvenience with the amount of time it takes to shine those big clod hoppers, Lieutenant J. G. Olsen. But no one told you to grow such a big friggin' feet. So too bad, Olsen, adjust and improvise. Is that clear?"

"That's affirmative, sir."

Malloy now walked to the end and spotted Lanny trying to hold back her laughter. "Ah, look at this. My highest ranking officer thinks it's okay to joke around in my formation. Get down and give me twenty pushups there, Commander Cromwell."

Lanny's face lost the grin and became a frown as she went down.

Malloy continued with, "Things are run my way and my way only. This is not up for discussion, but you may leave suggestions in the suggestion box – WAIT HOLD ON. That's right, we don't have a fuckin' suggestion box. Okay professor, they're all yours."

Pearson came up and said, "Well, Lieutenant, first thing first. Are you ready?" Orion replied, "Whenever you are, Doc."

The professor and Malloy stepped out of the way, as a curtain attached to the ceiling of the hangar descended. There, poised with a 30 caliber machine gun, was Carl Livingston. He immediately opened fire on them. They all flinched, except Orion.

All their special suits lit up with small amounts of tiny purple L.E.D. strobes all over them. A force field enveloped every one of them, and the bullets were deflected and fell to the ground without ricocheting.

Palladin screamed out, "What, are you crazy, Skipper? What would you done if it didn't work?"

Malloy looked sarcastically at Bobby. "Oops. Back to the drawing board, I guess. You dope, we had the suits tested earlier without all of you in them."

They began admiring how great the suits worked, plus they liked the way they looked on their physiques.

Orion explained that the force field power flowed from the electro-magnetic generator coming from the aircraft under the left hand tarp.

Professor Pearson interjected, "Ladies and gentlemen, I introduce all of you to THE VIKING AVENGER."

The tarp came off, and all were in a state of AWE. It looked like a cross between a Giant F-14 Super Tomcat and a commercial passenger-carrying Concorde. It was made of top secret materials conceived in the laboratories of Pearson Global Technologies. Pearson told them to go inside the aircraft so Claire and Professor Darfuir could show them how to operate their duty station.

Before Orion entered, he asked the professor what was under the second tarp. Pearson let him know it was an experimental Scram Jet that escaped the Earth's atmosphere, while creating fourteen Gs on the human body. They hadn't tried it yet because they had no one table to stand that amount of force . . . until now.

Orion felt a little scared at first, but the professor told him he'd have to learn how to fly it in a simulator for at least eighty hours. Maybe by then, he'd think of launching it into outer space from an electro-magnetic ramp.

Today they were going on THE VIKING AVENGER's maiden flight with Claire Vanderkamp in the pilot's chair and Carl Bingham in the co-pilot's chair. Lieutenant Commander Lanny Cromwell was stationed in the radio and navigator's chair behind Carl Bingham. This was being done for Lanny's sake, to get her acquainted with the aircraft that one day she would be flying, too.

Lars, also down the line, would someday fly the aircraft since he knew how to fly almost anything on the planet, anyway.

Malloy told them that the new name for their elite unit was the GLOBAL GARRISON. To be in the Garrison, one had to be selected by him and the two professors. If just one of them said no, that candidate would not be allowed in.

Malloy, checking his watch, announced to everybody to be ready to take off by 1830 hours. He instructed them to pack for a black tie event to be held this Saturday night in Berlin.

Everybody began to leave to prepare for the long journey across the Atlantic, or so they thought. For one reason, they knew the Viking Avenger attained supersonic speed once they reach forty thousand feet.

Malloy headed back to his office to say goodbye to Marilyn and her kids. The rest went to their homes on the base to get ready to deploy.

Orion and Lanny went back to the main house to let Mama Rosa know that they would be back in a week.

Time: 1540 hours. EST New York. December 2, 2010.

****

Time: 1710 hours. EST New York.

Lanny yelled to her boyfriend in the living room to hurry up. Orion, still with shaving cream on his face, looked at the television and saw a masked al-Qaeda leader talking with two more masked terrorists behind him. The print on the screen scrolled, AL JAZZERA NEWS NETWORK.

Orion turned it up so he could hear this bastard's words crystal clear.

The terrorist was sitting and proclaimed that the United States was lucky this time, because he underestimated their capacity to develop a cyborg robot. Speaking directly into the camera, he declared that it wouldn't do them any good because the cyborg was destroyed in the helicopter explosion. He gave a message to the West and threatened to destroy all of their technology so they would bow before Islam.

The house phone rang near Lanny. She picked it up and heard Malloy on the other end. He wanted to talk to Orion.

After Malloy's minute long monologue, Orion commented, "Well Skipper, I think they took the bait. After all, I'm supposed to be dead. Now we'll just wait for them to make one slip up, and we got them. Believe me, Skipper. I really want the kingfish that hides in the Tora Bora Mountains like a coward. I don't mind picking off the school of fish one by one until we get him."

Orion went silent for a minute, looking at the television to see himself throwing a car end over end at the terrorists in Times Square. Sarcastically smiling, he told Malloy, "Next time, I'll throw two vehicles to save jail space, so our taxpayers won't have to pick up the tab to feed and house these bastards."

After hanging up, Lanny said to him, "Johnny, that's not funny. Talk like that makes you just as bad as they are."

Orion pulled her into his arms and replied, "Honey I'm only kidding. I overheard the professor thinking I might become some kind of monster. I am now swearing to you, the woman whom I'm going to marry, that I'll never use my powers for evil against the good people of this beautiful planet."

They passionately kissed for about two minutes, then breathlessly broke away. Both of them took their luggage out to the curb for transport to the Viking Avenger and then headed back in. Orion saw a woman reporter on the screen showing footage of his incredible feats. Laughing, Orion pointed out to Lanny, "Baby I must be big in New York now. That really hot-looking Latino reporter, Darla Rodrigo, is now showing me off to the world!"

Lanny just replied with, "Yeah, yeah, yeah, Tarzan. Move your ass and help me with this luggage, or Jane will make you sleep in the tree by yourself tonight."

Orion grabbed everything in one shot and bulleted out the door to the car.

Time: 1730 hours. EST New York December 2, 2010.

****

Time: 1100 hours. Honolulu Time December 2nd 2010.

One half hour prior in the Hakeliah Observatory on the Island of Maui, two astronomers and scientist discovered strange purple lights behind a new star that had formed in the ORION NEBULA. They saw the light going on and off, which usually meant that whatever the lights were, they could be planets that were forming with the stars as they orbited around it.

Professor Theodore Bertram gave his colleague the signal to begin photographing the phenomenon just in case it stopped. His colleague, Professor Sato Yamaguchi, told him those lights are here to stay.

Time: 1106 hours. Honolulu Time December 2, 2010.

****

Time: 1745 hours. EST New York.

The phone rang in Captain Malloy's office. On the other end was Vice Admiral Fischer, telling him that the FBI had contacted him and were also on their way out to the base to ask him a few questions.

Malloy thanked his buddy for the Intel and began calling everyone to report to the Viking Avenger immediately. After hanging up the phone, he went outside his office and put his hand on the print scanner, then walked over to the eye scanner and peered in. He punched in a sequence code on the keypad next to it, and just like that, a door made of the indestructible elements descended to block the ordinary door.

He and Claire walked in cadence to the exit doors of the main building. At the back entrance, Professor Pearson and Professor Darfuir waited in the corporation's limousine. Malloy opened the door for Claire and they both got in the back with the two incredible scientists.

Pearson, with a smile, said to Malloy, "Well, Jim, you were right. You said they'll probably come earlier than expected."

Malloy laughed wholeheartedly. "I've been around these idiots for years. They're all creatures who repeat their same habits time after time. So what's the big deal? We leave a half an hour earlier."

Pearson smiled and said to his daughter, "You nervous there, sweetheart? You must be all excited to be the first one to ever fly an aircraft with the capabilities of THE VIKING AVENGER."

Claire replied to her father, "I've been waiting all my life for a moment like this, Papa. Believe you me, I'm ready."

As they went through the woods they looked over and spotted the amazing aircraft waiting at the edge of the tarmac for them.

Pulling up, Orion informed Malloy that Gail was being swamped with reporters at the main gate. She doubled the guards and was waiting to see the Viking Avenger airborne so she could relax before getting off duty in two hours.

Malloy yelled to Ensign Queen to get everyone strapped in, because they would be taking off right away. All of them were wearing their BDUs and strapped themselves in as Lieutenant Commander Claire Vanderkamp sat in her pilot's chair.

Claire put on her headset and winked at Lanny, who smiled proudly at her. Claire spoke into her mouthpiece. "Tower, this is One Zulu Tango Five. I am proceeding to Runway Two and requesting permission for takeoff."

Over the radio as she began to taxi to Runway Two came, "Ah, One Zulu Tango Five, your airspace is clear and ready for your deployment."

"That's a Roger, tower; now getting into position for takeoff."

While this is going on, Orion shook his head to the iPod's music streaming into his earphones.

Bobby told him, "C'mon, Lieutenant, share the music with everybody else, damn it."

The jet began to taxi down the runway as the FBI pulled up at the gate. Within thirty seconds, the Viking Avenger lifted off into the sky.

Orion, at the same time, plugged the iPod into the aircraft's console so everyone could enjoy Aerosmith's song, "No More, No More." It was just finishing with Joe Perry's incredible guitar solo.

People down on the ground could not believe the sight of the incredible looking jet taking off into the sky, climbing at an incredible speed. Inside the cockpit, Claire and Lanny smiled at each other as they ascended into the heavens. People looking up saw the same eerie purple light that was in Times Square the day before. The VIKING AVENGER slowly disappeared into the Horizon.

Time: 1810 hours. EST New York December 2, 2010.

ABOUT THE AUTHOR

I am a former serviceman for the greatest country, the good old USA, and a former construction worker living in New York State. Unfortunate events have left me with a disability, and because of these unseen circumstances, I discovered my love for writing and have been addicted ever since. I have been a fan of science fiction for as long as I can remember. When I am not writing or enjoying playing my guitar, I enjoy spending quality time with my grandson Devin and the rest of my family.